THE RISE OF DARKUS: AWAKENING

By

JOSH R. HAMILTON
"TICKER TWIZTED"

COPYRIGHT OF 2013

Creativity has endless powers. Those who cannot create can only criticize, take what they need and always bite the hand that feeds. Fear not the weird and the obscure for these traits do nothing more than pave the road for the sheep.

ACKNOWLEDGEMENTS

I would like to thank my fiancé Heather "Havoc" Mills for being incredibly supportive. I'd like to thank all of the fans, friends and family for downloading this book on Amazonstudio.com to support my wicked mind and to give me supportive criticism.

I'd also like to thank Spirit Halloween for giving me the idea to make my favorite holiday into a realistic, culture-filled quest full of familiar monsters with a twist of awesomeness.

Lastly, I'd like to thank Momma Lynn Management LLC for all of your help, my father Howard Hamilton for taking the time to edit this book, and Sarah "Eileen" for the amazing graphic illustrations.

CHAPTERS

Chapter I: The Rise of a Monster......pg. 12

Chapter II: Battle of Lanteria......pg. 31

Chapter III: Kursus......pg. 68

Chapter IV: Redemption Tower……pg. 100

Chapter V: Damned-sel in Distress……pg. 143

Chapter VI: The Philosopher's Stone……pg. 172

Chapter VII: A Taste of Blood……pg. 206

Chapter VIII: Reflections……pg. 295

Chapter IX: The Sea of Shame……pg. 352

Chapter X: Welcome to Robotica……pg. 385

Chapter XI: The Wish……pg. 416

The Rise of Darkus

AWAKENING

CHAPTER I
THE RISE OF A MONSTER

I rise up as quickly as physically possible, grasping my chest in my left hand as I gasp in my first breath of air. It feels like a hot knife had been driven into the center of my temple and my head starts throbbing with great pain. *What is wrong with my eyes?* I can't even open them; the light that shined intensely from wherever I am pierced through my eyelids. The after burn from lying on an ice-cold slab tingles in my back. I swing my legs over whatever it is that I was laying on and reached around for something to help me walk. I feel many wires pulling at my skin as I try to get off the slab. I reach down with both hands and tear out the wires and needles from my body and howl in pain. There is one more attached to the back of my skull. I reach back and feel a much larger wire pulling my head back. I take a deep breath and slowly pull the wire out of my skull as I bite down hard on my lip from the pain. I give it one last yank and a stud as long as my index finger rips out of the back of my skull. It nearly takes the breath out of me. I reach out to grab the edge of what I think is some type of chair. I push my weight onto it, but it quickly slides from under me and my face hits the floor, knocking over a bunch of beeping equipment around the slab that was connected to the wires. I lay there for a moment and I try to think. My entire body aches. Some kind of liquid oozes out of something I knocked over and slowly found its way to my face. Wait a minute; I have no memory. *Who am I? Where am I? What am I?* I try to get my eyes to open and focus. That's it. Just a moment more and I may be able to use my eyes.

As I'm trying to get my eyes to work, I flip over onto my back and began to run the tips of my fingers up and down my body to study its texture. Am I a boy or a girl? I reach down. Well I'm definitely a male. In all of my confusion and worry, a strange pinch of pride runs through my body; *very nice*, I thought to myself. I run my fingertips up and down my torso again but this time much slower to observe texture better. I'm not wearing any clothes. My skin feels rough and cold. Everything seems to be in working condition except my eyes. I strain again to move them. I can finally make out shapes and lights through the blur. As my eyesight finally gains focus I look over to where I once lay and I feel a little anxious as I realize that it's a cadaver slab. A little more in a panic I sit up once again this time on the ground and look down at my body. My body…it's all stitched up. My head slightly aches from hitting the ground as hard as I did. I'm so confused; I don't look human. I have human features and muscle structure. I reach up to touch my face. I slowly run my hands up my jaw bone, then slowly up to my cheek bone. It feels like an average human skull. I open my mouth to see what I have for crunch-ware. Wait…not crunch-ware…what are those called…teeth. I feel two very sharp canine fangs on top, but the rest feel like normal teeth. I look up a little where my head once rested on the cadaver bed and I see a reflective surface hanging on the wall next to it. A mirror! I become so excited that I stand straight up and nearly trip as I dashed towards it. I'm still a little out of it, but I made it to the mirror.

Oh my. I take a step back in shock at what I see in the mirror. Then, filled with horror, I crept up a little closer to check out the fine print. I pry my mouth open a bit to look at the inside of my mouth. I have many teeth and just as I had thought, my two canines were large and I had a long, purple tongue. I have dark blue skin, almost metallic, or glossy and an almost turquoise hue from the light reflecting off of my skin. I have a normal looking nose, but my eyes…my eyes are quite large. Vibrant, piercing neon green eyes and they almost look like they glow. My neck as well is stitched up. I reach out to tap the mirror to then reveal my long, black nails that I hadn't noticed before. I slowly run my hand down the mirror and create a high pitch screech as I drag my nail down the mirror, leaving a deep cut in its surface. I feel a little sick to my stomach as I register that at sometime in the past I didn't have a head; perhaps a different head? Taking this all in started to make me light headed. My stomach turns some more as I become overwhelmed with all of this.

    I reach up and run my fingers through my long, black hair that reached to the middle of my back. As I run my hands towards the back of my head, I stumble upon something sprouting from the back of it. Again, my stomach jumps in its place. What is coming out of the back of my head? I pull my hair aside and turn slightly to the left as I see a long, third arm looking device zigzagging its way out from my skull. On the very end there is a sphere. Is there a damn antennae sprouting from my cranium? I step back from the mirror; it's all too much for me. I feel sick and overwhelmed. Even at this very moment, I'm pondering how I know how to even think, or speak any language or use basic logic. I sit down on the end of the cadaver bed once more and stare into space. I think I'm slightly in shock. Everything kind of tunneled out and I become unresponsive.

I think I'm ok now. I don't know how long it's been, but I seemed to of spaced out for quite some time. Is time even relevant where I am? I then think about that for a minute then shake my head. I roll my head down into my arms and feel a heavy wave of sadness come over me. It just occurred to me; I don't know who I am. I don't know where I come from, or why I'm even here. All I know is that I look like a monster and someone at some point in time put me together. The only thoughts that I had left were; what was the motive behind all this? Was I assembled just for hobby? Do I even have a purpose? As I continue to bury myself in misery, I tilted my head up to the roof and stare at it. It's a very tall ceiling, about sixty feet high. The sound of water drops falling far into a puddle in the middle of the room, which then found its way in the crevice of the side of the wall where it was clear to me that the floor is slightly leaned and off balance. *Interesting.* I just realized that I've been so into observing myself that I haven't even taken a look around. I take my attention across the floor which is made up of old waterlogged wood of sort. I then take my focus up the walls, where I am overwhelmed by the mass amounts of highly stacked books, gadgets, doo-dads, tools, and scraps from mechanical pieces and parts. A spider slowly comes down from a massive spider web that looked very intricate, which hung from the lower part of the ceiling. It looked like it could catch your fall if you fell from the very top. The spider was rather large, probably as big as my clenched fist.

As I continue to look around, I notice a small red light blipping on and off behind some books and junk. I take to the floor and walk over to it. The wood was cool under my feet and loud cracks and squeaks from the old wood were made with every step. The red light had full hold of my curiosity. *Odd*; the light didn't seem to catch my attention before. Maybe it was because I was still in shock from all of this. I throw the books aside as well as the rest of the junk. To my surprise there seems to be a computer device. On the monitor was a disk that was labeled, "*watch me*." My heart raced and I became so excited that I grabbed the disk as quickly as I could with both hands and scoped the device out for somewhere to fit it, nearly slipping on the puddle on the floor caused by the leak in the ceiling. After pushing a bunch of buttons, I finally found one that opened up the device, where there was a slot that ejected and looked like it would fit perfectly. I stuck it in and shut it, waiting eagerly for something to happen. For a moment, all I could see was my figure in the black screen and my face, which looked so hungry for answers.

The monitor then blipped on and showed nothing but white noise for a minute. Right before I nearly destroyed it in total frustration, it changed. My eyes became glued to the screen for I didn't want to miss a single noise. I was so enticed that I had to even remember to breathe.

It was black, and then a man walked into screen from the darkness. He wore a long, white lab coat with big black buttons that ran from the collar down. He was a middle-aged fellow. He had long, withering grayish hair in the back and was completely bald in the front, and very polished looking. His face was long and his chin very thin and pointy. Big, shiny goggles covered his eyes, and the wrinkles in his forehead represented that he was at ease. He looked so miraculous and mad, but he had a long wide smile and he looked soft and caring. Finally, he cleared his throat and spoke in such a soft way.

"Hello there. You are probably wondering where you are. In fact, you are probably wondering *who* you are, *why* you're here; many things are running through that ticking mind of yours. I apologize for such an overwhelming display of birth. Allow me to explain, but before I do I must properly introduce myself. I am Professor Tinkarius, mastermind in all levels of Biology, Mechanics, and Alchemy. You, my gifted child-your name is Darkus,"

"Darkus," I said out loud. It just came out, probably in relief as to at least knowing my name.

"Yes," he replied, "your name is Darkus."

Wait a minute, is this live?

"Can you understand me?" I asked eagerly.

He continued, completely ignoring my question.

"You are a creation of mine-no, a *masterpiece*. I invented you. You are the very first of your kind. You see, I am the first to create synthetic life. I've mastered all types of life, through all kinds of science and magic, infusing them together for unseen and extraordinary formulas. But *you* are the first to be successfully infused with all three; Biological, Alchemical, and Mechanical parts. Your outer flesh is real flesh, and deep inside your core are strong bones that are purely mechanical, making you very indestructible, also a fierce line of defense. They are made of the hardest metals throughout the lands. Now to keep that all together takes some very potent, ancient Alchemy. Alchemy is a seemingly magical process of transformation, creation, or combination. Its power still not yet fully understood. The three formulated properly together has made you one *hell* of a monster.

Now, why would I make such living creatures for lines of defenses, you're probably wondering? You have most likely not stepped outside yet. This is a good thing. You see, you were born in a world full of much bigger, darker, hungrier creatures as yourself. Have you looked into the mirror yet? Though you may be a monster, you are of lifted heart and spirit, metaphorically of course. You may not have a soul but you represent the very meaning and are well conditioned in morality. There are monsters outside that door that can take souls from the living and use them against you or merely feed on them, killing you. You will learn that having no soul is just another way to survive out there.

Within the brain I have bestowed to you I have programmed the deadliest fighting techniques ever recorded, as well as everything else you know, such as thinking, language, movement, and so on. It also bares the tissue from an ancient race that hones curious and powerful techniques that you will later find to be quite useful. Lastly, your ability to charge your Alchemy is higher than anything ever documented. You are capable of summoning deadly amounts of ancient Alchemical powers that will both be founded in a time of need or be subconsciously triggered. You might even find your powers interacting with the land of Remains in curious ways without your consent. But beware, for triggering that much Alchemy can make you easily detectable by certain tribes in the field of battle. Power is an entity of its own, Darkus. Learn to balance it and unlock attributes within yourself that you never knew existed. Lose control, destroy the world, and yourself with it.

Now, outside of your shelter that I left you, the world does not approve of me, nor do they my inventions. My ideas are an abomination, and the cultures and tribes that thrive on our planet find what I do impure and disturbing; so disturbing that they have banned me and anyone else to do anything as such ever again including those close to me, but I find their ignorance wrongly accused and misguided. Of all the horror and fear out there, they fear my work the most. I still to this day don't understand it, but I believe deeply in my work and I refuse to stop. So, they've all decided to *kill* me. That's right; they want to murder me for creating you. Though you may be the only one with such remarkable infusions, there are many other creations out there that know that I am their creator and will do whatever they must to protect them, their comrades and I. Now I lie in hiding while I travel from location to location creating your monstrous, yet glorious brethren. You must find your allies and rid of the evil in this wretched planet. They will be easy to find once you see them. Each creation bares The Mark of Tinkarius, which is a swirly, twirling shape that comes out of each of my monsters left eye in a holographic form. for stealth purposes, it's only visible to other creations of mine. Only you and the others can see it. I'm counting on you Darkus. You will be the one that conquers. You are, and always will be, my masterpiece. Be safe Darkus, and watch your every move. They will be watching.

    Oh, and one more thing. This is most dire so you must listen. You have mechanical parts in your system. Meaning, you must find fuel. This is your one and only weakness. There is a very dangerous breed of plant life called the Creeple Tree. These plants are very hostile and look like any other ordinary tree, but they feed on flesh. You must destroy one and drink the sap that it contains. This sap acts as mechanical oil to your system. Now, you only have to drink it if you find yourself trying to recover from a battle. The sap will act as a powerful elixir in need of recovering from and you will be full of strength once again. Go without, and you will eventually shut down. The signs of a low amount of Creeple Tree sap will be ridged, stiff movement, which will soon turn to paralysis, and then lastly your system will completely shut down until more of the sap is digested. This is why it's very important that you find one of the allies that I've made for you. Do not try to locate me for it could endanger you, me and our whole operation. Besides, I am a master of hiding; all of the best hunters have failed to find me. It is your job to focus on the mission, for that is all you need to know. Good luck Darkus. It's a twisted and violent world out there."

The monitor starts to fade out. I grab it and hold my face close, "Wait! Where are you?" I pleaded. But it was too late. My creator was gone. I throw the monitor into the wall in a fit of rage, and it falls to pieces. How can this be? Why would they want to kill my creator? Why were the creatures outside so ignorant and so selfish? *Curious*; just a second ago I knew nothing about anything, and now I'm starting to get answers. I call Professor Tinkarius '*My Creator*' like some type of father figure. But he was; he gave me life and in an odd way, I was thankful to be alive because this humanoid follows his heart. It was quite admirable. But I'm far from pleased. He may be able to get his other creations out to the battlefield, but I want more than that. I want to know where he is, I have plenty more questions to ask. I want to know more about me, this world, and these beings that resent my creator and how I could possibly assist in any way other than fighting. I want to know more about what makes me tick, other than this Creeple Tree sap, which sounds like quite the pain in my ass. Hopefully I won't have to run into any of those anytime soon.

    I rummaged the building from where I was created for anything I may need. I gathered some clothing, a couple small pouches that I tied to my trousers, an odd-looking pistol of some kind along with a handful of ammo. Some books about Alchemy, Biology and Mechanics, and a diary from my creator that I found. I walked to the door and grabbed the chilled door handle and turned it slowly, but before I opened it I looked back at the cadaver table, the room that I spent such little time in, and even admired the massive net-like spider web one last time. I turned the door knob, and entered the vast, dark, hungry land called Remains, shut the door, and never looked back.

    Outside, there was a chilly, agitated wind blowing. I looked out far in the distance and there were nothing but miles of grey grass and some hills. The shelter I came out of grew distant in sight as I walked slowly down the hill it sat on, where a couple trees sat clustered together. I stopped and looked around. All was silent, except for the sound of the wind howling through the trees. I looked up into the sky and it was twilight. Dark oranges and purples shimmered in the distance, piercing through the darkness. For a world so dark and angry, it was beautiful. The grass crunched under my feet and the smell of the trees stayed with me for a little bit until I was far from my shelter.

    I reached a massive meadow that was flat and lifeless. I couldn't help but to feel like I was suddenly being watched. Perhaps it was because I was out in an open field and I felt exposed. *Maybe I should find a thick patch of woods, to act as cover and concealment.* My creator did say they were watching, and everything was out to get me. But how would they know what I am? They can't see my stealth hologram unless they are an ally so perhaps I have nothing to fear. Or maybe they could smell me? Or maybe they saw me come out of the shelter? I started getting a little paranoid so I walked to the edge of the field where there were plenty of trees.

    I made it into the woods, slowly entered and gave a look around. The sound of the wind grew quiet as it beat against the branches that were exposed towards the meadow. I stepped on a branch and it cracked and nearly startled the crud out of me. The crack echoed loud throughout the woods. Just great, if anything were out there they know I'm here now. *Way to go Darkus, real genius work.* I stood still for a few minutes hoping it would direct possible listeners elsewhere and continued to walk, this time more careful of where I walked. I have not a clue as to why I'm heading the way I am; I have no idea where to go, no lead whatsoever. All I have is a massive world full of potential haters and a hunch. But at least I know I'm a bit safer in the woods.

As I continue my way through the forest I came across an opening. I must have been walking for quite some time. It felt like I was in auto-pilot. *Just keep walking,* I told myself. But as I walked closer to the opening I could hear loud, violent sounds. Massive thud sounds, yelling, roaring. Something told me that I probably shouldn't go that way, but I couldn't help but to be ruled by my curiosity. I focused in on the loud noises cautiously, moving closer and closer.

Whack!

I hit the ground harder than I did when I fell from the cadaver table at the shelter. My face was now bleeding and I was a bit out of it from the surprise of blunt force to the back of my head. I got up and looked around. Nothing. I felt a rage within and all I wanted was to rip apart whatever hit me.

"Show yourself, you coward!"

Whack!

I was sent hurtling into a tree upside down, this time the attack was to my back. The force knocked the wind out of me and I felt long, dry twigs become tight around my ankles. The twigs pulled at me and held me upside down. From what I could see I was staring at an upside-down face in the tree. *This must be a Creeple Tree*, I thought. It shook me around for a minute then lifted me above itself as it contorted the whole upper part of its stalk back like someone lifting their head back with their mouth wide open, cracking and shattering the sides of its mouth to open it wide. It was going to eat me!

I reached for my pistol but it slipped from my trousers and right into the Creeple Tree's mouth. It lowered me down to its mouth as I reached for the branches that were holding me by the ankles. I grabbed one of them, snapping it from my ankle. It shrieked in pain and I hung from the one branch, but then it threw me out of its grasp. I flew in the air and landed in the branches of another tree.

Right when I was about to think I was safe, but the tree I landed in started shifting and animating to life. Its face appeared aside me and the branches I landed in started turning into ridged, cracking arms and hands. Before it could get a bite out of me I grabbed its upper jaw and with surprising force I lifted my arms above my head and pulled its jaw wide open and started ripping it from the corners of its large mouth. It shrieked in pain as it tried to resist until both sides of its mouth tore all the way around its back and met. The tree's top tumbled to the ground. I still hung in the branches of its lower stump and watched the trees upper half twitch and die as its last breath was given, and just like that it stopped moving and turned back into a normal looking tree once more. The other Creeple Tree reached for me as I tried to climb my way down the stump of the deceased Creeple Tree. I broke off a branch of the deceased Creeple Tree and started swinging it at the other Creeple Tree's long, extending arms. The closer I got to the ground the faster its arms extended and tried to grab me.

With this new-found strength I had, I decided that I would run up the tree's face and grab the top of its jaw and lift up as hard as I could to rip its top off like I did before. But it was as if it could read my mind because at this very moment it started shooting its roots up from the ground like jagged spikes my way. I ran to the nearest normal tree and started climbing it. The Creeple Tree's roots started wrapping around the tree I was climbing, much quicker than I was climbing. My foot slipped on a branch and the roots stop climbing up. They shot down to grab my ankle and caught me in midair. I was now face-to-face with the attacking Creeple Tree. It shrieked into my face as loudly as possible, covering me in some kind of creepy saliva. I took a look up to see that the Creeple Tree's root that caught me was caught around a branch from the normal tree, enabling me to pivot back and forth.

I continued rocking back and forth to build momentum so I could grab the normal tree I was climbing before, but to climb down towards the ground so I could pull the twig nice and tight. If I could pull hard enough, I could shoot upwards from the momentum, giving me only one shot at grabbing its upper jaw on the way up. It's either that or I become Creeple treats.

I sway towards the normal tree, and then swing back towards the Creeple Tree. The Creeple Tree gets ready to take a bite out of me on the way back, but I twist and lean my weight towards its side and successfully miss and start swaying back towards the normal tree. I reach out, but it barely touches my finger tips. I come back at the Creeple Tree once again, and it opens its mouth wide hoping to catch me this time but I have just enough time to twist and swing to its side once again. This time I can feel the momentum is strong enough to get me to the other tree. I'm sent flying towards the normal tree and wrap myself around it. I got it! I start crawling down the tree as the Creeple Tree tries to pull me closer with its roots; just what I was hoping for. If I pull down and it pulls me towards itself I will swing high up like a rubber band. I crawl as far as I can and hold onto a lower branch as the Creeple Tree pulls with all its might. Finally, the branches I was holding onto snap, and I go flying right up the Creeple Tree's face. I turn to face it, and reach out for its jaw, successfully grabbing it. The branch that snapped flew out of my hands and stuck straight into the Creeple Tree's right eye as it screams in pain. The force is just enough to crack its jaw wide, and its top is cracks sideways. I go flying into the air, and down into the top of another tree.

Crashing down through branches that barely catch my fall, I hit the ground with a good thud. The pain spreads throughout my legs, my feet, my back, and up to my arms and head. I lay there, motionless. I'm conscious, but it is hard to breath. I look up where the Creeple Tree and I once fought. A wave of relief and accomplishment tend to my wounds as I witness the Creeple tree continuing to fall backwards as it gives out it's last shriek. The weight of it's top is too much, and the remaining threads that held its top up crackle and give out. It's top falls to the ground with a finishing thud. I put my head back down onto the ground in exhaustion, and I black out.

I lift my head up. It's covered in soot. I spit it out, wipe my face off and get up to my feet. I'm a little off balanced, but quite alright. My first victory with a Creeple Tree, and I took two of them on to boot! I look over at the stumps that once held flesh-eating trees to find my pistol lying near one of them, and I notice tons of black liquid gushing out of both of the stumps. That must be the sap my creator was talking about. I begin to walk towards the trees, but my legs won't function. The bottom of my feet become as heavy as led, and my legs are stiff as a branch. *Uh-oh*, I must have been out long enough to have the battle take advantage of my exhaustion and stiffen me up. I lift one foot like a sack of rocks and it slumps to the ground. I lift the other and the same tiring, ridged movement takes hold. This must be how the Creeple Tree's feel, quite ironic. I lift and lift as fast as I can. Closer and closer to the stumps I get. It gets harder and heavier to lift my limbs and right as I am in reach of the black substance, my legs become completely still. Stage two; paralysis; *Crud*. I bend down past my waist to reach the black substance, and it's just fingertips away. I barely get the end of my middle finger covered and I reach up and stick the cold, greasy black ooze in my mouth. To my surprise, it tastes delicious. I reach down to try and get more, and after a few reaches and a few tastes, I can't reach no more.

    Nothing seems to be happening with my body. It must not be enough. Drat! I look around for some assistance and I see that the pistol is just an arm-stretch away. I reach as hard as I can but nothing. At that moment, a small orange ball enters my location from the opening in the distance where the loud noises were coming from. It's glowing and it looks like it's got a face of some sort. The red light illuminating from the face gets brighter and brighter. That's when I realize that it's a bomb of some sort. Before I can even react, it blows up and sends me back into another tree. Exhausted and tired, my body starts climbing up to stage three; I was shutting down. I started getting tunnel vision and start to black out. This was it. I won't ever get to see my creator, or even defend for his honor. I was supposed to be the best, but I couldn't even get out of these woods. Without this liquid I was useless.

I accepted my fate, and as I saw a bright glowing blue silhouette coming towards me in my blurred vision, I closed my eyes and entered the darkness.

**CHAPTER II
THE BATTLE OF LANTERIA**

I slowly open my eyes. There is a bright light and my eyes are hard to use...wait a minute. Didn't I already do this? Was I just dreaming, or was I possibly having a premonition about what was about to happen? I was stiff and tired...no that's not right. I'm sitting up right against something that felt like...a tree.

"Are you awake yet? Hello? Are you coming to your senses yet Mr. Darkus?"

This bright light shining from this moving blurred silhouette was getting on my nerves. My eyes gained focus, and floating before me was what appeared to be some type of spirit. He had a long wispy tail, long, thin arms that reached below it's bottom. It had a long neck and face, and he had long hair that covered his left eye…wait a minute. His left eye-it's got a hologram of a swirly spinning mark shining through his hair. It's the Mark of Tinkarius.

"Oh, good you are awake! Oh man I was starting to get quite worried," he stuttered. He had a shaky, high pitched voice, and glowing neon orange eyes. "You are quite the weapon Mr. Darkus, taking on two Creeple Trees at once. It's a bloody miracle you're in one piece! Professor Tinkarius wasn't kidding about making one *hell* of a monster! Mmm-hmm, he most definitely wasn't!"

"Our creator," I muttered. I slowly got up. My head was a bit in the clouds. How was this possible?

"What do you know about our creator?" I asked.
"As much as you do, Darkus," he sputtered, "but unlike you, his newer inventions were warned about you. You are the top dog! The one that will guide us! Hooray! Oh, how exciting!"

He did a little spin in the air. There was something very off about this character. I began to ask him what he was talking about, but then it just occurred to me that the last thing I remember was seizing up and shutting down.

"How did you get me back into shape?" I asked firmly.

"Oh, right how silly of me! Well I took some of that Creeple Tree sap over there and force fed it to you. It sure is hard to open your mouth when you've been shut down. So, I had to possess your body momentarily and literally stick it in your stomach."

"You did *what?*" I yelled. He trembled in fear.

"Oh please don't be mad at me! I was only trying to help! Not that I'm holding anything over your head or anything Darkus sir, but had I not of done it you would have remained a corpse." I could tell he was telling the truth.

"No, it's fine. Say what is your name? Do you have a name?"

"Well of course I do. I am Ectus, the first synthetic man-made spirit ever to be invented!" His hologram blipped away. "Hmmm, I'm not feeling a soul in your presence," he said.

"That's because I wasn't given one," I answered. "Our creator said it would keep certain creatures from using me."

"Oh yes! What a brilliant man that Tinkarius is. Well, I could always be your soul! Are you better Darkus? Feeling energized?"

"Yeah, much better, thank you," I answered.

"Good! I guess that makes us allies!" Ectus looked so ecstatic. I felt as if I just made his day. "Then come quickly! Your assistance is greatly needed. In the clearing over there! Make haste Mr. Darkus!" Ectus nearly vanished he flew so quickly to the opening from before.

"Wait! Ectus, hold up!"

I started to run, but almost forgot my pistol. I ran back to pick it up and then took out the flask that I also nabbed at the shelter. I kneeled down near the Creeple Tree sap and filled it up as much as I could, screwed the cap back on tight and ran for the opening. My legs felt well lubricated and durable. I could run really fast. This sap is like a super elixir, just like my creator stated. I ran as fast as I could and jumped through the opening, hit the ground and rolled.

To my surprise, I was witnessing a massive war in this huge dirt clearing that expanded for miles. I stood in awe; I couldn't comprehend what I was looking at. There were these tall, thin creatures, who had giant pumpkin-like heads with burning flame inside of their skulls. They wore long, grey cloaks with vines running through them. They had a symbol on their chest that looked like a purple flame outline with an "L" in the middle.

I felt something grabbing my ankle. I look down to see vines wrapping around my legs. A face of the creature I was just observing popped through the ground and roared at me, ashes fluttering out of its mouth. I took my pistol and pointed it at its face but it slapped it out of my hand. I took my other foot and stomped its face into the ground as it squashed like a fruit. The fire in its face shot out and vanished. I tore the roots off and ran for my pistol. Once I grabbed it I hid behind a fallen tree to continue observing. Thousands of these pumpkin-like creatures were crawling out of the ground off in the distance like a ton of pissed-off fire ants. The creatures that they were fighting off were these quick little psychotic beings with red face paint all over their pure white faces. They had a huge red nose, and manic, discolored eyes. They wore clothes that had polka-dot like markings on them, but looked like they were once worn from someone else, all mismatched and sized differently. They stood on their feet but hunched down and ran with their fists to the ground. They were attacking the pumpkin-like creatures with many different types of weapons and gadgets that were also painted with polka-dots and different patterns of paint. I couldn't believe what I was looking at. Ectus flew out of the log and startled me.

"Why are you hiding?" He hollered. "Why are *you* hiding?" I replied.
"I can't fight! I'm a-I'm a-"
"Scaredy-ghost?" I joked.

"No! Well, maybe. Yes, yes I am. I'm terrified! That's why I need you!"

"Well which ones do I even attack?" I yelled over the loud fight.

"Well both of them, but mainly the Psychozoans!"

"What? Which ones are those?"

"They are the ones wearing the blood all over them!" He said simply.

"*Blood?* That's blood all over them and they're weapons?" I asked in shock.

"Well yeah! But the weapons aren't theirs, and neither is the blood. They paint the victim's blood on them in a humorous way to intimidate the enemy, and they only use clothing and weapons from the ones they kill. It's how they dominate and make it there own. It's their trademark in a sense."

"That's ridiculous!"

"It's psychotic!" He added.

"What are the pumpkin-looking creatures?" I continued.

"Those are Lanterians. They are a race of flesh eating plants. This is their territory; *Lanteria*. They were bombarded by Psychozoans early this morning. It's been going on all day. Lanterians are the keeper of a special type of fire, called The Aura

Flame. They empty out each others brains and hang heads at each entrance of their land to hoard off foe."

"Why do we have to fight them?" I asked.

"Until they quit this war and a side wins, the only way to get to the other villages are completely closed off. I was trying to get to Muckraid-"

"What's Muckraid?" I interrupted.

"It's a village of humanoids that practice very powerful magic and Biology. I was hoping maybe I could find a body there!"

"A body for what?"

Just as I asked, a Psychozoan jumped up on the log we were hiding behind and lifted up its large knife and began to swing it at me. I pulled out the pistol and finally shot the damn thing right in the face. It fell back off of the log. I looked around for Ectus and couldn't find him. I got up from behind the log and marched out into the battle field. I started shooting at anything that came at me. A Psychozoan jumped up on my back and started beating my head with a giant blunt object. I grabbed it the creature and threw it on the ground and shot at it. A Lanterian then wrapped its vines around my neck from behind as another came up and held its mouth wide open to shoot some of its fire at me. I kicked it in the face, threw the other over my shoulder by its vine into the ground, then started swinging the creature around to strike anything in my path. A Psychozoan then ran up from behind and stabbed me a couple times in the back. Furious, I turned around to shoot it with my pistol, but it was empty, so I pistol whipped it and knock it out.

"Darkus! Darkus, hey!" I heard Ectus calling me from a distance. I looked around through the battlefield to find him, and then found him back where the log was.

"Darkus! Use your pistol!"
"I can't! I'm out of ammo!"
"No, you haven't! Shoot it! Shoot it quickly!"

I didn't follow, but just then the whole ground shook. Most of the Lanterians and Psychozoans fell over from the massive movement of the ground. There was a minute of silence, and then I could hear the earth from under me cracking. The sound echoed through the lands and all grew silent. As I looked around, I could see where there was an opening happening in the distance. I watched in horror as these two massive vines, that were thicker than large Creeple Trees shot up high into the sky. They stood there for a minute about a couple hundred feet in the air, and then began to fall sideways in opposite directions. The one closer to me was lined up with where I stood. I started running as fast as I could, shoving

Lanterians and Psychozoans out of my way. I could see the shadow casted by the vines under me, growing larger and larger. I ran until I got right back where the opening was in the woods and jumped in. The ground quaked and shook hard from the vines striking the lands and the sound was deafening. The shockwave sent me flying through the woods from wince I came. The creatures out on the battlefield flew high up into the air and back down to their doom. I picked myself up from the ground and walked towards the opening to Lanteria. From there, saw that most of the creatures were dead or severely wounded from the force of the vines.

"Oh dear," Ectus stuttered. "It can't be,"
"What? What is it?" I asked.

Ectus flew away from the log and hid behind me peering over my shoulder in pure dread.

"It's…a Crophix."
"A *what*? What's a Crophix?"

To answer my question, a loud roaring howl came from the giant hole in which the vines escaped from. The vines started slithering closer to the hole, their ends pinned down into the ground for bracing as if they were being used to lift something even bigger.

From the hole, I could see what looked like a massive stem arising. Shortly after, a massive pumpkin-shaped head followed the stem. Its eyes burned red, and its mouth had millions of jagged tooth-like carvings. It was a massive version of the Lanterian's heads, but with no body. Two more giant vines came shooting out of the ground to join the other two. It used its vines to turn its massive body slowly towards me and Ectus. I then realized it was looking right at us. It howled again, a howl that filled the air as if it was calling us out. I couldn't take my eyes off of the thing.

"*That* is a Crophix," Ectus said in terror.
"Oh," was the only thing I could say.

The Lanterians and Psychozoans that were still alive regained consciousness and the Psychozoans immediately started attacking the Crophix. Thousands of them covered it trying to take it down. The Lanterians then attacked the Psychozoans that bombarded the Crophix. It seems that the Crophix was completely unaffected by the attack.

"Each culture within these lands has a Crophix. A Crophix is a guardian of tribes. A titan, but the Crophix only comes out when it's needed; a last resort if you would. My, it's treacherous," Ectus continued. "It must have sensed you in the mix."

"What? No way, I'm sure I wasn't the reason it came out to play," I said in disbelief.

"No, but with all of the Psychozoans, plus you, may have had something to do with it." Ectus said.

"Interesting, so now what?"

"We could always hang out in the woods until it's done and over with. That body I wanted suddenly doesn't sound too enticing. Yeah, that sounds pretty nice," Ectus said confidently.

I rolled my eyes. "If we do that we will never find our creator," I jumped out of the woods and ran towards the Crophix.

"Wait! Darkus, a Crophix is deadly! You're mad if you think you can take it on! Wait, why would you want to find our creator? We're supposed to be fighting for his sake!"

"Yeah, you're doing a stupendous job at that, by the way," I called over my shoulder.

Ectus looked taken a back and a bit flustered, but he continued to stay put. I didn't care. I wanted to get this giant squash out of the way so we could continue the quest to find our creator. Too much time being taken away from finding the answers that I need. It's just a giant pumpkin throwing a fit. What's the worst it could do?

I ran straight for it until I got about sixty yards away, then realized I didn't have much of a plan.

"Darkus! Use your pistol!" Ectus chanted.

"I already told you, you twit! I can't, its empty!"

"No, its not! Darkus, use it! Trust me! You've got what it takes!"

I had no idea what that meant, whatsoever, but before I could even deny it I turned around to see that just in a matter of seconds the massive Crophix somehow moved about ten yards closer to me. I looked up at it and felt a massive pit in my stomach; A fly taking on a fly swatter. *What was I thinking?* This is suicide. It looked down at me and howled. Bits of ember from its core swam past me in the air and singed by nose with the smell of burnt flesh.

"You want to yell at *me*, you big, irritated vegetable?" I screamed.

I raised the pistol and I pointed it right at the middle of the Crophix. What the hell am I even doing? I'm just winging it. A tiny bit of me going off of whatever Ectus is running his transparent yap about. It raised one of its vines and started lifting it over me. I took a deep breath and I held it. Its either something miraculous happens, or I become a soft serve for Lanterians. The Crophix howls again and the heat from its mouth was a little hotter than before. I start to pull the trigger but before my very eyes my arm began to glow a vibrant purple and blue. I feel this hidden power lifting from my core. All of this mysterious power rolls up my arm to my hand and goes right into the pistol. The pistol absorbs the power and starts to transform into a much more intimidating looking piece of hardware. It began to grow bat wings near the back where the hammer was. The size of the pistol grows larger and the barrel grows longer. It begins to charge and takes in so much power that it starts shaking vigorously in my hand. I bring my other hand up to assist holding it. Right before I can't hold onto it much longer I manage to pull the trigger. To my undying surprise, a massive beam of blue and purple light blasts through the Crophix like a huge spike from the barrel of my newly evolved pistol. The power continued to shoot through, and the Crophix screams in pain. Its face gargles away, as well as the Lanterians as they watch their Guardian being blown away by my hand gun.

In what felt like forever, the beam of light stops and I drop to my knees. I feel like the life got sucked from me. I look up to see that the Crophix no longer had a face; just a pumpkin with a giant hole through it. The vines fall to the ground, and there isn't a sign of any Psychozoans. The vines start to wither and die all the way up to the base where the core of the Crophix then begins to start rotting. It rocks backwards and falls back into the giant hole from wince it came. The vines follow quickly, taking Lanterians down with it that were in the way. A long fall and a distant thud that shook the ground once more and, without a doubt, aside from all the surprise and amazement I had just shot a massive beam of light through a pistol that took out a Crophix.

"Truly brilliant! My, what a site to behold! You are some piece of work, Mr. Darkus! Power beyond compare! What a day! Oh, what a day!" Ectus hollered in excitement. Aside from all of the power that took out of me, I felt pretty good. Not to mention a little in shock from the fact that I was a walking laser cannon. He helped me up to my feet and I looked at the pistol in amazement. It was back to its original form. I put it in my holster and celebrated with Ectus for a minute. That is, until I realized that all the Lanterians were staring at us without noise or movement.

"Oh, um…so hey, sorry about blowing up your Crophix," I said, half meaningful. They continued to stare. "Great, we're going to become a Lanterian side dish."

"Well, you are. You can't eat a spirit," Ectus added. I looked at him bitterly.

The Lanterians walked steadily towards us. Their faces still, aside from the bright flicker of the burning flame inside of their faces. Ectus was nearly inside of my skin from his terror. I reach for my Pistol and prepared for the attack. It was quite difficult to even focus; their faces were so still and bitter that it was somewhat distracting. *That's it, I'm making a move*. I pull out the pistol and just at that very moment the Lanterians drop to their knees, heads tucked down, completely still. I hesitated, and from my peripheral vision I could see Ectus looking around frantically from confusion. A loud voice then echoed from somewhere in the sea of Lanterians.

"That will be enough, creature."
I hesitated, and then spoke out loud, "Says who?"
"Says me."

The Lanterians ahead of us parted to reveal an opening and vines shot from the earth as a hole was forming from where the voice had come from. A much taller, bigger Lanterian pulled its way up from the ground. His big, spud-like feet touched the ground as his vines set him down delicately onto the ground and then entered his body without a trace. His stem was about a foot taller, and he looked much older then the others. His attire was black with red lines and markings around the sleeves, and around his neck was a necklace that had a glowing blue light illuminating from the clear sphere pendent that it held. He too had a fire emblem on his chest that hid behind the glow of his pendent.

"I am Lurt, head Elder of the Lanterian tribe and honorable guardian of the aura flame," The tall Lanterian spoke with a mighty howl.

"That's the aura flame," Ectus said in awe.

"Is that why you are here? Do you seek the aura flame?" The taller Lanterians voice boomed.

"Oh no. no, no!" Ectus repeated. I took the stage,

"We wanted this on-going battle to end so we could travel to Muckraid," I said, trying to match the tone of my voice with the Lanterian, which was much bolder than mine.

"I don't follow; many beings and creatures come from many distances to obtain our flame. Your power is but a fierce and intimidating source. You are the first ever in history to destroy a Crophix. Our Crophix, Bombadicus, is completely destroyed. Recovery may never see its fate, ever. We are now much more vulnerable than the other cultures and word will spread."

"Oh," was the only thing I could say. I wasn't sorry, not at all. The massive thing nearly tried to crush me into a fine dust.

"It singled me out and your kind was in our way. We don't have time to wait for a battle I can't even begin to understand. I need to find my crea-." Ectus nudged me. *Right, I forgot*. No one can know what we are or where we came from.

"-Err, what I mean is we need to get to Muckraid to find someone that we are looking for. Anyone who even stood foot in this place was brought straight into the battle. It was necessary to defend myself in the only way I knew how."

"You killed many of my people and my Crophix just to get by?"

"Pretty much," I answered. "I sure hope that Remains holds more forgiveness than these violent lands."

Lurt leered at us with an anger that seemed impossible to fathom, yet he continued to keep calm.

"And what of these ravaged lands, shrouded in greed and haunted sand? You will find violence and a lack of forgiveness in all corners of Remains. Your selfishness has brought misery and loss to our people. Though the Psychozoans lay in defeat they will be back and we will be low in numbers," Lurt continued.

"What do you want from me?" I asked bitterly.

"I want you to never come back to Lanteria ever again; for if you show your face here once more, there is a pretty good chance that you won't have a face anymore,"

"Well then it's a date. Then I'd be the second creature around these parts that would not have a face. We're starting a trend," I said with confidence. We looked at each other with dislike and then I turned my back and kept walking. The Lanterians on their knees bid their farewells by looking up at us with pure hatred. Some of them even hissed at me, but I kept walking. It seemed that I was damned if I did and damned if I didn't tell them who I was. But just as my creator told me; this world is an evil place and everyone was watching. Even if they didn't know I was invented by the infamous Professor Tinkarius, I was already making some new friends.

"Creature," I heard Lurt's voice boom from behind me. I stopped in my tracks and slowly turned on my heel and made eye contact with the elder of Lanteria.

"You never told us your name," He said curiously and calmly.

"Darkus," I said with a toothy smile to the right, "my name is Darkus. This is Ectus, my sidekick," I added. Ectus looked at me with distraught.

"Why you throwing names out there?" Ectus panicked. We turned around and kept walking.

"Did you call me a sidekick?" Ectus added.
"Well you are, aren't you? You're not quite the fighter,"
"Well I work alone, I'm not a sidekick," He muttered.
"Yeah, how's that going for you?"
"Well, I found you on my own, didn't I? I'd say I'm doing pretty well so far." *Right*, I thought.

As we reached the end of Lanteria towards the east the grass was again visible in the distance and the sky was starting to turn bright. I haven't had the feeling of drowsiness at all. Perhaps I didn't have to sleep, being a monster and all. Besides, I'm sure I slept for quite some time before I arose, I'm sure I'm all caught up on sleeping. Ectus was a spirit so I'm pretty sure he didn't need to sleep.

"Do you have to sleep at all?" I asked him.

"No," he said almost with a defensive tone, "I'm a spirit, do I look like I sleep?"

I shouldn't have even spoken. We haven't said much to each other on the walk. Then again, it's kind of awkward to build up a conversation with miles of Lanterians kneeling down watching you leave, drowning in hatred.

"I don't even need fuel," Ectus added proudly.

"Lucky you," I said glumly.

"Not really, it's a price to pay for owning the power that you carry,"

"True," I answered.

We walked off of Lanteria land and into another patch of woods. The Lanterians quickly got up and stood at the border of their land howling at us, looking hideous and hungry. Ectus nearly jumped out of himself from being startled. They looked so vicious and horrifying. Perhaps the moment we got off of their turf they were allowed to do as they please. Who knows, but it sure was a little intimidating looking at a wall of furious Lanterians blocking the way back, howling loudly.

"Well, looks like we're not going back that way," Ectus said, "which is a shame considering Lanteria plays out as a crossroads to other lands," he finished sadly.

"I wouldn't worry about that, I have a feeling that we're going to have no other choice but to revisit Lanterian soil," I said.

"That's fine as long as you have your mega pistol! But can we just wait a while to let things cool down?"

"Hope so," I answered. Ectus didn't look like he liked my answer much.

We were bathed by a bright grey light from the sky. The smell of burnt brush and wood filled the air as we continued venturing through the wooded area. The air felt humid and muggy. I felt a sense of dread pour over me like a bucket of glacier water. Something was wrong and my gut was trying to tell me but we kept walking. I could see that Ectus was oblivious to the sensation but I didn't say anything. If I was to tell him he'd get jittery and try to talk me out of going this way, whether he was looking for a body or not.

We continued through the odd wooded area. It felt like we were walking towards the opening of a volcano but everything looked crisp and live. It must be some type of illusion to throw unwelcomed visitors off their path. As we walked deeper into the mysterious muggy woods, ash began to be visible in the air. What a curious mix. Embers glowed like fireflies, but the greenery seemed unaffected.

"So where are we anyways?" I asked.
"Really Darkus? I mean, we just discussed this,"
"No, I mean, where *are* we? I mean how far does it go?"

"Oh, I see. This is Remains; land of savages. It has four corners, all in which have been ventured. North lies Psykya, East is where we are, which consists of Muckraid, Omitis, and Redemption Tower. South lies Cemetrica, and West is where your rising point was. Think of Lanteria as the center point; the crossroads. The name Remains came from the words of the Ancients who founded this land after its destruction; beings of ancient magic and lands whom gave us the gift of life and their knowledge. It is said that Remains used to be a land of reason. In the Book of Law, it quotes one of the original founders of Remains, who remains unnamed:

'What lies underneath our feet, Remains; a mystery. Unless the creatures of the damned can perfect structure and sustain purity, only wrath and war will remain. For the spill of blood is equal for the ultimate desire.'

Since the existence of the creatures you've seen, and yet to see, Remains has never had a ruler. Many have tried, but failed. The main reason is, every time someone attempts to claim the throne, a war nearly breaks loose. Tribes vote their own Elders to rule the lands, which conflicts with one another. Fights break out, and the discussion is stopped before the problem escalates. So, the Elders have decided that, in order to keep the peace, they would rule each tribe individually, with their own rules and regulations practiced by location. The only collective group that seems to have any sort of leadership is the U.S.P., or the University of Sacred Practices, which is located outside of Remains. They assist in regulating the rules of practice. They also assist with punishments to those who fail to follow their own practices.

The creatures of these lands crave war. Although they try to follow the rules, they tend to veer off the wrong path; preaching about guidelines that they hardly practice. The ancients left behind a sacred book called The Book of Law. The creatures worship the ancients, and try to follow the rules in the book. If they follow the Book of Law's guidelines then perhaps we can all find peace. That includes sticking to their own practices and not cross contaminating with others. Lanterians practice Biology as do the Flintkus. Each tribe has their own Book of Law. In that book lie rules and guidelines to how they must live and practice. If they were to disobey, they have shown their tribe that they do not believe the Book of Law or its prophecy and have contaminated the possibility of finding peace.

Say a Lanterian decides to practice Alchemy. That Lanterian would be prompted to stop immediately. If they continue to disobey they will be cut out of the tribe like a cancer to stop any chance of jeopardizing the future. You and I are nothing but walking sacks of mayhem in their eyes and nothing but terminating us matters to the creatures that thrive in Remains.

I personally think it's a load of bullocks considering we could all just throw away this book and shake on it. But those who have lost everything become desperate and will believe anything just to find self-peace. They also seem to find great fulfillment in using its words to their advantages, even rewriting it to fit their needs. The book's existence is nearly pointless and will never end war."

Interesting. I thought about what he said for a moment as I caught ash between my fingertips and rubbed it away in the wind. Tinkarius was a so-called *toxic thinker*. He didn't believe in this prophecy. He was a man of reason. His banishment ironically started a bigger war.

"I'm beginning to think we're entering Muckraid," Ectus said.

"What gave it away?" I added sarcastically.

We stopped dead in our tracks when we heard the sound of voices nearby. It sounded like a crowd-no, a riot? Ectus and I looked at each other to confirm we were both aware of the situation and sped up our walking pace. As we grew closer it looked like a volcano storm in the middle of a forest that grew thicker and started to smell like cooked flesh. At this point my curiosity was taking full control. We heard what sounded like an angry crowd. I could hear '*kill the traitor,*" and "*boil the forging harlot!*". I picked up the pace to a jog and Ectus floated right behind me at the exact pace. I could see a small village, and a crowd of people gathering just beyond the brush.

Muckraid, as Ectus called it, was a small village with thriving plant life. Dirt paths were aligned with exotic-looking flora. The shelters were made of logs of dark wood and elegantly decorated with a variety of plant life and cloth. Some shelters were a few stories high, built around the bases of large tree trunks. Wooden roped bridges hung high in the branches, crossing from one shelter to another. Most of the shelters had large gardens by their sides, where the Flintkus men and women harvested their crops. I could see a variety of large fruits and vegetables growing in their gardens. Some gardens grew odd-looking plants that didn't appear edible. I assumed they were used for medicines.

"The Flintkus are famous for growing hearty foods, and specific ingredients for medicines. Since formulating medicines are considered a branch in the study of Alchemy, the Flintkus are forbidden to use them. Instead, they trade the ingredients to tribes who practice Alchemy. Those tribes then trade the finished product back to the Flintkus for use. It's a very delicate, yet necessary process," Ectus explained.

Ectus and I entered the small village and joined the mob. No one seemed to notice that a glowing white spirit and a monster just joined the crowd. They were too busy hollering at something a little further in the middle of the village. I started moving my way more in site. They were humanoids of some sort. Knowing they are a dying breed I was a little surprised to see them gathering. Something was different about them though; it was their eyes. One eye on each and every one of them was colored white with nothing but the pupil. They all wore long dark robes with large black belts wrapped around them at their waist and they all wore long, pointy hats garnished with various roots and flora. The color of their skin was grey. Right above the brim of their hats bared an emblem that looked like a heart with a knife across it. They stopped yelling and stared at Ectus and me in a daze. Word got around quick and everyone we passed stared and whispered. The female humanoids looked at us in terror.

We made it to the front where a tall hunched Elder with a long pointy hat and long beard read from a very large book on a podium. There were a few others that joined the elder man's side up on an old dark green marble stage. They were all elder, except one. It was a much younger female. She was standing on a stool, and she had a noose around her neck. She was being executed. She had pale grey skin like the rest of the humanoids, but she had a neon purple mismatched colored pupil instead of white. She had long, dark green hair and had a pointy hat like the rest, only hers had little gears pinned to it and a gear logo instead of the heart and knife. She looked sad, her head bowed down in shame. As we walked closer we caught her attention. She stared at us with sudden desperation.

"Who are you?" She asked us from the stage.

"I am, Darkus and this is Ectus," I replied, looking around at all of the people staring back.

"Help me," she whispered loudly to us. I stared at her, reading her body language. She looked so young and harmless. What's the catch? I didn't reply. I wanted to hear what the elder man had to say.

The elderly man cleared his throat and suddenly all was silent. Ectus and I looked around, a bit surprised by the synchronized silence that just happened. The elderly man adjusted his reading glasses and opened the giant book, which also had the heart and knife insignia. He brushed it off, looked at it a bit closer, then drew his head back and took a deep breath, and then exhaled in disappointment.

"We have gathered here today because one of our kind has been tinkering around with man-made devices in which don't apply to our way of living. The individual you see here is, in fact, and unfortunately, my daughter."

"Eat Creeple sap old man! You've never claimed me as your daughter-"

"SILENCE!" The elder man yelled. His face then grew soft once again and he continued,

"She has been warned not to tinker with the science of mechanics, yet she continues to do so. As you know, our culture bans the use of any mechanics and practices magic and majors in Biology and Bioengineering only. It says in the Book of Law that anyone who continues to do so must be destroyed. This is to purify the evil that she has bestowed on our peace."

The crowd booed and threw rotting food and old footwear at the girl. She dodged what she could and spit at the crowd.

"I have the right to do so! I am a living creature! There is no rule against doing what your heart tells you to do! You're all a bunch of ignorant, close-minded bottom-feeders who are too scared of anything that is not practiced by our kind. That is not my fault!"

The crowd continued to boo. I suddenly chose a side. I chose the girls side. Just like my creator, she was being sentenced to death for doing nothing more than following her heart and passion. What is simple and pure is so complex and vexed to this world. I don't understand it. The girl looked down at us with dread in her eyes. Her eyes grew large and watery. I could tell she was innocent in this twisted world of law and order. But something quite shocking happened at this very moment. To my surprise, the Mark of Tinkarius blipped right in front of her purple eye. The hologram. The hologram that was to let us know who our allies are.

"Do you see that?" I said to Ectus.

"That I do. She's a humanoid who bares the hidden Mark of Tinkarius. How bizarre," He said staring into the girl's eyes.

How could that be? She's just a humanoid girl. The old man cleared his throat and stopped the chattering in the area, and carried on.

"She must be terminated. If anyone here is brave enough to side my soon-to-be deceased daughter, now is your chance."

Chatter filled the air and the girl looked at us with all of the pleading that she could direct at us. The Mark of Tinkarius started sparking in and out, it then faded, and blipped off. I took a step forward and spoke.

"I believe you should let her go," I said loudly. Anyone who had not seen Ectus and I before looked at us in awe. The elderly man even took a step back in shock.

"My word, what on *earth* are you?"

Before I could speak, the girl opened her mouth and loudly answered, "He is a creation of Professor Tinkarius. He's here to save me."

The crowd became outraged; throwing things at Ectus and I, trying to grab onto us. I looked up at the girl in spite as she smiled at me and then she gave me a wink. Was this some plan to catch us? Or maybe it was a plan of escape? The elder man took off his glasses and gave us a good look.

"How do you know that?" the Elder asked.

"I just do, you old fool," She snapped back. He took a good hard look at us once more, cleaned his glasses and then put them back on himself gracefully, then simply said, "Kill all three of them."

A majority of the angry crowd put their hands to their sides. Their hands began to glow with a bright turquoise color.

"Magic," Ectus said with discomfort. "Great, we're making some more friends Ectus," I said in return.

"Yes, we're quite the popular crew, aren't we?"

I put my hands to my side as well and just knew I could send some super charged juice down my arms. My hands glowed bright green.

"Looks like their fresh out of bodies for me now," Ectus sighed.

I looked down at my hands as they glowed brightly.

"I'm getting the hang of this," I said out loud. The humanoids instantly started throwing balls of magic at me. I jumped as high as I could into the air, which was pretty high, by the way. The sky soon became filled with flying balls of magic like stars in the sky, as I began to fall back down. I fell on top of a tree that blocked a majority of the magic. The elder man lifted both his hands up in the air. Green smoke shot from out of the sleeves of his cloak. The green smoke that shot out of his cloak started forming into two transparent, long arms and long tree-like hands.

"Let's arm wrestle," Ectus shouted. Ectus was finally going to join the fun. He stuck out his arms and they extended almost the same length as the elder's large, manifested arms, his hands burlier and thicker. He reached for the big green arms and they started pushing at one another.

"Go get that girl! I'll try to hold the old man off, but be quick!" Ectus yelled. For the first time, a rush of respect for Ectus filled me. I jumped down from the tree and landed on two male humanoids. I stuck my hands out in front of myself and my hands glowed bright green once again. I put both my fists together and slammed them into the ground as hard as I could. I watched in amazement as a wave of energy rushed through the crowd's legs and tripped them like a carpet being ripped out from under them. Before they could get up I stuck my hands out and showed them my hands and yelled,

"Stay on the ground if you know what's best for you! I'm a monster with a kick! I'm the first in history to destroy a Crophix." The humanoids gasped and stayed kneeled on the ground.

The old man became winded by Ectus. I jumped up on the marble stage and grabbed the rope that held the girl's neck. I yanked the upper slack as hard as I could, tearing it instantly. The girl fell off of the stool and I rushed to help her up. A look of gratitude swept over her face as I used my nails to cut the rope off of her neck.

"Thank you, monster," she said softly.
"My name is Darkus, remember? But don't thank me yet,"

I glanced up to see Ectus was starting to lose his balance. My attention was then directed up at the elder man. I ran up to him, shoving him as hard as I could. The elder man went flying into the wall of a small wooden shelter. I looked over at the girl and told her to make haste. Ectus withdrew his long arms and followed us out of the woods. The old man flew out of the small shelter and landed on the marble stage. I looked over my shoulder and saw him cooking something up.

The girl pulled out a handheld device with a big red button on it. Its antennae was made of a little branch. She slammed her finger into the big red button and threw the remote in the trees. There was a loud, gaining thudding coming from the forest that surrounded the village, followed by a howl. I recognize that sound. It was a Creeple Tree. But where? And why? The thudding grew louder and quicker, then all went silent. The old man stopped to listen. He quickly turned around on his heel to stare at a large tree. He stared at it and yelled, "You are an abomination!"

To my surprise, the tree uprooted and suddenly started sprouting long, swift mechanical arms. About six of these arms shot through the tree's bark and started reaching for the elder. The elder dodged, and the tree then grew mechanical legs and walked over the elder. It started running right at us. The girl jumped at the tree as it ran right at her. It extended one of its mechanical arms and caught her and placed her on a branch as it ran. It charged right at us.

"Jump onto the Creeple Tree!" She yelled.

Never would I ever want to do such a thing, but it looked like it was somewhat under her control. Plus I didn't have any better ideas. But before I could react the tree jumped over me and I barely had time to jump on. I began to run after the tree but the massive thing was much faster then me, with those long spider-like mechanic legs.

"Run faster! It's going to come in hot!" the girl called out.

The ashes came back into the air, and the mugginess entered my lunges, making it a little difficult to run. I started becoming stiff and slowing down. Ectus joined the girl riding on the mechanical Creeple Tree. They looked back to see me slowing down. I reached for my flask and opened it and poured the sweet tree gunk down my throat. It started to kick in and my legs started to speed up. But that was all the time the elder man needed. I could see his eyes glow red and his mouth opened abnormally large. He put his arms to his side and started yelling at the top of his lunges. His voice turned into a shriek and it filled the forest. Something big was about to happen.

"He's going to manic-zap us!" the girl yelled.

That doesn't sound pleasant at all, I thought to myself. The old man got down on one knee, fist in the ground, then shot his head straight up and pulled a rod out of his cloak. The top of the rod held a large sphere and it glowed bright red. I could see all of this through the brush as we ran. He's out of my site now but I can see a bright red light growing larger by the second. The light died down and I could hear what sounded like a massive bomb going off. The wind picked up about 100 mph and we were blown off our feet. Up ahead I saw the Creeple Tree trip and start to roll on its side, throwing mechanical parts all over from the impact, but I couldn't see Ectus or the girl. The burst of wind was followed by a bright light. It touched my skin and felt as if I was taking a bath in molten lava. I screamed from the searing pain and felt my body being blown into the air by a gust of fiery hot wind. I flew high into the air, then gravity took its toll on me and I started hurtling downward like a comet from the sky. I couldn't tell where up and down met and I was stunned from the searing hot burn of the blast. I could see the ground spinning below me, spinning closer and closer. I was going to eat soot again. I tried to get my brain to function but I seemed to be paralyzed. It wasn't from the fight. I had drunk half of my Creeple sap. The blast dug deep into my nerves. In seconds I was about to land on my face. I close my eyes and accept the fall and then suddenly, complete stillness. I was in the air like a feather. My eyes were clinched tight and my arms side by side with clenched fists. I was waiting for the ground to break my fall but nothing seemed to be happening.

"You can open your eyes now," a soft female voice said. I opened one eye to make sure the coast was clear. To my amazement, I was floating just inches from the floor, facing downward. I was hovering in mid air. I opened both of my eyes and stared at the floor. The girl had her hand out. She was keeping me afloat. Seconds later, she put her hand down and I hit the ground face first. I still managed to land on my face. It's becoming a habit that is getting old, quick. She giggled, then she and Ectus helped me to my feet. The sting of the energy blast was still aching through my veins. It felt as if I was held over an open fire for far too long, but no visible damage, whatsoever.

"Are you alright there?" the girl asked.

"Never been better," I joked. "Where is your mechanical Creeple Tree?"

"In pieces," the girl said slightly bummed. She pointed over to where its crash site was. I could see the tree was no longer living, and sparks shot from the base of where the mechanical arms once sprouted from. The sparks caught the oozing sap from the tree on fire. I ran over quickly with my flask to fill it up before the rest was turned to ash.

"How did you know we were creations of Tinkarius?" Ectus asked.

"Yeah, and why did you do us like that?" I added bitterly.

The girl giggled and looked at us. She tilted her body in a sassy kind of way. Her head tilted in opposite direction of her body.

"I had to think of something to get you guys to hurry up and save me," she said, "you guys weren't budging and I was about to be executed.

"I was listening first. I wanted to hear the details before we just played hero," I told her. She rolled her eyes at me and shrugged.

"You're welcome for breaking your fall, by the way," she continued.

"Yeah, well you're welcome for saving you from being executed. Got quite a nasty burning sensation out of this entire damsel in distress act, as well," I continued coldly.

"Well, don't you worry about that. It's got a hefty pay off," She said, walking up to the demolished tree and brushing the back of her hand over the bark as if it were some pet.

"Oh yeah? And what may that be?" Ectus demanded, crossing his arms.

"I know how to find your creator," she said. Suddenly she had our attention. I was not expecting that. We both became silent with anticipation.

"Hello boys. My name is Kursus. I'm the one that is going to help you find Professor Tinkarius."

CHAPTER III
KURSUS

The girl is a humanoid. At least, I think she is. She needed rest so I assume she's mostly human. The sky grew dark with orange and purples. I was drawn to the sky. It was so beautiful. Being as curious as I was, I couldn't help but to be easily mesmerized by such a sight. We set up camp on a hill between Lanteria and Muckraid, but far enough from both to stay away from our new fans. Kursus had walked just around the hill to bathe in a lake. On her way, there she took her clothes off and I couldn't help but notice what looked like scars, covering the center of her back and continuing straight up her arms and down her legs. Could Tinkarius have done that? Or perhaps it was from Muckraid? Something wasn't right about this humanoid, I could feel it. She didn't seem to be a creation of our creator, but she didn't seem to be all human as well. She came back from her bath. She sat down and picked up a brick of wood. She held it between her hands and closed her eyes. The brick of wood started smoking and then melted down into what appeared to be a bowl. It was like watching something physically impossible happening before my very eyes. She reached into her robes and grabbed a few random ingredients. She picked up a rock and used it to grind her ingredients into a powder, and then she took a couple of bones and grinded them up into a meal. She then picked up a small winged night critter and put its head on the edge of the bowl. Next, she took the rock and then smashed its head against the bowl, decapitating it and threw the body behind her. She began to stir.

"Staring is quite rude you know," Kursus said not even looking up. I looked away in embarrassment.

"I apologize. I'm just trying to figure you out," Ectus rolled his eyes.

"Oh brother," he mumbled. I shot him a glare.

"What I meant was, I can't tell if you are human or not." She started to stir her recipe faster. She took her hand and gestured it in a way that looked like she threw something small into the middle of where we were all sitting. Instantly a large, purple fire started. She pushed the bowl out in front of her, and it floated carelessly into the air as if gravity had been shut off. It floated right over the fire and became still. She stared into the fire. I could tell she had something on her mind.

"Don't mind my magic tricks. I'm able to summon an apport, or objects from thin air. It's a basic technique taught to us Flintkus. We're a tribe of magic, see." She took a deep breath and sighed, then continued,

"I am confident I am human. Although, I feel different. I know I'm special. I can predict the future semi-accurately. I can almost read minds, at times. These are not techniques taught to the Flintkus. My magic is average, but I have a fascination with mechanics. As you heard, the practice of mechanics is banned from the Flintkus tribe. That's my tribe; humanoids that practice only biology, a proud race that doesn't want to get our water muddy, if you catch my drift. But I find it preposterous! Who is to say what we can and cannot do? My passion is unique and never before seen. That's why I was a secret follower of Professor Tinkarius. He follows his dream and never backs down. He's an inspiration to all who dare to dream. I have to find him too, you see. He was my supplier before the world turned on him. His parts are what made that mechanical Creeple Tree you saw back there. But that tree was the last of the parts that I had. The damage is beyond repair. Without the parts, I cannot follow my passion. I know you guys are looking for him, and after hearing your names I remember him talking about a genius idea that would turn heads and bring him great fortunes. I don't know why he doesn't just use his well-mastered alchemy to gain his fame and fortune. Perhaps it's the pride of knowing he worked for it.

He talked about creating a one of a kind monster called Darkus. It would be the monster that would forever change the tides of the new war. The war that has swept over this land. I thought I'd never get to lay eyes on his creation, but then out of nowhere you just waltz into my village," she smiled. I couldn't stop staring at her purple eye. She cleared her throat and got up to grab her bowl. She took out a spoon from her robe and continued to stir.

"My father, Sulfus, was appalled when he found me using mechanical parts. Professor Tinkarius's parts, at that. He then disowned me and eventually got the town to turn against me. Such pride, and not nearly enough brains as those people think. I don't know where I got my independence from, but it certainly wasn't from him. It's sad, really. When we are young, we are taught to fear death. It is a perception that almost appears shatterproof. We humans are a dying race; the very bottom of the food chain in this nightmare of a world. Focusing on killing off what is left of our race to me, is plain stupid and just blind arrogance.

"Where is your mother?" Ectus interrupted. She stopped stirring for a second, and then continued.

"She was also sentenced to death,"

"Oh my," Ectus said.

"She had both brains and strength, and the men in the village found it threatening. It's important for the males to be the alpha. A woman with inspiration, alone, was hard for them to accept. It's pathetic. I wish I could just burn them all!"

The fire got large for just a moment, which startled Kursus. She took a deep breath and continued calmly,

"I'd rather be ridiculed for being different then to be riddled with the filth of ignorance. I am above my people's ignorance. By choosing to not fully open yourself to the possibilities around you, you are choosing to not fully exist. I'd rather just run away. It's a good thing I met you guys. Looks like we're allies now."

She stopped stirring the bowl and snapped her fingers. The fire's color turned blue. She sat down and started eating her odd mixture.

"But if you want my help, you're going to need parts," She spat, her cheeks puffed full of mush. "There is a way to find him. I can pin-point his location. I know because I'm a smart little girl and

I have done my homework. If this world knew what I know your Creator would be Monstrut soup."

"Monstrut soup?" Ectus repeated disgustingly. "What is a Monstrut?"

"You don't know what a *Monstrut* is?" Kursus asked in surprise while taking another huge bite of her weird critter chowder.

"Well you're going to find out soon enough, you will see. But for tonight I need sleep. We humans don't run off of Creeple Tree sap and synthetic energy."

She lifted the bowl over her head and opened her mouth wide getting the remaining fluids of her odd supper and threw the bowl in the fire. The fire turned green for just a moment then disappeared without a trace. She walked over to a tree with leaves that hid her from the lights in the sky and put her hand on the stalk. Roots came out gently from the ground and formed a small shelter for her to sleep in. She threw her hands over her as if she had a jacket and a velvet red quilt appeared out of thin air. She wrapped it around herself and crawled into the little shelter she had made.

"Good night monsters. We have a big day tomorrow," she said softly.

She slowly dozed off to the whispering of the wind and eventually fell asleep. I sat still looking up at the miraculous night sky. I pondered if there was anything out there. Being a creature that needs no sleep, you have a lot of time to think. I started thinking about Muckraid and their way of life. Eventually I started thinking about the battle in Lanteria and the fierce creatures that roam the lands. They were such hideous, soulless creatures; killing each other, and others, just to stay on top of one another to win. They preach upon a book that they barely commit to. This life that has been given to me I appreciate it, sure. the world I live in is fierce, but I'll never give up the feeling this night sky has made me feel; light, numb, calm, and at ease. It was the payoff that this world gave to us. A chance to revive our strengths and regain our confidence, and as far as I knew we only get one chance.

I started rambling there for a moment. That's what the sky does to me. I mind was at ease until the flicker of a bright blue light coming from the woods and had caught my eye from where I was facing. Ectus came floating through, humming to himself. He floated onto a large stone in front of me and appeared as though he was going to sit on his wispy tail, but just floated in the air above the large stone as if he was sitting on it.

"What's the matter with you?" I asked curiously.

"There is something about the woods at night that makes me feel at ease," he replied after a large sigh.

"Everyone has their private escape," he continued, "What about you?"

"I really like the sky," I answered as I looked back up into the dark abyss.

"Ah yes," he agreed.

"There is something very curious about that girl," I said, "I'm eager to know where she stands in all of this. What will come out of her joining up with us?"

"Yes, she's quite feisty," Ectus spat. I squinted my eyes to his tone but then nodded my head in agreement.

"I wonder where she will take us," I said, "I wonder what it is that she knows that we don't. The anticipation is killing me."

"She definitely plays a part in all of this," Ectus answered, "She knows a lot about Tinkarius. She used his parts and-Ahh!"

Ectus jumped and looked behind himself. He looked around for a minute. I stared at him in confusion.

"Did you hear that?" He said with a look of shock on his face.

"Here what?"

"Shh, listen!" he said. We both lay quiet for a moment. After waiting long and hard I said, "You're just a scaredy ghost."

"You didn't hear that?"

"No, I heard you scream like a wussy," I said. He snarled at me.

"There is nothing wrong with being afraid. Not everyone has powers like you."

"Yeah, but you're a ghost! You can turn invisible and solid objects can't touch you."

Ectus thought for a minute. "You know, you got a pretty good point there."

He kind of smiled and sighed in relief. I rolled my eyes and got up to walk towards the end of the patch of grass where the woods were. I stood still and kept watch. My eyes caught a very large face that appeared up in the air flying over from the woods in the distance and eventually into site. It had large bright white eyes and two large wings. It had small stubby feet and a large beard around its mouth. It looked creepy. It stared at me all the way from one side of the opening to the other and then disappeared.

"What are you doing?" Ectus asked.

"I'm going to stand watch all night; nothing better to do anyways."

"Good idea," Ectus replied.

"Did you see that?" I asked him.

"See what?"

"Well, it…it looked like a large flying face."

"What? Uh, no I didn't. Are you sure you don't need to sleep?"

I rolled my eyes once more, "Just shut up and keep your eyes peeled."

Ectus flew high up into the sky and floated steadily above our camp site and dimmed down the glow of his body. We kept our positions all night. Not one word spoken to one another, just silent and cautious.

I've yet to see the sun rise up from the end of the lands. It was beautiful, more than the night sky. The colors changed rapidly as it became brighter in the sky. I continued to stand until I heard rustling around in the vine shelter that Kursus had made. She sat up and yawned loudly to let us know she was awake. The shelter then slowly started deteriorating as the roots began to retreat back into the ground and just like that, Kursus was visible. She stretched her arms out wide, pushing her chest out and her head falling to her side, followed by a high-pitched grunting sound. Then she stood right up on her feet and started walking towards me. Ectus saw movement and slowly found his way down where we were and we regrouped. I waited all night to hear where we were going. I nearly drove myself insane obsessing about it. She walked up to us and looked at one another, smiled and said,

"I'm going to get me some breakfast." I sighed from lack of patience. She looked over at me and frowned. "Don't worry monster, we will get down to business soon. I know it's hard for you to grasp considering you don't need to eat."

"Humanoids are inefficient and needy is all," I replied.

"Wait until you deal with me being a woman," she snapped back, "you're just getting my basic humanoid functions. Just wait till you've got me in a bad mood," she finished and walked straight into the woods. Ectus and I watched her walk away.

"Why don't we just turn around and leave her here," Ectus whispered jokingly into my ear. I found that a little funny.

"I heard that!" Kursus yelled in the distance. Ectus and I were a little taken aback, then rolled our eyes and walked slowly behind Kursus.

We ventured a good few miles from our camp site through an area covered in dead trees and nothing else. She was looking for something in the higher parts of the trees. She went a long while without finding it and my patience were growing thin. She was so at ease and careless. It was kind of annoying me. I have things I need to do, and you're looking for something in the trees-

"Don't worry Darkus I'm growing close on its tail," she said from nowhere, as if she was reading my mind.

"I hope so because this is starting to get a little boring," I muttered. She turned on her heel quickly facing me, but was looking up behind us.

"There."

She pointed up to the top of a tree. To my surprise, the massive head with the large white eyes and large mouth with tattered sharp wings was sitting up right against the trunk of the tree with its eyes closed. It looked so odd. Its beard hung much lower than the branches.

"I saw that thing last night," I spoke, baffled that Kursus somehow pinpointed this thing.

"That's not good. Good thing I'm going to eat it today," she answered.

Ectus and I looked at her in shock. She caught onto our facial expressions and looked confused. "What? Never had a Brackling before?"

"Brackling?" I repeated in disgust.

"That's right, a Brackling. They lay eggs that look like giant cocoons. Because it's a lazy creature, they normally take over another critter's home. Oh, and they have the ability to instantly kill whatever makes eye contact with them the day after. Once they look into your eyes at night, you suddenly die at some point in the day. It can kill anything; even a Crophix, if a Crophix was dumb enough to look into its eyes. It's called the Evil Eye technique. The victim's heart will stop beating, and they will fall to the ground. The Brackling has no idea that it casts a fatal curse on anyone who looks at it; completely oblivious."

Ectus and I looked up at the Brackling in distaste. I couldn't eat that thing; it looked like a face with wings. Last time I checked, I don't eat faces.

"You can go ahead and have this one," I said, still looking at the Brackling,

"You have an odd taste in feasting."

"What can I say? I like the taste of monster flesh," she said as she looked into my eyes. Her eyes glistened and shifted then she turned her back to us and walked up to the trunk of the tree. She grabbed its branches and shook it as hard as she could. The Brackling nearly fell off and tilted back and forth trying to regain its balance as the thin dead tree wobbled back and forth. It flew off of the branch and looked down at Kursus. It made eye contact and tried to fly away. Kursus then pulled out a much smaller rod than Sulfus had and held it like a rifle.

"This is my ether rod," Kursus explained, running the palm of her hand up the shaft and grasping the ball on top, "Every Flintkus is given one in their teen years. It's made from the finest, toughest sludge marble found deep in the ground. It's brought to life by ancient magic. Normally they lose their magic once the owner is proven guilty of meddling. Fortunately, I rigged it to only obey my commands. It took a lot of voodoo but I did it. I even named her; Vengeance."

"You gave an object a sex and a name?" Ectus asked.

She looked up at the Brackling, which flew quite slowly. A green hologram of what looked like a bow and arrow appeared from thin air aside Vengeance. She locked onto the Brackling and the bow drew itself back. She then jerked the rod back as if she had shot a large caliber rifle and a long green dart, of what looked like an arrow shot straight through the trees. All of the trees suddenly bent sideways to clear a path for the arrow, magically, which hit the Brackling dead on. The burst of the hit sparked bright green and the Brackling instantly stopped flapping its wings and fell straight down to the ground. It hit a couple branches on the way down and landed with a hard thud. Kursus walked up to the Brackling and spoke some other language I didn't understand.

"*Nrub toh dliw gniw dna evig em ecnanetsus,*"

The Brackling suddenly bursts into flames and in seconds it turned dark enough to look well cooked. The fire died and disappeared. The smell of rotted flesh filled my nostrils. It didn't smell pleasant at all.

Ectus stared in awe as Kursus stood before the large Brackling.

"You know how to speak Ancient Voice," Ectus said in amazement. Kursus bent down and ripped off a big chunk of the Brackling's hide for herself. It looked well cooked and was steaming hot. She took a big bite out of it and filled both her cheeks. She nodded her head and tried to force a smile through her swelled cheeks. I frowned in confusion.

"Ancient Voice?" I asked. Ectus turned to me,

"Ancient Voice; It's a dead language that only people who have access to ancient scriptures or the blessing from the Mirror Elders. Mirror Elders don't leave those out in the open for the world to read. It is the language of the beings that lived here long ago. The Mirror Elders are what is left of the Old World, sworn immortal beings that protect the language. They are highly magical, ancient beings wearing masks that allow them to create and conceal spells in backward tongue, coating every word in magic."

I looked at Kursus in confusion. Kursus put her finger up to let us give her a moment while she chewed her way through the Brackling hide. She swallowed, licked her lips and bent down to grab another piece of the hideous looking being. Before she put it in her mouth she looked at me and said,

"My father had access to those scriptures. They are very powerful spells that I *technically* was never allowed to read. You just need to pronounce it right and you are well in business. It sounds easy, but I just explained it as simply as I could."

She was about to put the flesh in her mouth, but paused; her eyes looking up, thinking long and hard.

"Right, you can read those scriptures correctly all day long and not be granted its powers. You must be blessed by the Mirror Elders as I was. You must venture to their location and look into the face of the Mirror Elders, and stand up to your own reflection. Their faces are nothing more but cursed polished mirrors in which can manifest your darkest secrets into our physical realm. Kind of forgot about that part."

She shrugged it off and stuck that wad of cooked flesh into her mouth. She nodded her head in approval in the taste of the Brackling.

Ectus looked like he was thinking pretty hard about what was just said.

"Huh," he said.

"That is kind of clever, but why did you tell us?" I asked.

"Because eventually you're going to need to do the same. I did enough research to take myself through the trials of finding their location." she answered, "It's quite the power to use; pretty much a strong spell language, but you can only use it once a day, when the cycle of the moon rotates in full," she sputtered with a mouth full of carcass.

"In their faces, you can see the real you. If you are honest to the Mirror Elders, they will grant you this sacred ability. If you lie about your fear, the truth will reveal itself and your reflection can switch places with you, placing you in the reflections for all of eternity. Your true evil will literally come to life and overrule you. It's a powerful spell that results in a test of strength, courage and intentions. However, once you have made an appearance They will not allow you to make a second." She continued to chew, "It's kind of deep, really. It's like a living metaphor."

Ectus and I looked at each other in thought. *How curious*, I thought. I'd love to have that ability. But I couldn't really think of anything I was afraid of. I was afraid of the Crophix before I found out I could blow its head off. But does not being afraid make me courageous? I figured if you are afraid of something that you face, that is what real courage is. So would that even work for me?

"I'm afraid of everything, and I'm ok with that," Ectus answered with a smile.

Kursus and I smiled to Ectus's comment as well. Kursus flicked her hand like she was shaking a handkerchief and a velvet red napkin apported in her hand from thin air. She wiped off her mouth and threw the napkin on the Brackling.

"So, are you ready for this, monster?"

"You have no idea," I answered.

"Good, listen up close. This is big, and we're going to need to do this just how I say it or all will go wrong. We need to find two ancient artifacts; A Philosopher's Stone and The Elixir of Life. Are you two aware of these artifacts by chance?"

Ectus and I slowly shook our head in unison. Kursus closed her eyes and shook her head.

"Of course not, they are ancient secret artifacts," she slapped her head. She walked towards us. She crouched low, glanced around, and spoke softly.

"Long ago, in ancient times, there was a Master Alchemist, who created the stone and the elixir. His intentions, however, were not pure. In this time of peace, there were few who could not stand the quietness. They could not bear sharing equality with their own.

They wanted power beyond anything else. So, the Master Alchemist drew the power from the stars, using dangerous Alchemy. Using Metallurgy, he designed an unbreakable metal and infused it with the energy and metals of the stars with the most potent of magic. Finally, he completed the Philosopher's Stone.

He then took the stone in hand and murdered his own. He broke the peace that was thought to be endless, draining their blood to then mix into a divine concoction; the Elixir of Life. With a final spell, he turned the blood of his kin into a divine potion that could grant immortality. What he didn't know was that the magic he had used to craft the stone and the elixir reacted to one another when close together.

Although my tribe primarily practices Biology, Magic is our secondary practice. While studying Magic, we also study Magic Theory. In theory, Spell-on-spell friction happens when two objects bearing spells react to one another. Although we don't possess the tools to measure this phenomenon to confirm this theory, certain spells do seem to react near one another. Spells can resist one another, which can cause devastating reactions, while others can resonate with one another. This can cause two spells to combine and create a new spell.

It is rumored that one of the survivors of the Master Alchemist's attack had gotten her hands on both the Philosopher's Stone and the Elixir of Life during his slumber. The two artifacts when close together can supposedly grant any wish. Not knowing this, the survivor had wished that the two objects could be hidden, to be found never again by the Master Alchemist. As she had made this wish, the two artifacts vanished out of her hands, never to be found again. The Alchemist was then caught and punished for his horrible crimes. Thus, the rumor that bringing both of the artifacts together granted the beholder any wish he or she desired.

"That is incredible," I said, fascinated by this theory. "So, what kind of power would we possess if we were to find these artifacts? The same ones from the story?"

Separately, they do different things. The Philosopher's Stone gives the holder super strength. The Elixir of Life grants immortality. Since you both cannot age I will be obtaining The Elixir of Life for my own right before we put them together. Doing so gives the holder the power to make one wish that will come true no matter what, even if it defies science and reality. Most of the tribes that look for both of these don't know that the powers of both combine grant you one wish. That will come in handy for us just in case someone gets to it first."

"What's the catch?" I asked. Kursus smiled with the most mischievous grin I'd ever seen.

"Both artifacts are well hidden and guarded. Though they've never been found there is a theory that I am aware of about their locations. They were wished to be never found by the Master

Alchemist, which means they would have been placed where the Alchemist could never travel, due to the natures of the locations. They require the use of all three sacred practices; Biology, Alchemy, and Mechanics. Since most obey the Book of Law and practice their own, this makes it easier to keep these artifacts safe. It takes a 'toxic thinker' to obtain them. You just so happen to be a walking, talking, and breathing key and if anyone was to know of this, tribes from all over would be hunting you down. That's why it's best to keep this an ultimate secret."

"Well, then why are we talking about this out in the open?"

"We're not," Kursus said. "You're actually talking to me through telepathy right now."

I looked at her in confusion. Just as she said that Ectus asked,

"Why are you two just staring at each other like that? Is everything alright? Because you both kind of freaking me out."

"We were communicating telepathically," Kursus answered. Ectus slightly frowned.

"Why wasn't I invited?"

"Because *we're* talking telepathically right now," Ectus looked at me in confusion.

"I didn't hear any of that," I answered to his obvious question.

"How do I know when you're doing that?" Ectus asked.

"You don't, but we're not now. Secret time is over. We must head to Redemption Tower. It's a massive land in the sky held up by an endless, twirling flight of stairs."

"Uh, Kursus? I don't think that's a very good idea," Ectus added.

"Why not?" I asked.

"What he's referring to is the natives that live there are geniuses. They are an evolved race of humanoids with powerful minds. They are called Steinlocks, and they don't practice anything ancient at all. Unlike our mechanical, biological, and alchemical powers, they practice an advanced form of what's called robotics and humanoids with robotic innards. It's a large step above mechanics, a life form with the same concept of artificial intelligence that you have, Darkus."

"Wait a minute, so does that mean," I stopped to think.

"Yes Darkus. Where we are going is where Professor Tinkarius is from, our creator's homeland. Professor Tinkarius is a Steinlock."

It all clicked. These people hate our creator. They are the ones who pushed him out and banned him from using ancient technology; the first to cast him out. Another race who thinks they can push their kind around and tell them what to do. But from what I gathered, this meant that they possibly know what he is doing. They probably know that I am is a creation of Tinkarius.

"Do you get it? Do you see why it's going to be a challenge?" Kursus added. I nodded my head.

"If anyone knows how to shut you down, it's the Steinlocks. We must be very diligent when we are passing through or the Steinlocks will catch onto us and do who knows what."

"How do we get through?" I asked.

"Although the idea is intimidating, the concept is simple. The Steinlocks hold much confidence in their design that they don't feel that they need protection from our ancient studies. This gives us the upper hand since I've got a book full of sneaky spells that will allow us to slip right in. The downfall is that we have to go back through the boarder of Muckraid."

I didn't like the sound of that. I wasn't what you would call ecstatic with the thought of reuniting with my Flintkus friends.

"As long as we stay on the boarder," Ectus demanded. "We'll be fine. That scary, old bat of a dad of yours sure is rather forceful for such an age."

"He's actually 1,487 years old," Kursus said.

"Does that mean he has taken the Elixir of life?" I asked.

"Yes, he did. But anyone who drinks it only gets a sip and the treasure is returned to its hideout. Being a guardian of his lands, he's been granted a sip by the Mirror Elders."

"So why must we go to Redemption Tower?" Ectus asked.

"The Steinlocks possess a device that will show us the path to these artifacts. Each artifact is hidden well. Darkus will act as a key to unlocking the path."

"Why am I a key?" I asked.

"You hold all of its powers in your design. You're invulnerable to most powers and attacks, making you quite useful. There is an ancient key hidden elsewhere, but having you here cuts out time for us since we won't have to locate it. Normally it would take three people from each practice to find each artifact. Although there are three of us, we only need you."

I could see Ectus looking at us in confusion again. We were talking telepathically once more. She was smart with when to do it, making sure every detail of secrecy was kept hidden. Ectus rolled his eyes and floated away a couple feet to look around.

"Without law, there would be no control, and the artifacts would be destroyed or used. So, in its own way, it benefits us that law is practiced," I stated.

"Very good monster," Kursus said proudly.

"Very good what?" Ectus said out loud. She obviously turned off the telepathy, which told me she was done with the secrets once again.

"So, are you two ready? We have a date with the Steinlocks," Kursus finished. "What exactly is your plan?" Ectus asked bitterly.

"We are going to give you a humanoid body." Ectus's face lit up. "Wha-really?" He asked in disbelief.

"Yes, but the bad news is its only temporary. We don't have the technology to make it permanent."

"Oh," he said glumly. "Well I guess I will get the feeling for just a moment," he added.

"You will be disguised as a Steinlock. Doing so will grant access to Redemption Tower. Darkus will then consume a potion that I've mixed for just the occasion." Kursus stuck her arm straight out, hand out flat, her palm up and a bottle instantly appeared in her grasp.

"This will make you odorless, invisible, and even block your system from every type of scanning device. None of their technology will be able to detect you. But it doesn't last for long. Darkus, you and I must find the leader of the tribe and look for a device called the NaviBox. It looks like a plain cube but can be opened to reveal any secret that you desire. With this cube, we can find the exact locations of the hidden treasures. It will be a great challenge, considering many have tried to nab it and failed. But we have a solid system."

Kursus began walking towards Muckraid. Ectus and I looked at each other and then began to follow. This plan sounds pretty solid, but I couldn't help but to wonder how she knew so much.

"So, how do you know so much?" Ectus asked the moment I thought it.

"When your dad is an Elder you tend to listen. I wasn't like the rest; following orders, joining the herd. I wanted to be heard and I wanted to go on adventures and get out of Muckraid. So, I listened to everything around the corner and kept it all up here," She took her index finger and tapped it on her temple.

"I memorized every detail and listened carefully, playing the innocent young daughter. Elder's obtain knowledge of mostly everything. They must know as much as they can to defend their lands and be prepared for the worst. Knowledge is power."

As we continued to walk, the smell of burnt wood came back and the air became muggy and hot. My gut turned as the smell reminded me of my last and only unfortunate visit to Muckraid. I could tell Ectus was quite disturbed as well by the look on his face and how he tapped his finger tips together whenever he was nervous, which was quite often. Kursus walked until she came to a sign that I had not seen before. The sign was tall and tattered; covered in mold, but the words were still big and black. An arrow pointed left saying *"Glirbettes,"* and an arrow to the right that said *"Muckraid."*

"Glirbettes?" I asked in confusion, eyes still on the sign to make sure I read it correctly.

"That's right! Glirbettes; they are mischievous little green creatures that look similar to humanoids, only they are much smaller, and have large noses. They wear little stocking hats and have long black nails and big long feet. Fortunately, they don't eat human flesh. They eat the skulls of Lanterians. But they are quite nasty if you disturb them while they sleep. Which is why we are going there during the day," Kursus answered cheerfully. She then continued to walk in the direction that warned, "*Glirbettes*."

"You never said anything about dealing with other creatures," Ectus complained.

"Well deal with it, night light! You're going to be dealing with all kinds of creatures on this quest. You haven't even seen the worst yet!" Kursus snapped back, then turned on her heel and walked a little faster. Ectus sighed.

"She's not my most favorite person," he muttered.

"She's definitely all business, isn't she?" I added.

It wasn't too long before the smell of burnt wood and the mugginess went away. We were then welcomed by a rotten vegetable type of smell. The air grew much cooler, but the woods were silent. Creaking of trees in the wind were the only things you could hear, other then our footsteps. It wasn't long before the source of the rotten vegetable smell came into site. Looking up and around, I wasn't paying attention to where I was walking. I had stepped in something mushy. I stopped, and looked down to check my feet and almost jumped back. I had stepped on the head of a Lanterian. I shook my foot off and before my eyes were dozens of Lanterian heads that looked like they've been chewed on. Unlike the ones in

Lanteria, these ones had no fire burning hot within. They were empty, cold and hollow. It was an eerie site.

"They are around here somewhere," Kursus said, bending down to pick up a Lanterian's head to look face to face at it. She stared into the skull, and then softly said, "These heads are fresh." Ectus and I tightened up a bit in defense. We looked around and saw nothing. We continued to walk down the path, but then I got that feeling again, like I was being watched. My natural instinct was to look up at all the trees to make sure they didn't have any faces. The last time I felt this way was when I encountered those terrible Creeple Trees. Something suddenly ran quickly behind us. We all three stopped dead in our tracks and looked back. Leaves that had fallen from the trees to the ground were kicked up by a gust of wind from whatever ran behind us. The sound then came from the front of us and we all looked ahead. Again, more leaves got caught up in a gust of whatever was running around.

"Its just one of them," Kursus said irritated, "it's just checking us out."

We then began to walk some more and suddenly we heard howling from above the trees. It sounded like hundreds of little voices. The howls were followed by laughter and then we saw little green men sliding down on vines. They hit the ground and surrounded us. Some fell head first, slowly standing up on their feet and retrieving their purple stalking caps. They were all laughing and chuckling. They were definitely small and green. Most of them wore hats, but some of them were wearing Lanterian skulls.

"Get out of our way, we mean you no harm," Kursus yelled. They all began to giggle and chuckle as they moved in a little closer at us.

"Ouch!"

I hollered as a sharp pain came from my behind. I turned around to see one of the little green creatures holding a small spear and chuckling at me. I yanked it out of his hand and held it over my head and was about to smash the little critter with it, but Kursus stopped me.

"Stop!" She hollered.

"Why would I do that?" I demanded, my behind still pinched by the prick of the spear.

"If you attack one of them, then all of them will rush us. Just continue to walk through and ignore them."

I would much rather like to blast all of these little annoying critters to hell. They yanked at our clothing and tried to trip us as we walked.

"They are actually kind of cute," Ectus said blissfully.

"That's because they can't touch you," I said, bitterly. We continued to walk until they stopped following us. They started to throw Lanterian skulls at us until we were too far away. Then they all waved at us in goodbye while they stood there watching us. I was relieved to pass through them. I didn't know how much longer I could have held my temper. The loud cackling and laughter grew silent as we walked further away, and then a distant echo of giggles, until finally, silence once more.

"So far, I do not like the creatures in this world," I said coldly, my rear still throbbing with pain.

"Does that include us?" Ectus asked.

I smiled and answered, "You have your moments, but I certainly like you two a lot more than everyone else I've seen."

"Aw, how sweet," Kursus said sarcastically.

The woods started to clear out and in the distance through the trees I could see something shooting straight out of the ground, but couldn't see where it ended above because the brush of the trees were still in the way. I picked up my pace and we made it out of the wooded area. About five miles ahead of us was a massive rod that came right out of the ground. It shot up so high that the mist above blocked off the view of whatever it was, and what it held. Adjusting my sight, I could see thousands and thousands of stairs. Stairs that spiraled all the way up the shaft.

"There it is," Kursus breathed, "those are the stairs that take us to Redemption Tower. And yes, they are just as exhausting as they look," she said slightly discouraged.

"Good thing I float," Ectus said.

"Yeah, and I don't get tired," I added feeling relieved.

"Good, then you can carry me on your shoulders," Kursus implied. She then continued forward. I thought about arguing that statement, but she really was just a humanoid. A fragile, needy humanoid. I didn't speak, Ectus and I just followed her lead down the grassy, rolling hills that were at the end of the clearing.

As we walked closer, my monster heart pounded with intimidation as the tower appeared much more massive. We walked towards it, looking straight up for a couple miles. It was so huge and impressive. There was no way humanoids had built this.

We finally made it to the base. We all had to touch it and look straight up. It was quite an incredible site to behold. A sense of honor and pride was felt for whoever built this tower.

"It's so massive," Kursus said in awe. The beginning of the stairs wasn't visible so we walked around the massive base of the tower while still touching it until a flight of stairs came before us. We walked up to the first step of the tower and stared at it. We looked at each other and took a deep breath and sighed.

"Are you ready, monster man?" Kursus asked me. She walked up to me and turned around and stood there, waiting for me to place her on my shoulders. I grabbed her by both sides of her under arms, lifted her above my head and placed her on my shoulders. She wrapped her calves around my sides and both feet locked on to each other. She was very light, and she smelled real nice. Ectus and I then looked at each other once more, looked forward, and took our first step onto Redemption Tower.

CHAPTER IV
REDEMPTION TOWER

Up the stairs we climbed, higher and higher. What felt like hours were only minutes. For entertainment, I started counting from the first step, but after I got to two hundred thousand and eighty-four, I became bored with it. The air pressure changed a couple of times. The first time my ears popped and the air got a little chilly. I looked down to see that we've only traveled up about five miles. The second time the pressure changed, my head became a little tight and it started to ache. I held my breath and pinched my nose closed and pushed the air out of my ears to relieve the pressure. Kursus started to cough from the air's dry iciness. She pulled out her hand from her pockets and snapped it back as though she was whipping a cloth to apport a large scarf. She unfolded it and wrapped it around her neck and covered her mouth. She then put out both of her hands and muttered something that was muffled by the scarf. A glowing hot little ball of orange fire appeared before her face. The heat was hot, to the point where it felt good on my face.

I stopped for a moment to look down again. Every time the air pressure changed I was curious to know how far up we were. We must have walked miles and miles around the massive rod. If we were to lay out the stairs straight I'm sure it would be thrice as long as Redemption Tower. My legs actually began to ache and grow stiff. I stopped for a moment, and Kursus asked through her big scarf,

"Do you need Creeple Tree sap?"

"I think so," I said, slightly surprised. We must have really been exerting ourselves for me to need Creeple sap. She pulled a flask from her robes and handed it down to me. I opened my mouth and closed my eyes tight and let the warm black sap run down my throat. I took only as much as I felt I needed and handed it back. She stuffed it in her robes and waited to see what I'd do. I began to walk again, regained my strength and continued on.

We were finally entering the mist in the sky. I took one last look down at the ground and my chest felt anxious as the length of how far we traveled made my stomach turn. *That would be a pretty hard fall*, I thought to myself. We entered the blanket of mist and we continued to walk. The mist was so thick that you couldn't see the next step ahead, or even the base of the giant tower. I reached my hand out for the base and felt its coldness. I kept my hand there as I continued to walk. I could see the glow that Ectus radiated from his body faintly aside of me and the glow of the hot ball of fire Kursus had summoned. She muttered something under her scarf again and the ball of light grew brighter and slightly bigger, brushing away a little more of the mist from our presence which allowed us to see a little better as we walked.

We walked, and walked, which felt like an eternity in this icy, blinding mist. I was about to stop and complain, until I saw the top of Kursus's head reach the end of the mist. It bellowed past her as her face reached light. I got excited and put an extra pep in my step. Soon after, the end of the mist reached my face and we were bathed in a bright, warm light. It was the most incredible sight I've ever seen. I looked up to see what looked like a massive shadow a few miles higher above our heads. It looked like a giant slab of ground made of a polished metal with millions of bolted layers, which glistened in the light. As we walked a little higher, I looked down at the base and mist from which we submerged from and I looked out to the sea of soft, fluffy mist all around us that seemed to have no end. It was an amazing site.

After walking a little longer, we made it to the very bottom of the massive base. We hung back a little before getting to the entrance in order to catch our breath. Kursus climbed down my back and she pulled out her potions as we huddled.

"Alright boys, this is it," she said loudly under her scarf. She handed each of us a potion, then kept one for herself. The one she kept was like mine; in a thin vial with a brownish metallic coloring. Ectus's vial was fat on the bottom and held a liquid that was just as blue and bright as his glow.

"Ectus your potion is mixed with a spell to make you a shape shifter. It has Steinlock extract in it."

Ectus looked at the vial with disgust. "What part of the Steinlock did you exactly extract?" He asked.

"You don't want to know," she answered, "and Darkus and I have the Cloaking potion. Its key ingredient is ectoplasm from Ectus. I harnessed some of his energy when he was distracted," she continued. Ectus shot her another dirty look. "Since it's synthetic, it won't last as long as the original recipe. And since I could only get Steinlock extract your potion as well will not last long.

"I got the butt end of both potions," Ectus said bitterly, "you could have asked for some of my energy you know."

"Well, here goes nothing," I said. The three of us drank the potions at the same time. We coughed and hacked from the burn and horrible taste of the potions

"What is in this?" Ectus said with a disgusted look on his face.

"Again, you don't want to know," Kursus answered with the same disgusted look on her face.

We waited for a few moments, and then Ectus started flickering.

"What's happening to me?" He panicked.

"Don't panic Ectus this is normal," Ectus looked up like he was going to yell at Kursus, but he looked around for us.

"I can't see you guys," he said as he continued to flicker. I didn't even feel a thing or notice anything. I looked down at my body, and then over to find Kursus and I were both completely invisible. I looked at Ectus and before our eyes, muscle tissue and organs began to reanimate over and inside his transparent body. The organs sprouted within his core like quick growing fruit. His flesh filled in like a bucket of paint was being dumped over his body. within minutes, he looked like what I assume a Steinlock would look like.

He wore a long white lab coat, black buttons running down it just like our creators. On his face he had a long, hooked nose, and big black reflective goggles, with metal rings around them. He had some type of head gear that sat atop his head with all kinds of gadgets on it. From the gadget on his head he had a mouth piece attached to it that looked like a surgical mask with a visual digital equalizer that moved up and down when he made noise. He wore long, black rubber gloves and big heavy black boots. His hair wired out from the gadget on his head and was long and grey in color. Strapped to his back was a device that looked like a jet pack.

Ectus looked at his body with glee.

"I'm a humanoid!" He said with excitement.

"Don't get too carried away, Ectus. I don't want to be a killjoy but we don't have much time. We must quickly run up to the entrance and enter Redemption Tower."

Ectus took his attention off his body. In his eyes you could tell he was excited, even through the goggles and the equalizer mask. He nodded and ran as fast as he could up the remaining stairs and stared at the door. I walked up next to the new Ectus and waited for Kursus to talk.

"What are you waiting for?" I heard Kursus yell from the opposite side of Ectus. Ectus jumped from Kursus, startling him.

"Let me know next time you're going to yell in my ear! I can't see you remember?" He said back in a voice that sounded much older and accented.

"Place your hand on the door," Kursus replied. Ectus reached up above his head and touched the door above him. The door shot steam at us and opened up with a loud metallic noise and clanked open. A beam of red light doused us and before we knew it we were hurtled up by a pulling force.

We were flying through a clear tube that was barely shoulder width at high speed. I looked up to see us hurtling right into what looked like a large metal wall with emblems and markings. The emblem looked like a Steinlock face with goggles and equalizer mask. Right before I thought my brains were going to meet my rear end the metal door's core spun, lit up and split apart to open. The speed of the tube slowed down and just like that we were standing on the horizontal door that shut beneath us and its core spun once more, locked and dimmed. Ectus was still trying to get used to his legs, so he kind of fell over. He got back up and joined us in awe as we looked up into what looked like a completely different world. It was far too advanced for me to calculate; my brain was temporarily spaced out by the site we were beholding.

The ground was a polished black metal that had orange and red lights that ran through it like veins. The vein-like lights climbed up most of the black, polished towering buildings that covered most of the land; hundreds of large buildings that reached the sky. Steinlocks floated by on devices that looked like half circles that just floated in the air. The devices also had orange vein-like lights covering its dark, polished metal finish. They had a glowing core similar to the door and had bright white lights that circled the brim of the bowl-shaped ships. The Steinlocks had both hands on what looked like two levers that guided them where they pleased. The smell of the devices, using some type of unusual fuel, burnt my nostrils.

The sky in this land was grey and gloomy like stormy weather, but without the rain and thunder. I didn't understand since I knew that we were above the mist. We were dead center of this giant futuristic village, and here in the center seemed like the only opening for a walkway. Tons of Steinlocks walked quickly in all different angles as their attention were directed in many different types of handheld devices. There was a large clock tower near us that didn't hold a clock at all, but some type of fuel meter. Above it was the words '*The Dose*.' There were only a few Steinlocks on foot. They all bared the emblem that we saw on the large door on our way up. As I finally took my attention away from the technology, I could see that there weren't just Steinlocks on foot, there were monsters as well. They were tall and very masculine, all different sizes and colors, with mismatching parts. Some of the Steinlocks had monsters beside them as they held a device that seemed like it was controlling the monsters. Loud noises came from behind us. We looked around at the sound of a monster going berserk. The Steinlock was hitting his device as the monster was roaring and hitting the ground. I could see electrical arcs purging through the monster. The sound of quick flying mechanical objects buzzed past us and circled around the monster that was going berserk. The mechanical flying objects looked like insects of some sort, pure glossy black in color. The end of their abdomens glowed red with light, and in unison, shot the monster, which then quickly melted, flesh and all. A voice boomed over the busy atmosphere.

"Monstrut five nine three eight seven has been terminated. Carry on," it said.

As quick as they came, the futuristic insects flew away, except one, which stopped to look at me, just a foot away from my face. It tilted its massive, insect head with glowing red eyes. I realized they had no wings. They just flew around on some type of pulse-propelling technology, like the flying devices the Steinlocks flew in. It was analyzing a presence. I held my breath in fear, and then it flew away. I let go of my breath in relief.

"Alright, listen up," I could hear Kursus speak quietly somewhere close by, "Darkus and I need to act now and find the elder of this place. Darkus, where are you?"

"I'm over here," I said, reaching out my arms.

"Where?" Kursus asked once more a little closer. I reached out and felt an invisible object.

"Watch where you're grabbing there, sir!" Kursus quietly hissed at me.

"Sorry, not like I can see you or anything," I joked. I felt her hands take my hands off wherever I was grabbing her and she wrapped her fingers around mine and pulled me in her direction.

"Wait, what am I supposed to do?" Ectus asked quietly,

"Oh, um, stand here and act natural. When we come back, you will know it," Kursus said, and continued to pull me quickly past a crowd of monsters.

"Act natural?" Ectus said in disbelieve. A Steinlock stopped him, then looked at him oddly for talking to himself.

"You alright there, chap?" The Steinlock asked Ectus. Ectus began to speak but cleared his throat and spoke deeper, even though his voice was already altered.

"Why yes, chap, never been better. I seemed to have dropped my…hand…thingy," Ectus sputtered. The Steinlock looked at him, raised a brow and repeated, "*Hand thingy?*" Ectus nodded.

"Yes, I apologize. I'm having a moment," Ectus replied nervously, in his deeper voice. The Steinlock than smiled and put his hand on Ectus's shoulder.

"No worries. That just means you need to stop by the lab!" He said kindly, "stop on by and get yourself a Dose. Come, I will take you. I just finished completing my monster anyways. I can tell you all about it; it's one of a kind!"

The Steinlock laughed out loud. Ectus laughed as well, much more blandly than the Steinlocks'. The Steinlock put his arm around Ectus's shoulders and walked with him.

"I don't think I've met you yet. Are you a newcomer?" The Steinlock said.

"Oh yes, very new," Ectus replied.

"Well allow me to properly introduce myself; I am Professor Zint. I major in robotics, like most of our kind. I am also the runner up Elder here aside of the great Dante Alighieri. How about you?"

"Well, my name is Ectus, and I practice all kinds of robotics!" Ectus said quickly.

"Very impressive. So you do many things. Let us go get a dose at the lab," Zint said cheerfully. Ectus nodded and followed, looking quite scared. He looked back as if to see Kursus and me, but we were long gone.

As Kursus continued to yank me around corners and Steinlocks, monsters and odd robotic living creatures, every now and then one of the monsters would stop what they were doing to look right at me, but not acknowledge me.

"What are those monsters here for?" I asked, "They look kind of out dated for the Steinlocks to have them around." Kursus stopped for a moment. I couldn't see what she was doing, but I heard something beeping from her.

"Oh, those are the Monstruts I was talking about earlier. The Steinlocks created them to do most of their grunt work. They are programmed just to obey and move objects. They took the concept from your creator. They practically stole Professor Tinkarius's design. It's quite hypocritical. They stick to one practice to invent

110

them, but reanimating is still frowned upon. Leave it to the elders to bend the rules to their needs-aha!" Kursus yelled. Steinlocks nearby heard her and looked around in confusion, then carried on their way.

"I found him," Kursus finished.

"How are you doing that?" I asked.

"I pocketed a tracking device from one of the Steinlocks."

"Won't that give us away?" I asked.

"Sure, if we kept a hold of it, but I only needed it for a moment," The device suddenly became visible in the air and flew into the back of the head of a Monstrut. The Monstrut looked behind straight at us once again, but then ignored us and carried on its way. Kursus grabbed my hand again and began to pull. As we continued down the alleyways of the massive robotic city I stated,

"That Monstrut looked right at me-"

"They know we are here, but the potion specifically sweeps your system. They can still feel you, but they aren't able to alert the Steinlocks or even acknowledge you other than just to feel you. Do not worry," Kursus said confidently.

"I wish we could catch a ride on one of their gravi-tones," she finished bitterly. I assumed a gravi-tone was the name of the devices they were flying around in.

We made it to another clearing. This spot was much different. The lights in the ground turned green, and they climbed up only one building. It was a large building that had those little flying robots buzzing around the top of it. On the ground were what looked like spherical clear containers full of red fluid. They had six robotic legs and a massive saw blade on the front.

"Those robots flying around are called Tech-Z's, and the floor robots are called 8-Bits. They take care of malfunctioning Monstruts and clean up the mess, nice and quick. They also are a basic line of defense, only programmed for clean-up and defending the level they are assigned to, but they are very quick and give you only seconds to react," Kursus explained,

"Long ago the Steinlocks invented an advanced robotic life form that they called Mechids. Mechids were highly developed and intelligent, and were made to build this Tower. They only built Redemption Tower in six days; *incredibly impressive.* Steinlocks thought they had the ultimate weapon and creation for easy living. But with their ignorant minds they never thought of the Mechids taking control. The Mechids got smart and started to attack the Steinlocks. Then in seconds, a brutal war happened here on top of Redemption Tower. The Mechids killed off more than eighty percent of the humanoids, which made up both my people and the Steinlocks. As quickly as they could the Steinlocks had to invent Crophix called *Wings of Famine,* to kill off the Mechids. It was developed and infused with a spell that made it mysteriously invulnerable to Mechid attacks. The spell had backfired since the

Steinlocks were practicing something they weren't familiar with. Too proud to ask for help and too ignorant to do it right. Not to mention breaking the rules, which created a curse that also rotted sustenance in the Crophix's presence, hence the name Wings of Famine.

They failed for they had to rid of the Crophix. It was destroying all of their food supply, causing even more Steinlocks to die from hunger. After losing so much, the elder of these lands pleaded for help from the others to build a prison made out of a material that was completely unbreakable. Something strong enough to put the Mechids into. They were so desperate that they were able to swallow their pride and put all of their beliefs aside to beg the other cultures to assist. The only reason anyone helped was because the elder spoke of the Mechids destroying the whole world just as fast as they built Redemption Tower. Other than the Wings of Famine, the Mechids had only one weakness; large amounts of water. It never rains here on Redemption Tower, since it sits high above the mist so the Steinlocks didn't find it necessary to make them water resistant. The storm you see above us is self made and generated for appearance. They believe storm clouds stimulate their creativity.

If it wasn't for their mistake, they would have never successfully rid of the Mechids. But the Mechids were never destroyed. Our cultures gathered and used all of our powers to place the Mechids into an unbreakable material and pushed out a massive piece of land, which came out of Lanteria. We shoved the piece of land far into the Sea of Shame, which is a large body of water just off the north-west coast of Lanteria. They thrive there, isolated and full of rage. I wouldn't doubt them plotting to eventually come back and annihilate us. The robots you see here are all basic with the same programming as the Monstruts. Build. Destroy. Rebuild. I find it ironic how we built things only to tear them down, and repeat history."

Kursus grabs my hand once again and pulls me towards the large building with green vein like lights glowing all around it. We walked right passed an 8-Bit. Just like the Monstruts, its front noticed our presence and it watched us enter the building. When we arrived inside the smell of dust was in the air. I didn't like the smells of this place. It all smelled toxic and made it a bit harder to breathe. Judging by the way Kursus sounded when she talked, it appeared that she still seemed to be wearing the scarf.

"Ok we're in," Kursus whispered. The walls were tall and metal, but looked a bit rusted. Thousands of multicolored wiring decorated the ceiling as they went to their sources. The flooring was a polished green marble similar to the stage in Muckraid. There were computer devices everywhere, and Steinlocks were flying in and out of the building in their gravi-tones. A hologram coming from the steering area. The Steinlocks would run their fingers across the hologram and whatever they did on it, the same would appear on the computer monitors. As we walked closer into the building, I could see that the monitors were displaying images of what was going on outside. The cameras were flying around really quick, some of them still, others looking at Monstruts as they were terminated.

"This is the control room," Kursus whispered, "whatever the Tech-Z's or 8-Bits are looking at, the Steinlocks are looking at as well. Each robotic creature has a security system installed into it and the Steinlocks watch and record." I thought about what the Steinlocks were possibly thinking when the robotic creatures were looking at me. Were they curious to know why they stared into space for a moment? Apparently not. No one seemed to care. Straight across from the door was some type of robotic creature in a large glass casing with internal light fixtures. A plaque hung on the lower casing which read,

To remind us of an error that soon became redemption.

It had a large head with a lower jaw drilled in its skull that hung open with big hollow eyes. It had antennas on either side of its skull that looked like ears. Its face was long and narrow with markings in it that looked like it once held the veiny lights that were around the city. I wondered if that was, or used to be, a Mechid.

I worried a bit about Ectus. Hope he was doing alright. He's not really the brave kind of creature. We entered a lift that was propelled by the same pulse-propelling technology in the gravi-tones and the Tech-Z's that took us up to the top floor. The lift opened and we were in a large hall of some sort. Everything was made of stone rather than metals and fancy hardware. It was like a whole new world, inside of a whole new world. It was ancient and dusty; clashing with the technology below. As we continued down the hall we could hear talking echoing from the distance. Kursus grabbed my hand and pulled to stop me from walking.

"You keep yanking me around like that I'm not going to have an arm," I hissed.

"Well fortunately for you I majored in bio engineering. I can stitch a limb back up faster than I can eat a Brackling." she replied.

"That's pretty fast," I said sarcastically. My arm took a punch from her invisible fist and she continued to hush me.

As we continued to enter the big empty hall we grew closer to what looked like a cult gathering. They were gathered around a giant statue of a man holding up a robotic head that looked identical to the one hanging from the first floor. He had a wicked evil face and a long beard. The way he was hunched and grinning made him look like a cynical man. As we walked around the corner, to my surprise the man that was the statue was hovering in a much larger gravi-tone that was much more detailed then the ones flying around below. It bared green vein like lights and had all sorts of devices and weaponry on it that dangled from about a dozen long, robotic arms. There was a man on his knees, head down in a middle spotlight, his back towards us. The man in the statue was yelling at the man down on his knees. A couple dozen Steinlocks hovered in their gravi-tones all around the one on his knees.

"That must be the Elder," Kursus said quietly.

We walked right in as if we were apart of it all, but no one could see us. It was a little worrisome to walk in there so confidently.

"Where did you say you were from?" The Steinlock Elder demanded. The man on his knees stayed silent. A robotic arm shot out from the elder's gravi-tone and revealed an advanced saw blade of some sort with lights that blipped all around it. It began to spin as the man continued to be silent, not even showing fear.

"Was anyone with you? Are you a spy with some pathetic tribe from below trying to steal our technology? You slipped by us, I'll give you that, but nobody gets past the Steinlocks. *Nobody!*" The blade shot towards the man on his knees and began to saw through his arm. The arm shot blood all over the place, but to our amazement the man stayed silent. I became curious as to why the man showed no pain until Kursus spoke in shock,

"That is Ectus!"

"What?" I said in surprise, "How do you know?"

"He can't feel pain because Ectus is still only a spirit. He's not attached to his physical form. It's only a camouflage shell."

The man stopped cutting and Ectus's fake arm fell off slowly, strands of flesh trying to keep it together. It slumped to the floor and continued to gush. Ectus lifted his head, smiled and said,

"Owe," in the most sarcastic way.

The Elder grew even more irate and then snapped his fingers. The gravi-tone's robotic arms grabbed onto the ceiling like a spider. The bottom of his floating device began to lay mechanical-looking eggs that had a glowing sphere in the middle. They fell to the floor with a large metal thud and laid there for a moment, covered in a shiny film.

"Not going to talk, are we? Well that is just fine, I will drain every ounce of your blood, slowly and painfully, I assure you. If you have anything of ours you will never return it to wherever you came from. They will soon know, and we will continue to be untouchable," The metallic eggs began to shake and shift.

"Now is our chance," Kursus said, "Ectus is a total distraction. Look over behind the elder," I looked over to see a small, shiny silver little box.

"The NaviBox," I said in excitement. We made a run for it. I could see legs sprouting from the metallic eggs.

"I don't ever use the thing, but just for today I may please myself," the Elder said. We grew within arm's reach of the NaviBox but the Elder had reached over and quickly swiped it up. We backed up to the middle of the room next to Ectus and looked up at the elder in his large gravi-tone. The elder cleared his throat and spoke,

"Where did this creature come from?" A beam of light shot from the top of the NaviBox dowsing his face in light and then just as quick as it lit up it disappeared. The elders face suddenly became outraged.

"Impossible. How could that be? So, be it, what is this creature?" The top of the box lit up once again, and quickly faded.

"So, you are the very first synthetic spirit to have ever been created by the one and only Tinkarius, huh? I should have known better; sending his little toy soldiers to fight his battles." For the first time Ectus looked up in shock in his Steinlock body and became terrified.

"Oh no," Kursus said out loud. The man curled his forehead in anger and went to ask the NaviBox another question.

"Tell me NaviBox, does he have accomplices here with him?" Suddenly, Kursus and I started to flicker in and out of invisibility.

"Oh no!" Kursus said much louder. It was clear now that there were two creatures sneaking around the room because everyone's eyes were directed at us, including the Elder.

We finally stopped flickering and became solid. I grabbed Kursus and put her behind me. She grew terrified. We were in the middle of the nest, totally stripped. The elder smiled a long, wide evil grin like he did from the statues and began to laugh in the most diabolical fashion.

"What a lovely surprise," the elder grinned, "if it isn't the one and only Darkus. And what's this? It appears we have ourselves a member of the Flintkus tribe with us today. *Fascinating*." The elder brought his gravi-tone low enough to become eye to eye with me.

"And my, what a curious creation indeed. I've heard all about you Darkus. Actually, you're the very idea that got your creator banned from his kind. He must have made you in a run-down shelter somewhere below," my fists clenched with anger. I wanted to destroy this man, and I knew I could.

"Tell me little monster, what has brought you here today?"

"I'm here for your NaviBox," I said loudly. The elder man lifted up the NaviBox in front of his face to show me.

"This little thing? Why on earth would you want this? You think this is going to help you find something you need? Or perhaps you'd like to get even with your creator? I would be most thrilled to give this to you for such a reason. Too bad it won't locate him directly, but you already knew that, didn't you?"

"I'm not getting even with my creator. I don't need to tell you what I need it for. Just hand it over and I may spare you your life." The Steinlocks around us started to laugh as well as the elder.

"That is *adorable*. You really think you can defeat us? We are far too powerful for even the best creation of Tinkarius. Why don't we ask the NaviBox why you are really here?" the elder looked into the NaviBox once more. It lit up and dimmed once again. The elder's face grew long. He grew silent, and then said,

"You don't even know what Professor Tinkarius did, do you?" I looked at him with anger, but was all ears.

"What are you talking about?" I demanded.

"Enough, I don't need to explain anything further to a mere slab of Tinkarius flesh. You will die only knowing what you know. Death to Tinkarius, and those who stand by him! I am Dante Alighieri! Leader of the Steinlocks, creator and destroyer of the Mechids and ultra controller of the Monstruts! Let the name burn within your mind while I rip it from your petty little skull!" the elder yelled.

One of his robotic arms, shaped like a massive hammer came hurtling down towards me. I grabbed it, ripped it off and through it at a group of huddled Steinlocks. Dante's gravi-tone flew back from the impact and his saw blade was thrown over at the barricaded Steinlocks. The saw ripped right through them, their blood splattering all over the walls. The eggs then completely hatched and 8-Bits came from the shells and went right for Ectus. They devoured his body and nothing was left except Ectus. He screamed in horror and flew away.

"Ectus!" I yelled. A second arm reached behind me and grabbed Kursus. She kicked and screamed and Dante disappeared into the ceiling.

"Darkus!" I heard Kursus scream from the distance.

"Kursus!" I Yelled.

I grabbed one of the 8-Bits that ran at me and through it at another group of Steinlocks. I then jumped as high as I could out of the top of the opening Dante had made in the ceiling.

I landed on the floor below outside of the building. Total chaos broke lose. I could see Tech-Z's coming for me by the dozens and Steinlocks running towards me with devices in their hands. 8-

Bits crawled aside of the walls and Monstruts thudded towards me with mighty strides. Steinlocks in gravi-tones propelled towards me. *Full house*, I thought to myself with a smile. A Monstrut threw its weight at me. I caught it in mid air by its arm and spun around a couple times in order to build momentum to throw it at a crowd of Steinlocks ahead of me in order to clear a path. The Monstrut knocked them over and laid there on top of a dozen yelling Steinlocks. I jumped on top of the Monstrut and gained way. I could see Dante flying above in the air a good length ahead of me. As long as I could keep my eyes on him, I can find Kursus and the NaviBox.

Whack!

A Tech-Z sideswiped me and I lost my sense of direction and fell to my side. It zipped around to look right at me and its abdomen glowed bright red. It zapped its ray at me but I put my hands out and made a protective hologram shield in front of me. I held as long as I could but the force of whatever was shooting from the Tech-Z was highly charged. I had to let go. I got pushed back by the burning force. Steinlocks gathered all around me, reaching down to grab me. I screamed as loud as I could and they all let go and covered their ears. I let out a piercing scream that made the nearby Steinlocks start bleeding from their ears. I got up and looked around frantically into the sky. I lost sight of Dante and Kursus. I became furious. I put my fists together as Steinlocks, 8-Bits; Tech-Z's and Monstruts jumped me and tried to hold me down. I hit my fists on the ground as hard as I could. I made such an impact into the ground that the force of the shockwave scattered all that was near me within a thirty foot radius. I watched the ground lift, and the buildings nearby me started to sway back and forth.

All that anger I released had nearly leveled the location I was at. I could see pieces of Monstruts and robot parts sparking in scattered locations. The Steinlocks that were near me had disintegrated. I looked up and saw that the buildings had become still and had stopped swaying. Then a loud cracking sound had echoed throughout the area. I looked up again and saw that one of the buildings had cracked at an angle, and started to lean. I then saw Ectus flying in the sky.

"Ectus!" I yelled. The ground rumbled beneath me. Ectus stopped and looked down at me. He looked manic and flew towards me. Right behind him the large building structure started to fall into another. It went right through Ectus and continued to fall. It hit a group of Steinlocks flying in their gravi-tones, sending them spinning out of control. They came crashing down around me like comets. Ectus joined my side and watched the building fall with me. It landed right on the building with green veiny lights from whence we came. The ground beneath us shook once more and Ectus and I took a moment to look at the destruction that we had created.

"It seems wherever we go we leave a trail, completely destroyed," Ectus said, staring at our mess.

"Kicking ass and taking names," I answered, not taking my eyes off of the destruction.

"I know where Kursus is!" Ectus said snapping out of it. "Follow me!"

We began to run until we were covered by a massive shadow. It passed over us and we slowly looked up to see nothing. We looked at each other for a moment and then continued heading towards the direction in which Dante had taken Kursus.

More Monstruts had spotted us as well as the Steinlocks. The Monstruts formed a wall of death and began to charge at us. I ran as fast as I could towards their formation and smashed my way through. I kept running, not looking back. I followed Ectus as he took me to where Kursus was supposed to be. All I cared about at that exact moment was finding Kursus. Not until just then had I realized how much I cared about someone else other than just finding my creator. I needed to find Kursus. She was our navigator and our guide. She was also our friend.

"More Tech-Z's!" Ectus yelled from above. They zipped right by him, sending him spinning. Within seconds they came to a halt right in front of me. I hardly had a moment to gather myself but all I could think of doing was jumping straight in the air. Two of the Tech-Z's ended up zapping each other by my swift jump and I began to fall again until a Tech-Z flew right under me and I landed right on it. I started yelling, hardly able to keep on the thing. It was trying its hardest to buck me off. I grabbed its antennas and without my consent my hands glowed bright purple and I felt energy draining through me into the Tech-Z. The Tech-Z's eyes went from bright red to purple. It just flew in place, steady. I think I had control of it somehow.

"Uh, forward!" I yelled. It shot forward so quick I nearly flew off. My legs were behind me from how fast we were traveling. We zipped by Ectus, sending him spinning again.

"Hey wait!" Ectus yelled. He sped up his pace, slowly passing us. He looked over at me in confusion. I looked over at him and smiled. He brushed it off and continued to look forward and slowly pass me.

We reached another ancient looking building. I climbed off the Tech-Z and patted it on the head.

"Destroy the rest of the Tech-Z's," I told it. Just then a swarm of Tech-Z's approached us from the sky. The Tech-Z in my control turned around and zipped up to the swarm and started blasting them out of the sky. We quickly ran into the building.

Everything was made of stone and ancient ruins once again. Narrow walls and a low ceiling made of un-carved stone; almost like a cave. Another statue of Dante was upright in the center of the room in the same pose with the Mechid skull. We slowly entered observing the area before entering any further. I tip-toed behind the statue to hide and peeked around it. There was an even darker, narrow tunnel up ahead. Ectus took the lead and lit up the tunnel, lightly. I joined his side and we walked slowly into the dark abyss.

As we walked I could hear things crawling around. They sounded like they were just outside of the light, slithering and clicking. I looked around to try and get a glimpse but I could see nothing.

"Do you hear that? I asked Ectus.

"I do, but I cannot see what it is. Whatever it is, it isn't bothering us," Ectus said.

The creepy crawly sound followed us all the way to the end of the temple. Flickering fire light could be seen in the distance in an opening. Ectus and I made it to the end of the temple. There, chained up to the wall, was Kursus. I ran to her side as quickly as possible.

"Kursus! Kursus we are here! Can you hear us?" I yelled. She didn't respond.

"Let me try," Ectus said.

He dissolved into her body as he once did mine. She twitched a little, and her eyes opened wide while glowing bright blue, then her eyes shut and Ectus appeared in front of me.

"She's alive, just unconscious, but I cannot wake her," Ectus said. I felt relieved. We heard something mechanical above our heads and behind us. I turned around just in time for a massive fist hitting me and sending me hurtling towards the ancient walls. I went through the wall and landed in a pile of mechanical parts. The sound of giant robotic foot steps came stomping towards me, rumbling followed with every foot step. I looked up through the hole I created to see what I was up against as it smashed through. The impact covered me in debris, but before I could take another look I was lifted by my leg and hung upside down. I was looking at Dante sitting in the chest of what looked like a massive robot. One that he had complete control of, with two levers similar to their gravi-tones. The arms and legs were massive and held many emblems and bright lights. With a closer look it appeared that he was in his hovering craft that was sitting in some pod that had legs and arms.

"Darkus! I knew you'd stop by for your little tinkering spell caster. Please, have a seat," he yelled, then lifted me above his head and slammed me into the ground.

"Oh wait, my apologizes, your seat is over *here*!" He lifted me above his head again and slammed me against the opposite side of himself into the floor. I felt my head crack from the force of being slammed against the stone floor. He left me there for a minute. I pushed with my arms to get up but I was starting to get stiff after all of the fighting I've been doing. Dante laughed, and then continued to throw me around like a toy.

"You know what? You're a special guest, how about you take the balcony seats!" He threw me up into the air and I went crashing through the roof and into another room. I landed on my shoulder and my neck was sent sideways.

Crack!

I heard my upper spine go. I couldn't move my neck or head, just my arms. I tried to push myself up, but it was no good.

"Give up Darkus! You may be a powerful creation but you're still nothing but a monster! You've lost. You have finally met your match. I hear you defeated a Crophix! Sure, that is impressive, but a Crophix is still made of flesh and bone, monster! We Steinlocks have real power that come straight from our minds, which can create technology that cannot be easily destroyed!"

I spat some blood from my mouth and smiled, looking at him with my head sideways and contorted by the break.

"You may have invented some nice toys, but without all of that you're just a humanoid with a large brain and thin skin. You had to invent something to defend yourself against a world that has been eating your race whole ever since you stepped foot in Remains. All you are is monster bait to this place and there is nothing you can do to eek your way up the food chain."

Dante laughed as loud as he could. "This may be, but we have done something about it. We have invented a force that has brought us to the very top of your food chain! Tinkarius was a fool to create you and think that you could stop us! I'm going to dismantle you limb from limb and scatter your pieces all over Remains to show him how despicable his inventions really are and destroy him with our new found technology!" Dante gave out a loud and proud cackle. Ectus came up through the surface below and entered Dante's body.

Dante squirmed and yelled, "No! Get out of my body!"

Dante's head suddenly twisted all the way around and the sound of his neck was heard shattering. His body was then reanimated. Dante looked up at me with bright blue glowing eyes, his head tilted sideways and his jaw hung low from being dismantled from his skull. Ectus's voice slurred through the broken jaw, "Grab Kursus and get out of here!"

The sound of Steinlocks running through the building was heard.

"I can't, my spine is broken," I yelled, not moving. Ectus moved Dante's arms to control the robot he was sitting in. Dante's head hung sideways and his jaw was hanging out, but Ectus was looking at me through his newly glowing eyes. He was controlling a dead man like a contorted marionette to get to me and the sight was a little disturbing. He walked the robot to me and pushed a button that suddenly started to leak a lot of black goo that smelled familiar.

"He's using Creeple Tree sap to control this robot. It must be an older device before they used whatever it is they are using now," Ectus said. The ooze hit the ground and started to flow towards me. I stuck my hand out to reach the ooze. It continued oozing slowly towards me as it dumped out of the bottom of the robot.

The Steinlocks came pattering upstairs with long rod looking devices that glowed bright blue. Attached to the bottom were pipes that went up to a type of back device. They all flipped on a switch and shot the robot with a beam of blue light that came from the rods. Ectus started to howl in pain and came out of Dante's body. He shot out and hit the ground. He was hurt. The Steinlocks circled Ectus. I was watching from behind the robot. They fired up their devices again and began to zap Ectus. He screamed in pain for the first time ever. I started to drink the ooze. In minutes, I heard my spine reconnect and repair itself. I could feel all the pain and tire rid of my body as the sound of bones popping back in place vibrated through my body. I picked up the massive robot and lifted it up and over my head, with Dante hanging out of the cockpit. The Steinlocks saw their elder dead as a door nail in my arms and gasped. They turned on their devices and blasted me. I endured all the energy, in fact it kind of tickled. They stopped and looked at me with shock as I stood there before them, still holding the huge robot.

"How's that new technology doing for you boys? I assume you want your Elder back," I threw the robot as hard as I could at the Steinlocks as they screamed. The robot landed on the Steinlocks and forced them back into the wall. I looked over to find Ectus but he was nowhere to be found. A spark jumped from their mysterious weapons, the ones that affected Ectus and caught the Creeple sap oozing from the machine afire.

"Ectus! Ectus where are you?" I yelled. I broke the chains off of Kursus, then I picked her up and put her over my shoulders. I looked around for the exit and went down stairs. The machine exploded and soon after I heard a loud sound that I've never heard before. It was like a loud screaming hiss that tickled the inside of my ears. From what I could see through holes that were created by the battle, the outside grew dark and then bright again. It was that massive shadow that flew above Ectus and I earlier.

I made it to the outside and I was ambushed by more Steinlocks with Monstruts and robots closing in on me. I stood there with Kursus over my shoulder trying to think everything through but before I could muster up a scheme the loud hissing screech filled the air. The back of my eyes rattled from the loudness. I looked around, and even the Steinlocks and their living weapons stopped paying attention to me to take a look around.

"It can't be," said one of the Steinlocks.

The building that we were at was at the edge of Redemption Tower. The walls were tall but I bet if I was to stand on the top of the walls I could look straight down into the sea of mist. Redemption Tower grew silent except for the sound of humanoids muttering and the clanking sounds of weapons and mechanical parts; everyone was looking around waiting to see what was making that noise.

The sound of massive, slow flapping wings was heard just outside the walls of Redemption Tower. The corner of my eye caught some of the mist being pushed up from the side of the wall. To my amazement, the head of an incredibly large creature was seen peering over the wall. Its wings blew heavy winds into the land of Redemption Tower. Everything was being blown away and sent outward from the massive flaps of the wings. As it flew higher and higher into the sky it revealed its body, which bared a mark on its side. The mark looked similar to the Mark of Tinkarius, but it was a little different. It flew higher and it revealed its tail which had a small head on it that looked down at Redemption Tower and screeched at us all. The massive flying creature started to turn around in the air and focused its attention straight towards the edge of the tower where the ancient building stood, with Kursus and I in front. It had large, angry eyes, and a massive eye ball in the middle of its head. It had ears that looked like giant bat wings, and its mouth was wispy and looked as though it's been stitched up at one point.

It opened its mouth and hissed loudly as it flew its way down towards us. It was gaining speed and I just knew it wasn't going to stop. It was going to ram itself into the side of the building where we were. It locked itself right into me. It looked like it could be a Crophix.

All of the fire power that Redemption Tower had was taken off of me and thrown into the giant Crophix. I felt Kursus's head slightly lift up, and I heard her quietly whisper,

"The Wings of Famine."

The winged beast flew over the Tower and covered all in darkness. I noticed that the food supply that was out in the open began to rot. As if time had moved forward; even the blood inside of the 8-Bits started to deteriorate and soon turned to dust. This massive Crophix definitely looked man made. Its curse was clearly still in tact. I grabbed my flask to take a sip of my Creeple sap, but got a mouthful of dust instead. I coughed out the dust and turned my flask upside down to pour out the remaining dust. Crud, my fuel supply had run dry from the curse of the Crophix.

I started to run towards the inside of the building I had just came out of. Most of the Steinlocks stopped firing and ran for cover. I jumped into the building with Kursus over my shoulder, and right when I did the ground beneath me shook from the impact of the Crophix's strike. The walls started to fall and crumble and the ground felt like it was starting to shift. I fell; dropping Kursus, then got up to pick up her up once again and began to run up the stairs. The whole building was shaking, making it difficult to conquer the climb. I ran to the very top and made it to the roof. I ran to the edge and looked down. *Oh my*.

Parts of the building and the ground that was struck by the Crophix was falling from the edge of Redemption Tower, taking us with it as I stood on top of the roof with Kursus as we were thrown downward. The Wings of Famine was flying just under the debris of the building. We landed on top of it, the debris following and striking it hard in the back. It screeched in pain and stopped flapping its wings, causing it to freefall with us and the debris riding on its back. I fell back and Kursus was sent flying above me in the air out of my reach.

"*Kursus!*" I yelled.

I watched her fly up into the sky above me. I had a good grasp on the edge of the building as it was twirling around. The Crophix managed to shake me and the debris from off its back. Its tail reached back and grabbed Kursus with its mouth.

"No!" I yelled.

I tried to climb my way up, but it was too late. The Crophix flew away above me and off in the distance, and I was sent tumbling down with the buildings remains. I held my hands out and looked down at the ground that was coming at me quick. Debris from the base of Redemption Tower was passing me by to my left. All those stairs that took hours to climb passed me by in seconds. I turned to face upwards and lay there; falling through the sky with my hands stretched outwards and my hands relaxed. I closed my eyes, and then opened them again. To my advantage, there was one of the Steinlocks gravi-tones hurtling down with me. I began to swim in the air towards it and I managed to grab a hold of the edge of the cockpit. I looked behind my shoulder to see the ground coming at me. It began to spin in the air from my weight tilting it. I spun sideways a few times with it then managed to get inside. I started pushing a bunch of buttons and pulling levers but got no reaction as I continued to spin in the air, but I remembered what I did with the Tech-Z prior. I put my hand on the control panel of the gravi-tone and it lit up with a purplish hue. I hollered in excitement and pulled one of the levers. It stopped free falling and slowly started to gain levitation. It found its balance and I hovered in the air. I watched all of the debris fall and hit the ground. I looked out to find the Wings of Famine. It was flying slowly towards Lanteria. I put the gravi-tone in full throttle and raced to catch up to it.

    The tail of the Wings of Famine watched me catch up with Kursus tight in its mouth, unconscious. I held the gravi-tone's controls with one hand and pulled out my pistol with the other. fueling it up with my alchemy, I shot a ball of purple energy at its wings. It burned straight through its wing, as it screeched in pain. The tail that had Kursus in its mouth whipped back to take a swing at me, and missed. I ducted into the gravi-tone and sprung back up, pulled out my pistol again to take another shot at its wing. I missed. The tail swung back and hit the gravi-tone. I spun around and it began to malfunction and sputter. I tried to keep it energized but the craft was too damaged. I started to slowly fall, engulfed in a sudden puff of smoke that blurred my vision. I gave up on getting the gravi-tone to work properly and pulled out my pistol, held it with both hands and filled it with enough energy to blast the Wings of Famine out of the air. A massive wave of energy shot out of my pistol and a huge beam sliced through the air like it once did to the Lanterian's

Crophix, Bombadicus. I reached down to control the gravi-tone once more to keep it from spinning from the power of my pistol. I moved the pistol's giant laser towards the Crophix and managed to line it up with its neck. The beam of light cut its head clean off. The head fell passed me. Its eye looked right at me, my reflection quickly seen through its massiveness. I looked up and the body was still gliding ahead. The tail was screaming in pain as it flailed around, but still not letting go of Kursus.

I watched the corpse glide into the distance as the gravi-tone fell further and further, still trying to function until it finally hit the ground. I was still looking up in the distance even though I couldn't see the flying corpse of the Crophix anymore. I stared blankly as I rested my arms on the gravi-tone. For the first time in my existence, I had lost. Not just a fight, but everyone I cared about, and the mission, were no more. I had nothing to go by; Ectus and Kursus were gone. Dead, for all I knew. I put my head down into my arms that rested on the gravi-tone. I felt pain and sadness. I felt something wet come out of my eye and roll down my face. I lifted my head and rubbed it off my face with my finger and rolled it between my fingertips and observed it. It must be a tear drop. It was still a fake tear from a fake monster that had a fake dream to find his creator. I'm alone, lost, and broken.

I sat there and thought hard, still sitting in the gravi-tone. After I had sulked for a while I felt a little better. Just a little. I took both of my monster hands and put them on my face and rubbed good and hard. I finally got out of the flying craft, which felt like years of sitting in the thing. I paced around it pondering for a moment, got really angry and I ran up to it and kicked it as hard as I could. The gravi-tone went hurtling towards where I saw the Wings of Famine take Kursus, and a pinch was sent to my toes. I grabbed my foot in pain, jumped around a moment, but then I had an idea.

The mission is dead, at the moment, as it is. What harm would it do to go find my friends and see with my own eyes if they were really alive or not? A sudden burst of hope was sent through my body. Yes, I don't know for sure if they are dead. Not like I'm getting any older. I got years to find my creator. What good would it be to do it alone? I needed allies. That is why Tinkarius made them after all; to work together. I suddenly got a burst of motivation and I stared into the distance, then started heading towards Lanteria. I've needed to make an appearance anyways. What would it hurt?

I made my way through the woods and looked back once more at the gigantic rod that shot up into the sky that I once scaled with my friends and took off, not looking back again. As I crept through the woods, the sky began to get darker. I wasn't too worried since my eyes adjusted quite well in the dark. I stepped on something sharp that made me jump back. I took a step back and looked down.

"It can't be," I said out loud.

I bent down to pick up what had jabbed my foot and to my amazement, in my hand was a shiny polished cube device.

"The NaviBox!" I said out loud.

But how? I thought about it for a moment looking at it curiously. Perhaps Kursus had made away with it while she was being kidnapped. Then, when she got carried off by the Crophix she must have dropped it. Yes, that had to of been what happened. I closed my fingers around it tightly and looked up into the sky with pride.

"Way to go Kursus," I said softly. I looked at its shiny plated exterior for a moment. This could answer all of my questions right now! I wanted to ask if my friends were alive, but I didn't have the guts to do it. So, I thought long and hard, and then I lifted the NaviBox up close to my face, as I watched Dante do, and I asked,

"Where is Kursus?"

A beam of light filled my face and on the top of the NaviBox I saw an image of what looked like a small village. The village was full of little creatures with big swelled noses and blood painted all over their face. They were jumping around in a crazed manner.

"Psychozoans," I said out loud. The light vanished quickly and I tried to remember what Kursus may have said about their location. I couldn't think of anything, but I did remember Ectus saying that Lanteria was like a cross road for villages. So, to get Kursus I'd have to make someone talk in Lanteria. That shouldn't be too hard since they all know I'm quite the powerhouse. Then I remembered that I needed to find Ectus. I looked down at the NaviBox and demanded,

"Where is Ectus?"

The device did nothing. I waited a bit longer, thinking maybe it needed to warm up or something. I shook it a little, and after no reply I repeated, "Where is my friend Ectus?" Nothing once again. *Curious.* What does that mean? Does that mean that Ectus is nowhere to be found? Is he…dead? The thought kind of worried me, but I knew that Kursus would have the answer. I put the NaviBox in my pocket, picked up my stuff and continued on my way.

Not too much further I stumbled upon the Crophix's head. I walked up to it, and stared into its big eye that was wide open, but still. I could see my reflection in it. As I stared into its decaying eye I saw something move quickly behind me in the reflection. Something quickly stuck its hand in my pocket and took the NaviBox and then tripped me. I fell on my back and the small critter ran away. I looked up to get a quick look at whatever it was. I saw a small body, wearing rugged polka-dot clothing. Then the critter turned to look at me. It laughed and snarled at me. It had a big swelled nose and that manic look on its face.

"Psychozoan," I muttered through clenched teeth. I got up on my legs and started to run after it. It ran away quickly as it laughed at me. Well, it looked like I didn't have to stop by and ask for help in Lanteria after all. I have a lead, and I was going to follow this Psychozoan as long as I don't lose sight of him. Then when I get to his location I'm going to squash him myself for taking the NaviBox out of my pocket. No one sticks their hands in my pockets and gets away with it!

CHAPTER V
DAMNED-SEL IN DISTRESS

The Psychozoan was very agile and light on its feet. As fast as I am, I had to constantly cut corners to keep up with him. Eventually after making it to the end of Lanteria, and not seeing a single life form in sight other than the Psychozoan, I followed him to the entrance in which he came from. It disappeared in the distance but lead me right to its tribe. I slowed my pace and walked towards the opening. I almost walked off Lanterian soil, barely passing the large spears in the ground that held a dozen of stacked, hollowed Lanterian skulls. A hand of some sort shot through the ground to grab my ankle and held me there. I looked down to see pale blue hands reaching out of the ground. Its grip was super tight. I couldn't shake it. It looked like a humanoid hand. I yanked and yanked, then pulled out my pistol to shoot at it, but then I was blown over by a gust of forceful cold air. I fell to the ground with the hand still grabbing my ankle, slightly twisting it.

Dozens of hands shot through the ground around me and wrapped their cold, clammy arms around my body. I filled my body full of energy and yelled as loud as I could. My body released a burst of energy and the pale blue hands were torn off my body. I stood up and looked at the pale blue arms squirming and flopping on the ground in confusion. In mere seconds a spirit rushed down from above and stood just inches away from my face, and then looked into my eyes.

"Hello Darkus. We've been expecting you."

The spirit pushed me with great force and I landed on my back and skidded back a few feet. The spirit rushed me once again and floated horizontally above me. It had the appearance of a female humanoid with glowing green eyes, her hair bellowing in the air. She had a smirk on her face.

"We have been re animated by the Lanterians to keep you out of Lanteria," the spirit said. I could tell this spirit was pure, unlike Ectus.

"And where are your friends? And that joke of spiritual energy, Ectus. Man-made spirits just aren't made like the real ones."

"I came alone," I said through my clenched teeth.

"Oh, that's too bad. They won't be here for the celebration."

The spirit entered inside of me and started tugging on my organs. I screamed in pain and I gave out another large burst of energy. The spirit was sent hurtling out of me. She stared down at me in shock.

"How did you do that?"

"I'm full of surprises," I said, "batteries not included!"

I jumped to my feet and put my fists down to my side and pushed out another wave of energy that pushed her back further. The ground began to rumble, and I looked back to see hands ripping out of the ground once again.

Before my eyes arose more humanoids digging out of the ground. Their skin was pale as death and they had hollowed out eyes. Their jaws were hung open and they groaned in the most disturbing ways. Somehow the Lanterian's managed to bring back dead humanoids and revive spirits; must have been some pretty good alchemy, which is something they don't practice. The humanoids stood on soil and stared at me with their blackened eye holes, then started slowly walking towards me with their arms reached out at me.

"I am Ladidya, the Elder of the Ectos tribe; gathered spirits that were once living. The animated humanoids you see here are a new breed of humanoids; dead-brained and easy to control. They do dirty work and don't care to be used as meat shields. They are called Voids. Do you like it? The name came from the emptiness they hold inside of them. Only their shell is active."

I looked at them in disgust. "What a desperate, wicked way to go," I said, looking at the Voids.

"Don't sound so full of yourself. You idolize your creator for doing what he wants, what's wrong with what we want?"

I looked at her with anger.

"The difference is these Voids and you are going to die again. *I cannot die*," I said with a smile. She lifted her head and scowled at me.

"We shall see about that!" She screamed and then dive-bombed me. I rolled out of the way, forgetting about the ground full of who knows how many Voids. I stood up and looked around. The ground shook with a mighty force similar to when the first Crophix I encountered here came out. I stood in waiting to see what was about to happened. Then a familiar voice was heard behind me.

"Hello, Darkus."

I turned around to see Lurt, elder of Lanteria. He stood alone.

"Really? Reanimated humanoid corpses? Could you not be anymore pathetic? Isn't this all against your stupid little book?" I yelled.

"Desperate times call for desperate measures, monster. Besides I wasn't the one who did this. Got to stick to our own practices, you know. I had a little help." he hit the ground with the bottom of his staff. It sent shockwaves miles around where we stood. It was silent for a moment, and then I heard the ground grumble.

"What did you do?" I yelled at him.

"Jump started the lifeless living, miles of Voids. I had to find everything I could to take down the creation of Tinkarius."

I glared at him, "so now you know, huh?"

"Word travels fast monster, especially when you're reckless. When the creatures of Remains catch wind that a great threat comes near it brings them all together. *Unity*. We work together to take out the big threat, like humanoid white blood cells attack a virus, then we continue to eat each other alive."

"What is the point of any of that?" I asked desperately.

"It is in our nature to become the alpha male. Whoever stands above the rest will soon be respected and feared. It is practiced to try and keep it peaceful but when we are pressured to survive we have to bend the rules. This land doesn't have a master, Darkus. So we fight until there is peace. Once there is peace, then we can all be civilized. But until then, we continue to climb our way up the food chain in this land of insanity. You wouldn't understand. You're not organic. Only your shell is. The rest is synthetic and humanoid crafted. You don't have the instincts that this land hands out because you are a bastard. You don't belong here, so we must destroy you. Don't you see? You are not pure. You are only an object."

"Yeah, I'm an object that is going to bury you where you stand." I put out both my hands forward with open palms and built up as much energy as I could, and then the ground shook harder than the last, throwing off my balance. I regained balance and to my horror, the hands of thousands shot from the ground from miles around as far as the eye could see. I couldn't even see the end of them. Hundreds of thousands of arms digging their way up and revealing what was once a deceased humanoid now called Voids. They all arose to their feet and all honed in on me, reaching out and groaning out of their long gaping jaws.

"Perhaps you should worry about burying all of your new friends first," Lurt said calmly. He cackled and continued as the Voids moved in on me.

"You see Darkus, we figured that the best way to take you out is to settle our differences and fight fire with fire. Perhaps the only way to end you is to make another monster! Only this time we made millions! We're just working the system. I don't practice alchemy, but I know someone who does who was kind enough to lend a hand. So, we all play the game as foretold and we still get to stomp you out. Everybody wins!"

Well, I guess I should give it a shot. I was outnumbered by endless counts, but one thing is for sure; I am definitely one tough monster. I put my fists in the air and they glowed hot, then I slammed them into the ground. About a hundred of the voids were sent back, but they stood back up, even though they were mangled and torn. Lurt almost fell back from the impact and then decided to hide once again in the dirt.

How are they functioning? I thought. I analyzed them quickly. Let's think; like anything I've seen both flesh and metal, they all have a brain or computer that keeps them going. Remove the computer and you remove their function. I thought about trying to take the heads off. I put one hand aside of my head and the other on the opposite side, both with palms facing out and the back of them touching my head. I put my heel deep in the dirt to push myself to spin. My hands glowed hot with bright purple light and I let the energy flow out in large beams as I spun on my heel and kept my hands head level. I became a living laser-copter.

I stopped spinning and saw that the heads of the Voids had been cut clean off all around by a couple hundred foot radius. That space gave me time to recharge. I reached into my pocket to grab my flask, but it was empty. *Oh crud*, I forgot that the Wings of Famine drained my sustenance. I panicked because I knew I'd become stiff soon, but then I took another look at the liquid oozing from the Voids. I don't believe it; its Creeple Tree sap. He did say that they made a monster like me. I got down on the ground and lifted one of the decapitated heads of the Void. The eyes closed and the body shut down, but the mouth still twitched. Decapitating their heads worked! I looked at the sap oozing from the severed neck and hesitated. *This is going to be quite a disgusting experience*, I thought to myself. I closed my eyes tight and opened my mouth wide. My long, pointy purple tongue rolled down to my chin. The Creeple Tree sap oozed from the neck of the head into my mouth. I got a little on my face.

I drank enough of it from the decapitated head and threw it aside, distastefully. I wiped my face and felt the power running through my veins. If all these Voids are full of Creeple Tree sap, I can go until the very last one is down! I smiled to the thought, knowing I had a field of unlimited power supply and ran through a crowd of Voids with my arms out wide and stiff. My arms knocked the heads off of a few dozen Voids as I ran at them, arms out wide. The bodies fell to the ground, followed by the heads. I could see Lurt in the distance. He came up once more to watch me with fear in his eyes. He sank into the ground once again to hide from me. *That's right, hide coward!* Guess it wasn't going as well as he had planned.

I found myself having too much fun knocking all the heads off of the Voids. I'd run out of a little fuel and then hold one of the heads over mine and drink the sap from their severed necks then repeat. I did this for a long while. Cutting the heads of the Voids off until I got stiff, filled my system back up as well as my flask and slaughtered some Voids.

It wasn't until it seemed like I took on half of the Void population that they suddenly stopped movement and slowly dug their way down back into the ground. I was then revisited by the Ectos as they came from behind. A few dozen of them appeared in the sky as glowing white balls then turned into their form to stare me down.

"Impressive, monster," Ladidya called out, "but you can't get Creeple Tree sap from an Ectos!"

They all rushed me at once. I crossed my arms in front of my face and then threw them out on either side of me to release a burst of energy. The force pushed the Ectos, sending them backwards.

They floated for a moment, analyzing me. I kept my arms out wide and stared at them.

"What's the matter? Can't touch me?" I asked sarcastically. I felt a yank on my feet and I was suddenly pulled into the ground fast.

I couldn't breathe. The dirt was suffocating me. I heard the Ectos laughing above the surface as I was plummeting down. I tried to reach down and cut off whatever was grabbing my ankle but I was surrounded by a sea of soil which made it very difficult to move. I was pulled far enough down until the dirt around me was ice cold and the weight of it all was crushing me. I couldn't see or breathe. I felt hands crawling around my face and body. The Voids had me stuck in the dirt like a spider held its prey in a web. I felt jagged teeth bite into my neck and torso. About seven mouths biting deep into my skin and sucking out my Creeple Tree sap. I felt the life draining from me. I pushed out every last bit of power I had and shot straight up towards the surface like a giant monster drill. I reached the surface and shot high into the air, flapping my arms in front of me as Void arms still held onto me.

Gravity kicked in and I began to fall. The Ectos were below and I fell right onto them. My hands glowed hot and I somehow managed to physically grab Ladidya and bring her to the ground with me. I could feel the cool, windy surface of her body. It felt like I was able to grab a ball of mist; all cool and dry with a pinch of electricity surging through my fingertips. I threw her to the ground and held her there. She looked into my eyes with horror.

"What are you?" She said trembling.

"I'm just a monster," I replied, "a really scary monster."

The other Ectos came to her aid but I turned around and held my hand out and shot them full of my energy. The Ectos began to smoke away as they screamed in pain. In just seconds, they faded away like mist. I turned around again and looked deep into Ladidya's eyes.

"You ever try to come at me again and I'll turn you into nothing but a memory, like I did your friends. You understand me?", I said firmly. She nodded frantically and began to whimper. I stood up with Ladidya still in my grasp and threw her as far as I could into the air. She spun around for a second then regained her balance. She looked down at me for a moment, then flew away as quick as she could.

I stood up slightly off balance, clothes torn, sap oozing from the deep bite marks. I had taken quite a beating this time. My neck felt weird, like it was kind of off balance. I touched my face and felt nothing abnormal. I reached down to touch my neck and felt that a seem had came loose. *Great*. Its bad enough I have to drink tree sap to stay alive, but I have to sew myself up, too? I grew irate. I looked around in the cold.

"Anyone else want a piece of me?" I beckoned.

I was the last one standing. I earned my so called *alpha male* dominance. Not that I really cared; to me that was just a stupid game that these beings played. It didn't have to be as important to them as they thought it had to be. In all reality, if we just worked together and just went along our way, we really could. It was as though they were all programmed to dominate. If they could just see passed that and live as their own, there wouldn't be a war, or a fight, or anything like that. They would just do what was really important; they would just live. Enjoy the chance to be here, like I did. But I was just a monster; a creation that supposedly wasn't given that. What do I know?

I made my way back towards where I saw that little Psychozoan take my rightfully stolen NaviBox. I walked over to the entrance and enjoyed the feeling of the purplish grey grass under my feet. I spent way too much time on Lanterian soil for my own liking. I walked over to the way the Psychozoan ran. Everything looked like the forest near my shelter. I found a comfortable spot up against a tree. I checked to make sure it didn't have a face and sat up against it. I reached into my satchel for the books and diary that I had taken from my shelter and looked for the one titled Biology. I located it and opened it up to the table of contents and looked for anything that covered sewing and putting seems back together.

I found it; it had a birds-eye image of what looked like a group of Steinlocks circling a Monstrut on a cadaver table. In large fancy words it read,

"Biology Section B2:
An understanding of the living and the reanimated."

I located the page number and started to read. To my relief, there was a needle and thread pressed between the pages of the chapter. Taking the needle in hand, I began to read.

Step eight in reanimating process: The Stitching Process.

"This is one of the most basics of the reanimating process. Take the needle and press firmly between your thumb, middle, and index finger. Take your other hand and pinch the flesh in the area needed to be sewn and pull it out slightly enough to make it possible to run the needle through," I read out loud.

I put the book down on my crossed legs and continued to read. I cocked my head to the side and pinched my skin on my neck.

Then I ran the firmly placed needle between my fingertips through the pinched skin in the area I was falling apart.

"Pull until thread is tight, and then repeat until it has been completely sewn together. Cut thread and tie off well. Let flesh rest together long enough to begin healing. If you are a holder of a welder, melting the skin together is highly recommended to speed up healing process, for better sealing," I finished reading out loud as I finished sewing.

Well I don't have one of those, I thought. I ripped the thread between my teeth and tied it off and jerked my neck back and forth to feel the strength of the thread. It felt good, but I could feel where it needed to rest. To give myself a moment, I pulled out the diary I had found at the shelter with my Creator's name on it. His name was engraved in silver lettering. The book was dark grey with a string attached to keep track of recently visited pages. I opened the diary to where the string was tucked and began to read.

"Last day of the reanimating process, my newly crafted creature has accepted the Creeple tree sap. All is in good standing. The most difficult part of the process was keeping the powerful alchemy in its system; it had rejected the power multiple times but the genius that I am I successfully harnessed it within its system. A

new era of the living is born. I must continue my studies. Tonight, I give my most ingenious creation yet, Darkus, his power supply. It will take many months for the process to complete. By then I will be long gone continuing my plot to dish out my revenge through the lands."*

Curious, I thought to myself. So, it took a long while for me to be juiced up. I continued towards the beginning of the diary and continued reading.

"Today is the beginning of my Darkus creation. The other Steinlocks have warned me not to continue to do so. Meddling with ancient technology is prohibited in Redemption Tower but I can't help but to be so obsessed with this technology. The futuristic technology up here has too many weak points due to my cultures large ego. They do not understand that the ancient technology hoarded powers that no humanoid can comprehend. If we do not continue to research the older technology then we lay in danger of what is to come by an unexpected force."

I decided to turn a couple more pages towards the end and read once more.

"I've been sentenced to death. I must take my equipment to a hidden area in a place no one would think of finding me. It's a genius place, but I cannot say for I may risk it all. This is my last day being a Steinlock. It's been a hard, long trip but I must follow my own path and not fall into the line I'm forced into. I can't believe my kind would sentence me to death for following my beliefs; they will regret the day they betrayed me. That goes for every creature in Remains as well! I must go; they plan to kill me once the sky turns dark, and it's turning twilight. Farewell diary."

I had hoped to read something about his whereabouts or more about my system but it seemed like it was only a log for thoughts. I tucked the Biology book and the diary back into my satchel and sighed, resting my neck a little longer.

I rested until I became antsy, then got up and continued to walk towards the Psychozoan's path. I saw a sign that told me where I was heading. It read *Psykya*. So, Psykya is where the Psychozoans live. *Sounds about right.* I just remembered Ectus had mentioned such a place. I read the sign once more to make sure I read it right, and then continued to walk.

As I continued to walk I started seeing a large amount of a red substance painted all over the place. It was thrown up into the tree branches and tree trunks, dripping down into large puddles. I was so busy looking up that I nearly slipped and fell. I looked down to see even more of it on the ground. It was all over the place as if there was a massive slaughter. But as I looked closer it was smudged around by what looked like large fingers. There wasn't a slaughter. This was put here as a decorative of sorts. My stomached turned from the lack of sanity. Of all the things I've experienced, there was something different and eerie about this.

I tried not to think of the fact that I couldn't find a single reason why these creatures would keep her alive. I picked up the pace a bit and I found myself approaching an opening. I became so worried and walked so fast I nearly walked straight out into their village. I jumped back into a bush and observed, nearly being spotted. Far in the back of the village was a massive wheel that looked like it had seats all around the frame, as if it was used for some kind of amusement. The only type of shelter I could see was little tents that were covered in blood, pin striped red and yellow. The Psychozoans wandered around aimlessly and made chuckling noises. Every now and then I witnessed one bumping into another and they'd start slaughtering each other until one was nothing more than mush, then they'd reach down and cover their choice of weapon and face with the blood. I swallowed hard as I continued to be sick to my stomach.

I looked all around but couldn't see anything like the Crophix. I decided to continue along the brushes on the outskirts of the village and get a look from a different angle. I walked quickly through the trees and kept my eyes out on the village, staying low to the ground. I found a spot I liked and crouched down to looked around. Behind the giant wheel structure I saw what looked like the Crophix's tail, but no Kursus. I walked swiftly along the edge of the shrubs, staying hidden, until I got close to the tail. I ran to the tail to find nothing, but I saw a blood smear track that came from the mouth of the tail where Kursus was. I followed with my eyes until I saw it go to the giant wheel structure. I nearly choked on my heart when I saw with astonishment Kursus hanging from the very top of the wheel structure, on the backside. She wasn't conscious. At least, I hope that's all it was. I walked passed the tail, and then looked down at the body of the Crophix in horror. There was nothing left of the Crophix except mush. The Psychozoans must have beaten it like crazy. This was by far the most horrific site I've witnessed yet; just a large pool of grinded down innards and flesh.

I stepped around the mashed up Crophix and walked towards the back of the giant wheel. I grabbed onto its mechanical parts and thought a moment as to how I was going to get up there. I realized that the best way to do it was to climb, so I jumped up on the bars and started to climb. The giant wheel was made by a bunch of mechanical bars that were shaped into a wheel with many frames that went from the outer frame to the center of the wheel. It made climbing quite easy. I nearly reached the top where I could barely touch Kursus feet, as I heard a silence grow from under me. I looked down at the village. Every single one of the Psychozoan's were looking right at me. I didn't move for a moment, hoping they'd go back to their business of rubbing blood everywhere, but that was just wishful thinking.

They all started jumping in the air and yelling, making weird noises. Some of them would punch each other in the nose and scream at one another. Then my eye caught a big slow moving object coming at me to my left. It was a giant Psychozoan. It looked very large and stout, and was dragging a large, mallet looking weapon behind it. Unlike the little ones with their wide smiles, this one had a long, sad looking face. It too wore face paint and had a large nose. It looked up at me and tilted its head.

"Why you steal our saint from above?" It yelled. *Wow; it speaks*, I thought.

"You steal our saint and we don't like that not very much," it said slowly.

Judging by its choice in word placement and its speech impediment I could tell it wasn't that bright. It was obvious that it was the leader. I don't think it was an Elder; that would be giving it too much credit. I think this clan just had a big berserker with a large hammer. I didn't know what to say.

"Um…this is *my* saint!" I yelled back, "So, back off!" It continued to stare at me.

"Why are you stealing our saint?" It repeated. I grew tired of trying to talk to a brainless boulder. I shook my head and continued to climb up. I reached the top and untied Kursus and dragged her into one of the seats attached to the giant wheel. I held Kursus in my lap.

"Kursus! Kursus you in there?"

She was breathing, so that was a plus. She was just unconscious. I was relieved and didn't even care that I was trapped by a bunch of mindless murderers. I held Kursus close. A loud clank came from the base of the wheel that vibrated up where we were sitting. I poked my head out to see the massive Psychozoan swinging its hammer at the rod holding the wheel in place.

"Hey! Do you mind?" I yelled, "I'm having a moment with Saint-I mean, Kursus!"

The giant Psychozoan looked up slowly at me with its blank face, and then he looked back down at the base of the wheel and continued to hammer at it.

"Hey don't do that!"

I grabbed Kursus and put her over my shoulders. I climbed out of the seat and got to the very top of the wheel. I then put Kursus in my arms and looked down at the Psychozoan whom continued to hammer at the wheel.

"Hey genius! Knock it off before I come down there and-"

The wheel tilted. The sound of bending metal echoed throughout the village. The little Psychozoans jumped with excitement and pulled out their sharp objects. I think they actually had a plan. The giant Psychozoan looked up at me and said,

"Point that….that's the point," it stuttered, then smiled at me with a big toothless grin.

The wheel began to tilt where all the Psychozoans had their sharp objects held up high, but then their plan went wrong. The other side of the wheels base broke from the weight, and the giant wheel was grounded. It started spinning forward towards the Psychozoans and I was running backwards as fast as I could on top of the towering wheel as it spun out of control.

It ran over a large amount of Psychozoans and headed straight for the woods. I was running backwards trying not to fall and get Kursus and I squished by the massive wheel. We were catching speed and we wheeled our way far from the Psychozoans village. I looked back and could see the large Psychozoan waving good bye at us. I didn't know what to do! There was no way to stop this thing and I could tell the ending results would be unpleasant no matter what. Just at that very moment, Kursus's eyes started to open. She looked up at me and then frowned.

"Darkus? What's going on? Why are you holding me?"

I looked down in shock to see her wide awake, but doing so made me almost lose my balance. I caught my balance again and she looked ahead. She saw the wheel under us and the trees brushing by and shrieked out loud.

"Darkus what are you doing?!" She yelled.
"Would you stop yelling at me? This is harder than it looks!" I yelled back.

She grabbed my antenna, pulling me sideways with her and off of the massive wheel. We started to fall into the trees, as the branches were helping to slow down our fall.
We finally hit the ground. I landed on my stomach which knocked the wind out of me, and Kursus landed on her back. She yelped in

pain. I slowly lifted my head to watch the wheel catch speed and tear through the woods and vanish as I laid on my stomach. The sound of cracking trees and destruction grew distant, until it was silent. I got up on my feet and then helped Kursus up. I pulled her close to me by accident. She looked up into my eyes. Well, that's a feeling I haven't felt before. Her eyes glowed and she smiled slightly to the right. Her body was pressed up against mine and her hand on my chest. My heart started to beat fast. She then pushed me away and turned around and crossed her arms.

"What the blazes was going on back there?" She demanded. Her face was a little red. I realized she was a little embarrassed.

"Do you not remember anything?" I asked her. She let her arms drop to her side as she lowered her head.

"Not really…last I remember was…wait! We're not on Redemption Tower anymore! So that means-"

She checked herself for the NaviBox. "Oh no! It's gone! Will you please explain to me what's been going on?"

I told her everything; the Crophix, the fall, the Voids and the Ectos. How the NaviBox was found but then taken by the Psychozoan, and how Ectus isn't anywhere to be found and how the NaviBox won't tell me where he is. Then I told her about how I saved her and how we got on the giant wheel.

"Oh", is all she replied.

She sat down and stared into space. As she was trying to catch up to the present. Her face then looked concerned as she glanced around.

"Wait, where is Ectus?" she asked. I looked at her and shook my head.

"He was attacked by the Steinlock. They had a weapon that could hurt Ectus, and he just disappeared. I'm worried about him," I replied.

"Well then, where is the NaviBox?"

"It's still in Psykya," I told her. She frowned, but then she looked up at me and her face began to soften.

"Thank you for saving me," she said. She put her head down and ran her foot in circles in the ground. She began to twirl her hair between her fingers. She looked up at me again and smiled,

"I may be damned but I was still a damsel in distress! I'm actually quite relieved that you're ok."

"Yeah, but I wasn't man enough to save Ectus. Had I been better, I…"

She got up and gave me a hug. I put my arms out almost not knowing what to do, but then I wrapped my arms around her and gave her a hug back. She then pushed me off and looked at me with one eye brow up.

"You're not getting soft on me, are you?"

"Me? No way," I said. "I'm a monster, remember? I'm not programmed to do such things."

"Good. Don't strife to be a better *man*, Darkus. Strife to be a better *monster*. Now, let's go get that NaviBox!"

We followed the path that was made by the giant wheel and made our way back up to the village of Psykya. We decided that hiding was over rated. We both walked into the clearing and Kursus whistled. All of the Psychozoans looked up and started to charge at us. Kursus pulled out Vengeance and it glowed bright. She pointed it towards the charging Psychozoans and yelled,

"*Snaozohcysp tsum edolpxe!*"

A majority of the Psychozoans exploded, like little meat bombs. Pieces flew everywhere. The only visible Psychozoan left was the big dopey one. It walked into the clearing and stopped in its tracks and slowly turned its head at us. It stared for a moment and yelled,

"Why are you stealing our saint?" Kursus looked confused.

"Oh yeah, since you came down from the sky, you apparently are a saint," I said sarcastically.

"Well this saint has one big appetite after being kidnapped. I'm going to cook this one up real good," Kursus growled.

She charged at the large Psychozoan. The Psychozoan drew back the large hammer, and swung with brute force. Kursus ducked in perfect timing and spun in circles, with rod out and drove it right into the Psychozoan's stomach. It let out a groan of pain and hunched over. She jumped over its head and faced its back. She drove the rod into the back of its legs, sending it onto its knees. She winded the rod back behind her and swung it horizontally, ripping the head clean off of the large Psychozoan. The head flew right towards me, landed a couple feet away and rolled up to my feet. It was looking right up at me with its jaw open in what looked like shock. I looked at it bitterly. I drew my foot back and kicked it right back towards Kursus. It flew into the sky back at Kursus and she caught it with one hand. She held the rod under it and muttered something under her breath and the head suddenly was engulfed in flames.

She let it burn for a moment then she blew it off until the flames were extinguished. She then opened her mouth wide and took a large bite out of the side of its face. The sight of that made my stomach turn. I walked up to her slowly, trying not to focus on the fact that she was chewing off the face of the large Psychozoan.

"What did you say you were again?" I asked her.

"One really hungry humanoid," she said with a mouth full of face flesh. I turned as to not watch her raunchy appetite, but I could still hear her eating it.

"One thing I can't stand about you is your bizarre taste for creatures," I said, looking away with my eyes closed shut, trying not to heave.

"Well don't look," she simply said, and continued to tear away at the skull of the psychozoan.

"Even if I look away, your manners can be heard from a distance," I replied.

"Well don't listen," she simply said again with another mouthful. I couldn't help but to take another peak; the crazed eyes of the Psychozoan staring straight into my soul as she ate its face off. And I thought the *Psychozoans* were mad.

After Kursus finished up with her odd supper, we began to rummage through the tents of the Psychozoans. We found nothing except some mangled body parts from both creatures I've seen and some I haven't even seen yet. There was even the head of what Kursus called a Moon Walker, a breed of deformed humanoids that took on a beast like mutation in the night. Its head was completely covered in fur, and its nose was long and pointy with a full set of razor sharp teeth. Its eyes were missing and it was covered in blood. Just like everything else we found. There were all kinds of weapons that were covered in blood. There was even a pistol of some sort I saw the Steinlocks using up on Redemption Tower. There were some power rods from Kursus's Flintkus tribe. Some long hatchets and meat cleavers covered in paint and polka-dots. I couldn't believe the high levels of crazy that these Psychozoans held deep in their brains. It was truly a site.

After searching through all of the tents, we couldn't find the NaviBox. We worried that maybe that giant wheel had it possibly in the carriages that were all around it. We looked high and low, and decided to follow the trail that we left with the giant wheel. We walked through the exploded carcasses that once stood Psychozoans, but then something caught my eye. There, in the mess of flesh, lay the NaviBox glistening in the light. I bent down to scoop away the flesh with my hands and dug it out. Kursus saw me digging and rushed to my side. I scooped out the NaviBox and stood back up. Kursus's face glowed and she jumped with excitement.

"Great going monster! You found it! Why, that silly little Psychozoan must have eaten the damn thing! What a nut!" She said, looking over my shoulder.

She grabbed the NaviBox from my hand and cleaned it off. She held it with a big smile and stared at it.

"Finally, I can set eyes on it. Ever since I grabbed the damn thing I didn't have any time to ask it anything! What should I ask it?"

"Ask it where Ectus is. I want you to see what it does," I said. She looked down at it and concentrated.

"Where is Ectus?" Once again, nothing happened. She pondered for a moment.

"I don't know what that means. You see, if Ectus had been deceased, it would still tell us that much."

I felt a bit relieved knowing that if Ectus was dead it would tell us that much, possibly. That meant that there was still a chance he was out there somewhere. Kursus concentrated real hard once more and asked it another question.

"Where is the Philosopher's Stone?" The top of the cube lit up and bathed her face in light. Her face was in awe; she was so blown away by its wonders. The light quickly disappeared. She continued to stare at it as if the light was still there. She turned at me with a big smile and said, "Let's get some rest tonight monster! Tomorrow we venture off to Cemetrica!"

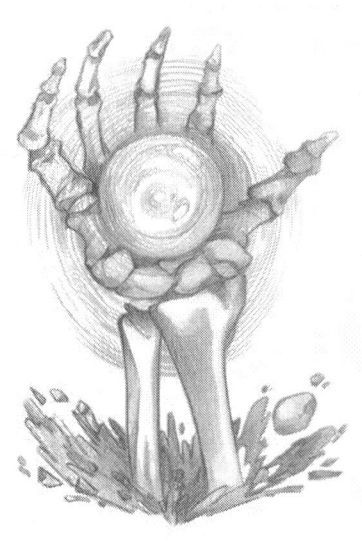

CHAPTER VI
THE PHILOSOPHER'S STONE

After waiting all night for her to get her much needed rest, the sky came out from behind the hills. Purplish green to grey and red was seen across the skies. The one good thing that comes out of waiting for humanoids to rest was watching the sky change. She walked up to me and put the NaviBox in my band.

"Ask it where the Philosopher's stone is," she said. I frowned.

"But I thought you already did?" I answered. She rolled her eyes and answered.

"Right, but I'd like for you to see where it is as well so you have an idea on where it's at."

I see, I thought. I nodded my head and looked down at the NaviBox without question and asked.

"Where is the Philosopher's Stone?"

The top of the cube lit up and covered my face with light. I saw a land that was vast and very similar to Lanteria, only there were old stone buildings scattered about and small slabs of stone here and there with writing on them. The ground was dirt just like in Lanteria. The view panned out and sped forward passing many stone buildings and took me to the very beginning where Cemetrica met Lanterian soil. There was a massive gate entrance. The gate appeared to be very old and ridged, up at the top read *Cemetrica*. The light disappeared and the image faded. I looked up at Kursus to let her know I was finished.

"Good," she said. She took the NaviBox from my hands and put it in her robes.

"I will hold onto this since you have greasy fingers."

"Uh, sorry but whom was the one who dropped it from the sky?" I retaliated.

"I was unconscious, what's your excuse?" She sneered back.

I had nothing to say to that. It was in fact, a good point. I remembered back when it happened, how I was mesmerized by the large eye in the center of the forehead of the Wings of Famine right before the Psychozoan pick-pocketed me. I stood up to join her side and we then started yet another quest. I had successfully rescued Kursus and felt quite pleased about it. It was enough to get me motivated. Kursus was sharp and keen and she made me feel like we were on the right track. She hadn't been wrong yet. I missed Ectus, but wherever he was I had a good feeling he was around somewhere. I'm sure if he's alive he's terrified, floating around trying to find us. Now we could focus on the main goal; finding my creator. We had a lead on where the Philosopher's Stone was.

We crept up to Lanterian soil. In the distance, we could see the giant wheel lying on its side where it lost its momentum and finally rested. It dug up quite a bit of soil in Lanteria. The sight of this kind of made me smile. It seemed no matter where we went we were bound to destroy something. I was quite ok with that. It's not like anyone liked us, so I had no respect for the land or its creatures. They were all against me, and now that the word had been spread out that I was an invention of Tinkarius, things were just going to continue to get heated. So much for secrecy.

It was cold and silent; not one word or sound. At this point I would rather be greeted by a bunch of nasty Lanterians, or those obnoxious Ectos, but nothing. We walked a little farther into the middle of the land and then stood still once again to listen, but nothing had happened. I couldn't help but to feel like I was walking right into a trap.

Cemetrica was located on the south end of Lanteria. We walked all the way until the south end of Lanteria. I could see a massive gate entrance coming into view from the distance. We walked about a mile longer to find that the gate was actually quite large. It towered up high above us. The gate continued to cover Cemetrica as far as the eye could see. I had a hunch that Cemetrica was heavily gated for a reason.

We walked up to the gate and tried to open it but it wouldn't budge. There was a large lock on the handles. I placed the massive lock in my hand and closed my eyes to channel my energy through the lock. The lock glowed bright and shattered into dust in my hand. I dumped the ash to the side and pushed the gate slowly. The screech of metal on metal pierced our ears as the door slowly squealed open. My ears began to ring loudly from the horrid sound. We took one more look behind us in Lanteria to make sure we weren't being followed, but there was still silence. It was a bit eerie. Each time I've came into Lanteria I was met with a rude welcoming, but this time was different. What disturbed me the most was I knew they were aware that we were traveling across their soil. We entered the massive gates into Cemetrica and shut them behind us.

The slam of the gates echoed out into the distance of Cemetrica. The air here was very icy. The volume levels in the air were so low that I could see my breath. Dead silence filled the land. Even the sound of breathing and foot steps could not be heard. I had to clear my throat to make noise just to make sure life wasn't just switched to mute. You could feel that the land was dead, and it filled my stomach with dread. I looked over at Kursus to let her know I was concerned. She walked alongside me, staring out into Cemetrica and began to speak.

"These lands hold the most horrific monsters that you will encounter yet, monster. They are terrifying and fearless. They are creatures that have already been deceased and reborn to suck the life right out of you. I would rather not be here, but it has to be done. The silence acts as a defense mechanism for the beings that live here. There are no tribes, just a mess of damned souls that roam endlessly throughout these lands. The Lanterians despise the creatures that live here, but they aren't the only ones.

Some time ago, Cemetrica used to not be gated. The gate we passed is actually a force field that keeps them locked inside this vast land. As you can see the ground is the same as Lanteria. This used to be a part of Lanteria until a mysterious force from the darkness arose and began to attack all living creatures. They spread out of the land and took the souls of thousands. Like the Mechids, the creatures in this land brought us all together to create a massive lock to keep these creatures away from civilization. Your alchemy is some of the few that could break open the lock. Even if I tried I couldn't open it.

There once was an Elder who was bold enough to watch these lands, but the living had found out a secret he had kept from all and banned him to another world. In my opinion, he was no different than your Creator; inventive, open minded. It's been a long while since anything living entered these lands. If I were you I'd keep your eyes sharp. We must stay close. You won't be able to hear anything come at you. The air is so thin from the dead silence; death even lingers in the air you breathe. We may have broken the lock but that was only to keep civilization out. They cannot pass the gates."

Kursus looked behind herself quickly as if she saw something, but there was nothing there.

"These creatures like to play with your mind. They will cause illusions if they get too close to us. Let's just hurry through. The Philosopher's Stone is located in one specific grave. It will be labeled 'gnivig fo enots' which is Ancient Voice for Stone of Giving. As you can see it's well hidden in the sea of graves. Not knowing Ancient Voice, we would never be able to find it. This place is a perfect hiding spot for the stone, for not much of the living enter hear and return, alive."

She stood still for a moment and hesitated moving forward. I walked up beside her and grabbed her arm.

"Now it's my turn to guide," I said with a smile. She smiled back then looked out in the distance and bit her lip anxiously. She let go of my grasp and grabbed my hand instead and we joined sides, looking out into the vast land of Cemetrica once more before trailing.

We walked as carefully as we could through the lands trying not to step too close to a grave. Kursus explained to me that the graves act as summoning devices, and if we got too close to one it would revive a creature that lived within the grave. The giant stone buildings she told me were called crypts and they held even darker beings. We must not go anywhere near a crypt. The silence was causing a ringing in my ear that I had never noticed before. It was quite annoying. We looked at each grave carefully. After we passed each grave, Kursus would summon a small black flower of some sort and put it close enough to the grave to let us know we had read it. The land was covered with possibly millions of graves. It would be impossible to know which ones we had read if she had not thought of this tactic.

We walked for what felt like hours. I started to become impatient from the lack of progress. We were covering so many graves but it looked as though we had hardly made a dent. I turned to ask Kursus if we could come up with a better tactic, but just as I did I felt the back of my foot catch something sticking out of the ground. I tried to catch my balance but it was no use. I began to fall backwards. Kursus reached for me but failed to grab me. I hit the ground and laid there on my back with my head tilted up. I heard a weird noise right above my head. I looked up and saw a grave inches from my nose.

"Darkus, no!" Kursus hissed quietly through her teeth.

I got up quickly and stepped back next to Kursus while looking down at the grave. It started to shake violently, and it made a noise that sounded like it was being switched on.

A wisp of black smoke came pouring out of thin air above the grave. The smoke hissed as it soon bared two glowing red eyes. It stared right at me, forming a mouth with large daggered teeth and then screamed into my face. The noise then awakened about twenty graves in a close radius around us and they all did the same; black smoke poured out from the graves and joined the black floating mass. Instead of keeping separate, they all bunched into the mass floating in front of me, making it grow larger by the second. I took a couple steps back, Kursus now holding my hand and stepping back with me. We looked up at the mass as it started to form a shape.

It started to solidify and it formed a massive floating cloak that had a large hood with glowing red eyes and a long, wide smile with large, sharp teeth. It held a massive scythe with a long, jagged blade hanging from the top. Its blackened face became a large skull that still showed its glowing red eyes. After the creature finished forming, it floated above us. It leered at us and let out a deep, quiet laugh. It opened its mouth and said,

"Darkus," in a low growly voice.
"Oh no. That's a Soul Collector," Kursus gasped.

The Soul Collector put out its massive boney hand, palm out and attempted to suck the life out of me. I floated in the air a couple feet above the ground. Even though I couldn't resist, nothing seemed to happen. The Soul Collector frowned and threw me to the ground. I got back up and dusted myself then and quickly joined Kursus' side. It continued to try to suck something out of me. It then lifted its massive scythe high behind its back and swung it right at me. I braced myself for impact but the blade of the scythe hit me and turned to smoke. It formed back into itself once it went through me, failing to suck my life source dry.

"This creature has no soul," the Soul Collector boomed, "Beware where you step, creature. Had you bared a life source, I would have eaten it right out of you. I am but a Soul Collector, nothing more. Step on the wrong grave, and your shell could be shattered. Beware the Damned. If you are not foolish, you will turn back now, never to return."

The Soul Collector slowly vanished back into the ground, staring at me until it was no more. Silence joined us once again. Kursus punched me in the arm just in the right spot to give me a good pinch.

"Owe!" I said looking at her in irritation.

"You're lucky you don't have a soul! You don't want to run into one of those with a soul. Fortunately for you it was just a Soul Collector. Trust me, you don't want to meddle with the Damned."

"What's the Damned?" I asked.

"Some say they are creatures from a darker realm. They are made of pure evil and feed on the living. That includes you too bucket head!" She snapped. "The only way to hoard them off is speaking Ancient Voice, but I've already used mine for today. There isn't anything out there to keep them away. Not even your powers," she finished.

I didn't like the sound of that. There is actually something out there I can't destroy? Yeah, I'd rather not run into those things. My confidence lies merely on the fact that my powers so far have been able to destroy everything. If I ran into something I couldn't destroy, I wouldn't know what to do. It's a good thing I found Kursus before coming to Cemetrica.

We searched and searched for the right grave, and we were starting to give up. Kursus sat down on the ground and pulled out the NaviBox once again.

"Where is the grave that holds the Philosopher's Stone?" she asked.

The top of the NaviBox lit up into her face, and then quickly disappeared. She looked out into the distance as though she was looking for whatever she saw, then her face lit up and she pointed out into the distance.

"There!" She yelled.

She got up on her feet and quickly walked around the graves ahead. I followed her, keeping a closer eye on the ground and the graves.

She walked up to a grave, and my heart started to pound. Seeing her walk right up to a grave nearly freaked me out, but to my surprise it was the grave that read, 'gnivig fo enots.' I was so surprised. I kneeled down beside Kursus and looked at the grave.

"What do we do now?" I asked her. She was reading the fine print on the bottom of the grave in Ancient Voice.

"Evarg siht sdnif ohw eh,
Reklats wodahs eht fo sesha tcelloc tsum
Esime d fo tpyrc eht ta em ot meht gnirb dna"

She swallowed hard, squinted her eyes in deep thought and then stood up straight to look around. She spotted what she was looking for then spoke without taking her eyes off of what she had spotted,

"We have to kill a Shadow Stalker and bring the ashes to the Crypt of Demise. There is a big problem with that," she explained, "A Shadow Stalker is almost impossible to kill; it's complete suicide. Secondly, entering a crypt is exactly what I said we weren't going to do."

"What can we do?" I asked. She grew silent as she thought some more, closed her eyes and took a deep breath and exhaled and said,

"We have no choice. It's the only way to get what we need."

"Why don't we just dig it up ourselves?" I asked curiously. She looked at me with one eye brow raised.

"Because if we were to do that, something much worse would happen to us. Doing this deed would be less of a suicide than just digging it up. Believe me; I've heard stories about those who just dig it up, if they can even find it. It never ends well, and it's real messy."

She looked back at the crypt, and I finally followed her eye sight. Just over the rise, past some jagged graves was an oblong shaped crypt with the writing, *"Crypt of Demise"* on a large stone that was seperate above the door. I continued to stare at it, and then let out a sigh and said,

"Well, we better find ourselves a Shadow Stalker."

Out at the far corner of Cemetrica, the land grew dim. As we walked a little further it became pitch black. We walked beside one another. I was just about to step over the visible line that separated the dim light from the pitch black when Kursus put her arm out in front of me to stall my steps and stopped.

"Don't go any further," she said quickly, "do you hear that?" I stopped to listen.

I heard a familiar noise creeping around in the pitch black, but I couldn't remember where I've heard it.

"That noise is a Shadow Stalker. Just like the ones in the tunnel deep in the temple where you found me up inside Redemption Tower." *That's right*, I remember now. When Ectus and I walked through that tunnel there was a noise that followed us all the way to the end.

"Shadow Stalkers are one of the most mysterious creatures in these lands. They live in pitch black and cannot enter light. Only a couple beings have ever laid eyes on one. They only live here in Cemetrica and sometimes with the right kind of skills can be summoned into an area using a sacrifice and the consent of a Mirror Guardian. They are rarely summoned but are most commonly summoned to guard sacred places. They capture you in the dark and make you completely disappear. Nobody knows where they take you. If you're too late, you never will be found even if you bring light. You just vanish. Same goes for the Shadow Stalker; if you brighten up a place where they dwell they disappear in thin air like they never existed. It is said that if you trick a Shadow Stalker into the light they become visible for only a moment then instantly turn to ash. Problem is it's nearly impossible and suicidal. Most people can't trick them. Its rather difficult," she finished unconfidently.

We stared into the darkness for a moment, listening to the critters crawling around just at the outside line of pitch black and light. I thought for a moment, and then had a crazy idea. I looked over at Kursus and asked, "what if you go in there yourself?"

Kursus snapped her face over in my direction with a look of shock.

"What? No way! That would be complete suicide," she said loudly.

"Just hear me out," I said as she turned her back at me, "if I held a bright light of some sort in my hand and brought it out when they touched me, they will be looking right into it and they would burst into ash!" I said confidently. She turned and looked at me with worry.

"But what if you don't make it?" she said much softly, "What if they take you away? Then all of this would be pointless. There's just…there has to be another way. You don't realize how slick they are. You wouldn't even know when to light them up, and besides, We don't have a light that bright! Even my glowing energy torches aren't bright enough."

She had a point. But then I thought of the NaviBox.

"What about the NaviBox?" I asked, "It lights everything up around it real bright. I think it would be just bright enough to do the trick."

I could tell she knew that might work but she didn't want to admit it. Hell, I didn't want to do it, but I was willing to risk it. It was the only thing I could think of. Might as well skip the hard long thinking process and just go for the obvious. She began to bite her nails and stared into her thoughts. Then she looked over at me and sighed,

"Ok fine, but I swear if you don't make it, I'm going to find you and when I do I'm going to turn you into a Psychozoan!" With a bit of a tantrum she reached in aggressively into her robe to grab the NaviBox. She slammed it into my palm and crossed her arms, staring at me. "Well, what are you waiting for?"

I looked at her for a moment as she turned away. She obviously was concerned about my well being, but I had no other idea. I turned on my heel and stared into the darkness. I swallowed hard and lifted my left foot up, slowly placing it over where dim light met pitch blackness and placed it into the darkness. I then slowly lifted the other and entered the pitch blackness. I turned to face Kursus again, who was now looking over her shoulder in worry. She couldn't see me; it was far too dark.

A moment went by, and I could suddenly hear the slithering, clicking sound of the Shadow Stalker drawing near. I closed my eyes tight and stood stiff, grasping the NaviBox as tight as I could with both hands. The sound grew closer and closer, and as quick as it came I felt long, clammy tentacles run over my shoulders and down my torso. I opened my eyes wide and stared at Kursus. She was now facing completely towards me and leaning in to listen. I wanted to let her know I was ok but I didn't want to make any noises. As quick as it came I felt two more tentacles wrap around my neck. I started to gasp for air and I lifted one arm up to yank on one of the tentacles.

Kursus could hear me gasping for air. The pressure was getting real tight. I started to see spots.

"Darkus!" She called out. But I couldn't speak. I pulled as hard as I could on the tentacles and had just a little elbow room to speak. I could feel the creature breathing in my ear, its breath hot and moist. It ran its tongue up my face and snarled.

"Where is…the…where is the…Shadow Stalker at?" I spat out at the NaviBox.

The box lit up the darkness and the burst of light revealed me and the Shadow Stalker. Kursus was looking over my shoulder in fear, and I could see why; down in the NaviBox I could see a hideous, black creature with dozens of tentacles that danced around in the air behind me. I could see myself in the NaviBox, and the Shadow Stalker was attaching itself to my upper back. It screamed in agony and let go of my shoulders and covered its eyes. For a moment I saw its giant, red eyes and its long, jagged mouth full of sharp teeth. It had two long black ears that flopped down on either side of its head. It had a long neck and four big arms. The tentacles let go of me and I fell on my face. I dropped the NaviBox and crawled out of the darkness backwards to see the Shadow Stalker that had attached itself to me struggling to get out of the light. It screamed and continued to cover its eyes from the NaviBox that I had dropped on the ground. The beam of light imprisoned the Shadow Stalker in its beauty. It fell to its knees and reached out one arm into the sky as the other covered its face, and it began to turn to ash.

The tentacles began to disappear and it began to fall to its face, but before it hit the ground it was ash. The pile of ash began to blow in the wind. I got up on my feet and ran to its side and began to grab handfuls of the ash into a large piece of cloth I tore from my clothing. I filled it up as much as I could and tied the cloth and the NaviBox shut down. Kursus walked up to my side to grab the NaviBox. I got up and held the cloth full of Shadow Stalker ash and handed it to her.

"You hold onto this," I said, "I had its slimy body all over me. I don't even want to hold its ashes." Kursus smiled slightly to her side. "You know you liked it," she joked.

We walked up to the Crypt of Demise and looked up at its sign. We looked at each other with disapproval, but then walked up the old stone stairs and up to the door.

"Why are we not supposed to go into these again?" I asked.

"Well, normally they imprison some of the deadlier monsters of Cemetrica. Perhaps this one is nothing more than just a Crypt," she had said hopefully.

"Yeah probably not," I answered bluntly, "when have we ever been that lucky?" I finished.

I reached out to open the large, stone door. It took a bit of strength to push open. We both put our shoulders on the cold stone door and pushed it open. We walked inside and saw nothing but pitch darkness. I reached out to stop Kursus.

"You should create one of your energy balls to check and see if the coast is clear," I said. She put her hands out and created a large ball of light that was a bit dim. It glowed orange and I could feel the warmth emanating from it on my face.

"For the record they are called torches," she muttered, "not energy balls." I looked at her bitterly. *Like it even mattered*, I thought to myself.

The "torch" lit up the room enough to see. No critters or slithering clicking sounds. It was a bare stone room that held a podium in the middle. Up at the top was a large book that had a large marking on it.

We walked up to the podium that bared the large book and Kursus ran her hand over the cover to dust it off. She opened the large book to see what was inside and then pulled out the ashes of the Shadow Stalker and handed them to me. I looked at it with caution. She looked at me in disbelief.

"Are you actually afraid of something, for once in your life?" She asked.

"Uh, no..." I lied. She dumped the wad of ashes into my hands and faced the book to read it.

"It's dead, no less. Afraid of something that is dead is a little ironic, don't you think?" she finished. I glared at her from behind. *Someone's feeling a little feisty*, I thought to myself. Not like she was the one covered in a cold, slithering creature that was immune to mostly everything in the dark. Oh, and not to mention it had the power to make you completely disappear.

As she continued to read to herself, she shut the book once again to look at the emblem on the front.

"It looks like Ancient Voice," she said. The emblem looked like a wheel of some sort. Kind of like the wheel in Psykya. It resembled a stone-carved wagon wheel. She opened it up once again and began to read. We both were hunched over the book. I heard something clatter on the stone floor behind us in the corner so I quickly turned around. Kursus was startled by my movement and looked back and followed my eyes.

"What?" She asked. "I...I was certain I heard something-" the clatter happened again. This time she heard it as well.

We looked around, but there was nothing. After waiting a moment, she went back to reading the book. I continued to stare in the corner. The corner was dark, but not pitch black.

"Interesting," She said, "I found a spell that requires the ashes of a Shadow Stalker, but it's not like the summoning one I'm aware of. This one must have the ashes but in a building made of stone. It summons…it summons an Elder," she said in confusion.

"An Elder?" I asked. The clatter happened again behind us, but this time twice. We looked at each other in surprise. That time it almost sounded like something was trying to answer.

"How do we know if it's going to bring us fortune or trouble?" I asked.

"We don't, but it says here this spell is the only way to get the Philosopher's Stone," she said, "It…it may even summon the ancient elder from long ago. But that couldn't be…or could it?"

"Well, I guess we have to do it then," I sighed.

We opened up the ashes from the cloth on the ground and Kursus cleared her throat as she began to read.

'*Ecaf on htiw erutaerc a fo ecifircas a,*
Ecalp siht ot gnirb I efil ym fo hpmuirt a,
Retlehs tliub enots a ni sehsa eseht gnirb I,
Redle daednu eht em ot nommus,"

The pages of the book began to flip through vigorously and the ashes on the ground flew up into the air and entered the dark corner. The crypt began to rumble and the room began to fill with a black mass from out of the corner of the area I once looked upon. Kursus grabbed my hand and pulled me out of the crypt entrance and we ran down the stares. Just as we did, the black mass shot out of the entrance with such a force that it made the black smog look like raging waters coming out of the crypt. Once we got off of the steps we turned around to get a better look at the crypt that was shooting out the black mass from every opening and crevice it had, like steam.

The smoke stopped and there did not appear to be a trace of the black mass anywhere. Kursus and I looked around in confusion. She began to slowly walk towards the crypt and I followed. We crept up the stares and walked up towards the large stone doors. We looked at each other in hesitation and then entered the crypt. The book was face down on the ground. Kursus walked up to it and picked it up, then held it to her chest. I followed her in and looked around. The stone doors shut quickly behind us as if they were much lighter and a loud booming sound echoed through the small stone crypt, causing my ears to ring for a moment.

"Greetings and salutations," a voice announced from the corner. We turned quickly and looked over in the darkness. "Do not be afraid, Darkus. I am not an enemy. Unfortunately, I cannot say the same about the creatures that live among us here in Cemetrica."

"Then why don't you show yourself?" I demanded. The voice chuckled,

"Of course, how rude of me; I'm still standing in the shadows."

A foot stepped out of the shadows. A polished black boot, attached to trousers with pin stripes. A humanoid suddenly appeared into the light. He had a long black dress coat that went passed his knees, a long boutique and a long curly mustache. His pupils glowed bright yellow, with black rings around his eyes. He had long black hair, and appeared to be in his middle ages. Everything appeared to be human, with the exception of his hands. His hands were skeletal; long, boney fingers that he had grabbing onto the collar of his coat. He bent down in a bow, then stood up and smiled, running his boney fingers through his long, wiry mustache.

"Hello Darkus. Hello Kursus. My name is Rip Van Lorenzo. I am the elder of Cemetrica." We looked at him in confusion. How could this be? He's just a humanoid. "What is the catch?" Kursus asked, "And what's with looking like a human? And your hands…"

Rip chuckled. "Of course, allow me to explain. You see, I am not just a human. I'm also a spirit. I'm split right down the middle.

It's a gift that some see as a curse. I am gifted with the powers of both humans and spirits. But with such a responsibility I do have a weakness. I can be casted out of the physical realm and into the spiritual realms. I have been imprisoned here by the humanoids and other cultures because they didn't like what I was and thought it was impure. I was a friend of your creators before you were created. I lie on the other side but lay in watch of what has been happening. I know that you've been to Redemption Tower, and I know that you are seeking the Philosopher's Stone."

He walked towards us and reached out for Kursus's hand. Kursus gave him her hand cautiously and he lifted it up and kissed it gently on its backside. Kursus took back her hand slowly and held it in a disgusted manner with her eye brow lifted up.

"So, it's true; you *are* the Elder of Cemetrica," Kursus said in awe. He than began to look for something near us.

"Interesting. I felt the presence of three people drawing near. I only see two of you," he said, running his boney fingers across his boutique, "Oh well. Sometimes my senses are inaccurate," He shrugged it off.

"You see, I am not affiliated with the creatures that live here. No, putting me here was part of my imprisonment. I'm much older than I appear. I watched these lands long ago before the dark creatures were summoned by the darkness. I was able to keep them out, but out of pride the other cultures had casted me away, willing to risk the dangers to let rid of me. Doing so brought the darkness amongst these lands. They replaced me with a large powerful gate, the one that you crossed on your way inside. How ridiculous; being replaced by a giant gate. I suppose a gate can't defend itself or talk back, it's just an object!" Rip chuckled again, "It was one thing to cast me away, but to do it in a land where most do not come back- how preposterous! I share the hate inside like you do, and would like to be of assistance. Those creatures need to be knocked down a peg or two. Of course, if that is acceptable with you two."

Kursus and I stared at him in silence. He smiled and closed his eyes as he bowed his head a little.

"I know this world is full of haters, Darkus. I am aware that your comrades are few. Well let me tell you, I am definitely an ally. I have been a supporter of Tinkarius as long as I can remember. He's an incredibly intelligent being. You know this, for you are quite the creation. I don't know if you are aware but has it ever occurred to you that he created you, perfectly? All of the cultures and creatures that thrive in Remains, most of them you are immune to, aside from the few mysterious creatures that seem to be able to take anything out like a Brackling or a Shadow Stalker, of course. They all practice just one type of study, leaving them vulnerable. You have it all, Darkus! Your mechanical bones make your strength superior and resistant to most biological attacks. Your outer body is made out of a thick hide which makes you somewhat human. Sadly, you have no soul, but makes you immune to some of the most horrific creatures out there, as well as having the most powerful, most ancient type of alchemy running through your veins. That makes you nearly untouchable. You are in fact, a masterpiece." Kursus and I looked at each other oddly, and then looked back at him.

"So, they casted you away for being different?" Kursus asked.

"Yes. I don't know where I exactly came from, I have no memory of family or my beginning of existence but somehow, I'm half human and half spirit. I'm one of a kind. The power I hold allows me to protect these lands. It's odd though; they had known about me for centuries. They never seemed to care until they decided to cast Professor Tinkarius as well," he said, scratching the top of his head with his boney index finger.

"Can you help us get the Philosopher's Stone?" I asked. Rip bowed once more and answered,

"It can be done. There is one last task that you must complete, but it's not a pleasant one. Bringing out the Stone you seek will raise the army of the darkness. Those creatures out there are exceptionally powerful and their numbers are in the thousands. Fortunately, I have the power to keep them at bay. You will be flushed away by their grasps. This land is theirs now. I cannot rid of them forever, so you have to be swift!" Rip said putting his finger out.

He walked towards the stone door and put his boney hands out at them. The doors swung open with ease, as if they were weightless.

"Let's go get your stone," he said looking back at us.

We walked the short distance it took to get to the grave that had the Ancient Voice written on it. He walked right up to it, held his hands down and closed his eyes. He muttered something and lifted his hands up high in the sky. He looked back and beckoned,

"I have lifted the curse of the Philosopher's Stone. Quickly now," he said. He walked behind a tall grave and pulled out two shovels and handed them to us. Kursus and I quickly stuck the tips of the shovels into the ground in front of the grave. We started digging. As we continued to dig, we constantly looked around to make sure we wouldn't be jumped by anything.

We dug until Kursus's shovel hit something hard. She lifted the shovel to strike it again but was stopped as Rip reached down to grab her shovel.

"Ah-ah! That is the stone! You don't want to break it now, do you?" He asked. Kursus pulled back her shovel and scowled at Rip. She joined my side as we looked at what appeared to be a small rock that was as large as my fist. We bent down and dug it out with our hands. It sat in a skeleton's hand, which then shot up, startling us. The skeleton hand opened its fingers and the stone sat firmly on the skeletal palm. Kursus lifted the stone in her hands and her eyes glistened. We both smiled at the very site of it. The skeleton hand sucked back down into the dirt, and disappeared.

"Here it is! The Philosopher's Stone!" Kursus said excitedly.

We climbed out of the grave to take a better look at it. It glowed bright green, and from the looks of it, it wasn't that heavy. Kursus handed it over to me so I could look at it. The green light was mesmerizing.

The ground began to quake, throwing us off balance. This caused the Philosopher's Stone to jumped out of my hand. I Immediately juggled to catch it, which I did. *Oops*, I thought to myself. Kursus fell back into the grave. I ran over to make sure she was alright. I looked down to see that she was fine. She was just a bit irate.

"Get me out of this filthy hole," she growled. I helped her out and the rumbling ground stopped shaking. We looked out into the distance.

"Was that a Crophix?" I asked Rip.

"No, worse," he answered. I didn't like the sound of that. What could be worse than a Crophix?

To answer my question, all the graves as far as the eye could see came alive, just like the one I tripped over earlier. They all sprung to life and I could hear a wind blowing our way, and it was coming in quick! I looked back at Rip.

"Go!" he yelled, "Run as fast as you can and don't look back! I can hold them only for a moment. Wait!" he stopped us, "Catch this!"

He reached into a pocket within his coat and threw something that glistened in mid air towards me. I reached out to catch it. I opened up my hand to reveal a pendant of some sort. It was made of thin, cold chains. The pendant that hung from the chains was an emblem of the wheel that was on the book from before.

"That emblem is a signature of the Mirror Guardians," he yelled over the howling wind, "The Wheel of Misfortune; you can contact me through this pendant. If you ever have any questions, do not be afraid to ask," he shouted. "You must go back from wince you came! Through the entrance of Cemetrica, then you must find a small village called Omitis! You will not make friends with the locals there. They are a mutated humanoid breed who feed on humanoid blood. You will be once again immune to them, but they will do everything in their power to stop you!"

From the air, a large mass of blackness started to form over Rip. Creatures began to appear from graves. Ones I haven't seen yet.

I could see that one had a long face that looked like it was melting. It howled and a few others appeared nearby along with many other new creatures.

"Wraiths," Kursus shouted.

Just then, the stone lids of two nearby crypts shot straight up with a powerful force as more black mass came to be absorbed by the large ball of blackness. The lids came crashing down. He paused to look up at the large mass and then looked back and yelled,

"Go now!"
"What are we going to Omitis for?" I yelled back.

It was too late. Rip reached out with his long boney hands up at the giant mass. which then began to absorb all of the creatures within the graves by a trail of the black mass, which looked like hundreds of tentacles. A loud, booming voice echoed from the mass. It simply said, "Lorenzo." Kursus grabbed my hand and pulled me. We began to run as fast as we could. The wind was picking up, pushing us back towards the large mass, making it very hard to run at full speed. As we ran I looked back at the mass but it was completely gone. Kursus stopped me and I looked forward as a giant fissure had cracked its way across the ground. Graves and Crypts began to fall into its abyss. We backed up a little, and then gained a quick sprint to jump over it. As we jumped over I looked down to see black and red silhouettes flying up from the pit caused by the fissure. The silhouettes had red eyes and wings. The shrieks bounced off the walls from below which caused my ears to vibrate. We landed on the other side and rolled into a run and continued forward.

"The Damned!" Kursus screamed back at me, looking back at the fissure in horror. I looked back as well and suddenly a giant tidal wave of red creatures came shooting out from the fissure into the sky. The sky had quickly filled up with these creatures, creating a reddish black color of the land underneath and at the same time causing a large typhoon in the air around us.

"Don't let them touch you! If they do they will drag you down and not let you go!"

We continued to run forward, continuing to dodge graves with creatures rising from them. A few Soul Collectors had formed and watched us go. One of them reached out to grab Kursus but I picked her up, threw her over my shoulder, and ran as fast as I could. The ground began to crack and I had nearly fallen through. I jumped up on top of the graves and started to jump from grave to grave. Just as I had readied myself to jump on another, it suddenly sucked through the ground as if something had pulled it quickly under. I landed on the ground and continued to run as I watched the other graves began to do the same; disappearing into the ground in seconds. I made it to the top of a crypt and jumped as far as I could with all my might. I hit the ground and ran some more.

Kursus was screaming at whatever she could see behind us but I didn't look back. Finally, I could see the gate far in the distance.

"They are coming!" She yelled.

The gate was just yards away. The ground began to lift up in the air, causing me to lose a bit of balance. The ground then sucked back down and turned into a massive whirlpool, and we began to spin around. We got caught right in the giant whirlpool. I jumped on top of a grave that had been pulled in the mix and began to spin in circles with Kursus still on my back. She was screaming so loud, we were spinning so fast. I could see the Damned growing closer then go out of sight, the gate, and repeat as we spun around. Kursus pulled out Vengeance and screamed something that sounded like a spell. We were thrown out of the whirlpool, along with the grave, and was sent hurtling towards the gate. As the grave hit the ground we began to surf on it as raw ground passed graves, crypts, and critters. I stood up and steadied my footing on the grave and rode it hard as we caught speed quickly to the gate. I held my hands out to keep myself balanced.

It slowed down then stopped about twenty feet away. I jumped off of it and made a run for the gate. I looked back to see a tsunami of black mass coming at us. The gate was in reaching distance and I jumped for it, busting right through it. I landed on my face and skidded forward, then got up to realize Kursus wasn't on my back. I looked back towards the gate and saw that Kursus had fallen off of me right at the entrance. Her arm reached out as her other arm held onto the gate as I ran to her aid. I grabbed her arm, but it felt as if something was pulling her back in fighting and pulling with tremendous strength. One of the red glowing creatures poked its head out and screamed in my face, took its claws and slashed me across the face, then screamed some more. Upon close observation, I noticed that they had no eyes, and they also appeared to have large horns on the front of their skull. They looked quite muscular and carried large chains that hung down from their wrists that clanked against each other. They displayed ancient markings all over their bodies that were black in color. I could see more and more of them piling up as they collectively tried to grab onto Kursus. I pulled with all my might.

"Darkus!" She screamed.
"Hold on! I've got you! I won't let you go!" I yelled back.

She began to slip. She was grabbing onto the end of the gate as tight as she could with her other arm. Just when I thought I had lost her, someone, or something, grabbed me from behind and began to pull, causing us to gain strength. To my relief Kursus began to be pulled from the gate. I almost had her, almost there!

I pulled her through. She made it. We flew back and she landed on top of me. We made eye contact for a moment and smiled. We had a moment. Oddly, it felt like something warm and fuzzy was in my monster stomach. Honestly, I didn't like it. I tried to ignore the situation and looked over her to see that the gate had shut. The giant mass hit the gate with blunt force, causing an enormous sound that thundered like a giant tidal wave against a rocky shore. It echoed in the lands of Lanteria and we watched it subside. Kursus looked back at me and smiled, but her attention was directed to something behind me. She got up and helped me to my feet. I turned around. What I saw truly amazed me.

"It can't be," Kursus said quietly.

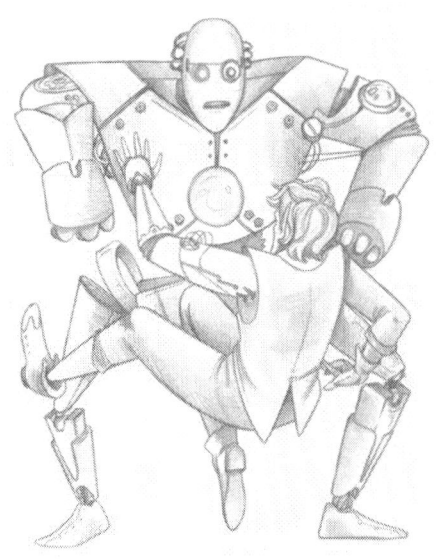

CHAPTER VII
A TASTE OF BLOOD

There, glowing as bright as the Philosopher's Stone, with the look of concern in his face, was Ectus.

"Are you guys alright? What on earth was that?"
"Ectus!" Kursus yelled.

She rushed to go hug him but then stopped. Lost in her excitement she realized you can't hug spirits. She stood there and smiled at him. But then she began to frown and took a few swings at him even though she knew she couldn't actually hit him. He still backed up in surprise.

"Where did you go? Where on earth have you been? And why can't we find you on the NaviBox?"

"You guys obtained the NaviBox?" He asked surprisingly.

"That's not all," I said with a smile on my face. I reached in my clothing to find the Philosopher's Stone. I couldn't feel it.

"Uh-oh," I said. Had I really dropped the stone?

"Don't worry about it, monster," Kursus chuckled. She reached into her robes and in a presentative fashion, pulled out the glowing green light and simply said, "behold, the Philosopher's Stone."

"It can't be," Ectus said, unable to remove his eyes from the stone. He reached out to hold it, but Kursus withdrew it.

"First tell us where the hell you have been hiding!" She demanded.

"Oh, I wasn't hiding," he replied, "I've been looking for you two ever since Redemption Tower. I had teleported myself to safety after being attacked by those Steinlocks. They have powers that are able to cause harm to Ectos, so I made haste. I teleported to Lanteria because that was the only place that came to mind in the midst of my fear and chaos."

"You didn't see me pass?" I asked.

"Of course not! Don't you think I would have let you know? I must have barely missed you."

I felt relieved to see both my comrades beside each other again. There was scared ole Ectus, and Kursus the tempered right beside him giving him a lecture. I couldn't help but to smile.

"Hey you two," I said. They both looked at me. "I'm just glad you two are ok. We're a team again! Before we go and look for the Elixir of Life, we should take a day to ourselves."

"You mean like a break?" Kursus asked in surprise.

"Sure, but just one day. There is nothing wrong with that, right? I'd say we earned it," I perceived. They looked at each other and then me and shrugged.

"Sure, I guess so," they both muttered.

Crossing the lands of Lanteria were silent once again but not as silent as Cemetrica. The silence of Lanteria was somewhat soothing after being in those lands. Ectus kept looking at the pendant I had put around my neck. The one I had gotten from Rip.

"What's that?" He asked.

"We met the Elder of Cemetrica. His name was Rip Van Lorenzo. Unlike our other experiences meeting Elders this one was on our side, not to mention we had to summon him," I continued, "this pendant holds the emblem of the ancients; The Mirror Guardians."

"*Whoa*," he said with great enthusiasm, "what does it do?"

"It allows us to contact him in the event we need to ask for advice. He was a good fellow, just a bit odd. He was cast away for the same reason as us; for being *impure* and being affiliated with Tinkarius. He had been cast into the spirit realm, even though he shares the characteristics of both human and spiritual."

Ectus looked forward and nodded his head, lost in thought.

"Can I touch the Philosopher's Stone now?" He said, completely off topic. Kursus stopped, rolled her eyes and pulled out the stone. She handed it to Ectus.

"Only because we missed you so much," she answered sarcastically. It glistened in his eyes.

"It's so beautiful," he said. He gave it back to Kursus.

"Can I see the NaviBox, too?" Kursus switched them out of her robes and handed Ectus the NaviBox.

"I think I know why you guys couldn't find me," He began. Kursus and I listened carefully. I think we were both equally curious about the reason behind this.

"When I teleport, which can only be done a limited amount of times, I leave this realm and enter another. The NaviBox must not be able to see me when I have teleported. When someone dies they still leave a physical shell behind. All I am is energy so when I go, all of me goes, leaving nothing to find." he looked at it then asked, "Where am I?"

The NaviBox lit up bright into Ectus's face and he looked down on the top. He could see himself sitting where he sat with the NaviBox in his hands glowing into his face. The light dimmed and he looked at us and smiled as he handed back the NaviBox to Kursus.

"Very peculiar," Kursus said looking at the NaviBox, then stuffed it away in her robes.

We walked to the west of Lanteria where the woods held the Creeple Trees and my shelter. I thought it may be a good idea to take them back to my shelter to show it off and stay warm. We walked to the edge of Lanteria and I had that feeling that someone was watching me. I turned around to see Lurt standing in the distance, and watching us. His head bowed down a little but his eyes stared right at me, burning with fury. I stood there and looked at him for a moment. Once I felt we understood each other, I continued to follow the others through the opening of the woods.

"Did you know that this particular forest is named Creeple Forest?" Kursus informed us as she grabbed branches and moved them out of her way. She let go of one and it snapped back at Ectus who flinched, even though it went right through him. I didn't know that but I guess it makes perfect sense. I looked around and up in the trees, keeping a close eye on each tree. This being the location of my first experience with a Creeple Tree, I easily formed the habit of looking up at the trees. To my surprise, I saw a face form on a tree up ahead in the distance. It watched us as it breathed heavy. I checked to see if I had any sap left in my flask. My stomach dropped when I realized it was empty.

"Uh, guys," I called out as they turned towards me, "I'm out of Creeple Tree sap." Kursus sighed,

"Well I guess we will have to get ourselves some sap. Perhaps we should stock up on other things we need as well. Unfortunately, I need a spell that I had left in Muckraid. Omitis is just around the corner from there we will have to stop by there. I was thinking about finding some Milderoids as well."

"What is a Milderoid?" I asked.

"Milderoids are mechanical plant life. They were seeded throughout this region by a mechanical tribe that is less advanced than the Mechids. They don't have a village so they tend to be dispersed throughout the lands. They were an invention by a man who was murdered for his successful attempt in creating mechanical life to live amongst us. His name was Professor Milder. This mechanical plant life is able to live and thrive like any other plant life. It's infused with metals through biological engineering. Milder was a secret idol of mine, since he was fascinated with the same interests as mine. Personally, I'm totally obsessed with the Milderoids. They gave me the idea to make the Mecha Creeple Tree. The one that carried us out much earlier, do you remember?"

I nodded my head. "Unfortunately," Ectus answered. Kursus snapped him an ugly look. "What does that mean?"

"Oh, not your tree, I meant Sulfus," Ectus answered.

"How will the Milderoids assist us?" I asked. She turned her attention away from Ectus to look at me, her face turning soft again.

"The Milderoids are a form of natural and useful metal. If I can collect a few, I can create a few things to help us on our quest. Like minions or devices for traveling."

"That's quite fascinating," I said happily. I really liked the idea of traveling with someone who could create such devices. I hoped to learn a thing or two as well. It would be nice to learn a few techniques myself, just incase I get left alone again.

"Well, shall we take down a Creeple Tree?" Ectus stopped and asked as he stared at the Creeple Tree. We joined him at the Creeple Tree and stared at it as it smiled wide, leering at us.

"Might as well. We can't afford to have Darkus seize up on us again," Kursus teased. We began to walk towards the Creeple Tree, the tree keeping a close eye on us. Kursus and I drew out our weapons and got ready to take it down. The tree began to shake violently, and then it chuckled. That's odd; I didn't know they were vocal, other than the screeching. I pointed my pistol at its face, closing one eye to take aim. Its smile grew wider. Suddenly, it spoke, causing me to open both eyes in shock.

"There is no need for violence, traveler." the Creeple Tree said with a deep, raspy voice. I lowered my pistol and looked at Kursus and Ectus to see their reaction to this. They too were surprised.

"You can talk?" Kursus asked.

"We reserve talking when a negotiation is at hand, and this one appears to be of importance. We too have a structured society where we communicate and keep one another informed, just like your kind. I've heard about you, Darkus. You serve but an evil deed," it said with a wide smile.

I glared at it as I raised my pistol and took aim once more.

"There is nothing wrong with following your heart," I said through my teeth. I pulled the pistol's hammer back, letting him know I was serious.

"True, but it appears you don't know the real story," the Creeple Tree replied calmly.

"Why don't you shut your mouth, stump," Kursus snapped at the tree. The tree began to frown, leered at Kursus and said, with a much lower voice,

"You're no better, traitor. You too serve a darker purpose," the tree shook violently again, then directed its attention to me and began to smile once again,

"Even as I try to reason, you point that gadget of destruction at me. Don't you find that interesting?"

I stared at him for a minute, then said, "well, last time I met your kind, they weren't the friendliest to me. In fact, they attacked me first. I'm sure that has something to do with it," I answered back.

Before I could finish what I had just stated, a vine shot from the ground and smacked the pistol out of my hand. I jumped back and held my hands out to charge-up just as the vine whipped down at my flask and nabbed it. The tree extended a branch towards the lip of my flask, twisted the lid off and began to gush out sap. I watched in confusion as the tree smiled and dumped out its sap for me in my flask.

"All you have to do is ask," the tree said softly in its raspy voice, "not all of us are hot tempered. I know how powerful you are. You destroyed the Lanterian's Crophix. I watched it with my own, hollowed eyes. I figure why fight when I can just give you what you need? Life is but important to us Creeple Trees as well. It's not like I'm low on sap or anything," the tree explained.

The tree brought down my flask and handed it to me. I waited a moment to grab it as the tree dangled it in front of my face. I reached out slowly, and then quickly grabbed it out of its vines. The tree chuckled and took a deep breath and exhaled.

"If you find yourself in need again, you know where to find me. Beware of the outcome of your decisions, Darkus. There will come a day when you may learn the truth behind your quest. I'm quite sure you will not like it." The tree's face began to slowly disappear.

"Wait! What does that even mean? What do you know about my quest?" I asked, but it was too late. The Creeple Tree had turned back into its dormant state. I turned to Kursus and Ectus with a look of concern on my face.

"Do you think that Creeple Tree was trying to fill my head with nonsense?" I asked them.

"Of course it was, it's a Creeple Tree," Kursus answered as she began to walk towards my shelter. I began to follow, but looked back at the Creeple Tree for a moment. That was the second time someone, or something, had said that to me. But why wouldn't I like the outcome of finding my Creator? I know in my heart he has the best intentions. I should know; he made me. For a moment I grew concerned, but then I had realized that everything has been against me, living or undead, and will stop at nothing to prevent me from completing my quest. I glared at the tree and then continued to walk away.

We had walked through Creeple Forest and we came across the vast, beautiful meadow that I had walked through just outside of my shelter. As Ectus and Kursus continued forward, I stopped in my tracks to take in the view once more. This field felt like a giant yard in front of my home. The grass was grey and glistened in the dark skies' colors of purples and oranges. My stress had lifted and I felt a big smile growing on my face.

"Are you coming Darkus?" Ectus called out, his glowing body shining off of the dark grass underneath him. I nodded but didn't look at him. I was still dazing up in the sky. I took one last breath and soaked in the worry-free grange, and then continued to walk.

We had made it to the beginning of the hill that led up to my shelter. We walked up the hill for a good minute. I noticed that where there should have been a tall roof, there was nothing. I picked up my pace and walked passed my two friends.

"Darkus, are you alright?" Kursus asked. I walked faster and faster, and I could see nothing coming over the hill. I began to jog and then ran to the top of the hill. I don't believe it. How could this happen?

The shelter had burned to the ground. There was nothing but a giant black mark on the ground, and some of the building's remains. I bent down on my knees and threw some of the debris aside hoping to find something, but there was nothing. I stood up, closed my eyes, and held my fists clenched tight to my side. Someone had burned my shelter down. Someone who had to know I was coming here.

"Darkus, what is this?" Kursus asked in concern. I didn't turn around to look at her. I was so filled with anger that I felt my hands grow hot.

"Darkus steady now, your hands are radiating black," Kursus continued. I opened my eyes and looked down at my hands. She was right; my hands were radiating black. I've never seen that before. Normally they were colors of purple and greens, sometimes blues. I looked at Kursus; I could tell she was a little worried.

"Black energy is pretty potent," she began, "mixed with your alchemical powers, that could be quite devastating," she finished, backing up a little. I calmed down and took a couple breaths and watched the black color disappear from my hands. I turned towards my friends and sighed.

"This used to be my shelter. Someone had burned it down and I think I know who did it," I hissed through clenched teeth and my face feeling tense from the anger.

"Who do you think did it?" Ectus asked, floating above the burn pile to look around. Kursus walked up to the pile to kneel down and touch the ashes.

"I think Lurt had something to do with it," I answered.

"The Lanterian elder?" Kursus added.

"When we were walking into the Creeple Forest he was watching us from afar. I'm sure that…"

I was stopped by the site of a figure walking out from behind a tree a bit lower on the hill. I pulled out my pistol and shoved Kursus behind me. Ectus floated a bit off to my right, suddenly turning around from the sound of my pistol. It looked like a humanoid. It gracefully walked towards us, but maintained its distance. The shade from the tree hid its face, but it soon walked into the light, given off by the dark sky's colors.

"Hello, Darkus," he said through his smile. His skin was a pale whitish-yellow. He had long white hair and piercing red eyes. He wore what looked like goggles on his head. On his hands he wore long leather gloves and his clothing displayed gears and cog designs. On his chest bared an emblem that looked like a blood drop with a skull inside. From his robes hung vials of multicolored formulas. He wore a satchel and a long belt across his robes and had on big boots. His gloved hands were together pressed up against his stomach. In his hands looked like some type of container. He smiled wide to reveal long pointy teeth. He almost looked like he had been mutated. The very moment that I had realized what he was, Kursus had answered it for me.

"Its a Noctria," Kursus said through her teeth. She grew angry and pulled out Vengeance and shot at him with spite. The creature moved so fast that I didn't even see which way it went, and then Kursus yelled, "It went down the hill!"

She ran towards him as I reached out and grabbed her arm to stop her.

"Let go of me!" She yelled. "How do you know it went down there?" I demanded.

"My tribe has spent centuries watching those leeches! They are nothing more than a parasite," she pulled her arm out of my grasp and looked out towards where she said it ran.

Kursus stopped just ahead and looked back at me and growled, "Those are the creatures Rip was telling us about from Omitis. It seems that they are the ones who burned your shelter down. When I was examining the ashes, I found a chemical known as E.L.F., or 'Eternal Liquid Fire.' It is capable of burning anything it touches. The Noctria are highly advanced chemists whom are always finding a way to blend deadly Biological Warfare formulas. They must know your one of Tinkarius's creations," she stopped to think, and then her face lit up and looked at me with wide eyes.

"Oh! They are also known to work for other creatures for a good price. You said that Lurt was watching us enter Creeple Forest. He must have given word to the Noctria's," she theorized. I grew angry again. It all made sense. Even if we were wrong, it didn't matter. Everyone hated us, anyways. I was willing to destroy anyone or anything standing in my way, and I knew that I could. This time it's much more personal. But it was late and I could see that Kursus was exhausted.

"Let's take shelter for now. No use of tiring yourself out. We can start fresh in the morning to Omitis. But before we do, let's continue to gather the things that we need. I have plenty of Creeple Tree sap, so let's find those Milderoids that you spoke of. Then we can head to Muckraid for your spell. We will set up camp here. I'm sure the Noctria had made it to its destination by now. Lets catch up on your rest and then we can give them hell," I said, putting my hand on Kursus's shoulder.

She looked up at me with large, tired eyes and nodded her head.

"Then you can fill me in on the story of the Noctria," I finished. She gave me a big hug and waved at Ectus, then she turned around and casted a spell into the ground that uprooted vines into a cozy little tent like she had done before, crawled in and not before long, she was sound asleep.

The sky began to turn bright. Ectus and I had all night to plan our attack. Talking about it all night had gotten the both of us quite ecstatic. I walked over to Kursus's vine tent and began to nudge it with my foot.

"Wake up princess," I joked. She moaned and groaned as I continued to kick the vines gently with my foot.

"Alright, alright I'm up, quit you're fussing," she groaned. The vines disappeared into the ground and she stretched her arms out and yawned, puffing her chest out. Then she stood up and punched me in the arm.

"You can be so annoying sometimes," she snarled. I chuckled, and then walked towards Ectus and stood by his side. We both looked at her with excitement. She looked back and forth at us with eye brows switching one up at a time.

"It must be riveting to be a creature that needs no sleep," she said bitterly.

"Hold out your hand," I demanded. I had a hand behind my back. She looked at me with distaste.

"Why?" she asked cautiously.

"It's not like that, just put your hand out," Ectus insisted. She looked at us both once more with unpleasantness then slowly put out her hand and held it palm up. I placed what I had in my hand into hers. It was a small critter that I caught during the night. I had remembered her eating one the first night we met. She smiled and held the critter up by its wing. It was a small, furry critter with long, windy wings and a long tail. She held it up to her face as she smiled and sniffed it, then put her hand out and started a fire.

She looked at us and said, "You made a mistake letting me know that you two can fetch breakfast," she said as she winked.

Kursus ate her critter and then we all huddled in a circle to talk about our plan.

"Alright boys, we have a long day ahead of us. What are we doing?" Kursus asked, wiping her mouth off as she ate the last bit of her critter.

"Well, first we need to know where the Milderoids grow. We're trying to do everything efficiently so we don't lose the light in the sky. I'd rather not enter Omitis in the dark," Ectus muttered.

"Well, Milderoids grow here and there, and they are everywhere," Kursus answered. "We've actually walked by many of them you just haven't been looking for them so you never noticed," Kursus explained, "So don't worry about that, I will scout for them. I assume we are going to visit Muckraid first?" she added.

"Yes, and while we are walking there I'm going to actually try to communicate with Rip with this," I continued as I lifted the chain of the pendent around my neck. "I'm going to ask him about the weaknesses of the Noctria and the best way to enter Omitis."

"Great. We may have to set up shop before entering so I can craft and infuse a few fun toys. Let's get down to business boys."

We walked down the hill and through the meadow. I looked back at the location where my shelter once stood one last time as we entered the woods. The moment we entered Creeple Forest I saw Kursus scouting for Milderoids. I was really curious to know what they looked like, considering I had been overlooking them. Ectus even kept his eyes out. We walked for a little while on the trail. I remembered that the Creeple Tree stood where we currently were. I looked at the Creeple Tree that I had once communicated with, but it did not reveal its face. I was nearly startled when I heard Kursus yell "I found one!" Ectus and I looked at each other and rushed towards where we heard Kursus holler from.

She was bent down looking at what appeared to be a Milderoid. I could see something sticking out of the ground that was eye level with Kursus. As she bent down, there in front of her was what she called a Milderoid. It looked like a tall metallic tube that had shot up from the ground. It had polished metallic leaves all around it, but on its sides were little rotating gears. On the very top was a large metal flower-shaped object with long petals that touched the ground. It sounded like it was quietly sputtering as its gears squeaked softly. It then puffed out a small ring of black smoke from the center of its flower slightly above itself. Kursus giggled and ran the back of her hand across its leaves, passionately.

"*This* is a Milderoid. There are many kinds of Milderoids. This one in particular is a Cog Flower. It supplies cogs, obviously, as well as other types of gears. When we cut one down, plant one of its cogs back into the ground. It will start to grow in just a couple of nights," Kursus explained. She reached down to the base of the Cog Flower with both hands and twisted the bottom of it. It snapped off and the cogs that it bared began to slowly stop spinning. The flower stopped puffing smoke and the squeaking sound that it made quietly ended. Kursus held out her right arm as if she was waiting for something to fall into it. Just then a large sack appeared out of thin air and landed in her palm. She took the stalk of the Cog Flower and stuffed it in the sack. She then put the cogs in her robes and bent down once more to place a cog in the dirt where it once stood and buried it. She put the strap of the sack on her shoulder, stood up, and looked at us with a wide smile.

"I need eight Cog Flowers. I also need three other types of Milderoids. One is called a Sparkler, another is called a Piston Stalk, and the last is called a Scrap Cabbage," she explained, "I need a good amount of them, but no worries; I can stash some of the heavier pieces in thin air," she said as she tilted her head at us. She then turned on her heel and almost seemed to be prancing. If it couldn't get any worse, she started to hum. Ectus and I looked at each other in disapproval.

"I liked her better when she was at my neck," Ectus said from the corner of his mouth. "I heard that!" Kursus yelled.

Kursus continued to hack away at Milderoids, which seemed to suddenly appear everywhere. With all of the time traveling in all these areas, I had not noticed all of the interesting types of Milderoids. What's even more disturbing is how I didn't hear them. A Piston Stalk was just that; a stalk of three to four pistons that pumped up and down in a cluster as they grinded against each other on the surface. This caused a screechy metal-type sound. The Scrap

Cabbage looked to be a large pile of scrap metal. It displayed a nice, yet rugged spherical shape. They sat neatly on a small pile of metallic leaves. Kursus would take her rod and bash it on top of the plant and it would just split down the middle. By doing so, it would give her many layers of scrap metal, some of them she just pulled off of the small piles of leaves, as a whole.

The Sparklers were the ones that caught my attention. I found the Cog Flower quite interesting, but the Sparkler was a stalk of what looked like hundreds of wires. These wires made a small tree with many branches that were bellowed down by the hundreds, touching the ground. The branches would spark and send out an arc of light throughout its branches. Kursus had to time it just right in order to chop it down between the arcs of light. If she failed, it could fry her into a crisp, as she explained. Again, I can't believe I did not noticed such lively creations. Most of them were on the path that we had walked as well. I must have really been in "the zone" thinking about our mission.

We had made it to the end of the Creeple Forest and Kursus had more then enough Milderoids to set up and create, but we decided that we would wait until we were closer to Muckraid. We had entered Lanteria and all I wanted to do was to wrap my hands around Lurt's viney little neck. I walked slightly ahead of Ectus and Kursus and stood there with my hands out.

"Where are you Lurt?" I shouted. My voice echoed throughout the lands. We all looked around. Apparently, for an elder Lurt was quite the coward.

"Yeah, that's what I thought. Your silence answers my question. Maybe the real reason why your tribe is at the bottom of the food chain, next to humanoids, is because you hide in the dirt. Maybe that's where you should stay, alive or not, you're going to end up in the ground." I yelled. Again, nothing. I knew he could hear me, but he was smart enough to not show himself. Lurt was more of a technical player. He didn't have the pride to override his technique. I wanted him to at least know that I was onto him. I looked back at Ectus and Kursus and tilted my head towards the direction we were heading to let them know that we were to continue our walk.

As we continued through the silence of Lanteria, I grabbed the pendent on my chest and held it in my hand. I decided that now would be a good time to ask for Rip's aid. But then I thought about how I didn't really know how to ask for him.

"Uh, Rip? Can you hear me?" I asked. I waited for a moment, and then Kursus looked over and stopped me. She removed the pendent and held it in her hand.

"You have to ask for him in Ancient Voice," Kursus said. I rolled my eyes, "I sure can't wait to be able to speak that language," I replied.

"No, you don't. It's quite the hassle and a heavy responsibility," Kursus continued.

"*Pir ew ksa rof ruoy ecnadiug,*"

She let go of the pendent. It glowed bright blue with a faded purple, outlining the pendent. It felt a littler heavier and as if Rip was standing right next to us speaking, we heard-

"Greetings, fellow comrades! I see you've discovered how to use the pendent. That is great news! Now, how can Rip Van Lorenzo be of assistance?"

"We need to know more about the land of Omitis," I answered.

"Ahh, yes. Now listen carefully for this pendent can only be used for short amounts of time. It takes quite a bit of magic to keep us all tied together, see." He cleared his voice and gave a cough, and continued.

"Now, the creatures that I talked about there are called Noctria. They are blood thirsty humanoids that have mutated by choice to start a new race of intimidating humanoids. All humanoids who dare to threaten the Noctria will be captured and then be forced to turn. It's a nasty process that involves a synthetic serum made from a deadly creature that lives in The Sea of Shame. It's called a Meenrale; a large creature that is nearly impossible to spot, that is unless it's about to devour you. Every few days it releases its toxins into the water, which then floats up to the top and can be used for this process. It has a foul affect on humanoids. It hasn't been used on any other creatures yet. The toxin is called Ghoul Grime type 3.0. It is the latest of its kind. The toxin is the key ingredient, used in a secret recipe. A majority of their humanoid victims have been taken from Kursus's homeland, Muckraid."

I see now why Kursus hates them so much. I made a nasty face to the very idea. I thanked Tinkarius for making me immune to this grime. Kursus seemed quite bothered by the idea though. I don't blame her.

"It's a deadly biochemical that they have been developing since who knows when. You'd be doing these lands a favor by destroying it if you are able to. Or at least somehow collect some so we can work on an antidote. But for now, what you want to do is find some kind of reinforcements to be used as a shield. I'm not sure how you are able to do that since you don't make friends easily," Rip added.

"Don't worry about that, I've got that taken care of," Kursus replied.

"Excellent! After that, you want to raid Omitis with all the power that you contain. I'm sorry but there aren't many other tactics to be used against them. This is going to be quite the attack the three of you," he added.

"No worries, we'll figure it out," I added.

"Good, good. Well then, now that you know what you're up against, I hope the best for you. I wish that I could help but as you can see I'm stuck here cleaning up the mess that was made after we obtained the Philosopher's Stone. Good luck, monsters!" The pendent shook and the glow dimmed and it became nothing more than just a pendent once again. I looked over at Kursus, whom looked a bit worried.

"Don't you worry, I will make sure they don't poison you," I told her. She looked over and forced a smile.

We headed east over Lanteria, speaking very little on the way. We made it to the edge of the woods, just outside of Muckraid. I remembered our last adventure here. We were ambushed by the Glirbettes, for their own entertainment. Oh, how I disliked those little annoying green bastards. The pain in my behind nearly came back as I recalled the sharp spear that they used on me. We continued further into the woods until the mugginess approached us, followed by the ash embers in the air. The discomfort in my gut came back as we walked towards the opening to Muckraid. As we drew closer we could hear what sounded like arguing and yelling. *De Ja Vu*, I thought to myself.

We made it to the brushes that outlined Muckraid and the muggy air disappeared. We could see Kursus's father, Sulfus, on the large, green marble podium. He was looking down on the Flintkus. I couldn't help but to notice that they were much smaller in numbers. The crowd was yelling at Sulfus as he answered their questions calmly. I could see that the area was still destroyed from our last visit, but no physical damage from his blast that burned my skin.

"What will be the fate of our tribe? We are running low on numbers. It will be quite difficult to defend ourselves against the Noctria!" a Flintkus shouted.

"We are currently under investigation for the chemical they are using to turn us against one another. There has been an increase in Flintkus magic and bio-engineering to better our defenses around the main premises of Muckraid. I promise you all that there will be no more abductions from here on out," Sulfus said calmly.

"What has happened to our kidnapped loved ones?" A female Flintkus pleaded.

Sulfus closed his eyes and took a deep breath and calmly answered, "They have been permanently mutated. I'm so sorry but your loved ones may not return." The woman began to sulk as she held her children.

"Once we obtain the chemical we can then work on an antidote. But until then, make sure you stay inside. We will protect you."

"What of your daughter, the traitor? What about the monster that she has sided with? The one that all has been talking about? Darkus…"

"Do not speak of those names!" Sulfus yelled. The tribe stepped back and grew silent. Sulfus looked around, then became calm, once more. "I can assure you they won't be around anytime soon. You have my word."

"Don't be so sure of yourself old man," Kursus whispered next to me. Sulfus put his hand up to the yelling crowd. He then turned and began to walk away. I looked at Kursus in curiosity. She noticed me facing her but continued to look forward.

"The Noctria have been kidnapping members of my tribe. I don't know whether to help them or let them be taken. They were going to kill me after all. I guess if we were to obtain this toxin I wouldn't mind placing it mysteriously in their grasp," Kursus said.

"That is really noble of you," Ectus answered. "Yeah, yeah," Kursus muttered.

Kursus continued to scout as the Flintkus slowly dispersed into their homes.

"Where is your spell?" I asked quietly.

"It's in that little cabin over in the back there," she pointed towards a bigger cabin than the others. I had not noticed before that most of their village had small wooden cabins for shelter. Some were up in the trees with roped ladders and bridges that lead to one another.

"The problem is my father," she said with a long sigh. "he has hired the best of his spell casters to guard every corner of the place. But I think I know how we can get past them. Ectus, you can still teleport correct?"

"Yes, I assume you'd like me to enter your home with your angry father?" He answered with distaste.

"Indeed, I do!" she said with a smile.

Ectus sighed and asked, "Where is it located?"

"Its locked in a small chest in a room with lots of plant life. Don't let my daddy see you sneaking around. He doesn't like surprises and especially guests in my favor," she answered. Ectus glared at her, then nodded in acknowledgement. Suddenly, he disappeared into thin air. Kursus and I waited for a moment in silence, listening carefully. We then heard a loud angry growl coming from the cabin and saw large balls of red magic cutting holes through it. Ectus floated out of the cabin quickly with his hands above his head. He had a thin book in his grasp. He screamed as he flew right passed us. We watched him in surprise, and then turned around to look at the cabin as Sulfus stomped out in a rage. He made eye contact with us.

"Uh-oh, its dad," Kursus gulped. "Time to run away from home again," I added as we ran after Ectus. Large red balls of magic were shot through the forest, each time barely missing us. The sound of Sulfus yelling at us was heard in the distance.

"KURSUS!" Sulfus screamed at the top of his lunges.

We soon made it passed the mugginess and the ashes and back into clean air. We waited a moment for Ectus. The book dropped from the sky onto the ground and Ectus appeared right next to Kursus, nearly scaring her skin off.

"Don't ever ask me to do that again!" He yelled in her face.

"How did he find you?" she asked.

"He had some type of force field that reacts to a sudden presence. He was practically waiting for me the moment I got your book," he answered angrily.

"Oh, right. I had forgotten about that," she said with a slight smile. Ectus looked at me with shock.

"Can you believe the nerve of this humanoid?" He asked manically.

We found a safe spot in the woods and Kursus put down her gear. She put her hands in the air and suddenly a bunch of scraps from the different types of Milderoids fell from the sky. It made a loud clank right in front of us.

"It's time you learn how to craft, monster," Kursus said to me. I was very fascinated by this. My creator was an incredible inventor, so I was interested in the idea of following my maker's foot steps. I stood beside her and she explained, separating the pieces.

"Now before we begin I would like to collect some biological pieces. In other words, we need to find living creatures, kill them, then reanimate them. Why don't you go do that while I get prepared?" Kursus asked. I nodded my head and looked at Ectus.

"Stay here and watch her," I demanded. Ectus gave me two thumbs up and I ventured off into the wilderness, but not too far; just in earshot of our camp.

I looked around for something living that would be big enough for crafting. I looked up in the trees, and I found something that filled my heart with pure joy; it was Glirbettes. Oh, how I waited for this. I pulled out my pistol and aimed at the Glirbettes that was sitting still. I cocked the hammer back and the Glirbettes heard the click, looking right at me. I fired without hesitation. I nailed the Glirbette right in the middle of the head, and fell to its doom. The other Glirbettes caught my eye and began to rush me. I charged my pistol a small amount, then aimed at the space between them. I fired. The energy ball was just big enough to take them both out. They slid to my feet and I smiled wide. *Karma is a bitch*, I thought. I picked up the Glirbettes and put one over my shoulders and dragged the other two and whistled all the way back to the campsite.

When I got there, Kursus was outraged.

"Glirbettes are harmless! You don't just go killing Glirbettes," she snapped. I rolled my eyes and sighed. *Whatever, I hate them and that is all that matters.* After she gave me a scolding, she took them and put them in a pile next to a cadaver table that looked similar to mine as she muttered in irritation.

"Might as well make use of their bodies; not like they will need them anytime soon," she continued to rant. *Damn straight*, I thought to myself with a smile. I walked over to the table and crossed my arms behind my back and watched. She brushed off her anger and put on her game face.

"Now, this part is important so pay attention. You must hollow out the body. You just need the shell, as well as the brain and heart. Leave in the nerves as well." she said. She pulled out a sharp knife made out of what looked like some type of stone and placed it on the chest of the Glirbette. She buried the blade into its skin and ran it all the way down to its large stomach. Its body opened up and all of its organs were visible. The smell was sour like rotten vegetables. She reached into its body and grabbed a cluster of its organs and began to pull them out and throw them on the ground. Ectus looked very sick from the sounds of the organs splashing onto the ground.

"You must take everything out to get just the flesh. We will be replacing the bones with mechanical parts," Kursus continued.

I began to help her take out all of its organs. *This is fun*, I thought. I smiled as I helped her remove all of its organs. Perhaps it was a bit concerning that I enjoyed this so much. Once we were done removing its organs we continued to cut down the legs and arms and pulled out the bones. We finished with the brain. She cut around the head and unscrewed the top of its skull like a lid and carefully placed the top of the head near the body. She reached in and pulled out its brain, shaking off the natural slime base that stuck to the inner walls of the skull and placed it next to the body as well. She then finished by taking the saw and decapitating the head. It hit the ground and rolled towards Ectus. He looked at it in disgust. She explained how the head will be screwed back on to make customizing the skull and brain easier.

"Congratulations, you just finished half the process of the biological part. Wow, I really could be a good teacher. You will be finishing your bio-engineering once the mechanical parts are inside by stitching up the body properly. Now, we're going to move onto mechanics; my favorite part," Kursus added. "This will give time for your shell to dehydrate and tighten up a bit."

She reached out and placed her hand, face down and flat about a foot above the table. She gestured like she was rubbing the surface of something. Right as she did this, there were two pairs of goggles, surgical masks, gloves, aprons, and some tools that looked like they were used for welding and cutting metals sitting on the crafting table. She put on her goggles, gloves, mask, and apron and handed me mine. I put them on and felt kind of official. She picked up an odd-looking saw and continued teaching,

"This is a Gizmo Saw; it's used to cut open Scrap Cabbage and trim pieces off of Cog Flowers and Piston Stalks. We can also decapitate heads with it." She placed it down next to me. She then picked up a small drawing utensil-type looking devices. She held it against the inside of her palm and the end was placed between her thumb and her middle and index fingers as if she was going to draw. It had a small motor that sat on top of it.

"This is your welder. It is used to heat the metals so you can infuse them. Stitching is much easier this way as well. We will be starting Mechanics today by first building its skeleton," Kursus explained, "We need Scrap Cabbage and Piston Stalk to do so."

She put on her goggles as I did the same. She walked over to the Scrap Cabbage and clicked on the Gizmo Saw and lifted it over her head and revved it up. She began to cut down the middle of the Scrap Cabbage. Tons of sparks came flying out of it. In no time, she managed to split it open. I didn't get why she didn't just use her rod like before. She put the Gizmo Saw down and grabbed both sides of the slit she had made and pulled it apart with all her might. She exposed plenty of thin pieces of metal that looked like it was just waiting to be used for a project. She pulled them out and placed them on her crafting table. She then grabbed the Gizmo Saw and placed it in my arms.

"You're going to cut up the Piston Stalk," she instructed as she walked towards the Piston Stalk. I followed her over there, looking at the device in my hands.

We walked up to the Piston Stalks that were laying flat on their sides. She pulled out a measuring device and started measuring them and then marked them where she desired. She then continued to explain.

"We need nine pieces' total; the spine, legs, calves, forearms, and arms. The legs will be a little longer. We will connect the legs and arm pieces with a ball joint that we will weld out of the Scrap Cabbage. The feet and hands will also be partially welded into smaller ball joints and then we will connect the nerves and tendons to Sparkler wire that will be connected with the welded scrap. Go ahead and cut it now, don't be shy," she pointed down at the Piston Stalk.

I started up the Gizmo Saw as I saw her do, lifted it above my head and lowered the saw on the marked areas. I could see her looking at me in admiration through my peripherals but continued to focus on what I was doing. Sparks flew from the saw touching the metal and slowly cut through the thick layers.

We brought the pieces to the table and laid them down. She pulled out a large piece of parchment that had drawings of the design and the basic idea. She called it a "blueprint." We began welding and customizing the metal parts to form the new and improved skeletal system for the Glirbette. We rolled up the scrap into little balls and then began to form them for the hands, feet, and ball joints for the knees and elbows. She saved the best for last; she showed me how to skillfully craft a hollowed skull out of scraps. She even explained how important it was to cut the same shape off of the top of the metallic skull for where we will place the brain. She took the top of the metallic skull and placed it neatly inside of the real top of the Glirbette's head.

For the first time in my life, as short as it may be, I had found that I have a talent for crafting and I had a new hobby that I truly liked. What was even more interesting was watching how I was actually made. I couldn't help but feel a relation to this new creation; every piece carefully crafted and cut, every piece made with passion and skill. I imagined the dedication and time it took to craft me. My creator spent a lot of time applying his knowledge into my body. It made me appreciate where I came from and I felt proud that I was a well-crafted creation. Ectus, however, was not enjoying any of this.

He kept his eyes focused on other things as to avoid watching the gruesome reanimation of the Glirbettes.

After a good long time, we had successfully crafted the skeletal system for the Glirbettes. We finished them off with cogs and gears from the Cog Flower that she had kept in her pockets. We carefully crafted them into the proper joints to assist in their movement. We placed the metallic skeletons next to the crafting table. After we got the other two Glirbettes gutted and cleaned, she cleared her throat and took off her goggles so she could see me better, and continued with her teaching.

"Now, we begin placing the skeletal system into the empty Glirbette. If you would please assist me in lifting the skeletal system into the body," she asked as she bent over to pick up the skeleton. I lifted the other side and we placed it right next to the Glirbette. It was fascinating to see the outer shell and the inner shell, side by side.

"Now we take the skeletal legs and tuck them into the real legs, neatly, just like putting on trousers," she explained in example. I found that example a little silly, but it worked. We took both skeletal legs and placed them into the real legs. Then with the spine placed in the middle followed by both of the arms and placing the new metallic skull into the head and screwing it onto its neck. She placed her hands inside of its chest and reached up to find where the skull and spine meet. She then demonstrated how to connect the two.

Once the heads were connected, we now had bodies with working mechanical skeletons inside of its skin.

"The reasoning behind keeping the nerves, veins, arteries, heart and brain is because they will be used to transfer fuel for the Creeple sap, which will bring power to its body," Kursus continued to explain, "we are now going to take sparkler branches and use them as wires and connect the nerves to the skeletal system. The brain will then be connected to its new improved system and we will give the heart and brain a jolt. This will cause the nerves to trigger the body's movement. The veins and arteries will then be reconnected to pump its fuel throughout the body to keep the body thriving. Kind of the same concept with your innards, Darkus. We must place a control device in the brain to command the body to our liking. Once that is done, we will then finish the final step of the bio-engineering, which will be sewing up the body. If the body works, we're in business. If not, we will have to completely terminate this project, for the corpse will be insufficient and we risk malfunctioning. Also, there could be *C.T.C.*, or Creation Turning on Creator, and even exploding," Kursus finished.

We then connected the wires to the skeletal system and outer shell. The heart was placed back into its system. We gently returned its brain and connected it, as she explained. She stressed how diligent we had to be to not make a mistake or we'd ruin the whole creation. She had supplied us with tweezers and an eye monocle which attached to our heads with a strap. This was to assist us in the careful placements with the small wire tips. We diligently connected its electrical system. Once that was done, we inspected it a few times. When she had felt confident that we had succeeded, we continued to connect the veins and arteries to the heart, brain, and system. The heart was like the fuel injector and the brain guided the fuel to the right locations, as the system burned the fuel. Kursus pulled out her flask full of Creeple Tree sap from the Creeple Forest. She opened the Glirbette's jaw and dumped the sap in all of the bodies.

"The electrical system and fueling system is now complete. We may now finish the final step," Kursus said. She pulled out of her robes what looked like clamps of some sort. She pulled the flaps of the opened skin together and clamped them; the stomach, legs, arms, and neck. *That would have been nice to have when I tore my neck*, I thought. She then put her welder in hand and began to melt the skin together.

"Feel free to join me," Kursus insisted as she melted the skin together. I assisted her on melting the skin. After we connected all of the skin together, she pulled out a needle and thread and gave some to me.

"If you don't know how to sew through skin by now, then watch carefully," she said, "Sewing over the melted skin will benefit as a secondary way to conceal the insides," she explained.

"I've already done this once before with my neck, only I didn't have all of these nice tools," I answered. She began to sew the skin together; she pinched the skin, ran the needle through both sides, then repeated the process back and forth, up and down the body. "It's really simple; you just pinch and push through, then repeat in opposite direction every time," she explained. I don't think she heard me. I helped her sew the bodies together. After a long while, which felt like it took nearly all day, we had finished our first project together. On the table lay three reanimated Glirbettes, ready to be deployed. I stood back and looked at them with pride. *My first creations*, I thought proudly to myself. I looked over at Kursus whom caught me staring happily at our project. Ectus floated over to examine them. I was so into my work that I had forgotten all about Ectus, he's just been so quite behind us and keeping to himself.

"Well what are you two geniuses waiting for? Fire them up!" Ectus yelled from between us as he put his arms on both of our shoulders. Kursus continued to screw something together.

"Hold on, almost there. Just need to finish the handheld device. Now Darkus, you saw how I made this with scraps, correct? The casing is Scrap Cabbage, the antenna is Piston Stalk. The button made by a small stump knot pushes the gears, which charges up the Sparklers through the antenna, giving complete control that strikes the brain." She reached over and handed me the control device. She then walked over to grab three sets of sparkler wires and placed them on each of the Glirbette's chests. The sparkler wires were attached to another odd gadget I did not see her pull out before. It was turning and charging to create electricity. The Glirbette bodies began to twitch from the exposed wires.

"The heart must have a jolt while you switch on the brain. Normally with our modern technology we don't need to do it this way, but we're cursed with using what we've got. Go ahead; they are your first creation. Light them up and see what they will do," Kursus said eagerly looking into my eyes with a large smile across her face. I smiled at her, put my goggles on once more and looked down at the control device in my hands. I felt so accomplished, so proud, and with all the irony they were Glirbettes under my control. I pushed the switch and watched in amazement as the heads of the Glirbettes lit up, starting up the device in the brain. The bodies twitched for a moment and I watched as they rose up from their slabs. I started to laugh out loud. I looked over at Kursus, whom was jumping up and down with her goggles still on.

"They are alive!" She yelled. Ectus even looked impressed. The mechanical Glirbettes turned to their sides and jumped off of the slab. I could hear their mechanical parts moving inside of them. The Glirbette's looked up at me, waiting for command. My body started tingling with excitement, for the first time since my awakening.

"Let's go ambush some Noctria," I said proudly with a big smile on my face.

Kursus welded herself a thick plate of armor, which included a helmet, gauntlets and a chest plate made of scrap cabbage. This would protect her against flying objects that may bare barbs with the GG3 toxin, but not so much in close combat. We packed up and headed towards the outskirts of Omitis with my three little decoys walking ahead of us. I was so amazed at the inventions and was very excited that Kursus taught me the basics of crafting and reanimating bodies. I felt a warm hand reach out and grab mine to hold. I looked over to see Kursus smiling at me, as she held my hand. Interesting, I felt attracted to her. I honestly didn't like this feeling. It was too fuzzy and warm. I kind of smiled at her, and then looked back at our creations in hope of avoiding this weird sensation.

We reached the crest of a hill and to our surprise just beyond it was a large village. We quickly hid behind a tree, the Glirbette decoys following our lead. We peaked around the corner to get a better look. At the bottom of the hill was the entrance to Omitis. The village of the Noctria was filled with wooden huts. There were mechanical devices that I didn't recognize throughout the village, located near their huts. Above the village was a giant floating mass similar to a large balloon. It looked like it had been patched up several times. It carried what appeared to be some sort of ship. Long, wooden wings came out from both sides. At the top, there were three sets of sails. Its propeller spun and creaked quietly from behind. There were Noctrian passengers on this large floating ship. It was very large; it seemed mechanical, but not entirely.

I could see little bursts of white mist throughout the land of Omitis. Most of them hid their hideous faces under a cloth of some kind, covering their mouths and noses, and a majority of them wore goggles similar to the Steinlocks. They wore strapped clothing and had all kinds of belts hanging from their attire, some with glowing vials that held all types of formulas, like the one that burned down my shelter.

"Those filthy creatures are the Noctria. They run a majority of their shelters and living devices on a technology that runs merely on steam. They practice flight with this technology and even a type of mechanics to protect them. Also, like I said once before, they are obsessed with science, mainly chemistry. Although I despise them with every fiber in my body, it is a unique and curious technology," Kursus ended softer than she started. *Steam huh*? I thought to myself. *Curious*. "They will try to use the toxin on us as well. I'm sure that will be a common plan of attack. If you look closely out towards the western area of the village there is a small shack. In that shack, you will find a large glass container that stores the toxin. That must be where they have the lab…what the heck?"

I saw exactly what she was seeing; to our surprise, a Steinlock walked out from behind the lab. He looked around and somehow none of the Noctria saw him. He then quickly ran into the bushes, located far on the other side.

"That was a Steinlock," Ectus stated the obvious. "How bizarre. Do you think he was here trying to steal a dose of the toxin?"

"Who knows? All I know is that he was sneaking around. They wouldn't have a reason to steal it, unless they created an antidote and are trying to black mail for the exchange of the cure," Kursus answered. Again, how *curious*.

"So how are we going to do this? Also, how are we going to get passed the floating thing in the sky? You know, the thing that keeps an eye out on everything?" Ectus asked.

"The long hard efforts we put into the Glirbettes are going to act as nothing more than decoys and distractions," I answered, "while they are distracting the Noctria, you must manage the flying device. It should be easy since you can't be harmed by anything other than ecto-resistant alchemy. I sense no alchemy here. Try to get it to strike the toxin storage." I finished. Ectus looked up at the big flying object and sighed.

"I suppose I can do that. I'm sure I can just pop the thing," Ectus answered.

"With the decoys bringing the fire power to the front and you taking down the flying watchmen onto the toxins storage, we will hit three feathers with one stone. It should be just enough to destroy a majority of Omitis and at least slow down their toxin production. The flying object is only made of wood and steam so it won't explode, but it should wreak havoc below. Kursus and I will wait until we hear them firing at the Glirbettes and then wait for the giant ship in the sky to fall. That will be the sign to ambush them from behind their land," I finished. Kursus pulled out the book I had nearly forgot about.

"Now I will cast a 'spell of finding' to locate the elixir," she whispered. Ectus stared at her blankly.

"Couldn't we have just done that with the NaviBox?" He asked a little irate.

"Yeah, but I felt that I was getting a little rusty on my spells so I decided to practice."

Ectus looked at me in shock. I could tell he was livid. He tried to focus and brush it off as Kursus opened the book and began chanting a spell.

A portal of some sort opened up in the ground before us and revealed the image of an ancient elixir container, that seemed to be hanging off the clothing of what may have been a Noctria.

"That's interesting, it appears empty. They must be storing it somewhere else. We need to find out where," she quietly pondered.

The portal disappeared into the ground and she stuck her spell book back into her robes.

Kursus, Ectus, and even the Glirbettes nodded to my idea. We then split up as according to plan. Ectus floated a bit up into the branches of the trees and waited for the Glirbettes to enter into site. Kursus and I rushed as quietly as we could around the outskirts of Omitis until we reached the farside.

Everything seemed according to plan until Kursus had tripped over something. We stopped for a moment to look down at what it was. High pressured steam began to shoot at us from under the surface, causing us to make a lot of noise. We got out of the steam and continued to run towards the back. I could hear yelling in a language I didn't understand.

"Intrusor! Intrusor!" they yelled.

It wasn't even Ancient Voice, I could tell that much. I pushed the button early to deploy the Glirbettes. We finally made it to our destination, but the Noctria were quick on our trail. They were clever; I had underestimated them. We hid low in the bushes as some of the Noctria walked around where the steam had been triggered. I watched as the Glirbettes run out into plain site; hands up in the air and yelling at the top of their lunges.

They shot darts that were filled with the brownish yellow substance that would drain into their system. Nothing happened, probably because they weren't normal Glirbettes. They yelled more at each other as the Glirbettes pulled out the darts and continued to run around and yell.

They were still perfectly distracted, even though there were a few coming close to us on our trail. I could hear one of them sniffing the air. I looked up in the sky, waiting for Ectus to attack the ship that was above us in the sky. I saw a glistening light shoot right at the massive balloon holding the ship. We heard a loud popping sound followed by high pressured air releasing from the mass. The air pressure shot out and the ship started to tilt. The Noctria that were hot on our trail suddenly became distracted by their ship that was now heading straight towards the toxin storage. *Great work Ectus*, I thought.

The ship hit the toxin storage with a loud crash as the Noctria jumped out of the way. Glass and that ooze splashed everywhere as the ship continued to slide across the ground, destroying huts, those steaming devices, and running over the Noctria, leaving a small trail of the grime. I waited 'till the ship stopped sliding and I gave Kursus the signal to jump out and attack. We jumped out of the bushes and I pulled out my pistol as Kursus pulled out Vengeance from her robes. The Noctria turned around and immediately were in our faces. They were lightning-quick. The first one had sunk its teeth deep into my neck and I could feel my sap running out and into his mouth. The Noctria stepped back and spat out the sap and looked at me in shock. I smiled then pushed him out of my way, using a large burst of energy from both my hands.

The second one charged at me, barely giving me seconds to react. I was taken aback and one of them grabbed my neck with no time for retaliation, slamming me into the ground. The ground cracked and dirt flew in the air from the impact. I felt the air leave my lungs. It reached in its pocket and pulled out a needle full of what I assumed was the Ghoul Grime and stuck it in my neck. I began to scream, which then became laughter. I watched the Noctria turn his smile into a frown. My skin began to bubble and hiss and it burned slightly, then it began to die down and my skin turned back to its normal state.

"I am Darkus, creation of Tinkarius! I am immune to your petty toxin!" I shouted.

I kicked him up over me and stood up. I placed my pistol against his temple and pulled the trigger. I looked back to see Kursus doing a much better job at fighting, than I. She did say that her tribe has been watching and studying their movements forever. Her armor was deflecting all of the toxin darts being fired at her. She'd bash and blast them in all-perfect timing; always a step ahead of their movements.

I stood up and pointed my pistol at a Noctria but before I could squeeze the trigger I got knocked down again. It stood above me and I tripped it. I quickly bounced up and jumped on top of it and began to pistol whip his face repeatedly until he was out cold. I stood up and looked around at all of the blurred movements that were the Noctria. *This kind of blows*, I thought to myself. I'm immune to their weapons, but I can hardly keep one in my grasp.

Ectus came swooshing down right into one of the devices that was blowing steam and knocked it over. The steam was so hot that it began to melt the skin off of some of the nearby Noctria's. They screamed and fell to the ground as their faces bubbled off. I looked over to find Kursus, and to my horror, the same Noctria that burned my shelter down had Kursus firmly by the neck. He pulled out a dose of the GG3 and stuck it into her chest through her armor plating.

"No!" I yelled. I ran to her aid but a Noctria rushed me, out of nowhere, and shoved me back. The Noctria that had injected Kursus stood there and smiled at me as I lay on my back. I took my eyes off of him for just a moment and I had seen something dangling off of his belt. It looked like an empty, ancient elixir container. One that he didn't have while at my shelter; the same container that the spell had revealed. He dropped Kursus and quickly disappeared. I felt the rage begin to take over me. My hands grew hotter than they ever had. I looked over to see the black flame taking over my hand

and shoot up my arm. I couldn't control the rage that was beginning to come out.

I heard a loud screeching sound that sounded like metal on metal. It was so ear splitting that I held my hands up to my head, the dark light faded away from my hands. The sound was mind-splitting. Although, it didn't seem to affect me like the Noctria. I opened one eye to look around and just as the Noctria had killed the last of my Glirbettes, the Noctria sank to its knees and covered its ears, screaming towards the sky. What looked like mechanical beings of some sort had jumped through the trees. They swung their massive arms into the Noctria, with full throttle, sending it into a distant hut. These couldn't have been Mechids; their parts didn't look advanced enough. Most of them appeared to had rust covering their bodies. They had small heads and long limbs that were rotated by large cogs and gears, and some type of glowing emblem on their chest. They were brownish red colored. They all displayed a hologram that transmitted out of their eyes that bore the Mark of Tinkarius. Relieved, I realized this was some sort of back-up team that knew we were in trouble.

I had instantly understood their game plan; the screeching kept the Noctria from running around quickly. They were also obviously immune to the toxins. *Oh no*! I forgot about Kursus. I looked over on my side to see her lying on the ground. I got up to ran to her but one of the mechanical beings swooped her up and ran for it with her.

"Hey! That humanoid is mine!" I yelled.

I ran after the mechanical being but I got sideswiped again by another Noctria. This one was wearing some sort of ear protection. I couldn't handle it anymore; these creatures kept knocking me down and it was doing nothing but boiling my insides. I stuck out my hands and released all of my rage. I formed some sort of invisible wall of pressure around me that kept the Noctria from coming any closer. They put their arms over their faces in hopes to stop the blinding light from burning its eyes. I walked slowly towards the creatures with my hands out. Small rocks and debris all around me started to rise from the ground and levitate. My entire body was engulfed in a giant black flame. The Noctria knew when to stop. They called out to each other and retreated into the woods. They knew what was coming; they felt it. I could feel my body convulsing from the high levels of power that was emanating from my corpse. I looked into the sky and yelled as loudly as I could, my arms spread out wide. My eyes began to roll into the back of my head. I lost all control of my powers. I could see arcs of electricity drawn near me from the sky. The ground began to rumble and I witnessed a shockwave that was pushed out of me shot up dust at high speeds all around me. The huts began to tilt and blow away as if in a hurricane. I jumped about twenty feet in the air. As I landed, I threw my foot down and drove all of my body mass into the ground.

A ball of energy shot out at high speeds from all around me, turning the village of Omitis upside down. The trees on the outskirts of the village were ripping out of the ground from the massive wave of energy I had released. I was like one pissed off atom bomb.

I looked up, feeling more tired than I ever had. I could see no living creature in sight. The village had become a crater; completely leveled. I tried to get up but I had no energy left to do so. I reached for my flask as I shook. I grabbed it, but the flask was even too heavy. It brought me back to the ground and I had fallen face first into the dirt. The flask fell out of my hand and rolling just inches away. I closed my eyes and all turned black.

I had slowly come to my senses. I was really out of it. I could see large mechanical heads looking down at me.

"There he is! Check it out, he's back," one of them chanted. I sat up quickly realizing I was awake and I was a little startled by the creatures.

"Kursus!" I yelled, looking around frantically. I stood up and fell back down on my face. That's odd; I seem to still be very exhausted. The mechanical beings helped me up, then I nudged them off.

"Where is Kursus?" I yelled at them.

"Over here, Darkus," I heard Ectus calmly reply.

I looked over at a nearby bed. Ectus hovered over Kursus's body, as she lay asleep with her arms crossed. I tried to run over to the bed but my legs were too stiff.

"Where is my sap?" I asked out loud.

"You have plenty of sap; you just really wore yourself out. In fact, our studies indicate that you can't use any of your energy for a passing or two," the mechanical being clanked. I looked at him for a moment, then looked to the ground. *No powers*? I walked more slowly towards Kursus. As I approached, I fell to my knees at the side of her bed. To my dread, she had mutation in her skin. I grabbed her hand and held it.

"She's been poisoned by the Noctria," Ectus answered. I felt my stomach turn in worry. I almost had that crying feeling again.

"Do we know if she will be alright?" I asked desperately. Ectus looked at me in worry.

"To our calculations, she will actually be quite alright," I heard a voice boom from behind me. I turned around to see where it came from. The mechanical beings moved aside to make way for a man walking towards us. He had black skin and wore yellow robes with gears and cogs hanging from it. He had many rings, all with gears and cogs on them, as well. As I looked closer some of his fingers were mechanical on one side, and his entire left arm was completely mechanic. The corner of his face from his skull down to his nose and around his jaw line was also mechanical, and he had a mechanical eye that glowed red. He was large and stout, about a couple of feet taller than me. I stood up but had a hard time doing so.

"No need to get up, I am your ally. As you can see, we rescued your friend from the fight. We are all quite impressed that you have such great powers. But it looks as though they have taken a toll on you, monster," the man said. I hesitated to talk, looking at all of the concerned mechanical creatures, and then back at the man.

"I've never let myself reach that level of power. I've also never been that angry before," I answered back, looking around. It seemed as though we were underground. The room looked like a hollowed-out tunnel with lanterns that hung about to give light. It was actually quite bright in the room for how little the lanterns were.

"Allow me to introduce myself, monster; I am the great Professor Milder," the man said as he reached out to shake my hand. I couldn't believe it; I remember Kursus gushing about this humanoid. He was a great man who had supposedly died believing in what he had believed in. After a couple seconds, I realized he was still waiting to shake my hand. I reached out and shook his hands in awe. He had massive hands.

"That humanoid laying down right there is a very good friend of mine. What is going to happen to her?" I asked.

He looked at me, a bit confused.

"Humanoid?" he repeated in confusion. I nodded my head. He smiled and looked over at Kursus, then back at me. "Your friend isn't human," he replied, continuing to smile. Ectus and I looked at Milder in shock.

"Excuse me?" Ectus spoke.

"Your friend is not human," he repeated, "She is like me; she is human with mechanical innards. At first, we thought she would have turned and attacked, but her body resisted the toxins. Normally the toxin acts quick enough to where we are given no time to react, transforming the body in minutes. Out of curiosity I ran a device I created called a Mecha-Detector over her. Sure as hell, she was a mechanical infused being!" He said in excitement. I looked over at Kursus in astonishment. *How could this be? Was she hiding this from me all along?* I felt a little blue from the news. Not because she was part mechanical; in fact, in any other case I'd be thrilled, but she kept that from me. What else would she be keeping from me?

"She didn't tell you?" Milder continued. I looked up at him and shook my head, then looked back down. The man thought hard and then his face lit up.

"You know, there is a good chance that she didn't know. When I was brought into this world, it took me eons to realize it. I mean, I knew I was different and had this crave to build mechanical structures but I never put two and two together. Not until one day during battle I got a severe face burn. What normally would reveal bone suddenly revealed a metallic skull. I was in shock for a bit but than I grew to accept it. If she doesn't know she's made of metal, she may not take lightly to this," Milder said.

My spirits were lifted a bit. I looked over at Kursus again, lying peaceful as can be. Something the man said convinced me without a doubt that she may not have known. I remember her talking about how she knew she was different but didn't know how and that she's always been into mechanics. It's in her system which also explains the Mark of Tinkarius that she bared, which means she must be a creation of his. Of course; now it seemed so obvious. I had totally forgotten about a story she had told me as well; how Tinkarius saved her once before from a deadly Psychozoan attack and fixed her back up. That explains the scars on her back. She must have been a normal Flintkus up until that point.

"How remarkable," Ectus spoke, "well I guess we should be thankful for this surprise discovery, otherwise our beloved Kursus may be a Noctria." I turned to face Milder and smiled. He began to walk towards another room. He looked back at us and gestured for us to follow.

"Follow me. Your friend will need her rest. I have something for you to see," he said as he turned back around and continued to walk. Ectus and I followed the man among a small group of the mechanical creatures.

We entered a smaller room just across from where Kursus was resting. The walls were made of dark red dirt, and this room had more lanterns than the other. There was a small dining table, a crafting table that bared some left-over scrap metal, a soft seating area up against the wall, and a small patch in the corner with Milderoids growing in it. Cog Flowers, Piston Stalks and Scrap Cabbage, but no Sparklers. There was even a Milderoid that I didn't recognize. I walked up to it. It had a long narrow stalk that was spinning in one direction. It bared a large bulb on the very top that was slowly spinning in the opposite direction of the stalk. I reached out to touch it and it suddenly opened and shot steam at me. I jumped back and Professor Milder laughed as the mechanical creatures followed. I scowled at them as I held my arm from the slightly burning sensation of the steam. I looked back at it.

"I haven't seen that one yet," I muttered.

"Obviously! That is a Steamer, for obvious reasons. It comes in handy when making steam-powered pieces of machinery," he explained, happily. "I had recently made that one. When I say recent I mean about five years ago. It's not as common as the others. There will be a few more out on the surface sometime soon," he continued.

He sat down at the dining table in front of a small bowl of what appeared to be bolts. He scooped out a handful and began to dump them in his mouth and chew on them. Loud metal crunching sounds came from his mouth. He pointed to the bowl and looked at me as if he was offering, but I kindly declined. He then pulled out a bottle from a bag, uncorked it and placed it on the table. He then pushed it a little towards Ectus and me.

"Go ahead, try it," he said with a smile. Ectus reached for it, but went through it the first time forgetting he was a spirit. He then picked it up carefully and took a sip. It went through him and pattered on the floor. He looked down in sadness and handed it over to me slowly, and sighed. I grabbed it and took a swig. What a bite it had! I coughed real hard and nearly dropped the bottle. I placed it on the table. I had to put both arms on the table, as well, to hold myself up. It burned going down, but then became cool and smooth. I wiped my mouth and leered at Milder, who was laughing so hard that he almost fell backwards in his chair. Apparently, Ectus and I were a good source of entertainment.

"You two are just too much," he said, finishing his laugh. He reached out and took a large swig of the burning liquid and placed it down. He wiped his mouth completely unaffected by its bite.

"What is that?" I asked.

"It's Aged Creeple sap. It becomes a bit toxic once you leave it out a while, but it will give you one hell of a buzz! Plus, it's stronger than the normal sap. You store the bottle of sap for a period of time allowing air to escape and it does the rest. Make sure it's air tight and allow it to ferment. I recommend doing so," he said as he pushed the bottle back towards me. I grabbed it and took another hit, more aware of its kick. I took a good swig and put it down. I made a bitter face. I liked it a lot, even though it burned. Why would someone like something that was so toxic and bitter? It had an odd, enjoyable feel to it. Apparently, I like pain.

"Go ahead, the rest is yours," Milder offered, "I've got plenty more where that came from. In fact, if you ever need more, you just let me know."

"That would be great, had I known where we were," I answered sarcastically.

"Oh of course, I haven't even explained anything yet. As you can plainly see, we are underground. We are *far* underground; perfect for hiding. The walls are all covered with a twelve-inch steel outer wall to stop possible surprise visits from Lanterians or those new Void things. Just like the great Tinkarius, I too am in hiding. When I was 'murdered', I faked my own death, with the help of some comrades from the inside. No one looks for someone who is dead-well, it depends on where you are, I guess. Had I lived in Cemetrica, that may have been a different story," he joked. "But in my hiding, I have been able to develop new plant-life. This allows assistance on the surface which provides scrap materials for those who need it. No one knows where they came from; they just think the mechanical creatures had planted them. This normally results in them being destroying since they are 'impure.' That is why more are brought to the surface regularly. I have also continued in the developing of the Mecha tribe that you see standing before me. Fortunately for you, there were a few wondering around keeping an eye on the Noctria for me. What you see standing before you are both my greatest creations, and your dearest allies, growing in numbers."

The Mechas stepped forward and saluted me. Being much closer I could see more of their detail. Most of them looked the same; they were a pale brownish red color. Most had moving cogs on the outer plate of their chest. Each one had an emblem of a simple gear in a circle, just like the one Milder has on the chest of his robes. They had long arms and legs, and each had a shield of some sort on their right arms. Their heads were large with silver-plated jaws that were screwed on from either side with large bolts, similar to the Mechid display from Redemption Tower. They had hollow eyes, but had slight abilities to use facial expressions but only in their foreheads. For cosmetic purposes I assumed, they had long Sparkler wires hanging from their head. An attempt to represent hair. They looked pretty interesting, to say the least.

Two stepped forward. They were uniquely designed from the rest to represent a sort of elite status, and appeared to be better suited for combat. They were both silver coated; one had drills for hands and one large cog that turned in the center of its torso. It looked like the Mark of Tinkarius, but still bared the wrench and gears emblem on their shoulders, like the others did. The other had the same large cog in its chest, but turned in the opposite direction. This one had no wired hair, but a metallic mask of some sort that had holes for eyes and breathing vents. I could see steam purging through the vents and its eyes glowed bright blue, and on top of its head were a few horns and an antenna. One of its hands was a large clamp and the other looked like a large cannon of some sort.

"The one with the drills is named Drill-Bit, the other is Triumphus. They are both higher rank of the tribe, but continue to look up to me for direction. They protect their allies when they are near and work against the tribes up on the surface. They are immune to the meenrale venom as well as most other biological warfare. Potent Alchemy is their only weakness. They are even immune to water, unlike the Mechids on the Island of Robotica," Milder explained.

"Aye, those insignificant Mechids must be destroyed. They will find a way to get off that island, and when they do we will be waiting," Triumphus spoke, the steam rising from his mask.

"All in good time, Triumphus. At least we are prepared for the worst unlike most of the cultures upstairs. Their pride will get the best of them," Milder answered. This was all quite fascinating to me.

I couldn't help but to feel a little tipsy from the Aged Creeple sap. I even felt a little loosened up and a bit happy through all of this mayhem. I reached for the bottle and began to drink again. I put the bottle down so I could wave and smile at the Mechas.

"Howrya doin?" I slurred. They waved back, which made me smile even more.

Ectus and I talked to Milder about everything; about our adventures and our hardships in finding the Philospher's stone and the NaviBox, as he continued to chomp down on his bowl of bolts. I explained to him that I had seen an ancient looking flask, that appeared to have been emptied out hanging from the Noctria's clothing. He rubbed his chin as he listened closely to me. I was surprised that he could understand me from all of the slurring I was doing. I had to push the bottle away so I could take a break from the delicious after-burn it contained. I was pretty sure I was quickly becoming addicted to it.

"They must be holding the Elixir of Life somewhere else," Milder explained, "and they are quite bold keeping the flask out in the open. For those who know what it looks like, they are much stronger than the average creatures. Only strong, wise creatures are given knowledge of its existence. Knowing that, they are like the Steinlocks; cocky and full of pride, which makes them vulnerable in all of the right places. They under estimate what is really out there," he slammed his fist on the table, startling me. I was fading in and out, my face leaning on my arm. *This must be what it feels like to be tired*, I thought. I felt hazy and a lack of energy. I was numb and careless. It was nice.

To my surprise, Kursus walked into view from the entrance to the room from across the way. I didn't even see her get up. To my relief, she looked well and no longer poisoned. Her skin was back to being soft and normal looking. *How long had it been*? Without seeing the sky, it was hard for me to judge how much time had passed. I stood up and kind of tilted a bit off balance.

"Kursus," I gasped, with a smile. She ran up to me and jumped in my arms. She pulled away real quick and looked at me with a frown.

"Are you intoxicated?" She asked. "I think so," I answered.

She kind of smiled. "Well, your breath wreaks of strong Creeple sap," she answered.

"You look great!" Ectus said as he floated up to her to give her a look. Kursus smiled at him and turned to look at Milder. Her face in complete shock, not even realizing he was in the room.

"It can't be," she said, "are-are you…"

"Indeed, I am," Milder replied. He stuck out his arm to shake it. To my surprise, bringing a sharp pain in my head, Kursus shrieked with excitement. She jumped up and down and grabbed Milder's hand with both of hers and shook it vigorously. She nearly knocked the large man over.

"Oh, my goodness! I'm such a huge fan! I have read all of your scriptures on alchemical transmutation. I have done a lot of metallurgy similar to yours but with my own preference of alloys," she gushed quickly, "and...and I've just-wait why aren't you *dead*?" she interrupted herself quickly, more concerned now. He chuckled and simply answered,

"It's a long story. Why don't you sit down and drink some Aged Creeple sap," Milder offered as he stuck his hand out towards the bottle.

"No thank you, I'm trying to quit," she answered. Ectus, Milder and I looked at her in surprise.

"What? I've got aged sap on me at all times. You guys never noticed?" Ectus and I shook our heads with one eye brow raised.

"Huh," she breathed. "Thanks for the offer though," she replied.

Milder told his story to Kursus and introduced the Mecha Tribe. She reached out to touch almost every Mecha. We then told her what happened at Omitis and she became very outraged; good ole Kursus.

"Those filthy balls of Glirbette waste!" she hollered, hitting the table, "just wait until they get what's coming to them! I just wanna-*oohh!*" She closed her eyes tight and wrinkled her nose. She shook her fists, then reached for the Aged Creeple sap, tilting the bottle all the way up and drank. We watched in amazement as she emptied the bottle. So much for quitting, I thought. She slammed the bottle on the table and crossed her arms. I reached for the bottle to take a sip, but it was all gone. I was a little bummed and put the bottle back on the table.

"Calm down Kursus. They will get what's coming to them. We need to utilize this time and be productive. We need a plan of attack. You *do* still have the Philosopher's Stone, don't you?"

"Of course I do, what kind of Flintkus do you think I..." she reached into her robes and paused, looking at us in terror as her eyes grew wide. Milder shut his eyes in disappointment.

"You don't have it," he muttered. He rubbed his eyes. Kursus looked at us in awe.

"That Noctria must have taken it from me," her voice shook.

"Well, there goes that plan. It's alright, as long as the Noctria doesn't know that with both the Elixir and the Stone he can grant any wish he desires, we will be fine.

"Way to go, Kursus," I hiccupped. She looked over at me angrily.

"Excuse me? For a monster with all of these powers, you sure were on your butt the whole time out there," she snapped back. I stood up and pointed my finger at her with one eye closed and said,

"Oh yeah? Well...they were *really* fast," I slurred, "I had no idea...what I was up against. But if it wasn't for me, they wouldn't have a crater for a village, now would they?" I flopped down hard in the chair and crossed my arms. I even stuck my long purple tongue out at her. She opened her jaw in shock.

"Why, how dare you? You stupid little-"

"Enough! Do not argue under my roof," Milder yelled. He looked at us both angrily. "Fighting each other isn't going to bring the stone back. We must go up there immediately. I will call for all of the Mechas. It's time to find that Noctria. He has both the stone and the Elixir. Who knows what could happen if he used them both. We must not fear his ever-lasting life but the stone will grant him great strengths. With his swiftness and his now improved strength he will be very difficult to capture. We must capture him. There are a few torture techniques that I know of that work specifically on Noctria. They cannot handle light directly into their eyes, which is one of the reasons they wear those goggles. Doing so will literally burn their eyes right out of their sockets. We can slow them down with the Mechas screech technique. We must go now, Kursus how are you feeling?"

"Better than ever," she answered, tilting her hips to the side and crossing her arms again. She reached into her robes once more and pulled out a vial of the brownish yellow toxins.

"Is that what I think it is?" Milder asked, standing up quickly.

"Yep, looks like the Noctria and I had the same idea. You do know what this means, don't you?"

Professor Milder walked up to Kursus as she held out the vial of the GG3.

"We can begin researching their formula and perhaps even create an antidote. Well done Kursus. The Mechas and I will begin working on an antidote as soon as possible." Milder walked over to a cabinet that hung on the wall and placed the vial carefully on one of its shelves, then walked back over to us.

"But for now, let's head to the surface."

Milder gave me a couple of bottles of his fine Aged Creeple Tree sap and grabbed a few of his own weapons. He had a pistol that was as large as the Triumphus's arm cannon. He loaded it with bullets that glowed brightly.

"These are flash rounds. They will enter the bodies of the Noctria and light them up from the inside. It's a beautiful sight," he said as he whipped back the pistol to load it and smiled. "Here, take this," he handed me a cubed item that looked like the NaviBox. I studied it and located a small button. I nearly pushed it and Milder stopped me.

"No! Don't do that! Why would you push that?" I shrugged, "I dunno, curiosity?" I answered. He shook his head.

"That is a Screech Box. Push that button this close to my head and you'll blow the eardrums right out of my skull. You don't have to worry but we humanoids have to protect our organs and such," he explained.

"Why do you gotta rub it in like that?" I answered as I stuck the Screech Box into my clothing, still kind of buzzed.

We followed Milder in a light jog as he marched us and the Mecha down a tunnel. The tunnel had a very fancy ancient designed flooring which followed down the length of the tunnel. It was polished gold with carvings throughout. The loud sound of clanking from marching Mecha beside us was all that I could hear. It looked like a runway of some sort. Here we go again; into another war. Only this time we have an army. I felt much more confident as they marched aside us.

We reached the end of the tunnel, where there was what appeared to be a giant bowl located in the center. Milder stepped into it and the bowl type device lit up with yellow and orange lights. These lights covered the entire bowl. I suddenly realized it was the same veiny-looking lights that were everywhere in Redemption Tower.

"What are these?" I had to ask before I jumped in.

"Those are the traces of what's called 'the Dose'. It's a more advanced fueling technique than Creeple sap. It's a chemical the Steinlocks discovered to provide better performance and to replace *ancient technology*. I got my hands on some sort of generator from the one and only, Tinkarius." He smiled as he pushed buttons and pulled levers. The entire inside of the bowl was rounded by a control board with endless buttons, gadgets and doo-dads. There were seats for some of the Mecha, where they instantly sat down and started pushing buttons and turning knobs.

"Now get your monster butt in here, we're going on a ride like nothing you've ever seen before."

I jumped in the large bowl-like device and the veiny lights grew brighter. A loud humming sound came from the lights. The Mechas piled in and began to yell, altogether, in some kind of war cry. I joined because it sounded fun, not to mention I was still catching a buzz from the Aged sap. Kursus then joined in and so did Ectus. Milder finished what he was doing and finally joined the loud noise making as well. The bowl turned a little and clicked. I fell on my face. I got up on my knees and looked over the edge of the bowl. The veiny colors reached out into the ancient looking runway. The bowl began to shake. I looked over at Milder as he put on a set of goggles.

"You might want to hang on for your life," he beckoned with a smile as he snapped the goggles on. He laughed and pulled one last lever that was bigger than the others, using both hands.

We were hurtled into high speed, flying up a large tunnel that seemed to have no end. I struggled to look up at the surface because of how fast we were hurtling upward. The surface was approaching us quickly. I've had a feeling like this before, when we were entering Redemption Tower. I felt yet again that we were going to hit the ceiling, but it opened and we were hurtled into fresh, clean air. We continued to fly up and I could see that we had been hurled out of a massive tree trunk kind of like a cannon. *Clever hiding spot*, I thought to myself. As we flew high into the sky gravity began to take its toll and we slowed down. We floated in the air for a moment and began to fall quickly. I peeked over the lip and my eyes grew large as my fingernails dug into the rim of the bowl. I could now see the ground coming at us quickly yet again but from above this time. I was trying to analyze what would happen next but it was hard to think over Ectus screaming like a hysterical female humanoid.

Just before we hit the ground, massive legs sprung out from the bottom of the giant bowl which stopped us from hitting the surface. The legs absorbed all of the shock and made the landing very smooth. The legs then extended up and we rose to a standing point.

"I think it's about time we say hello to some old friends," Milder called out. He laughed and began to walk the large object forward. I didn't know where we were until we walked walk over what looked like my old shelter. We had come up not too far from behind it and we then walked across the large grassy meadow I liked to call my yard. A smile grew on my face as I watched the meadow quickly disappear. I didn't need that shelter anymore. I now have new comrades and some cool new toys.

We walked onto Lanterian soil and looked out into the vast lands. Lands as far as the eye could see. As we quickly arrived to the middle of Lanteria, I could see the gate of Cemetrica and the entrance to Psykya. Creeple Forest disappeared as the giant mechanical structure stomped over the lands like a Titan.

"The Mechas didn't have a Crophix so I built them one," Milder hollered over the wind, followed by the loud mechanical noises coming from the massive legs, "this baby took me decades to create. I had a lot of free time as you can see. Its name is MechaTon. One of the toughest metals known to Remains is infused within this baby. It's got firepower, beyond belief. Just you wait and see. I've been saving it for a day such as this," He yelled, then tilted his head back and cackled into the skies as he marched MechaTon towards Muckraid.

"I hope you are all ready for this battle. As I've mentioned, The Noctria are quick. Their technology is built for silence. It would be wise not to mistake them for idiots," Professor Milder hollered over the cranking sounds of MechaTon's legs.

"I'm not afraid of anything!" I yelled over to Milder, with pride. Milder glanced over his shoulder towards me in the middle of pulling a lever.

"Courage is not being fearless, Darkus. It's being afraid, but fighting through the fear. Courage is manifested through experience, it cannot be brought to life on a cold cadaver table," Milder retaliated. I shot him a glare, then he winked at me and turned back around to pull more levers.

Within minutes we had arrived to the muggy woods of Muckraid. We couldn't see the town since it was completely covered in tree tops but we had a pretty good idea to where it was from the mass amounts of magic being shot through the tree tops. They hit MechaTon's metal exterior, which bounced right off. We had quickly left Muckraid and in just a few more seconds we had approached Omitis. To my surprise, it hardly looked like we've been there. The floating ship was in the air once again and the village was about 85% recovered. But to my satisfaction the storage for the toxin was still in pieces and none of the GG3 in sight. The Noctria spotted us and we began to take fire. We came in quick and hot, I was hardly ready. I stood on the side of MechaTon and pulled my hands out. I was all freshened up and full of spunk; I was ready for a come back. The Mecha hollered in unison as they jumped out of the bowl. They landed with loud heavy thuds and began to attack the Noctria. The ship in the sky began to turn towards us.

"Don't even think about it!" Milder hollered. "Kursus! Run over there and grab that locking system. The one with the large screen. Both of the control sticks, on either side, are the fire arms. Lock on with the screen in the middle and fire with the buttons on the side!" He yelled. She ran over to the large screen that sat out on a rotating stand with two control sticks on either side and started to move it around. It must have had a few ball joints throughout the stand because it moved smoothly as she pulled it up to lock onto the ship.

The ship in the sky began to fire on us, hitting the shell of the bowl. The metal absorbed the impact. Kursus continued to shoot rounds up at the ship and in just seconds the floating ship began to fall from the air and crashed yet again into Omitis, this time exploding. *They must have added some sort of new chemical fuel to the ship*, I thought to myself. Milder stepped away from the steering and leaned over the edge, pointing his massive gun down at the ground and fired a round of his flash-bullets. He didn't seem to aim, but I saw why as the bullet hit the ground and lit up the surface with a large flash. Most of the Noctria had goggles on but they turned away to not look, which helped as a distraction. Milder aimed much carefully this time fired a second round, sending the bullet into the stomach of one of the Noctria. He fell to the ground holding his gut as he looked up at us in horror. He began to scream, a bright light was exciting his body from multiple areas, including his mouth, his eyes, and from where he had been shot. He fell and landed on his face.

I put my hands up in the air, charged myself up again then began to shoot balls of energy at the Noctria that were on the ground. They began to climb the legs of MechaTon, in their nimble way. Milder reached over to a large blue button with a lightning bolt emblem displayed on the top. He lifted up the case that covered it and pushed the button. A giant shockwave shot out from the bottom of MechaTon. The Noctria dropped like flies.

"I call that 'pest control'," Milder yelled and cackled as he continued to stomp around the village of Omitis. He stomped on shelters and sometimes getting a bit lucky, stepping right onto a Noctria that was being held down by the screeching sounds of the Mechas.

As the screeching sounds continued, I had remembered that I had a new toy to try out.

"Ectus, catch me!" I yelled and began to run to the edge of MechaTon. I jumped off the edge, arms stretched wide, and began to freefall towards the surface. Ectus swiftly caught me in the air and flew me to a smooth landing. He dropped me about five feet before I hit the ground. I tucked and rolled, coming to a halt on my knees. I pulled out the Screech Box as I saw the Noctria quickly coming after me. I pushed the button. The screech was so loud that it made my head vibrate. The Noctria fell to their knees, putting their hands to their ears and yelled to the sky. I grabbed the Screech Box tightly and walked up to the Noctria, smashing it into their skulls. I walked up to the last one. I pulled out my pistol and shot it.

"Karma's a bitch," I said with a sharp toothed grin.

The fight went on and blood shed continued. Only a few of the Mecha were taken down. It took about two to three of the Noctria to overwhelm a lone Mecha as they began to quickly dismantle them and rip out their cores. A couple more of the Noctria stomped out into the battlefield. They were sitting in the cockpit of what looked like a much lower quality version of the robot that Dante had used to snap my neck up on Redemption Tower. They were much larger than the Mechas but weren't much of a fight for the Mecha. The Mecha were much quicker. The robots would shoot steam out of their backs every time they took a step. They would try to overwhelm the Mechas with powerful blasts of steam from their large robotic arms. This didn't work so well. The Mechas quickly took down the few mechanically enhanced Noctria, then they were no more.

This battle had been in our favor, with the use of better toys and assistance this time around. There was no sight of the Noctria that carried the flask. I looked up at the top of MechaTon and saw more Noctria climbing the legs up to the top. Milder, for some reason, wasn't firing his *pest control*. I insisted that Ectus go check it out. He came back to tell me what was wrong.

"Once Milder uses it, it needs time to re-charge. What do we do?" He asked desperately.

"Take me to the top," I demanded. Before Ectus could grab me, he was disrupted by a Noctria that started spraying him down with high pressured steam. Angered, Ectus entered the Noctria and possessed it. He turned the Noctria around and began to spray his own kind, melting the skin off of the Noctria as they fell to their knees. Ectus made his Noctria body lift the device up to its chin and pull the trigger, melting away the skin until the skull was visible. Ectus exited the Noctria's body to aid me. Ectus then picked me up and took me to the top of MechaTon. We passed Noctria that were climbing the legs. I held out the screech box and they dropped to the ground, to holding their ears.

I was then dropped and rolled once we reached the top and I got up to see a good number of Noctria had made it to the top. They were fighting Kursus and Milder. Milder was firing his flash rounds at the Noctria as they dropped. They were exploding from the inside. He grabbed a dead Noctria and used its corpse to beat off more Noctria. Kursus was in a serious sword match with one of the

Noctria. It held a small blade that Kursus kept countering with her Vengeance.

"Vultus tuus hos dies hominis sani," The Noctria said with his face close to Kursus as his blade collided with her rod.

"Quod homo non sum," she replied.

The Noctria looked at her in shock and she bashed her head against his and knocked him out cold. She then took his body and lifted it over hers in great strength and threw him off. I was a bit surprised, as well. *What language was that?*, I thought. That definitely wasn't Ancient Voice. She turned around and watched in horror as Milder had his throat slit by the Noctria.

"No!" She yelled. She ran up to the Noctria as it drew its blade. Her eyes glowed red, like her fathers, and she put her hand out and then chanted in Ancient Voice,

"Senob meht deelb niks ruoy yam!"

The Noctria grabbed his chest, ripped his flesh open and gargled as his eyes grew large. I watched the bones of the Noctria began to push their way out of the creature's skin, as if he was bleeding his bones out. The bones fell to the floor and its skin fell back like a fleshy quilt. Kursus's eyes became normal once again. She ran to Milder's side to lift up his massive body onto her knees.

"Milder," I muttered and ran to their side. Milder coughed and hacked as his neck continued to bleed. Kursus began to cry. She magically pulled out a cloth and patted it on his neck. I watched in shock as Milder lay there bleeding. He didn't bleed sap; he bled humanoid blood. I didn't know what to do or say. His wound was deep and we had nothing to help heal him.

"Is there a spell that can help?" I asked Kursus. She looked up with big watery eyes and shook her head, no.

"I don't know of any that would work on him. His metallic interior counters most spells," she sobbed as her lip quivered. She looked back down at Milder and held his head. He opened his eyes and smiled.

"My time has come. The village…the village is destroyed," He coughed up blood on his clothing. He reached up and placed the palm of his hand on Kursus's face. She began to bawl. I hated seeing humanoids cry. It was discomforting and awkward.

"Our friendship was short lived, but it was an honor to…to meet you. You must take care of my Mechas. Watch over them and guide them," he whispered.

"What? I couldn't…I wouldn't know how…" she said manically.

"You must. You are the only one that can do it. I'm...I'm not......"

Milder took his last breath as she held him He became still. My stomach turned, for I knew he had passed. Kursus held him close and cried. I watched her mourn and then I realized it was silent. Just the sound of her crying was heard. I walked over to the edge of MechaTon and to my surprise the Noctria had been defeated. All of the Mecha stared up at the top of MechaTon. Still, waiting. I looked over at Kursus as she wiped away her tears. She laid Milder's head on the ground. She got up and walked towards me, hugged me, and continued to cry in my arms. I put my hand on her head and held her, giving her comfort.

"There, there," I said not knowing what else to really say. She lifted her head up, wiped her face off, and looked into my eyes. She leaned over to press her lips against mine. I pulled back for a moment and looked at her in shock as her eyes were closed shut but I could tell it comforted her. I pressed my lips against hers and held them there. *This is awkward*, I thought. I didn't know exactly what we were doing; all I knew was that it made her feel better. Ectus continued to stare at Milder's corpse. He looked as though he was about to cry.

She stopped after what felt like forever. She looked up at me and then looked over the edge of MechaTon to see the Mechas all staring back at her. They saluted her as they all knew what had happened.

"All hail our new leader, Kursus," One of the Mechas hollered. Kursus looked at all of them in surprise. She stood there for a minute, looked out at them, became firm, and saluted back. They began to chant and holler. Kursus looked over at me. in discomfort, I smiled, shrugged, and then saluted her. It was obvious she felt uncomfortable.

"Well aren't you just Miss popular," I tried to joke. She smiled slightly then looked over at Milder's corpse. Maybe now was not the right time to be joking. I just wanted to ease the moment.

"We need to give him a proper burial," she said, still wiping tears from her eyes. "He will get the burial that he deserves," Ectus replied.

We lowered MechaTon and walked off to join the Mechas. We could hear shouting from a distance. We watched as Triumphus dragged a Noctria towards us as it tried to claw its way away from Triumphus's tight grasp. He threw it down onto the ground near our feet.

"This one will tell us where his leader is," Triumphus boomed. The Noctria hissed up at us and Triumphus. Drill-Bit walked up and started one of his drills. He pressed the tip lightly against its temple. The Noctria hollered as a trickle of blood came down from his temple.

"Or we will drill it out of you," Drill-Bit added.

"Tie him up," Kursus demanded while looking down at the Noctria. The Noctria looked up and smiled a sharp toothed grin. Kursus kicked it in the face and it fell back. The Mechas picked it up and dragged it onto MechaTon.

We tied up the Noctria to one of the chairs on MechaTon as we were lifted up into the sky. He looked over at Milder's corpse and laughed. We blind folded and gagged him. We walked MechaTon to the entrance from where it came, through Muckraid, Lanteria and Creeple Forest. After a good while, we had arrived at the entrance of the tunnel. We weren't controlling anything; it's as if MechaTon was thinking on its own. It jumped into the stump and we freefell down the long shaft. We landed in the spot where we first jumped into its bowl top. I looked up to see the surface shutting slowly, like the large door at Redemption Tower. Once again, the legs absorbed the shock from the fall and the tunnel crumbled with a bit of debris from the impact. MechaTon bent down and positioned itself and its legs retracted back into the bowl structure, bringing us lower to the ground. The bowl then turned and locked into position and the veiny lights dimmed, and then went out.

We dragged the Noctria down the long tunnel and into one of the dug-out rooms, and then took off its blindfold. It looked around and then looked up at me.

"Darkus," it said as it laughed, "A creatione, Tinkarius.", it finished in its native tongue. I grabbed it by the neck and brought its ugly mug close to mine.

"I don't speak scumbag. you'll have to clear that up for me, and don't you ever mix your filthy language with my Creator's or I'll feed you to that precious Meenrale of yours," I snarled, then punched it in the face. It spat blood on the ground and looked up and laughed.

"We've been expecting you, monster. How is that cozy little shelter of yours, huh? Oh, right, it burned to the ground," the Noctria joked. I clenched my fist and gave him a direct uppercut. He flew backwards in his chair. I stepped on the chair to bring it back up. I reached back to punch him again as he spat blood onto the floor. "Yeah, how was that nice amount of GG3 that your tribe had for your victims? Oh, right; we sent your ship into it." I countered back sarcastically. The Noctria began to glare at me.

"You think that was the only storage unit we had? You must think we're as stupid as your creator, monster." I took my pistol and smacked him across the face over and over with it until his face looked like a bloody infection.

"Enough," Kursus said. She walked up and reached into my clothes and grabbed the Screech Box. She put it in front of the Noctria, and his smile grew to a frown. He looked up at Kursus and hissed.

"Why don't you tell us where your elder is," Kursus demanded, "with all of that pride you have, you shouldn't have a problem doing so. See, by you not telling us tells me that deep down you are scared that we're going to win. If you were confident you would tell us," the Noctria stared at Kursus and then looked at the box, then up at Kursus once again.

"Do your worst humanoid. It's going to take much more than your little box to get me to crack," he said through his fangs. Kursus shrugged, and then turned the box on. The screeching echoed throughout the tunnels. The Noctria lifted his head high and screamed as his head shook violently. I could see the veins reaching the surface of his skin through his neck and face. His eyes bulged and became filled veins. Kursus let it go for a good while until I could see blood trickling down the Noctria's ears. She stopped and smiled at the Noctria.

"I can do this forever, see. I hate you and your race with a putrid passion. You killed the only man who had influenced most of my life, as well as kidnapped my tribe and turned them into walking eyesores. I'm the last person you want to meddle with. Either tell me where your pathetic elder ran off to, or I bleed you out through your ears."

The Noctria thought for a moment. I could tell he didn't want to keep doing this. Kursus was growing impatient. She sat up straight and gave me the box.

"Fine, I've got something much better than our little box," she said with a smile. She pulled out a couple of the glowing bullets that Milder had once placed into his pistol. The Noctria's eyes grew wide with fear. Kursus walked up to the Noctria and held a single bullet in front of his face.

"Do you know what this is? It's your favorite treat; pure light straight into your pupils.

"No," the Noctria spoke under its breath.

"Oh, what's that? I can't hear you, you'll have to speak up insect," Kursus said as she began to pinch the tip of the bullet.

The Noctria was jumping around in his chair trying to get away from Kursus.

"No! No!" it hollered. Kursus smiled as she bent down in its face once again,

"Then I suggest you start talking before I turn your eyes into Glirbette jelly," she hissed, inches away from its face. The Noctria hesitated for a moment, then sighed and looked up at Kursus,

"You won't come back alive, humanoid. He ventured off to Robotica, land of the Mechids," Kursus stood up straight and stared at the Noctria in horror.

"You…you're lying," Kursus spat.

"Unfortunately, I am not, humanoid. Looks like you are not finding my Elder," the Noctria smiled. Kursus glared at the Noctria and snapped the top off of the bullet. The blinding light shimmered on the Noctria's face, which grew long with fear.

"No!" he screamed. His eyes began to melt and hollow out as he screamed, shaking his head. Smoke rose from his skull as his whole body contorted. Kursus spun on her heel and round-house kicked the Noctria square in the chin. He flew back in his chair and twitched on the ground, his jaw open wide and his eyes still smoking.

We gently carried Professor Milder's body up to the surface to give him a proper burial. He wanted to be cremated and to have his ashes spread across the lands, to symbolizing the future triumphs that he and his inventions will overcome. None of us talked about anything. There was nothing left to joke about or laugh about; this fight for freedom was beginning to take a toll on us. We were losing new friends, we were facing dangers that were starting to harm us and we were starting to become a little lower on the food chain. The Noctria were swift and smart, although we now have an army of toxin-resistant Mechas and the possibility for an antidote. They were no match for what may lie in waiting for us at Robotica. The Mechas had our back here in these lands but we didn't want to lose them; they were the only real army that would fight for us other than Rip. Even though Rip was still part humanoid and though very powerful, he was far busy in Cemetrica. We were alone in a world full of hungry beasts who wanted a bite out of us. On top of it all, Kursus was now the leader of the Mecha. She could not deny it. Some things we just cannot control. I guess we should be happy that we were left with the assistance of some sort, and even a man-made Crophix. We still had the NaviBox and some new gadgets to aid us. We knew where both the stone and the elixir flask were located. Ectus, Kursus, and I had each other and we all shared a strong resistance to most of the creatures and creations out there. All we can do now is go with what we have, and continue to have each other's backs.

We lay Professor Milder's body in an opened-top coffin we had made out of mechanical parts and carved Creeple wood. Kursus had shed a few tears that trickled down her face as she pulled out a Cog Flower from her clothing. She placed it on his chest and crossed his arms. We laid the coffin in a pool of Creeple sap. Kursus placed her hands out above the sap and murmured something I couldn't understand. The sap suddenly caught fire. We stepped back and watched as flesh and bone from Professor Milder turned to charcoal. The Mechas surrounded the Professor and chanted in his honor. As quick as it started, the fire died and there was nothing more of Professor Milder. We stood there and stared at his pile of ashes as though the fire hadn't stopped. We were lost in thought. Lost in the idea that maybe Milder was still here, somewhere, watching over us. Of course, that could all be wishful thinking. But in these lands, I've learned to never question that anything is possible.

We collected his ashes and went back down to our newly given shelter. It was a long walk down that tunnel where we had parked MechaTon. The sound of slow marching Mecha feet echoed throughout the tunnel. We got to the room and gave a look around. The empty bottle of aged Creeple sap was still sitting on the table. Kursus walked up to her new Milderoid garden and slowly touched the Steamer. Unlike spouting steam at me, it continued to spin and steam slightly as if Kursus wasn't even there. Ectus floated over to the cabinet to take another look at the vial of the venom Kursus had snagged from the Noctria. Ectus then headed towards a chair, floated just above it and held his arms out as if he was resting them on the arm rests. I walked up to the table and slumped down to stare at the empty bottle. I picked it up and looked at it.

"Does anyone know where the Aged Creeple sap is?" I asked.

"He keeps it in the floor," Kursus said glumly and pointed to what looked like a carpet over a hidden door.

I walked up to it and ripped away the carpet, tossing it aside. It revealed a mechanical door with a cog wheel as its opening device. I reached down and turned it. Cool steam shot out from the sides and it opened up with a steady hissing sound. I looked inside and saw what looked like a few dozen bottles of chilled Aged Creeple sap. I kind of smiled to myself and reached down to grab a bottle. "You sure know how to live Milder," I said to myself.

I walked over to the table, slumped down, and pulled the cork from the bottle and smelled the liquid inside.

"To Professor Milder," I said as I raised the bottle, then tilted the bottom of the bottle high and chugged down the Aged Creeple sap. It felt good going down my throat; it was chilled so it was nice and cool, yet it burned as it went down. What an incredible sensation. I seemed to pacify the sensation more than the bittersweet taste. Kursus walked over and grabbed a bottle for herself and sat down at the table across from me. She raised her bottle and said, "to Milder," and followed my lead. She slammed the bottle on the table and sank down into the chair. It was quiet for what seemed like a long moment in time. We just continued to lose ourselves in thought. The sounds of gulping Aged Creeple sap and placing the bottles down on the table where the only noises heard, followed by the sputtering of Milderoids in the corner of the room. The Mechas separated into different tunnels and rooms, all with the exception of Drill-Bit and Triumphus. They stood side by side staring at us. They made me a bit uncomfortable since I couldn't read their faces. Still, solid Mecha faces. I cleared my throat and spoke to them.

"So, do you two normally just stand there and watch the room or," I said awkwardly.

"We are awaiting your orders," Drill-Bit clanked, "If we may, we would like to go with you to Robotica," he continued. Kursus turned around in her chair to face them.

"That wouldn't be a good idea. You two are the best line of defense that we have. Taking you against those fiends would be suicide." Triumphus's face shot a bit of steam.

"But that is why we are here; to fight by your side against the enemy; both mortal and immortal. Leaving us here would be inefficient for all of you. If we are destroyed then at least we would be destroyed in your honor. We want nothing more than to stand by you and help terminate those Mechids," Triumphus boomed.

Kursus turned around to look at me. I looked at her, then the two Mechas. What would it really hurt? Last resort, I'm sure we could rebuild them.

"I think that's a great idea," I said. I raised my bottle to Kursus. Kursus thought a moment, and then raised her bottle as well. We clanked bottles and drank. Kursus put down the bottle and wiped her mouth.

"What could it hurt? I mean, we could always rebuild them," she said as if she read my mind. She winked at me and drank out of her bottle once more. Sometimes I had wondered if she has been reading my thoughts all along.

As time went by, Kursus became intoxicated. Her face lay in her arms on the table, one arm out, still holding the bottle. I sat there staring at her, smiling slightly. *What a goofy little humanoid*, I thought to myself. I took another sip of the Aged Creeple sap and noticed Ectus staring at me, smiling as well. I stopped in mid sip and looked over at him.

"What?" I asked with one eye brow raised.

"You admire her, don't you?" He spoke with a big grin on his face.

"What? No way! ...well, maybe," I instantly interrupted myself. This Creeple sap made me a bit more honest with my feelings. That is going to be a side effect I won't be too excited about.

"She's just very interesting, is all. She's so human, yet she eats like a Psychozoan. It's just different is all and I happen to like different," I finished. I drank a little more out of my bottle.

Ectus smiled and chuckled, "yeah, she is quite interesting," he agreed. He watched me as I continue to drink.

"I sure wish I could enjoy one of those," Ectus said. I looked over, spilling a bit of it on my face. I wiped it off, then swallowed.

"Well, when we find you a body you will be able to," I said confidently. His glow lit up a little.

"You really think so?" He asked, hopeful. "I don't doubt it," I answered, and continued to drink. Ectus looked forward, deep in thought, smiled a little and sighed, his glow a bit obnoxious and radiant.

I finished the last of my Aged Creeple sap and walked over to Kursus. I took the bottle from her hands. I lifted up her arm and put her over my shoulders. I walked over to a large comfy seating area and laid her down onto it. She rolled over and curled up into a little ball. I'm assuming that meant she was cold. I looked around to find something to put on her. I found a large quilt that looked like it was large enough for Milder to curl up into. It was piled up in the corner of the room. I dragged it across the floor and threw it over Kursus. I looked down at her and smiled. walked over to the cooler, grabbed myself another bottle of Aged Creeple sap and headed to the chair. I sat down, kicked my boots up on the table to lean back in the chair and lost myself in thought.

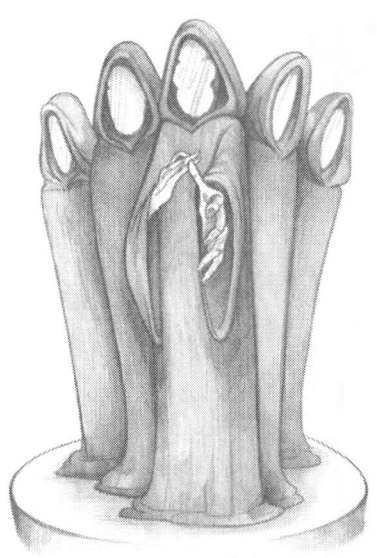

CHAPTER VIII
REFLECTIONS

Quite a few days had passed before we decided to talk about our plan of attack on Robotica. It was hard to get motivated after losing the Philosopher's Stone and Professor Milder, not to mention that we were about to head to Robotica. I've heard nothing but horror stories about that place. Robotic beings that made the Steinlocks look like Lanterians, and the Steinlocks were already too much to handle. We would need a serious plan. One that we knew in our hearts would be the best way to go.

Ectus, Kursus and I sat at the table in the middle of the room and got ready to talk about our plan of action.

"Alright boys, this is going to be no joy ride. You guys thought the Steinlocks and the Noctria were bad? Well suck it up because the Mechids are going to make those tribes look like a bunch of ninnies. They have power beyond compare and we have the Steinlocks to thank for that. They are programmed to practically read each other's minds and micro movements. Also, they are agile, and have a thick, yet light hide that is nearly impenetrable. As far as we know, there is no way recorded anywhere on how to defeat a Mechid, other than the use of water. If you're feeling brave you *can* rip out their core. If you two have any ideas, feel free to say something," Kursus finished. Ectus raised his hand; Kursus and I looked at him in confusion.

"Oh, right. Uh, so they are physical beings correct? So any chance we could find someone like, well I don't know, *me* to help?" Ectus smiled shyly.

"You mean like a spirit?" I asked. Ectus nodded his head quickly and smiled.

"Yes! Perhaps they cannot destroy what they cannot touch. Unless they have those ecto-resistant devices that the Steinlocks had; those kind of hurt," Ectus said glumly.

"That is a good idea, but we don't know anyone who would be willing to do that for us with that ability," Kursus answered.

"Actually, we do," I added. Kursus and Ectus both looked at me.

"We do?" Kursus asked.

"Well, kind of. We have Rip. Maybe he knows someone-or something, that would be willing to help." Kursus thought for a moment, and then shook her head.

"No, that would mean that we would have to go back to Cemetrica,"

"Well, sometimes we just have to…"

"Wait!" Kursus interrupted me, "There *is* something we could do, at least something to have in our arsenal. We would have to go to Cemetrica, but we'd have to make it across Cemetrica towards the *land of Sacred Reflections*." She gestured with her hands to make the name sound more dramatic. Ectus and I looked at Kursus without reaction. She raised her eye brow.

"You guys don't know where that is, do you?" She asked, with a hint of irritation in her voice. We both shook our heads. She sighed and said, "Do you guys ever listen to me? It's where the Mirror guardians are," she stated loudly.

"Ahh," Ectus and I answered at the same time.

"If we go there, you both can learn the Ancient Voice. You would first have to have someone present that has Elder or ancient blood lines running through their veins, which I do. Elder blood that is. Once you have that, you must venture through the back path of

Cemetrica, defeat all that you encounter and then finish the tests of the Skindria. Now, the aggravating part is that you have to go through Cemetrica the long way, which is through Shadow Meadows on the opposite side of where the Mirror elders are. You will find the Skindria there. The Skindria are tricky, malevolent creatures. They are reanimated humanoid skeletons that wear humanoid flesh as robes. It's a very foul sight. Unfortunately, these Skindria are the ones who will grant us entry to the Mirror Elders. You must find them in Shadow Meadows. Part of the challenge is that the Shadow Meadows is a land that is mostly pitch-black with no sky light. Fortunately, there are no Shadow Stalkers there. Once you find the Noctria, we must catch, but not kill them. There are three Skindrias and we must catch them all. Once we do, they will ask us to complete a difficult task. The task differs, depending on who stands before them. Once we have completed those tasks, they will open the path to the backside of Cemetrica, which is also full of fiendish creatures. Some more terrifying than on the regular route. We will then enter the Temple of Reflections.

 Once we are there, we must find our way through a mirror maze. I will inform the two of you on what we must do next. But for now, let's make this our priority. Being able to speak Ancient Voice grants you powers beyond compare, but as I said once before, you may only use this power once per day. We will at least have the sacred power to speak Ancient Voice. With the three of us being able to do so, we can bend reality to our will, for speaking Ancient Voice lets all physical impossibilities become possible."

I would love to finally be able to speak Ancient Voice. I'm not looking forward to meeting the Skindria; they sound pretty gruesome. Wearing human skin sounds a bit over the top, but it'll just be another horrifying creature to see. I will pass. All I will have are haunted images to add to my disturbed montage of horror clips in my head.

"What do we need?" Ectus asked. Kursus looked over as she tilted her hips to one side, placing her hands on them.

"All you need is a Flintkus with an attitude problem," she answered, "and maybe before we head out we can check on the Dose that Professor Milder had taken from the Steinlocks. I'm interested to learn a little about that technology," she finished.

We packed up to enter the surface, but before we did we approached MechaTon. We examined the veiny colored designs that are in the floor, and also the surface of MechaTon. We followed the lines from point to point but there didn't seem to be any connection. Kursus climbed up to examine the massive control board that lined the walls of MechaTon's interior.

"No fuel gauge or nothing," She said quietly, "Even though there is no connection from MechaTon to the tunnel floor, they both turn on when MechaTon is activated. This tells me perhaps they react to one another's touch or presence. Notice how the last time we ventured out of the tunnel, the floor dimmed down once we were thrown towards the surface," Kursus explained. She looked around the room, Ectus and I followed, looking for anything nearby.

"There must be a core of some sort, or a storage system," she continued. Suddenly, I remembered the large meter clock that sat in the tall clock tower-like structure in Redemption Tower.

"When we were up in Redemption Tower, there was a large clock tower that held the Dose meter rather than a clock," I explained. Kursus looked at me while raising an eyebrow.

"Interesting. So that means there must be…"

She started touching the walls and feeling for something. Ectus and I felt totally useless. Kursus was onto something and we didn't know how. She turned around and shot us a look.

"What are you waiting for? Feel around for a warm spot in the dirt."

Ectus and I began to feel around. Within minutes I had felt a warm spot radiating from the dirt.

"I found it!" I yelled. Kursus and Ectus ran over to see. Kursus removed the Vengeance rod from her robes and began to hit the dirt wall with the end of it. She dug out the dirt as it fell in a small pile on the floor. She continued to do this until a much smaller meter appeared in the wall.

"How did you know that was around here?" Ectus asked in awe.

"I'm sensing that this fuel technology somehow is also in fact, wireless. The fuel has no way to enter the objects around it. They react when one another is near. The fuel meter, that Darkus explained to us from Redemption Tower, was also not connected to anything; just a meter. So, I had a theory that somehow all of this fuel is sent to one another using some sort of wireless activity. This technology leaves a warm sensation caused by the levels of radioactivity it produces. I knew it would be warm where ever the meter would be."

Just like the meter up on Redemption Tower, it was labeled "the Dose" up on top of the meter. It also had a hand that was pointing more towards the right side. It glowed bright reddish orange, and it was labeled 'ON', which was on the right side, and labeled 'OFF' towards the left.

"The Steinlocks have invented a way to supply unlimited amounts of fuel to objects. How extraordinary. With that type of technology, you could run something forever, as long as you kept supplying it. The energy isn't running off of a substance, like the liquid Creeple sap. It's merely energy that is being summoned out of thin air. With that kind of fuel in your system, you could run forever without worry of losing your energy, Darkus," Kursus said in awe.

How incredible, I thought to myself. But why wouldn't Tinkarius have already made me run off of this? Kursus then answered my question as if she was reading my mind, once again.

"But it appears that it only works that way with pure mechanical or robotic objects. When infused with the living, I could see it vitalizing the mind and body to higher levels, but living tissue and organs would be quickly used and dried up, speeding up the process of our life span-oh goodness. That must be why most of the Steinlocks look so old." Kursus continued. I could tell that this was all clicking in her head, one by one, and Ectus and I became more and more curious with all of her sudden realizations.

"Yeah, in fact when that Zint guy pulled me aside before he found out I wasn't a real Steinlock, he told me that we were going to go to the lab and grab a Dose, as if we were going to drink it," Ectus answered suddenly remembering.

"Curious," I said as I scratched my chin looking at the meter.

"All of this makes sense to me now; all but one thing; I don't know where it's coming from or how we even harness it. As you can see here, the meter is slowly, but continuously refueling itself with what appears to be an endless supply. At this moment in time I have no idea where to even begin looking for its source. We will have to look more into it later."

We decided to leave MechaTon and the Mechas in the shelter until we needed them. It took much longer to reach the surface without our Crophix, though. We got to the end of the tunnel where MechaTon slumbered. We looked around to find ladders that would allow us to climb up the shaft. The climb was quite lengthy; it didn't seem so long when we were being catapulted up in MechaTon. It took a while but we managed to get to the top. There was a much smaller secret door out upon the surface in the giant tree trunk that normally would have shot us out like a cannon. We climbed out and shut the door, which looked like dirt on the ground; quite clever actually. We climbed to the top of the tree trunk and peeked around before coming out, then stepped over the top of the tree trunk and climbed down until we were on the surface. We ventured south-east, towards Cemetrica.

We walked over what used to be my shelter down the hill and through my favorite meadow and into Creeple Forest. The forest was always a reminder to check the amount of sap I had, even though it was now full of the Aged Creeple sap, which was much better in many ways. I looked over at the Creeple Tree that once spoke to us. It still would not show its face. As we walked away, I could almost feel it staring at us as we continued forward. We passed a couple Milderoids on the way out. Kursus had to touch every one of them and let them know that she was their new caregiver and how she wouldn't let them down. She picked herself a few cogs and gears from the Cog Flower as we continued through the forest.

"I read Professor Milder's scrapbook. The one that had a few of his designs for Milderoids. Apparently, there are many more out there to be discovered. Ones I didn't even know of. Like Bolt Bushes and Twine Vines. How exciting!" Kursus gushed with a smile.

We entered Lanteria and it was as quiet as ever. I looked around and grinned at the sight. I see miles of land, full of cowards. I stepped forward. To my surprise more Voids had begun to dig their way up from the ground as well as more Ectos that appeared out of thin air. Kursus and Ectus looked horrified.

"Oh right, you weren't here for this. When I was alone last, I was ambushed by these creatures. Those humanoids coming out of the ground are called Voids. They are reanimating humanoid corpses used as meat shields. Those spirits up there,"

"Those are Ectos," Kursus finished for me. Ectus glared up at the site of them.

"So those are the real deal huh?" Ectus growled, "might as well make it official."

"I thought I told you if I ever saw you again, I'd shock you out of reality," I hollered with my fist up at Ladidya. She lifted her head up in the air, her misty hair bellowing behind her as she laughed.

"Orders of a higher power. I'm working for a better, less pathetic breed than a Lanterian. I've got some pleasing to do."

"You could always please me," Ectus flirted.

Just as Ectus had said that, Ladidya came much closer to us. I put my hands to my side allowing them to glow.

"You must be Ectus," Ladidya cackled once again. Instead of looking angry, Ectus looked a little soft.

"Who are you?" He asked.

"I am Ladidya; elder of the Ectos, and you are a sad pathetic excuse for a spirit."

To my concern, Ectus didn't seem phased. In fact, he almost seemed like he admired Ladidya.

"Oh my. For an elder you sure are an attractive one," he continued. Kursus and I scowled at Ectus, and Ladidya looked appalled.

"How…inappropriate," Ladidya muttered. She threw herself into Ectus as they hurtled to the ground, in a ball of misty violence. The other Ectos joined in. Kursus and I began to fight our way through the sea of rising Voids. I could see Ectus was doing rather well at keeping away from the Ectos.

"Don't let the Voids grab you. They feed on our flesh," I yelled at Kursus. She nearly had been bitten, but held the Void back with Vengeance as it tried to reach for her, drooling all over the place. She raised her rod in the air. It released a shockwave that hurtled all of the nearby Voids back as they fell to pieces.

We fought until we were close to Cemetrica, fighting all the way there which slowed down our pace. When we got close enough, the Voids began to sink back into the ground. The Ectos withdrew the endless chase to grab Ectus as if someone had called for them.

"We will meet again," Ladidya yelled at Ectus.

"I do hope so," Ectus replied smiling. Ladidya was taken aback and then quickly disappeared.

"What the hell was that about?" Kursus asked. "I don't know; that was a sad excuse for an attack. The first time was way more devastating to me than this time," I answered.

"That is because you didn't have your comrades by your side," Kursus replied. She then looked up at Ectus and glared. "What is the matter with you?"

"What you mean?" Ectus asked.

"You were flirting with the enemy."

"Yeah, I think she likes me," Ectus replied, looking out towards where Ladidya had left. My stomach turned to the very idea. Great, just what we need; Ectus falling for the enemy.

We walked up to the Cemetrica gate and stared up at it. We looked at each other and I walked up to the gate to slowly push it open. It screeched from the metal on metal scraping against itself and we entered the lands of Cemetrica.

The silence hard returned and a cold chill ran up my spine. We looked around as we stood just a few feet in front of the gate. Everything was back to normal, like nothing ever happened from our last visit. The graves were all placed where they were before, and the ground was solid rather cracking and spinning like a whirlpool. It was a little eerie.

"Whoa, this place is cozy," Ectus said smiling. Kursus and I looked at Ectus in distaste as we continued to walk.

"Whatever you say, chief," Kursus muttered, "you weren't here to experience its fine line of defense, now were you?" she finished.

"No, but you have to admit; its coldness and silence is golden." Kursus and I rolled our eyes. We had a permanent grudge on the land that nearly swallowed us by blackness.

"I feel right at home here," Ectus finished gloating and he floated ahead of us looking around.

"Just be careful Ectus. You cannot touch any of the graves, especially you. You are nothing *but* a soul so please be cautious. You wouldn't want to run into a Soul Collector, now would you?" Ectus jolted in fear, and flew behind Kursus, and peeked over her shoulder.

"Th-th-this is where S-Soul Collectors are?" he chattered.

"Not too cozy now, are you?" I joked. I took the lead and headed east of Cemetrica, stepping carefully around the graves. Kursus followed with Ectus leeched onto her back peeking over her shoulder.

We continued on through the silence, doing everything in my power not to awaken a grave. I wasn't in the mood to deal with soul crushing creatures, or those things called The Damned. I was definitely not in the mood to be dragged down into the earth again and get stuck in the dirt. I just wanted to get these tasks done so we could find that filthy, good for nothing Noctria and then finally find my creator. Suddenly my pendent began to glow and vibrate and a voice cut through the silence.

"Darkus! I feel your presence! Are all of you here in Cemetrica?" Rip's voice crackled through the pendent.

"We're on a mission to seek the Ancient Voice," I answered.

"Oh, oh dear. That's quite a task you have going on there lad. Why ever would you seek that language?"

"Why wouldn't I?" I asked surprisingly, holding the pendent in my fist, which I pressed against my chest as I dodged graves.

"It gives me the power to do as I please, once per passing. That could be tremendously helpful," I continued.

"Indeed, it would, but you must not know of the creatures that hunt for those with Ancient Voice," he warned.

I stopped in my tracks and turned to look at Kursus, who looked to the ground, embarrassed.

"Oh, yeah I forgot about those," she said bashfully.

"Oh, did you now? And just what exactly hunts for anyone who can speak Ancient Voice?" I asked Kursus, but Rip answered,

"We call them Mimics; spiritual shape shifters that take on the image of those who are familiar to you to trick you into coming close. Once they have you, they eat every inch of you until not a morsel is left." I glared at Kursus.

"Gee, that's good to know Rip. I find that motivating and inspirational," I said sarcastically. I looked forward and continued to walk through the graves, quite irritated with Kursus.

"How do I avoid them?" I asked. I still wanted the ability to speak Ancient Voice, I wasn't afraid of a Mimic. I just need a weak point and I'll be happy.

"Well, the only way you can tell that one of your comrades is in fact a Mimic is that they don't speak, at all. They are completely silent and haven't been granted the ability to speak. But most of the time they don't need to. They come around when you really need to see an ally. It's like they know the precise timing to come around from what appears to be from out of nowhere. You must be cautious. They are considered a curse among those who carry the gift of speaking the language. My best wishes to you all and try to stop by once in a while, since you're in the area."

"Yeah, I'll do that. Say, do you like Aged Creeple sap?" I asked.

"Oh no, nasty stuff that is. I prefer a fine wine and a loaf of pumpkin bread from Muckraid," he answered.

"Good, more for me," I answered. Rip laughed. "Alright then, cheers!"

The light dimmed down and suddenly the ground shook hard.

"Oh no not again," I yelled. I did everything in my power to keep my balance. The ground stopped shaking and I asked Kursus to summon Rip to ask him what that was. A bit confused, she spoke into the pendent and it shook and began to glow once more.

"Everything alright?" Rip asked.

"You tell me; did you feel the ground shake?"

"No, I didn't...ahh I see. It must be the Grimarius," Rip answered.

"The what?" I asked.

"Grimarius; Cemetrica's Crophix. Also known as '*The Blot.*' It causes realistic illusions and hallucinations designed to mess with the living that walk these lands. If I were you, I'd hurry to your destination. You don't want to come face-to-face with the Grimarius. Grimarius attacks your thoughts, directly. it's capable of bringing the worst out of you and turning others against each other. Make haste and get out of the area. Grimarius knows you are visiting. Farewell," Rip finished and my pendent grew dark. I stood there quietly thinking, looking around. I turned around to look at Ectus and Kursus.

"Did you guys feel the ground shake?" They both shook their heads. "Huh, curious. Well, let's go, shall we?"

I continued to walk a couple feet ahead and looked back at Ectus and Kursus, who were still standing in the same spot.

"Come on you two, what are you waiting for?" They just stood there.

"Darkus, what are you doing?" I heard from behind me. I looked over and both Kursus and Ectus were ahead of me.

"Are you alright?" Kursus asked. I looked back where I saw them standing just a second ago and they were gone. I once again looked back at Kursus and Ectus. I suddenly realized I was being messed with. Those must have been mimics. I smiled.

"Very cute, Grimarius," I murmured. I began to walk towards whom I was sure were my real comrades and looked behind me once more to make sure I wasn't just seeing things, but I was.

There is a meadow in the distance and I could see that the sky was dark orange and the grass was black. I was very interested to check it out since it looked like my meadow near the old shelter. I kept Ectus and Kursus in my sight at all times. I wasn't ready to deal with illusions and another Crophix. I just wanted to obtain the Ancient Voice. Kursus looked over at me, worried.

"Are you ok Darkus?" she asked. I looked over.

"Oh yeah, I'm fine," I lied. She leered at me.

"Who are you trying to convince, me or you?" I looked over and sighed.

"The ground shook earlier and I seemed to have been the only one who felt it. Then I turned to talk to you guys, but it wasn't you guys. Well, it was you guys but it wasn't you, do you get it?" Kursus frowned and thought.

"Not really, but I guess they could have been Mimics? You know, those things I forgot to tell you about," she joked. "The ground must have been Grimarius. It was probably messing with you for a moment. It's in the past though; he can't enter Shadow Meadows because it is a sacred place; its part of the Sacred Reflections." She smiled and reached out to hold my hand. I reached out to hold it and we were suddenly standing in the middle of Shadow Meadows.

It seemed like we teleported. Ectus and Kursus were looking at me oddly.

"Darkus? Why did you stop walking?" She asked. I looked at her with confusion on my face.

"I-I don't know."

We were just standing in Cemetrica, and then-what the hell is going on? I looked at Kursus for answers. I was starting to worry.

"I thought you said I couldn't be messed with in Shadow Meadows?" I asked. She looked at me curiously and answered,

"No, I said we have to hurry because Grimarius becomes stronger in Shadow Meadows. We should probably hurry Darkus, I think Grimarius is messing with you," she said with the look of worry on her face. Her face suddenly split down the middle and ripped apart and she began to scream. I looked away and held her hand tight, then slowly peeked at her with one eye and she was totally normal. She looked even more worried than before. The hallucinations were so vivid and real. I nodded my head slowly and we continued to walk. I know for certain that is not what she said, but it had to be Grimarius. I just have to keep my head on straight. Although I was very worried, I broke down the problems in a basic simple form to remember; anything that isn't what it seems is nothing more than Grimarius, so I just go with it even if it doesn't make sense.

I looked up into the sky to take my mind off the illusions and keep a clear head. The sky began to tilt sideways as the ground began to follow as though life itself was turning upside down. When we seemed to be totally upside down I fell downward into the sky then hit the ground. I was looking up as Ectus and Kursus looked down at me. The sky was much darker than over at my meadow and the orange light burnt through the sky with such a vibrant finish. I got up and played it off as nothing happened and continued to walk forward with my friends.

The grass was black as the night; I loved the way it looked. So dark; so beautiful. Kursus looked over at me and smiled.

"Oh, you think so? I find it beautiful myself." What? *Was I talking out loud?* I smiled at her and nodded, going with whatever just happened. I looked over at Kursus carefully. Was she reading my mind? Why was she doing this? She shouldn't read people's minds, it's an invasion of people's privacy - *oh no*. I'm starting to get paranoid. I stopped again and closed my eyes. I lifted my head towards the sky and took a deep breath. Kursus and Ectus turned once again and looked at me.

"What is it Darkus?" Ectus asked. I kept my eyes closed and continued to breathe deeply.

"I'm certain Grimarius is messing with me," I answered. I kept my eyes closed but I didn't hear an answer. I opened one eye to see no one standing beside me.

"Kursus? Ectus?" I said out loud. Nothing. I began to panic. I had no idea where I was; I was in a pitch black meadow that looked like a sea of darkness. *Ok, just relax*, I told myself. I took a few deep breaths and pulled out my flask to take a few swigs of the aged Creeple sap. I drank enough to give me a good buzz. I took a little more and the taste became putrid. I spat on the ground and dropped my flask as I watched the brownish yellow toxin begin to ooze out of my flask. I picked it up and put it on my belt frantically. I was starting to lose it and become very irate. It seemed that whatever I did there was a prank to play. I looked around and saw Kursus and Ectus flicker in site for just a moment.

"Darkus your…" was all I heard Kursus say.

Was I still here and just not seeing it or was I somewhere else? I looked around and realized that I was in the same spot in the field that I was when I was with Kursus and Ectus a second ago. Maybe I was still physically here and just not conscious.

"Kursus, Ectus, if you're still right here I cannot see you, at all," I shouted, "I think I'm being tricked into thinking I'm alone. So, if I'm acting ridiculous just bare with me," I continued. I looked around and heard no reply. After getting an idea on what was happening I decided to go with the idea that I was still here, just not here, or something like that. Once I regained myself I became angry for being toyed with. I stuck my hands out and lit them up.

"Ectus, Kursus, if you are nearby back off because I may have to fight something."

The sky grew loud with a low, deep laughter as if all of Shadow Meadows was laughing at me. I began to shoot the sky with beams of energy I generated through my hands. The sky cracked like glass as I shot at it. I then heard Kursus shout from what sounded like ripples of water. I looked around, frantically. I felt like I was losing my mind. My ears began to ring so loudly that I couldn't stand it. I then saw a Brackling fly over my head. Its large face with bulging eyes staring at me as it flew above me. In a deep, disturbing voice the Brackling slowly opened its wide mouth and spoke.

"Welcome to my nightmare, Darkus." It cackled as it continued to watch me.

I began to shoot at it but it was as if my beams were going straight through it. Oh no, what if it gets away? Then I will die-wait, it's not real. It can't be; my bullets go straight through it.

"Come on out Grimarius! Or are you such a big coward that all you really got in that arsenal are a bunch of stupid magic tricks?" I yelled. I was then pulled into the black grass which became a sea of

Creeple sap. It was acting like quick sand. I tried to swim out of it. I saw a large fin in the distance. It looked massive! It gave a large screech and began to swim right towards me. Oh no, it's a Meenrale, I think. Wait, how would I know? I've never seen one before, but as it swam closer I realized it looked like what I thought it had looked like with my own imagination. The moment I realized this, it got close to me and opened its mouth. As if it was about to eat me, then it vanished.

It's a game; it's all a game. Perhaps Grimarius isn't a real physical creature; maybe it's a spirit of some sort. I began to sink quicker into the sea of sap. My head was now submerged. I held my breath and reached for the surface but I was sinking quickly. I couldn't see anything; only blackness. I felt cold hands grabbing onto my ankles and heard loud wining noises bubbling from under me. I was almost out of breath, but then in my last few seconds I realized that if I was going to really die right now why not try to breathe anyways? If it's really an illusion then that's all it is. I took in a deep breath and began to choke on Creeple sap.

I found myself, on my knees, on solid ground, coughing up Creeple sap. I was in the black grass again, and I saw Kursus and Ectus running towards me.

"Darkus!" Kursus yelled. They rushed to my side and picked me up. I coughed until I had nothing left in my lunges. I didn't have any sap on me or in my mouth. I stopped coughing and I looked at Kursus and Ectus for answers.

"What was I doing?" I asked almost out of breath.

"You disappeared for a moment but then you faded back and looked like you were swimming in the grass," Kursus answered, "It looked a bit ridiculous."

I looked at Kursus and began to laugh. She smiled a little and I hugged her in relief. It was just an illusion. I beat Grimarius's game. I kissed her on the cheek and reached over to hug Ectus and forgot he was transparent to only trip so I laughed again. I was so relieved to be back but I think my friends had thought I lost my mind on my little trip.

"Darkus, are you going to be ok?" Ectus asked.

"Yes, sorry, I'm fine. You have no idea what I just went through. I'm just glad to be here. Let's get out of here before I lose my mind completely."

I looked around and smiled as if Grimarius could see me. I beat his little game and now we're almost in the center of the Shadow Meadows. We stopped and Kursus let go of my hand for just a moment to look around. There were objects all around us, but other than us, everything else was a silhouette. I could see darker shadowed trees hidden in the darkness of Shadow Meadows. There were faint shadows of boulders and everything else that would be in a field completely engulfed in a massive shadow. It was like being on a totally different world. We heard what sounded like bones adjusting and rattling. The sound was growing near. Kursus muttered something under her breath and she created a torch that floated above her. Just inches away from her face was a skull. It was looking right at her. It screamed in her face then turned to get away. Kursus pulled out her rod and shot a bolt of lightning at it, which constricted it. It fell to the ground and growled.

"Not you again!" The creature hissed.
"There are two more around here somewhere! Find them!" Kursus yelled.

Ectus flew a little higher into the sky, his body glowing bright. In the distance, I could see two skeletal figures wearing human skin. The human's mouth was stretched out wide and used as a hood for the skeleton. It looked like the skeleton was being spat out of the humanoids mouth; it was a disturbing sight, especially in the dark. Ectus shot down to grab one but it ran very quickly, its bones rattling as it scurried away. I chased one down but it was just a little faster than I was. I pulled out my pistol and aimed for its legs. I took the shot but it jumped over it in perfect timing. I shot at its legs a few more times, then tried once more. With great focus I drew my pistol up higher to calculate an exact hit, aiming just a little ahead of the creatures pace. I fired. It was an exact hit and it fell to the ground and growled. I ran up to it and held it down. It screamed into my face as the eyes of the human flesh rolled around in the skin. I tore off some of my clothing and tied its arms and legs together. I looked up to see Ectus chasing down the last Skindria. After failing to obtain the Skindria he entered the Skindria's body and possessed it to throw himself into the ground. The skeleton looked up at me in the distance and yelled, "hurry and tie me up," The Skindria said in Ectus's voice.

I left the Skindria I was on top of and ran over to tie the other one up. Ectus faded out of the Skindria's body as it laid there.

Suddenly within seconds the sky lit up bright and all could be seen in Shadow Meadows. The grass was still black but the sky was bright orange and pink and everything that was in shadow became dowsed in light. We walked up to the Skindria as one looked up and glared at us.

"Let us go!" it hissed, "you play dirty, your lucky it's our duty to grant you what you desire or Id eat the flesh right off your bones!"

We untied them and they jumped up and pulled their human hoods down a little. What a disgusting site; the humanoid skin sat over their shoulders like blankets, the head covering their skulls. The flesh looked fresh and slightly oozed bodily fluids. The feet of the humanoid skin hung just below their waist and the hands and arms were used as sleeves for the Skindria.

"Where did you get those humanoids?" I asked. The Skindria's jaw chattered in laughter, "They were lost souls wandering across the lands. Such foolish humans only serve one purpose with lack of rational thought like that; food and clothing, Monster. You're in no room to judge since you are wearing humanoid skin yourself," the Skindria snarled. As much as I wanted to argue this, it was true. I try not to think about where my flesh came from. I just hoped it was someone who didn't need it.

The Skindria that was standing in the middle had walked towards us. We took a step back; they were quite intimidating looking. It was the human skin, more than anything, not to mention this was the first time I'd seen an animated skeleton. The closest I've seen was the Soul Collector, with its large skull head, but the rest was covered in a shroud of darkness that was in the shape of a cloak.

"You seek the secret path to the Sacred Reflections I presume," the Skindria hissed, "before we do such a deed you must first finish one last task. Find us the carcass of a large rare plant that feeds on human flesh. Do this, and the path is yours." Without a chance to understand what that meant, the Skindria spun and vanished. The sky became black once more. To our horror a familiar slithering sound drew closer to us.

"It can't be," Kursus whispered in terror. She created the largest of torches she had made yet and held it above us. Just outside of the light I could hear the clicking, slithering sound of what could only be a Shadow Stalker.

"Impossible; they aren't supposed to be here," Kursus said, as she was pressing up against me as close as she physically could.

"Perhaps someone had summoned them, knowing we would eventually be heading this way," I answered, "after all, this is a sacred place. I was actually a little surprised they weren't here from the beginning."

Closely together, we ventured through the darkness, using the torch light to find a flesh-eating plant in the middle of nowhere. *Just terrific*, I thought. This could take forever. Kursus cleared her throat and spoke.

"What they are referring to is the Plantimus. It is one of the few flesh-eating plant life out there. Fortunately, I know this specifically, considering the Flintkus tribes Crophix is Plantimus Maximus; a massive flesh-eating plant that comes out from the ground. Similar to the Lanterian's Crophix Bombadicus, but ours is much deadlier."

"Interesting. Had you not been from there, I would have never thought about the fact that your tribe had a Crophix considering you haven't had to use it against me," I replied.

"Yes, but we must be careful. One way to identify a Plantimus are it's spiny, striped vines that wiggle just a couple of feet above the surface. There must be more than we think here, considering they prefer darker locations. They are known as Nocturnal living plant-life. They use their vines as sensors for approaching food sources. Once it uproots itself we must instantly cut the head off." Kursus explained quietly, listening to the creepy sounds of the slithering nearby Shadow Stalkers. They are waiting for the right time to pounce on us, I could feel it.

We searched all over the place. We looked high and low. We checked behind trees and boulders that we sometimes tripped over or ran into in the pitch blackness, but no sign of this Plantimus creature. Kursus had made the task a bit easier by summoning a few more torches and placed them in areas that let us know we've searched that location. They would hover about three feet above the ground above each checkpoint. I had this urge or craving of some sort to drink more of the Aged Creeple sap that I had but I reminded myself that I must save it for important times.

I had that thought, we approached the wiggling vines Kursus had talked about. Excited and relieved, Ectus and I looked at Kursus for further instruction. She picked up a stick and poked at the vines. A large plant came out of the ground and sat on a pile of leaves, similar to the scrap cabbage. It had a fat, round body with swirly marks in its skin. It had a few tentacles and two larger, longer ones. It also had a gaping, wispy mouth and two large clear white eyes that were different sizes and a long neck with black stripes up it. It growled at us in a somewhat cute manner.

"The small ones are rooted to its location so we do not need to worry about it coming at us, just don't get within reach of its mouth or reachers, which are its longer tentacles that it uses to grab its prey." She reached for the stone blade in her pocket and quickly grabbed the neck.

"Grab its tentacles for me!" She yelled. Ectus and I searched for the tentacles in the dark and grabbed them. The three of us wrestled this plant creature in the dark, with the torch over our heads, totally ignoring the sounds of the Shadow Stalkers now. Kursus sawed off the head as it screamed in a high pitch sound. To my surprise it began to bleed red blood, like a humanoid. Its body sat in its leaves, motionless, and Kursus held the head by the neck.

"Sorry little fella. Your life has been sacrificed, allowing us to succeed in a greater good. Therefore, you will not go to waste." Kursus spoke. The Skindria suddenly reappeared out of thin air. The sky grew slightly brighter, looking more like a normal night sky. To our relief, the slithering, clicking sound of the Shadow Stalkers faded away. The Skindria took the head of the once living plant life out of Kursus's hands.

"Follow us to the path. Do us a favor and don't come back. Because if you do, we have decided to grudge feast you, understand me humanoid?" it hissed in Kursus's face. She pulled her head back in disgust. Although the Skindria had skeletal feet, they began to levitate just inches off the ground, dragging their toes across the blades of the dark grass and started to float in the opposite direction.

"This way, foul creatures," The Skindria hissed.

We walked until the Skindria took us to what looked like a massive pitch-black wall. It looked as if this is where the world had ended. It stretched as far as the eyes could see; like Cemetrica's gates, only this black wall appeared to have no end. It reached far into the sky.

"Enter with warning and beware, once you enter this black shroud you cannot come back. There is only one path to follow from here. To succeed on your quest and live, you must pass through in its entirety. Now get lost," The Skindria hissed. They turned around and flapped their humanoid skin and floated away back into the Shadow Meadows. The rattling sound of their bones faded away. We stood there, back within the silence.

We faced the massive endless wall of darkness. I stepped forward and began to walk through the wall. It felt like the wall was being moved around every inch of my body as I continued to walk through. It felt cool and heavy but at the same time movement was basic and easy. As I entered the other side, I continued to be amazed by the beauty of the twilight. Ectus and Kursus joined my side and we stared down what looked like a long, endless tunnel full of dead trees. There was a lit path to follow as the ground seemed to glow bright yellow. Just in arms reach on either side was more of this mysterious, never ending black wall. I waited until the others were ready and began to walk forward, slowly and carefully. I reached my arms out to touch the walls as I walked forward but my fingertips disappeared through it. I had felt something breathing hard on my fingers and quickly withdrew my hands from the walls.

"What the hell was that?" I shrieked holding my fingers in my other hand. Kursus stepped forward to listen.

"It feels pure," Kursus said, "Like pure darkness."

She reached out and lightly touched the walls as her fingers went through. Two large, yellow eyes suddenly appeared in the pitch-black walls, looking right at her. Kursus withdrew her hand and hundreds of different colored eyes appeared throughout the walls, all different shapes. The wall began to come alive. The eyes were all misplaced instead of having sets. They all watched us and blinked, continuing to stare as we slowly walked through. Soon after, pitch black hands began to reach out through the black abyss, then followed long distorted looking arms. Hundreds of them. All reaching out aimlessly. We huddled closely and watched in awe as the black walls came alive. We walked slowly through the walkway dodging the reach of these many long, oblong arms.

An arm reached out and grabbed Kursus's robes. She grabbed her robes and pulled as hard as she could, ripping her clothes in the process and bumped into me as the arms released her.

"What is going on?" she asked frantically.

"I don't know but I am quite disturbed," Ectus chattered. I held my hand out and it glowed bright purple. The arms and eyes quickly disappeared into the darkness from which they came. It grew silent.

"Curious," I said out loud.

I began to lead the way, walking through the old rotting trees. As we walked through the dead trees, I looked up where the sky normally would be. I could see what looked like a faint reflection of us and the ground beneath us. Where were we? None of this seemed real.Iit was all like a dream, or a different realm.

"We're in the Secret Path hidden by the pitch blackness that surrounds Cemetrica. Without finding the Skindria, this would have been impossible to find. Imagine trying to find a tiny fish in a large black sea," Kursus explained as she looked all around us.

The only sounds that could be heard were the sounds of us walking through crackling branches. We were so mesmerized by the scenery that we had not noticed the large mass about ten feet in front of us. I jumped back, finally looking ahead. The others were startled by my sudden movement.

Straight ahead of us was a large creature with long, thin, and boney spider legs. From the waist up it had an average looking humanoid body. Its skin color was purple, and it had a sleek female physique. She had long fingers, long black nails and long black hair that sat like a shaggy animal on her head. I could see one eye looking through her long, stringy hair. She appeared to have a stitched-up pattern on her mouth that ran up to each side of her ears. She had large white eyes that were enhanced by what looked like black eye make-up.

She slowly lifted her arms from her sides in the air side by side of her head. She smiled and began to speak.

"Visitors. How intriguing. I haven't seen a visitor in countless days. I suppose you would like to get by me? I suppose you'd like to get to your destination? Well here is the deal; I need to eat, so I see a negotiation is underway. You give me something to eat; I will let you pass. If you don't give me something to eat, I will eat you instead," she said simply.

"Nobody is getting eaten," I answered firmly. The spider lady spread out all legs to keep us from passing.

"Well someone is going to be getting satisfied tonight and it certainly isn't you," she snarled. She began to charge at us, her legs clattering on the ground and along the black walls. I stuck my hand out and it began to glow. She stopped in mid charge and jumped back in shock.

"My, such pure power," she gasped. She stood up straight and tilted her head.

"Definitely not worth dying for. Unlike many, I know when its right to stop. I do not let my pride override clear thought. I will let you pass," she muttered.

She stood close to the black wall and held her hand out to gesture passing through. We looked at each other for a moment and we slowly began to walk passed the spider humanoid hybrid, keeping our eyes on her every move as we passed. My skin brushed up against her ice-cold flesh as she winked at me as we became face to face. As we walked a little further, I looked over my shoulder and watched as she disappeared into the black abyss.

"Tell that good for nothing Rip Van Lorenzo a large purple spider said hi, won't you?" We heard her speak from the abyss.

As we continued to walk, I could see that we were coming to a dead end. A massive wall of pitch blackness was coming close, just like the entrance. We walked up to it only inches away and gave each other yet another look of consent.

"Well here goes nothing," I shrugged. I stuck my hand out slowly and dipped my fingers into the black wall. I began to step forward as I slowly entered the blackness. I experienced the heavy cool feeling again passing me by as I entered the opening. I could see what looked like Cemetrica. I stepped out and waited for the others to follow, and I turned and stood there in awe once again at the sight.

We were looking at Cemetrica, only there was pitch black grass like in the Shadow Meadows instead of dirt. There were graves that came out of the grass. I looked up into the sky to see that it too was a reflection of what lied under it. I could see the long stretch of graves and crypts reflecting off of the ground up into the sky. It seemed endless. It was a site to see.

"This is it; Sacred Reflections," Kursus said in awe, still looking up into the sky. She walked ahead of us and took the lead. We followed her up a large hill. Ahead of us was a large ancient looking structure. It had reflective surfaced framing all over its stone structure. Kursus walked up slowly to the doors, which were two large reflective surfaces.

"It's been so long since I've been here," she said softly. She reached out to grab the handle and opened the door. The reflective surfaces of the doors suddenly showed dozens of small creatures all around us, only through the reflective surfaces of the door.

Startled, I could see a small crazed looking creature with a long, crooked smile, wrapped up in bandages of some sort and small, curled feet, looking straight at me through the mirror, standing right next to me in the reflection. I looked down beside me to see nothing, and then looked back at the reflection to see the creature walking towards me. I began to run up close next to Kursus and she looked at me in surprise.

"Can we hurry and go inside?" I asked. We quickly walked through the door, shutting it behind us. The reflective creatures began to fade away.

We entered a large opening to where we were completely surrounded by reflective surfaces. The floor, walls and ceiling were all reflective. We continued to walk through, looking around at the fascinating site. In my peripherals, I thought I saw my reflection move on its own in a manner I did not. I looked over at my reflection and watched it as it did exactly as I did. As we continued to walk and observe our reflections I had caught Kursus's reflection moving on its own, not doing as she did. It turned around and looked at me, smiling with a large evil grin. It pointed at me and worded something I couldn't hear. Kursus looked over and jumped.

"Oh!" she gasped. The reflection shook her head and finger at her, and then morphed into her normal reflection.

"That's odd; your reflection looked like it was disappointed in you Kursus," Ectus said. She shook it off and rolled her eyes.

"Yeah, everyone is disappointed in me, remember? It's just a reflection of how I feel. If you see a reflection moving, it's because they mimic your secrets and insecurities. So, no secrets are kept here," she finished. I kept an eye on my reflection, curious to see if it would move. It did not. Only the one time I could have sworn it moved.

We walked until we came to some type of reflective entrance. It looked like a maze.

"This is the Reflection Labyrinth. Its reflective surface makes it nearly impossible to finish. We must enter it and find the end." She said. "I memorized most of it. Just follow me," she finished. She reached over and grabbed my hand pulling me through with her. Ectus followed. The walls were incredibly tall. There was no way to view over them.

As we walked, Kursus kept her free hand reached out in order to touch around. With all of the reflective walls, it gave the illusion that most everything was a reflective surface, even thin air. Every now and then she'd bump into a wall and growl with irritation. She kept on going. Finally, she stopped after what felt like forever.

"This is where I become confused," she said, "I don't remember much from here. Ectus can you by chance enter through and take a peek? Remember where we are or you will easily get lost," she said. Ectus looked a little hesitant, but nodded his head and disappeared through the wall. We waited a moment, and then heard him shout.

"Ectus?" Kursus yelled. It was quiet for a moment. Ectus came back and looked manic.

"There's...there is something coming this way! Through the reflections," he said, panting. I looked at Kursus in confusion. Her face looked a bit terrified, and her reflections began to turn and face her as they shook in fear. She was obviously frightened.

"What is it?" I asked. Kursus turned to me and swallowed hard.

"It's a type of mimic. It lives only in reflective surfaces. You don't want it to find you. The only way to tell it's here is when your reflection stays still while you move on." She looked over at her reflection and moved. It followed to make sure it wasn't too late.
"I'd rather get lost than have the reflection mimic find us. It will drag us into the reflective dimensions. We don't want to be there. They will fight to switch places with us between the reflective world and the real world."

"There is a reflective dimension?" I asked.

"Yes, but we'll talk later about..." she looked over my shoulder in horror.

I felt a cold chill up my back. I slowly looked over at my reflection. It stood there looking at us. I moved to check and to my surprise it did not move. All it did was stare at me, completely still. I reached my hand out slowly to touch my reflection and the reflections hand reached out of the surface and grabbed my arm trying to pull me in. Kursus and Ectus began to pull me back and I became more afraid to realize that both Ectus' and Kursus's reflections did not move either. They just stood there next to my reflection.

"There are three of them!" I yelled as I did my best to resist being pulled through the reflective surface. I took my other fist and slammed it against the reflective surface and the reflective mimic let me go. The reflective surface began to crack up towards the top and we ran for it. I looked back once again and could see the three reflective versions of us standing together watching us run.

We ran around a corner and came to a dead end. We then turned around to go the opposite way. I felt suffocated being in a thin walkway full of reflective surfaces with creatures looking like us running around trying to find us. We were in their world and they knew it all like the back of their reflective hands. We could see the reflective versions of us coming towards us through the sides of the reflective walls. I ran ahead and stuck out my long fingernails. I scratched the walls as I passed them, cutting our reflections in half.

Kursus and Ectus quickly followed behind. We ran to a four-way intersection and stopped.

"Wait, I remember! This way," Kursus yelled and began to run to the right. We followed, running as fast as we could. We ran until we hit a reflective surface and fell backwards. We fell hard on our backs. I looked up to see the reflective versions of us running towards us through the walls. They were moving so fast that their movements were contorted and unnatural. Kursus grabbed my hand and pulled me up. We continued left from the spot in which we hit head on.

"There! It's the exit!" Kursus pointed straight ahead as she pulled me. I looked behind us to check and saw nothing as I ran into Kursus. Two arms were reaching out and grabbing her from either side of the walls, both looked like the reflective mimic of herself. The arm on the left was much stronger and pulled Kursus into the reflection.

"Kursus!" I yelled throwing myself against the reflection. I pounded on its surface. Damnit; they got her.

"Hold on Kursus!" I yelled and wound my fist up and threw it against the reflective surface. The surface cracked but didn't budge. I began to pound at it repeatedly, hoping to break through some type of barrier. Ectus grabbed my arm to stop me.

"Don't! If you open a door, they will enter this world and find us."

"They can already do that!" I yelled back. I continued to beat at the reflective surface and Ectus stopped me again. I looked at him with irritation.

"Let me go in and find her," he volunteered, "I'm a spirit; I can enter without difficulty," he explained.

I hesitated for a moment, looking at him, then my reflection, which was staring back at me with fear. My reflection began to nod its head. It must be how I really feel. I wanted him to go find her. I looked over and nodded my head. Ectus pulled back and threw himself into the reflective surface. I stood there for a moment in silence, feeling paranoid, looking all around me. My reflection was currently back to normal. I looked over at the exit and thought about at least getting into a clearer spot. I put my face up against the reflective surface and screamed,

"Ectus! Ectus, if you can hear me, meet me near the exit!" I touched the wall for a moment and my reflection was pointing over at the exit gesturing for me to go. I ran for the exit. I made it! I turned around to look at the reflective outer surface of the labyrinth.

I waited for what felt like forever. I paced back and forth, not taking my eyes off of the large reflective wall on the outside of the maze. I couldn't take it anymore. The anticipation was killing me. *What if they got caught? What if they died or are trapped and are waiting for me to come get them?* I took a deep breath and ran towards the reflective surface. I put my fist up, hoping to break through.

I was a few feet away from the surface when my reflection stopped mimicking me. It put its hands out and shook its head. I stopped in my tracks and looked at it. It looked like I was trying to tell myself not to do it.
I put both my hands on the reflective surface and got nose-to-nose with my reflection.

"Well, what else am I supposed to do?" I yelled at it. My reflection began to mutate like the splitting of a nucleus. I backed up and watched Kursus and Ectus get thrown out of the reflective surface. They fell onto their faces. I ran to help them up. I was so relieved.

"Are you guys ok?" I asked, helping Kursus up. The moment they stood up my heart sank as I looked into the eyes of someone other than my friends. Their bodies flickered and their coloring was just a bit shaded darker then my real friends.

"Where are they?" I demanded.

The Kursus mimic lifted her head and tilted it sideways and her arm pointed behind her towards the reflection not taking her eyes off me. I had forgotten that mimics cannot speak. I looked behind them to see that they had no reflection. I put my hands to my side and the mimic Kursus walked up to me and hit me, cutting my face. Her arm felt like a large razor to my flesh. I began to bleed sap. I looked at her with anger and wiped the sap off my cheek and sucked it off of my finger.

"It's going to be like that, is it?" I asked in a low voice.

I pulled out my pistol and began to release large balls of energy at the Kursus mimic. The large balls of energy ricocheted off of her reflective surface of the labyrinth wall as she walked towards me. *You've got to be kidding me.* Her body acted as a reflective shield. It looked like blunt force was the only option I had at the moment. I charged at the Kursus mimic and threw my fist into her chest. She flew back into the reflective surface, leaving a large cracked area on the reflective wall. She looked up and I could see that her chest began to crack.

"Found your weak spot," I said with a smile.

The Ectus mimic came up from behind me and slashed my back. I stuck my hands out and screamed in pain. The feeling of a hot blade sent pain diagonally across my back. I turned around and head butted the Ectus mimic. It fell back. I heard a loud crack followed by the metal clank sound that my skull had made. I tilted back slightly, a little dizzy from the impact. I shook my head and looked at the Ectus mimic, who had a cracked face. I looked back at the Kursus mimic who had gotten up and ran at me.

She reached out to swing a slicing punch at me. I ducked and grabbed her by the waist and neck and threw her over my shoulders, head first into the Ectus mimic that was lying on the ground. Her upper body shattered into hundreds of pieces. The loud sound of glass breaking filled the air. Her lower torso and legs fell to the side of the Ectus mimic in defeat. The Ectus mimic looked up at me in rage. I could see its lower body was cracked pretty well.

Slash!

His arm went across my chest, another across my neck. They went pretty deep. With one hand on my neck and the other out in front of me I backed up against the reflective surface. I could feel warm sap gushing down my hand from the cut on my neck. The Ectus mimic sized me up and got ready to run at me. I waited for the right moment. I side stepped as he went right through the reflective surface, like magic. The moment he disappeared, the real Kursus and Ectus flew out. Kursus landed on her face and Ectus was sent floating in circles across the air. They regained their focus and found me sitting up against the reflective surface. I was gushing sap all over the place and I could feel my body quickly rushing through the phases of shutdown.

"Darkus!" Ectus yelled. They both came to my side to see my wounds. Kursus pulled my hand away from my neck and the sap came gushing out. She reached into her robes and pulled out a pin and thread and her welding device.

"Hold still and let me close this before you lose all of your sap," she demanded. She pulled my hand back and began to send a searing hot pain through my neck. I gargled in agony and closed my eyes tight. She finished welding my neck and put the needle through my wound and began to quickly sew me up. The pain began to fade and I became lost in Kursus eyes; she was so worried, so caring. I felt relieved and began to slow down my breathing.

"There," she said with a smile, "how do you feel?"

"Like I need some Aged Creeple sap," Grinning from ear to ear.

She stood up and held her hand out to help me up. I took her hand and she helped me up. I reached down for my flask and took a large swig, and then handed it to her. She took a quick sip and breathed through her teeth. She screwed the lid back on and then handed it to me. I stood there for a moment looking at her. She stared back.

"What?" she asked. I looked down and experienced a feeling I hadn't felt before; embarrassment.

"Well um, thanks," I said, "you've fixed me up quite a few times now! I just thought you should know that I appreciate it." Ectus groaned but I ignored it. Kursus smiled and punched me in the arm.

"Don't feel so appreciative. You've obviously saved our butts a lot too. It's what we do. We've only got each other. Now, let's get out of here. I will never look at my reflection the same ever again," she finished, looking over my shoulder and into her reflection.

"What was it like in there?" I asked, as we headed further into the mysterious Sacred Reflections.

"It was like looking into a reflection, only to see everything else happening outside of the glass. We could see your fight and do nothing. We pounded on the surface as loud as we could and yelled but you didn't hear any of that, did you?" Kursus asked.

"No, I didn't. What a curious place," I said.

"The louder we yelled the more we brought other reflections near us. Your mimic stood beside us and watched you suffer. It enjoyed it. It didn't hurt us though. Maybe because we were in its dimension. It seems like they just wanted us to suffer and be separated away from our realm, as well," Ectus said. He shivered and shook his face.

"It's all too much to take in. I hope we only have to do this once. I don't think I will stick around for the next lesson of Ancient Voice, if there is one," he finished.

We walked through an open area that was large and empty. We had entered a large hall that was circular shaped. In the middle, there was a rounded slab of stone. As we entered into the light, I realized that there wasn't one thing with a reflective surface. I felt safe and relieved.

"The Mirror Elders are beings that have lived since the ancient times. They have created a spell similar to the reaction between the Philosopher's Stone and the Elixir of Life, using mirrors to store the energy. It is called Ancient Voice. This magic was used to punish the Master Alchemist who created the artifacts. An equal power was the only way to defeat him. Normally, teaching your tongue these spells can take centuries. Now, only those who can survive this deadly quest can be granted such power to avoid years of practice. The magic is so potent that it can be only casted once a day.

The Mirror Elders cannot look into another reflective surface. By doing so, their own reflection may act against them, grabbing them into themselves, creating an instant black void that would cause them to completely disappear. They are forbidden to look at one another. There are but five Mirror Elders," Kursus explained, as she looked around.

The room grew dark as the middle stayed lit. The empty lanterns that were around the room began to light up of green and purple flames. We continued to walk. We came to the stone slab in the middle. Kursus reached out to touch the stone and the Ancient Voice emblem glowed on top of the large round slab of stone. Right before our very eyes arose large hooded figures out of the emblem, slowly, as if the stone was water. They were long and tall with no arms that I could see; just tall, hooded figures. They stopped rising and the glowing emblem disappeared from under their feet.

They stood there, still and silent. I looked at Kursus for direction but she was looking up at the figures and smiled.

"*Sredle esiw ho, sremocwen emos thguorb I,*" Kursus spoke.

One of the Elders in the middle floated towards us and lifted its head up. To my surprise, the elder didn't have a face at all; only what looked like a reflective surface, just like Kursus had said. I now understood what Kursus was ranting about a second ago, how they couldn't look at themselves in a mirror for their reflective mimics would literally pull them into themselves. *What a twisted process*, I thought.

It looked down at Kursus. I could see Kursus looking back into her reflection. For a second, I thought I saw her smiling devilishly into the reflection. I looked again and tilted my head to see but I couldn't see no more. *Curious*; was that really what I saw?

"*Dlihc suktnilf, ynapmoc ruoy revo dnes,*" the Elder spoke.

Its voice echoed and somehow it faded and reversed; it was an interesting speech pattern. It sounded unworldly. I began to be even more interested in all of this. I listened carefully; the words sounded so familiar, yet so alien. Kursus looked over at me and gestured to come forth. I walked towards Kursus and then in front of the towering Mirror Elder on the stone slab. I took her place and looked up at the Elder. Ectus did the same beside me. Two of the Elders reached down quickly with hands that shot out of their robes, grabbing both sides of our faces tightly. They held their reflective faces inches away from ours with cold, long boney fingers. Ectus gasped from being startled from the swift movement, not to mention something that was able to physically grab him. I looked over at Kursus with difficulty from the Elder's tight grip looking a bit nervous. She bowed her head, closed her eyes and smiled. She lifted her head up and opened her eyes, indicating that it was alright. I looked back into the reflective surface.

"*Ecnetsixe fo gninaem ruoy si tahw dna uoy era tahw?*" The Elder asked; I could tell it was a question by the way it was spoken, even through its windy unnatural voice pattern.

"Uh...I don't understand you," I answered.

I was at a total loss of what was going on. I couldn't understand a thing it said, but then I saw my reflection changing. I could see my eyes glow red with rage. I looked so evil. I began to moan in fear; I looked so hideous. Then I saw Tinkarius standing there looking happy. He crouched down and looked evil and began to laugh.

"I'm afraid," I spoke out loud in sudden terror. The terror took over my body and as I was freaking out, somewhere in my head I was thinking to myself, *why am I so afraid? What is happening to me?* I had never been so scared during my existence. The images were burning into my head and my eyes were beginning to roll into the back of my skull. I could see the memories before me of my haunting experience with Grimarius and the reflective creatures. Ectus began to scream at what he was staring at as well. he began to whimper.

At this moment, a beam of light dispersed from its reflective face and entered my face. An ice-cold chill entered throughout my body and I almost felt as if I was beginning to float a little off the ground. The Elder let go of my face and I fell back, landing on my behind. I looked up at the Elder and shook my head. Ectus was let go and he flew back. The fear had left and I felt both relieved and shocked. The elder joined its brethren's side and the long, gangly arms were sucked back into its body. They all bowed to us. The middle one spoke once more, this time I could understand what it was saying,

"*Erutaerc ylesiw ti esu .tfig laiceps ruo detirehni*

"*evah erofereht dna traeh ta erup era uoy .tfig siht rof raf emoc evah uoy.*"

"You have come far for this gift. You are pure at heart and therefore have inherited our special gift. Use it wisely creature," he spoke.

The Elders bowed once more. The stone slab lit up with the emblem and then began to slowly sink into the stone slab from where they came. The emblem disappeared with the elders and it grew silent. I stood up a little dazed and confused.

"What the hell just happened?" I asked.

"Yes, what was that all about? What is necessary for me to have to see," he stopped himself. I looked over at Kursus. She was smiling.

"You two are a bunch of big babies; it's just a part of the qualification process. Had you not faced your darkest fears and was true to yourselves, you would have never obtained the ability to speak Ancient Voice. Didn't you realize that you understood what the Elder was saying at the end there?" she asked. It's true. I did understand the Elder. I looked over at Ectus and he looked at me.

"Interesting, I totally understood the Elder," Ectus said.

Kursus laughed, "Very nice. Try this out;

Acitobor etanimod ot gniog era ew,"

We are going to dominate Robotica,"

"We are going to dominate Robotica!" Ectus said it before I did. We both smiled. At last, I could speak and under stand Ancient Voice.

"*Reve gniht tselooc eht si siht,"*

"This is the coolest thing ever," I spoke. As I did, my tongue vibrated in a way that felt unnatural.

"*deedni,"*

"indeed," Ectus replied.

Kursus rolled her eyes, "Ok, ok I get it you can speak Ancient Voice. Don't burn it out," she said, annoyed. The ground began to shake and the ceiling began to be painted with what looked like a reflective surface. I looked closer to see that it was Cemetrica upside down, and gravity became reversed. We started to fall upwards towards the ceiling. We went through the ceiling and entered Cemetrica, falling down right out of the sky. We hit the ground with a hard thud and the air was knocked right out of me. Ectus slowly floated to the ground and I became a bit jealous of him for just a moment. I coughed hard and slowly made it to my feet as well as Kursus.

"I forgot about that part," Kursus said, shamefully. I scowled at her.

"Yeah you tend to do that," I answered coldly dusting myself off. My attention was drawn to a freakishly tall figure standing in the distance. It slithered towards us in the most obscure way.

"What is that?" I said. But Kursus and Ectus didn't hear me; I must have said it quieter than I thought. Its head lifted up and revealed a ghastly face that stretched and distorted like some kind of melted plastic. As it walked closer, it grew smaller and smaller until I couldn't see it anymore. I stared for a moment wondering if what I had just seen was what I really saw. I turned around and was struck in the face by what felt like a massive hammer. I flew backwards and slid across the ground, striking a grave, causing it to crumble. It began to glow but then died off from its destruction. I stared forward in a daze as I saw the creature extend a large shape out of its body. it looked like a massive hammer.

"Grimarius," I said to myself.

Its head began to turn slowly and it bent itself backwards, real low to the ground, but its head stayed straight and looked right at me.

I got up and realized that Kursus and Ectus were gone. *Not again*, I thought to myself.

"Why don't you give it up? I'm not interested in playing games," I yelled. Grimarius sank into the ground and disappeared. I stood still, keeping my clenched fists at the read. I was suddenly sent into the air Once I figured out what had just happened, I was already falling. Grimarius had shot up from under me, causing me to shoot up. I fell hard to the ground. I slowly got up but couldn't see where he was. I thought quickly and pointed my pistol under me.

He began to rise from under me again but I began to shoot at him. He wailed and screamed then went back into the ground. I lifted my fist up high, elbow behind my head, and shoved my fist into the ground. I sent a wave of energy into the ground. Its full effect could be felt for at least 20 feet in all directions. I heard a screech. Grimarius began to climb out from underneath me wrapping himself around my arm. He began to crush my arm. I sent enough energy though it to have him blown off, but it was too late. He somehow managed to enter me through my skin.

I felt a strong loss of control through my body. I was then sent back into my subconscious. I could see through my eyes like windows, but it wasn't me controlling my body. I could see Ectus and Kursus again and they were looking at me in worry.

"Get away from me!" I yelled at them through my head, but they couldn't hear me.

"Darkus what's wrong?" she asked. I saw my hand stick out and glow and Kursus and Ectus stepped back in fear.

"Darkus isn't with you anymore," I heard my voice say. Kursus stuck out her Vengeance and spoke in Ancient Voice,

"*Yrekcirt fo dneif uoy sukrad esaeler,*"
"Release Darkus you fiend of trickery," she yelled.

I was thrown out of my head and back into my body. I was sent to my knees as this black mass oozed out of my mouth like smoky gunk. I held my hands out and watched as the smoky ooze left my mouth and ran down my hands and entered the ground. I stood up and looked around. I was so irate that Grimarius took over my body.

"Where are you, you pile of waste?" I screamed, but there was nothing. Kursus reached out to grab me and I flinched, pushing her aside. I looked at her and she looked at me in shock.

"Darkus is that you?" She asked.

"Yes, it's me. I-I want to kill that foul creature so badly," I said out of breath.

"We must go. Grimarius is a very hard and tricky creature to fight. Sometimes you just need to walk away Darkus," she said firmly. Every fiber in my body didn't want to leave; I wanted to teach that thing a lesson.

"I can speak Ancient Voice now," I replied.

"Yes, but now that you're here and alive and Grimarius is gone you should focus on using it on something else that may come into play. You must know exactly when to use it or you may lose an opportunity. You should only use it at life threatening moments," she said.

I looked back into the distance and the silence made my ears ring. I sighed and looked back at her and nodded my head. She was right. I just needed to cool down. Although I did just have my body possessed by Cemetrica's Crophix, I should focus on the fact that he's not near and I am alive. I walked forward into the silence of Cemetrica as my friends followed me.

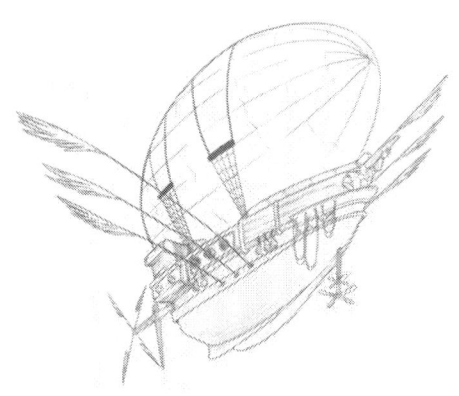

CHAPTER IX
THE SEA OF SHAME

We ventured as quickly as we could to Rip Van Lorenzo's crypt. Throughout the lands of Cemetrica came a new feature; Voids were starting to rise from the ground. We'd run up as quickly as we could to their rising hands, punching their way through the surface. We quickly stomped them back into the ground. It seemed as though something underground was being patiently planned; I could feel it every time I walked over the lands of Lanteria. The living dead humanoids were growing impatient and rising further throughout the lands, beyond Lanteria. We kept a mental note of this odd phenomenon and continued forth towards Rip's crypt.

We proceeded up the stairs and placed our hands on the stone door of Rip's crypt. The door swung open and there stood Rip hands together and pleased to see us. His large smile was as wide as his long curly mustache.

"Hello again! Oh, do come in, please!" He gestured us to come in. He shut the door behind us and we entered a much more vibrant living arrangement than before. He had a bright red velvet carpet. The windows that once looked empty and bare, now hung deep purple curtains and the walls were pin striped black and white. The roof hung many different trinkets, pendants, gadgets, bones and such. There was a large stone fireplace with skulls that sat on either side of the frames and the fire burned purple and blue. He had a large, cozy purple chair near the fire. He even had a dining area that was all nicely straightened out and ready for company; the plates were empty but they looked ready for company.

"Please have a seat," he gestured towards a large comfy sitting area. We looked at it with distaste. It was too bright and too soft; quite obnoxious, really.

"We're good," I answered. He walked over and poured us wine of some sort and gave us each a glass. He handed one to Ectus and then quickly took it back.

"Oh, I'm sorry I didn't mean to…"

"No, it's alright," Ectus said. Rip studied Ectus for a moment and smiled.

"I knew there were three of you! We haven't properly met yet; my name is Rip Van Lorenzo; elder of Cemetrica," Lorenzo bowed and Ectus reached out to shake his hand, who was then shaken up pretty good by the power of Rip's hand shake. Rip let go and straightened himself out.

"I'm Ectus, nice to meet you," he said bashfully.

"Ah yes; Professor Tinkarius's first and only synthetic ectoplasmatic experiment; very impressive," he said, checking out Ectus.

"Uh, thanks," Ectus replied, feeling a bit uncomfortable from how closely Rip was inspecting.

I smelled the liquid in the glass and could smell traces of whatever made the Aged Creeple sap so tasty. I took a bigger sip then planned and coughed at the foul taste of the wine. Rip lifted up his glass, drinking most of it. He finished and let out a gasp of refreshment, raising his glass to us.

"Delicious, isn't it?" He asked proudly. I nodded my head, raising my glass to join him. Kursus had already drank hers, but still raised her empty glass. He turned around and continued to sip on his wine. I threw the wine in a small pot with a plant that I didn't realize was a Cog Flower until after I tossed it in. The Cog Flower began to puff oddly, rejecting the wine and made a fuss. Rip ignored it and moved onto a conversation.

"So, you three, where are we off to now? Also, what have you accomplished since we last talked?"

"Both Darkus and Ectus obtained the ability to speak Ancient Voice," Kursus said. Rip ran his fingers through his curly mustache.

"Ah yes. I bet that was quite the difficult task. I'm sure you ran into Webra,"

"Who?" We three asked at the same time.

"Webra, the spider-humanoid hybrid. She guards the narrow walkway through the Secret Path. She is on our side."

"Didn't seem so much like it," Kursus muttered. Rip looked up in confusion.

"What ever do you mean?"

"Well what she means is she tried to eat us," I said firmly. Rip continued to look confused.

"Well didn't she bare the Mark of Tinkarius?" he asked. We shook our heads. His cheery feeling dropped suddenly into despair.

"But she did tell us to tell you hi," Kursus added as she helped herself to another glass of wine. She then gave it back to Rip.

"This cannot be; she must of…" he stopped and looked up at us.

The wine glass in his hand turned into a bright greenish blue flame and then vanished. He slammed his fist on the table.

"I must go. I apologize for having to leave so quickly. Now that you have the ability to speak Ancient Voice, you're close to being unstoppable. Your lack of concentration will be your true weakness. Use it wisely. If you fail, your trip to Robotica will become horrendous. Farewell friends," he lit up just like his wine glass, in a large turquoise flame, and he was gone. The sound of the crackling fire and the dying Cog Flower was all he left us with.

We exited his crypt and walked down the stairs. The silence joined us but fortunately Kursus broke it with a question we were all thinking.

"I wonder what that was about?" she pondered.

"Yeah, that was a little weird. Until now I didn't realize that you could possibly leave your allies and join the others. Wouldn't that process seem painful? I mean, you abandoning the Flintkus is one thing, but us creations have markings and holograms built into our system. She had to of pried all of that out of her body. What's even more curious is that she was a hybrid, which is something those cultures don't appreciate," I added. We stepped carefully passed the graves towards the entrance. We were extra careful not to awaken anything so we wouldn't relive our past experiences.

For once we left Cemetrica without rattling a nest or running for our lives. I was most excited about not running into that wicked Grimarius. We exited Cemetrica and shut the gate behind us, its piercing screech rattling our brains as we shut it slowly. We turned and began to walk through Lanteria. The more we entered here the more anxious I got from the silence. I cleared my throat and spoke my mind.

"Every time we come here I feel like something big is being put together," I said.

"What do you mean?" Ectus asked.

"Those Voids rising from Cemetrica, our last ambush here, as well as the silence. Lurt only showing himself before something happens. I can feel it in my cold metal bones. Something big is going to happen. I just hope it's after we find everything we are looking for," I finished.

Ectus looked out into the endless lands of Lanteria. He looked a little nervous, and then sighed.

"I remember us first meeting here. Don't you Darkus?" I smiled a little.

"Yeah, that was a whacky time. The land was so alive and brutal but we put a stop to that real quick, didn't we?" Ectus joined in a smile and we both looked out and admired the lands. Kursus rolled her eyes and walked through us.

"Ok you too, go find a shelter or something."

We headed west towards our new shelter. We had to make big plans for entering Robotica; a fierce and fleshless island full of hatred towards the living. We marched to the stump from across my old shelter. We took a quick look around and entered. We climbed down the long, large opening that was used to hurtle MechaTon. After spending a long while climbing down, we got to the top of MechaTon. We then climbed down its bowl-like features onto the tunnel, where we then walked forward much longer to the living area.

We entered the living area and there was no trace of the Mechas, Drill-Bit or Triumphus.

"They must be on the surface keeping an eye out," Kursus assumed. She sat down at the table and began to think. She noticed that the Steamer Milderoid was missing.

"Huh, that's odd; the Steamer Milderoid is gone," she said. Ectus and I entered the shelter to take a look but the moment we had a seat there were loud banging sounds and clanking coming from the tunnel. We got up quickly and ran towards the sounds. The sounds grew louder and louder; smashing followed by loud drill sounds. It sounded like hundreds of workers building something. We ran as fast as we could down the long tunnel towards the ruckus. All I could think of was someone or something dismantling our MechaTon and finding our hideout.

We reached where MechTon sat. To our surprise there was a hole that led to another large entrance near MechaTon.

"Has that always been there?" Ectus asked.

"I don't think so," Kursus answered. We walked towards it slowly, and followed the sudden silence.

To our amazement, the Mechas were large in numbers, working around what looked like a larger replica of the floating ship that the Noctria had. The ship was massive and had much more mechanical parts than the Noctria's. It had the whole package; the pronounced foaksul, the main deck, quarter deck and the poop deck. Its bow was long and narrow. It had a massive mainmast, Foremast and mizzenmast that held large tan colored mainsails and jib sheets that were assisted by many battens, spreaders and stays. Under the boat you could see its propeller that was where its rudder would be, as well as its large keel in the middle of the hull. It had a large thin patched balloon material holding air from the steam that was shooting out of a large Steamer Milderoid. It was tied by dozens of ropes that were then attached to the deck beam. *That's where that Steamer went*, I thought. It had wings that could expand and was tied to the ground by many ropes. We walked towards it in awe and admired the large flying object. Triumphus and Drill-Bit walked up to us. The Mechas stopped building, turned and gave us a holler.

Triumphus began to explain, "We thought perhaps a surprise gift was underway. Professor Milder was a great captain. We've sailed many skies with him. To honor his death, we figured the construction of a flying vehicle was needed for our next quest. Being our new leaders and all, we thought maybe something to help motivate would be necessary, didn't we boys?" All of the Mechas hollered, throwing their parts in the air.

"What you are looking at is not a Crophix but a source of transportation. Of course, it wouldn't be a good idea to use often since we're much more vulnerable and visible to the enemy. Not to mention, we don't plan to visit Robotica on a daily basis, but it will get us where we need to go. We call her Milderia, after the great Professor Milder, who started this underworld. The Professor gave us hope and promised peace, as well as you three. Now to pay us back you must take us all for a test ride. I hope that won't be a problem."

"Of course not," Kursus replied through her large smile.

We entered the large ship and looked up at the large balloon that held the air control. I walked up to the steering wheel and held it, looking down the body of Milderia and feeling powerful.

"Does it have any firepower?" I asked Drill-Bit.

"Doesn't need it; you have a large army of Mechas with built in fire power; not to mention you and Kursus whom have the capabilities of shooting large masses of energy out of your body."

"Fair enough," I said with a grin.

"Won't the army be hard on Milderia's delicate weight?" Kursus asked.

"Again, no problems there. We Mechas are bullet proof, but made of a super light metal material that is feather-light, making it easier for us to jump high. Milderia will hardly notice," Drill-Bit answered.

"We have extra Steamer Stalks just in case the one above goes out. We may not build as quickly as the Mechids, but fast enough for living creatures such as you. We built all of this just as long as it took for you to run through the tunnel. We're quite handy, you see," Drill-Bit bowed.

All I could think of was how incredibly awesome it was to have an army of metal minions who could build structures lightning fast. As they had hoped, this surprise lifted our spirits and solved our problems into how to get over seas to Robotica.

"Will we be heading out now, or later?" Triumphus asked.

"I think everything is at hand," Kursus replied. Ectus and I nodded.

"As you wish; cut the ropes, boys!" The Mechas below cut through the ropes. A Mecha above us pulled another rope that was attached to the Steamer and it began to gain altitude, quickly through its own vast tunnel. A tunnel similar to MechaTon's. Below the ship, the Mecha held onto the ropes that they cut loose. They all began to holler. We joined them once again in a loud shout of what felt like freedom that echoed through the tunnel. This is what freedom felt like; this was why it felt good to be here. For every pinch of pain and agony we endure, this is what made fighting for, what we stand for, supreme.

I looked up and watched the surface come quickly towards us once again. The above ground began to crack as debris fell downwards onto us from the splitting surface. We raised high through the surface and into the air, continuing to gain altitude. I had noticed that another massive stump, similar to MechaTon's, appeared from nowhere. I was a little curious to how that got there and how they brought it there so quickly.

We continued up, high into the air until the stumps looked like tiny little dots. The Mecha that controlled our air power let go of the Steamer and we gained longitude, coming a bit closer to the surface. The Mechas ran to the large levers on either side of the ship's deck beams, causing Milderia's wings to spread wide open. The wing span was massive; at least twice as long as the size of the ship. We were airborne; what an incredible feeling. The cool air brushed by us as we cut through the sky. It was incredibly silent; great for sneaking around, though it was quite obvious that we were a large ship floating in the air. Ectus went high up to the top of the mainmast to keep an eye out while Kursus stood next to Triumphus who piloted the ship in the cockpit. I stood on the bow of the ship arms stretched out; it felt incredible.

We headed south-west to an area I had not visited yet. We saw the lands of Cemetrica, Creeple Forest, and Lanteria in the distance. To our surprise the Lanterians arose from the dirt and began to throw little explosives at us that looked like their skulls. They burned bright with multiple colors. I remembered my first experience from when it hurtled me across the Creeple Forest.

"Fire!" I yelled. The Mechas were all stationed in their respected areas. If they all ran to one side, the ship would tip and dump us all out. They were evenly spread throughout the ship. The

Mechas on the right side of the deck began to fire rapidly, for Lanteria came into site far to the right. I could see Lanterians getting turned into mush as the bullets tore right through them. I lifted my hands over my head and formed a large purple ball of energy and hurtled it across the sky. It curve balled towards Lanteria, hitting the ground and exploding, throwing Lanterians across the lands. I put my fist up in the air and yelled out.

From the distance, I could see the Lanterians digging out what looked like a catapult. They put large versions of the small bombs in the catapults and fired them high. Large Lanterian skulls flew through the sky right at us. I shot what I could down with my alchemy and the Mechas fired them out of the air. They turned to crumbs and the fire that burned within the large skulls puffed into smoke. We reached far enough away to where they could not fire at us anymore, and we cheered for the win. We watched as they stood at the edge, watching where we were going.

"That could be bad, they could be warning who ever works with them," Kursus yelled.

"Not to worry. By the time they come around, they won't want to come this way. Nobody likes to enter the Sea of Shame. The only ones daring enough to do so are the Noctria. We will be halfway there by the time they even head this way."

As we cut through the air, I saw a massive body of water coming in quick. It reached as far as the eye could see, like Lanteria.

The waters were lively but not angry, but it looked dark and hungry. I could see that some type of fuel had been dumped into the waters for what looked like centuries.

As we came closer to the water the Mechas pulled two large levers on each side to slowly withdraw the wings. We lowered down and the ship's hull skimmed through the top of the sea with ease.

"We've made landing, boys!" Drill-Bit yelled. The Mechas began to holler. Triumphus climbed up the foremast and began to quiet down the Mechas.

"Quiet! We don't want to bring attention to us. The last thing we need is to meddle with a Meenrale," he spoke.

The Mecha cheered much quieter, almost to a dull roar. I walked over to the deck beam of the ship and looked down into the waters. It was so black and blotchy. I could see a thin layer of some type of chemical on the surface of the water. I could see my reflection looking back at me. Kursus joined my side.

"What do you think?" She asked.

"I think I never want to fall in there," I joked. She laughed.

Her hair bellowed in the wind from the velocity of the ship's speed. I found myself analyzing her physical features more and more everyday. The truth was I found her attractive. I just grew sick of the idea of being intimate. I don't know if it was how I was made or what but it wasn't by choice. She caught me looking at her and smiled.

"See something you like?" She asked. I cleared my throat and looked over her shoulder. "Nope just admiring the sea," I lied. I smiled a little and turned around and walked away.

As the ship moved forward, it began to lull me to a daze. I sat down against the base of the foremast and analyzed my surroundings. I watched the Mechas focus on the water. They were crafted so well. I admired their creation. Milder was such a bright humanoid. I looked over to the right to see that Ectus seemed a bit sick. He was hurling over the deck beam, and then I wondered; what exactly did he have that he could vomit? Triumphus was now where I was at the bow of the ship standing tall with his massive tools of weaponry by his side. Drill-Bill wasn't in site but I knew where he was. He was steering the ship. I bet that was tricky for him since he only had drills for hands.

Bang!

I had dozed off into thought. It seems that we had struck something. But it wasn't that. To my surprise we saw a ship coming in close from the direction of where Robotica supposedly lie.

"It's the Noctria!" Triumphus yelled, "To your battle stations!"

I got up as quick as I could and stood at the edge with my hands out. They fired their cannons and shot cannonballs into the side of our ship, causing large impacts and creating giant holes.

"Start the battle recovery process! I want to see Mechas heading down to the gun deck to patch us up, and fire at will! Everyone up on the deck, stand your ground!" Kursus yelled. *She sure is getting the hang of this*, I thought.

The Noctria were coming in quick. I could see the Mechas below patching up the holes. It was an unbelievable site to see how fast they could seal the holes. They began to return fire as they quickly patched up the holes. I started shooting large amounts of energy at the ship. I could see the Noctria standing on the edge and firing at us with pistols. Some of the Mechas took fire, but their metal skin was too tough. We had more luck fighting them on water than on land.

They pulled up beside us, firing all of their cannons at once. Milderia took heavy fire and tried to sink, but the Mechas in the gun deck quickly spat out the water and fixed up the patch. It was incredible to have such sufficient assistance. The Noctria threw down large boards, running over to our ship and began to attack us. I pulled out the screech box, but the Mechas beat me to it and began to send out loud, shrieks of metal screeching. The Noctria that were in the middle of infiltrating our ship had fallen off into the black abyss. I looked over the edge and shot the ones I could see in the head as they sank.

Drill-Bit stomped his way to the edge and ran his drill through a couple of the Noctria's. Their organs began to spin and fly around from their backs as Drill-Bit ran his drills completely through them. He was quickly ambushed by three of them, trying to dismantle him. Kursus ran to his aid and shot a ball of light at Drill-Bit, who then began to glow bright red. The Noctria's skin began to melt by the touch of Drill-Bits hide. Kursus had turned his metal skin scorching hot. The Noctria fell to the floor holding their severe burns and wounds and Drill-Bit kicked them all off of the ship.

This went on for a good while as the fight eventually ruled out in our favor. The remaining Noctria that were still alive called out in retreat. They all ran to their ship like cowards and withdrew their planks. They began to rise from the waters until a mysterious tentacle shot straight up through their air balloon from the abyss. They fell to the surface of the sea, hard, causing their boat to crack a bit. Two tentacles shot up once more and pulled the Noctria's ship down into the abyss quickly with nothing left except their balloon. The balloon came up from the depths of the sea and floated atop of the surface.

To my horror I heard a Mecha yell; "It's a Meenrale!"

…And just like that, the ship began to panic and fire into the abyss beneath us. Large tentacles reached up onto the ship and grabbed Mechas, dragging them to their doom. I jumped to my feet and held my fists out, ready for charge. Ectus grew larger in size and began to wrestle the Meenrale's tentacles to keep the Mechas from being pulled down. Kursus ran to tell the Mecha on the mainmast to raise the ship from the sea and into the air, but the Mecha had fallen into the abyss. It went up for air but was crushed by the tentacles.

Kursus climbed up to do it herself as the ship shook again from impact. She slipped and fell and headed for the water.

"Ectus, catch Kursus!" I yelled.

Ectus reached over and caught Kursus, and set her on the ships main deck.

"No, we need to get to the Steamer!" She yelled. She held out Vengeance and pointed it at the Steamer. She tried to lock on but the ship was shaking too much. Ectus pushed one of the large tentacles into the sea and quickly reached over to turn the Steamer on with his large fingers. The ship began to rise as the tentacles reached for us. The Meenrale grabbed our ship and pulled it back down. The ship hit the surface of the water with a large splash. The Meenrale wasn't going to give up. We needed it to let go of the ship. I ran to the edge of Milderia and looked down. To my horror, it began to release the familiar yellow toxin called GG3. It filled up a large spot around our ship. I hesitated, not wanting to dive into it but I knew I was the only one that could survive all of it. I took a deep breath, closed my eyes tight and dove into the water. I could hear Kursus call my name.

I dove in and felt the ice cold, greasy liquid engulf my body. I opened my eyes they began to glow bright purple. They acted like bright lights and helped me to see through the muck. I looked around and could faintly see the large tentacles squirming through the thick liquid. To my horror, the Meenrale's large eye looked right at me. I turned around and began to swim back. The eye was much larger than me, and I could see my reflection in it. Its pupil dilated from the light that had struck it from mine, and it closed it in pain.

The sea echoed with its scream and I felt my body shake from the vibrations that were sent through the waters. It started to calm a little, then I heard something heading my way from behind through the sea. I turned around just in time to witness a large tentacle flying steadily at me. I quickly swam down just enough to dodge it. I pulled out my pistol and began to glow vibrant purple. immediately I shot an energy ball right into the center of the Meenrale's eye. It clenched its eye tightly as it gushed out with what I assumed was blood.

I heard the ship rock. I looked up and saw the bottom of the ship slowly begin to rise. I swam quickly towards it but a large tentacle wrapped itself around my body and started to squeeze. I felt all of my organs trying to force their way out of my mouth. I began to send all of the power that I had stored through my body to blow this sucker sky high. It dragged me close to its face, as its large mouth began to open wide. Its tongue reached out and snagged me with what felt like sharp teeth ripping through my chest and back. It pulled me into its mouth. My skin began to burn and I felt very sick all of the sudden. I felt hot liquid running though my veins. It must be the toxins that perhaps came from the teeth of its tongue. I felt so close to death that I hesitated no more and lit my body up like the sun. I could feel my body being sucked through the greasy liquid in its mouth, trying to swallow me down its throat.

I sent a massive wave of energy through my body. I felt the creature's skin and flesh burst as I was hurtled upward towards the surface and out of the water. Underneath me, I could see the ship trying to lift up from the surface of the sea. I could hear my comrades calling my name as I soared into the air. I began to fall, nearly missing the edge of the ship. I grabbed a rope that was hanging from the bottom of it. I held on tight as I looked below to see a spot of red and yellow in the black abyss. Guts and body parts rained down from my large underwater explosion. I was covered in some kind of saliva and it smelled like rotting flesh. My knuckles were bubbling from the venom that was in my system. I was losing my grip. I tried to hang on with all the strength I had left. Thankfully the rope was then pulled up by the Mechas.

I reached the ships deck beam and felt relieved from the struggle in the water. I flipped over the edge and laid on my back. Above me, I could see everybody rushing to my side. I began to fade out. I could hear Kursus holler.

"He's been poisoned, his skin is peeling off," As I laid there, I could feel my system slowly shut down.

I awoke and sat straight up, with my hands straight out. I found myself rising from my slumber quite often. I was in what looked like the captain's deck. I was in a large bed and there were large cogs and gears that were working on a wall across from me. There was a large table that looked like a dining area. The only sound I heard was the calm ticking sounds of the gears doing their job and the distant sound of Mechas pacing around on the deck. There was a slight turning sound of a knob and one of the large doors on the right of the wall of giant cogs began to slowly open. Kursus peeked her head in and gasped in relief. She came in, shutting the door behind her.

"Oh Darkus, you're safe," she said as she ran to my side. She got on her knees and held my hand. "How are you feeling?" She asked. I let out a long, deep sigh and looked around.

"Good. I just can't believe I survived down there. It swallowed me and just filled me up with those toxins. If I had waited any longer, I would have been Meenrale chow." Kursus punched me in the arm.

"What were you thinking? Doing that was complete suicide," she snapped angrily.

"Well hey, you're welcome," I replied sarcastically. She stared at me with worry.

"I just don't know…" she stopped then continued, "I don't want anything bad happening to you. You're cocky and too bold for your own good. You may be powerful Darkus, but you're not immortal," she said much calmer.

I looked at her for a moment and smiled.

"Well, I'm *almost* immortal. Actually, I think I *am* immortal. I'm not a real mortal; I'm more like a machine." She smiled and lifted one eye brow.

"Whatever floats your boat, monster. So, you should come outside when you're better. You have quite the crowd of inspired Mechas out there waiting for you. Apparently, you're the first creature ever recorded to take out a Meenrale. You may not be immortal, but one thing you sure are and that is a miracle worker." She finished, with a wink. She slowly let go of my hand and walked to the door. She opened it and looked back seductively, and then left the room. I put my head back down on the large pillow and stared at the ceiling. I let out a sigh.

It's true, I'm not careful. I push myself like I'm a machine. In this world, I feel that I have to let everything know that I am a threat and to not meddle with me. I'm on an important mission and there is nothing that can stop me. So far, I'm proving that point.

After waiting a moment longer of being conscious, I rose to my feet and stretched out my arms, feeling for any weak points or tears. I looked down on the bed and saw a sewing pin and a thread. I hadn't noticed that earlier; Kursus must have patched me up again. She sure is a good friend. I walked to the door and took one more look at the large cogs on the wall, spinning busily. I exited outside.

Before closing the door, I heard Triumphus yell,

"Well if it isn't Darkus, the Meenrale demolisher! Ha!" He laughed. His large metal body clanked towards me. He reached down and put me in a headlock, which actually hurt considering his large metal body was grinding against my fleshy face. He rubbed the barrel of his large cannon over the top of my head and messed up my hair. I pushed him off and he laughed once more.

"Hey fellas, check it out! Darkus is up!" The Mechas all stopped working and turned to face me. They all lifted their hands up and started rooting to me. I looked around with a smile.

A Mecha called out, "You all saw it; he turned that Meenrale to mush! What a true Comrade!" The others cheered. I looked up at the top where Kursus and Ectus were and Ectus saluted me. I saluted him back. I jumped up on a higher deck and shouted,

"Were any of you smart enough to bring Aged Creeple sap?" The Mechas cheered, and Triumphus came up to me once more, putting his large arm on my shoulder. My knees bent down from the weight of his arm.

"You really think we'd forget to bring some fuel? Lets celebrate the Mecha way!" The Mechas cheered out loud and so did I. I had almost forgotten about the Noctria ship.

"Wait a minute. Where did that Noctria ship come from?" I asked.

It seemed like everyone else had forgotten about that ambush as well.

"It came from Robotica. Perhaps that was the ship the Noctria took that we were looking for, which means that he won't have a way back now, will he?" Triumphus implied and laughed, steam shooting out of his mask. "That just means that we are in fact on the right track in finding that Noctria. Even more of a reason to celebrate! Taking down Noctria ships and gutting Meenrale's is what we do! This calls for a pint!"

The Mechas brought out what looked like a large keg. They sat it upright. Drill-Bit walked up to it to drill a hole in it. It began to gush Aged Creeple sap. Another Mecha walked up to it, screwed its hand off and entered its tube-shaped arm into the keg. He used his other hand as a spout. The Mechas lined up with cups that looked like they were molded out of scraps. They all got their cups filled to the brim with dark, tasty sap. They chugged away, chattering and laughing as if there was not a care in the world. I walked up and got me some of that sap. I drank it as I walked around and talked with the Mechas.

Drill-Bit jumped up on a wooden table, but it broke and he fell through. Everyone began to laugh. I caught Kursus dancing with one of the Mechas with some Aged Creeple sap in her hand. She tried to mimic the Mechas crazy mechanical dancing but she fell, everyone laughed including her. Triumphus ran up to me and put his heavy cannon arm over my shoulder and began to sing.

"Oh, Darkus man or monster,
In the end he will not fail,
Raise your glasses upwards,
To the man who killed the rale!

All hail Darkus, he will never fail!
All hail Darkus, the one who killed the rale!"

Everyone began to chant and cheer as Aged Creeple sap was spilled everywhere. There were Mechas slipping and falling into the wasted Aged Creeple sap. Two Mechas began to wrestle in the sap, knocking over more of the Mechas. I couldn't believe how much fun these Mechas were; not a care in the world. It was kind of nice to have around.

As the night carried on, the Mechas didn't relax for a moment. All night they went singing and dancing, singing the song that they had dedicated to me, who apparently (if you didn't hear) killed the Meenrale. It was so much fun. I had to step outside onto the deck and enjoy the peace and quiet for a moment. I walked to the deck beam of the ship and let my arms cross and rest on the beam. I kneeled down, crossed one leg over the other and looked into the endless black Sea of Shame. Other than the "man-eating giant", it felt nice to know there was nothing that could dig its way up from the ground and grab my legs. No sneaky Lanterians or Psychozoans, Voids or Noctria; just me, my comrades and beautiful Milderia.

The only sounds that could be heard was the greasy water slapping up against the ships hull, as it sliced through the sea, and the Steamer above. The Steamer kept the massive object made of cloth full of hot air. I closed my eyes and took a deep breath of cold air, then released a cloud of moisture from my mouth. I had nearly forgotten that I had a cup of Aged Creeple sap in my hand. I lifted it up and took the last swig, and threw the cup in the water. I heard a door open and close. I looked over to see Kursus walking awkwardly towards me.

To my surprise she reached out and grabbed me and gave my body a big squeeze. She let go and looked up into my eyes. Her breath wreaked of Aged Creeple sap and she had a big, goofy smile on her face.

"Hey you," she slurred followed by a hiccup. She giggled and covered her mouth with the back of her hand. I laughed with her. I did what I could to keep her upright; she was apparently intoxicated. She looked up at me again to slowly give me another intimate kiss, but I pulled away. She looked at me in wonder for a moment, then let go. She turned around and walked for a moment. She turned around again and put a strand of her hair back behind her pointy ear.

"Darkus...do....do you like me?" she asked. I rolled my eyes and looked out to the sea.

"Kursus...I.... it's not like that..." I sighed.

"Well then, what is it? Because I can't figure you out. You're giving me mixed signals," I looked over at her; she looked concerned. I felt obligated to tell her how I really felt; how I wanted to be with her and how she was the most beautiful creature I had ever laid eyes on, but I just couldn't.

"I really do like you Kursus, but...but maybe I just...wasn't programmed to admire like most are. It's not you, it's just...I want to find what I'm looking for before I think of anything like that, do you understand? Maybe then we could possibly, I don't know, try to work something out."

She looked at me for a moment; I felt terrible. Honestly, there was nothing I'd like more than to do than to be with such an interesting, fascinating, and caring humanoid. I had a mission. One that is important to me, and I didn't want to lose my focus.

"I guess I understand," she answered, looking a bit confused and a little hurt.

"Besides, Kursus, I'm…I'm a monster. What do you even see in me?" I added, asking a question I've been meaning to ask the entire time I've known her. She looked over at me, her face full of sincerity.

"Darkus, when I look at you I see a monster, just like everyone else. But when I feel you near me I feel something humanity had lost long ago."

She drank the rest of her Aged Creeple sap and threw the cup in the water. She walked up to me, looked at me once more, and sighed.

"Regardless, monster, we make a great team. No matter what happens, I've got your back. When that time comes, when you want to maybe hold my hand, passionately, you just let me know, ok?"

She said and smiled, patting me on my shoulder. She leaned in for another kiss, but kissed me on the cheek instead. Her lips were warm and human; they soothed me so. She drew back, smiled and joined my side. We looked out into the endless sea, together. We didn't talk for what felt like forever; just admired the abyss.

Kursus eventually entered the captain's cabin to rest. I stared into the darkness taking advantage of my alone time. I'm definitely one of those who enjoy my private thinking time. I thought about what we would expect from these Mechids, and relived the dreadful fight I had with the Meenrale. Of all of my troubles and battles, the Meenrale was by far my least favorite experience. The feeling of suffocation while my skin was boiling from toxins, not a good feeling whatsoever.

I snapped out of my deep thought to the site of something large and tall, far, far into the distance. It appeared through the mist. It must be…it can't be; but it was. About eight miles ahead lay a dot in the clearing; it was Robotica. I could see large structures that reached high into the sky. My nerves ached and my mouth hung open in surprise. I turned around and began to yell. I stomped on the ground.

"Robotica, up ahead!" I screamed.

Drill-Bit, Triumphus and the gang busted through the door after a long night of celebrating in the dock below.

"What's going on out here?" Triumphus boomed. I looked over to the site of the Mechas covered in Aged sap.

"You guys may want to take a look in the distance," I suggested and pointed forward. The Mecha team walked up and joined me as I looked out into the distance.

"That can't be. According to our coordination's, we aren't supposed to be heading towards Robotica. Not for another whole passing," Triumphus explained, puzzled.

"Perhaps we were wrong," a Mecha spouted. Drill-Bit knocked him on the back of the head with his large drill hand.

"Don't be such a bucket of bolts, tin head! Everyone knows exactly where that island is supposed to be," Drill-Bit snapped, "something is screwy here. Triumphus, what says you?"

Steam arose up from Triumphus's mask and his eyes glowed in the dark as he stared at Robotica still as a statue. He stood up straight and stuck his cannon out towards Robotica.

"They must have somehow found a way to move the island," he said. The Mechas gasped.

"How can this be? They cannot enter water," one of the Mechas yelled, "we're all going to die!" another hollered.

Triumphus shot his cannon in the air to shut everyone up.

"No one is dying. That island is not reaching our lands. We have a new mission on this quest boys; we need to find whatever is causing that island to move, and destroy it. If the mission is failed, we must warn everyone in the lands, even those we do not associate with. It is in our well-crafted bones to work together with the flesh in times like this. We must only work with those we despise when all is at risk; you know the drill," he finished.

"Aye," Drill-Bit answered, as he stuck his left drill in the air and let it rip. Kursus came out from the captain's deck to see what the fuss was all about.

"We've got a problem," I said to Kursus as I pointed out in the distance. She yawned and rubbed her eyes, then squinted into the distance. Her face then grew long and her eyes wide.

"Wha-but, but how," she stuttered.

"Looks like our crafty little Mechids finally found a way to push their island towards civilization. As you know, this is not good chief," Triumphus said.

Kursus stared blankly into the distance as the island drew closer and closer. It seemed that we were gaining speed, but it was clear that the island was also moving towards us. It moved with tremendous speed. It grew larger by the moment.

"Well, physically that's impossible. They must have some special force helping them out. They couldn't have done it themselves. Perhaps they built something massive and were smart enough to make it water proof, or maybe they got their hands-on alchemy somehow?" Kursus theorized.

"That couldn't be. They had no strand of any magic sent with them. It was well inspected before doing so. My bet goes towards them finding out how to make a water-resistant device and using it to push. Only question is how did they get it in the water, and how did they get it to push and keep hold?

We continued to theorize silently, and then Ectus broke the silence.

"They must have built a large living device," we all turned to look at him. He became nervous from the sudden attention. Ectus cleared his throat.

"Well, think about it. They couldn't have gotten it into the water themselves or drop it in. It would just have floated away. They must have built something that allowed itself to enter the waters and push. It's the only way," he finished. I swallowed hard. Everyone grew silent which told me they felt that perhaps Ectus was right. We continued to stare, thinking about a quick plan as the island grew closer and closer. We couldn't just drift to shore; there may be something in the waters protecting them. If we take to the air, we will be recognized. We had to choose the lesser evil.

"The best option would be to risk Milderia. If we get to shore, we can build another force of transportation quite easily. If we go to the skies we will be recognized and blown into the water faster than you can say five hundred ton MechaTon," Triumphus boomed, "we have to try our damnest to sneak up to the edge of the island and enter with caution. Get ready to reach shore boys. Things are going to get a little hectic tonight. Looks like we're going to cancel the celebration. We've have arrived to our destination sooner than expected."

Kursus, Ectus, and I gathered what we needed and watched the island draw near. The Mechas collected the greasy waters from the Sea of Shame and entered the liquid into handheld devices that looked like little pistols. Some of the Mechas dumped the greasy waters into their arm magazines to be shot from their arms.

"Gather as much water as you can. This is the only line of defense we know is effective. We do not know any other line of defense other than finding their power supply and shutting it down. If this is possible, it will be informed to do so. If it is possible to get close enough, you can also rip out their cores. Even though I suggest not doing so. We will be arriving on shore in five minutes," Drill-Bit yelled from the top of the deck.

I was the most nervous that I have been yet. This whole attack was last second planning and the Mechids did nothing but intimidate me just by hearing about them. I filled up a few pistols full of the greasy waters and handed them out to Ectus and Kursus. Kursus looked at me biting her lip; I could tell she was scared.

"Just stick close to my side and nothing will happen to you, you understand me?" I told her. She nodded her head and slightly smiled. I turned to Triumphus for more information.

"Do we know where this power supply is?" I asked.

"We do know that it lies in the center of the nest. It's almost impossible to get to but with some muscle and smooth planning we can make it happen. A line of close quarter combat and some sneaky assassinating will have to be done. What you all must remember is that it's incredibly important that we do not let them know we are there. Doing so will spread word quickly and before you know it we will be surrounded. So, make note to be very, very quiet…Ahhh!"

CHAPTER X
WELCOME TO ROBOTICA

The ship was inches from the shore, but something had grabbed our ship from below. The ship shook and began to make loud cracking noises. To my surprise the ship began to sink.

"Everybody off of the ship!" I yelled.

All of the Mechas, Kursus, Ectus and I ran to the bow of the ship as fast as we could as the stern of the ship began to sink. The ship tilted and the bow began to rise. We began to run up towards the bow as it quickly rose. With quick running and right timing, we jumped off the nose right onto the edge of the shore. A few of the Mechas sank with the ship. We all stepped back on the shore and watched in horror as something bubbled its way up to the surface.

"Is it another Meenrale?" Ectus asked.

"Possibly, but I get the feeling its something else," Triumphus said.

"How can you get the feeling? You don't have feelings, you dip rod," Drill-Bit snapped back.

"Are you trying to say that mechanical living creatures can't have a hunch?" he yelled back.

They were interrupted by a large, robotic tentacle shooting out of the water. It stopped high into the sky. Its claws at the end opened up and held a large red eye that looked down at us. It began to glow red.

"Mother of Milder," Triumphus gasped, "it's a robotic Meenrale."

"Jump!" Drill-Bit yelled.

Everyone jumped to the side as the tentacle shot a hot red laser down into our area. We barely missed. We all scrambled to our feet and ran towards Robotica. The laser was as wide as Milderia; such power.

As we ran, I looked over my shoulders to see about a dozen more robotic tentacles rising from the waters. It screeched underwater. The sound could be heard throughout the lands and in seconds shot right back down into the abyss. We ran until we found some large robotic trees that covered the outside of the island. We hid behind them to catch our breath for a moment.

"I think we found what has been pushing the island," Triumphus yelled from behind a large metallic tree.

"So much for making a silent approach," one of the Mechas said.

"Ah, shut up you idiot," another yelled back.

"Quiet!" Drill-Bit whispered loudly, "this is the last place we want to be arguing, comrades. We are in the belly of the beast. We need to all keep calm and be as diligent as we can be. We're in robo-hell so don't piss off anything or attract attention to any of the locals."

Triumphus and Drill-Bit took the lead. We waited until the coast was clear and they began to run lightly into what looked like a forest of robotic plant life. The plant life looked like giant tin trees and shrubs that resembled ours except carved out of a darker, heavier metal. Throughout all of these plants, they had lines that went deep inside of them. These lines gave off a low blue glow that shined through their carvings.

"How curious," Kursus said, admiring the plant life, "they are like an evolved form of Milderoids. But they look like they are just for show; no real use for these things, whatsoever, other than they appear to have a harder metal. It's a shame we won't be able to bring any back."

Triumphus and Drill-Bit ran behind, tree to tree, checking ahead as we followed their lead. As we kept this up for a good while, the sound of machinery drew nearer and nearer. But it wasn't the normal clanking and tinkering I was used to; this sounded much more advanced. I began to have flash backs of Redemption Tower. My stomach turned and ached.

We got through a couple more trees when Triumphus and Drill-Bit stopped to get a longer look at something up ahead. I could see lights flashing on their faces.

"Oh, you guys gotta see this," Drill-Bit muttered. We slowly walked up towards them and peered through the metal shrubbery. My jaw nearly hit the dirt when I saw what they were talking about.

A massive, robotic city had come out of nowhere up ahead. Large metal towers that glowed red with the Dose towered into the skies, much higher than the ones in Redemption Tower. Everything moved much faster and efficient then normal. I could see the Mechids for the first time. They were much larger then the Mechas. They looked just like the one hanging in the security room in the building we had entered in Redemption Tower. The Dose veined all throughout their bodies and their eyes glow red. Their mouths were aligned with sharp teeth and large metal jaws. The center in their torso glowed hot with the Dose. It looked like their very own personal power source. They were tall, moved smooth and almost humanoid like; it was a little eerie. They looked hideous, angry, totally ruthless, and full of hate for the living.

    In the far, far distance there was what looked like a massive castle that glowed with many of the veiny lights, only they were green just like up in Redemption Tower. That must be their core and where their leaders were. They lived like the Steinlocks only much more evolved and not fleshy. Everything here was much larger and efficient and with no Monstruts walking about. They talked to one another with a voice that sounded monotone and lifeless, also super quick. One looked quickly over at where we were in the middle of conversation with another and we quickly ducked. We waited a moment and peeked up to see that they were gone. We waited a moment longer until we heard a Mecha yelp. We looked over to see a Mechid had ripped out the chest of one of our Mechas. It held its parts in its hands and looked over at us. Its eyes glowed hot.

"The living are among us," it blipped.

Everything that had lights glowed hot red and I could see the green in the castle in the distance turn to red as well. An alarm that sent chills down my back began to go off. Very fast speaking was heard throughout the lands. I heard the words '*living*' and '*lockdown*' specifically in there somewhere.

"Damn it, they know we're here," Triumphus yelled. Drill-Bit walked up behind the Mechid and grabbed it by its neck and drilled through its chest, destroying the Mechid's core.

"The core is its other weakness. Don't go assuming that's easy though. They are quick, *real* quick," Drill-Bit yelled, "which is why it's important that we practice the element of surprise. Here, find a way to wear this," Drill-Bit said, handing me the Mechid scraps.

"They are programmed to detect the living, but they are easily fooled by disguise, like us. They look at one another, as we do, so they don't feel the need to scan one another unless you give yourself away. It is the only way we can get through here. The Mechas, Triumphus and I need to find some of the Dose and take it. It will temporarily give us a disguise, which will make the Mechids think we are one of them. It also gives us extra strength, so there is no need for worry. But we won't have much time. Once we find the Dose, we will go with you to the castle. From there Triumphus will go with you living creatures to find that Noctria and find out where your elixir is, while me and the Mecha go shut down their power supply."

Triumphus, Drill-Bit, and the Mecha ventured off to find themselves some of the Dose. Kursus walked up to me and took the Mechid pieces from me.

"I can turn this piece of junk into a suit for you," she said, "You and Ectus go find two other Mechids and spray them with liquid or destroy their core. I will be here in hiding. I will cast a spell of detection in a ten-foot radius around me, so if anything comes near I will be able to react, so do not worry. Go find two other Mechids," she kissed me on the cheek. She turned around and set up for transforming the Mechid into a suit.

Ectus and I ran through the metal trees quietly as we looked for nearby Mechid victims to snag into the shrubs. Ectus stopped me and pointed up into the trees. There were electric eyes watching, looking around. I took my pistol out and aimed but Ectus stopped me again.

"We have to be quiet, Darkus. Here, let me take care of it," he disappeared into thin air and then appeared behind one of the electric eyes. He pulled and ripped it off of the metal tree. Just then, the other eye locked onto him and there was another siren. I took out my pistol and shot them all down but the sound of quick moving metal raced to the scene. Four Mechids appeared to scout and spoke to each other quickly. Two began to walk around fast, looking for us while the other two quickly replaced the electric eyes. We dodged behind some metal shrubbery, waiting for them to get close. We jumped up behind them and held them by their necks. The other two Mechids turned at us and pulled out weaponry. I held my water pistol out and they began to fire into the other Mechids. I aimed at their cores and shot them as well.

As quickly as they came, even more came for the bodies. Ectus and I made away with the two Mechid bodies we had and headed towards Kursus. We could hear the Mechids appear at the scene and began to find out what had happened. We rushed to Kursus, who had already finished the Mechid suit and we threw down the two Mechid bodies.

"We've got company," I whispered. Kursus put away her crafting equipment, "Apparently there is no time to craft. I must do this much quicker.

"Hself retuo ruo emoceb tsum sdihcem eseht,"
"These Mechids must become our outer flesh," she spoke in Ancient Voice.

The Mechids that we destroyed rose up to their feet. Their innards poured out like magic; the parts swirled around our bodies and connected, fitting snug onto our bodies in seconds. Just as we had done so, the Mechids that were hot on our trail came through the bushes. They looked at the three of us, standing there awkwardly in our new Mechid suits.

"Where did the living go?" One Mechid quickly spoke. We looked at each other for a moment and we all pointed towards the shore. They moved with great agility towards the shore without question. We waited until they were gone, and took a deep breath in relief.

"I could go for some Aged Creeple sap," I said, moving around and feeling out the Mechid suit.

"I have an itch that's killing me and I can't itch it," Ectus hissed violently, scratching his robotic fingers into his robotic bottom.

"Spirit's have itches?" Kursus asked.

"Well yeah, you ever heard of a phantom itch before?" Kursus and I looked at each other. We couldn't see each other's faces but the gesture alone implied that we found that quite ridiculous.

"We must wait for the others to return. While we wait for their return, I think that we should ask the NaviBox where that wretched Noctria is hiding," Kursus said.

She opened a latch from the Mechid suit and reached into it. Reaching into her robes, she grabbed the NaviBox, shutting the latch.

"Where is the Noctria Elder?" she asked. The top of the NaviBox glowed bright. We huddled together and looked down into the light. There he was, shaking hands with what looked like the Steinlock Elder, Dante. There were Mechids all around them and we could see green, veiny lights that were within a building. The Noctria handed Dante the green ball, which looked like our Philosopher's Stone. The light on top of the NaviBox stopped glowing and we continued to stare at it, trying to figure out what the hell we just witnessed.

"Was…was that Dante, the leader of the Steinlocks shaking hands with that Noctria?" Ectus asked, in shock. "And wait a moment…didn't we *kill* Dante?" He asked, with even more surprise.

"There were Mechids watching them, totally doing no harm to them. They were…they were working together. Ectus, that must of not had been the real Dante you killed earlier. The Steinlocks are capable of making what they call Capsules; robotic mimics that are spitting images of living creatures. Unless he was revived by alchemy, which I highly doubt since he was blown to smithereens up at Redemption Tower," Kursus finished with her eyes wide with surprise.

There was rustling from the metallic shrubbery behind us. We turned around and stood ready for attack. Triumphus, Drill-Bit, and the large group of Mecha came into view with a new look. They had the red glowing veins all over their bodies. They drew their weapons at us, but we quickly took off our Mechid head gear to reveal ourselves. They drew back their firepower and walked towards us.

"I apologize for that. Never can be too sure," Triumphus said and laughed.

"What do you think of the new improved Mechas?" Drill-Bit said confidently.

"Looking good, guys," Kursus answered as we put our Mechid headgear back on.

"We have a problem, comrades," I said, "we think there is a bigger picture being painted here. We just asked the NaviBox where that Noctria was. Get this; he was shaking hands with Dante and surrounded by civilized Mechids."

"How…deceitful!" Drill-Bit hollered. The Mechas all shushed him. He continued to talk quieter.

"How could this be? Ectus, didn't you kill Dante?"

"We think he killed a Capsule of Dante," Kursus answered.

"Mother of Milder, we got ourselves something big in the works here boys. We need to find these no-good flesh walkers and tear them limb from limb until they bleed out the truth. I take it they are all in that castle towards the North side?"

"Yes, we're going to head that way. Since the power supply is there as well we all need to head that way. Is that Dose going to do the trick?" I asked.

"Until we get inside of that castle. From there it doesn't matter if they know or not. They will find out soon enough since they are already on high alert. We must quickly make it there before our Dose runs out and they catch on to your movements. The key is to not walk like mechanical beings. The Mechids are smooth walkers, so just walk natural," Triumphus boomed. He ran to the entrance and gestured for us to follow him. He jumped out into site and we followed.

We entered into the opening. All of the nearby Mechids stopped and looked at us. We stood there for a moment awkwardly and then remembered to act natural. We all started walking quickly down the metallic paved streets and headed straight for the castle. One of the Mechas even started to whistle. We walked fast, avoiding any conversation with the locals. As we got a closer look at everything, I realized that there were 8-bits and Tech-Z's about, but they looked much more advanced with more armor and they moved smoother. They all watched us as we walked by, quietly and swiftly.

As we made down the streets one of the Mechids stopped us.

"Where are you all off to?" the Mechid buzzed.

"Oh, well, um, we were told there was a celebration up at the…the uh…castle?" I answered without confidence. The Mechid tilted its head at us and stared at us. It looked over at the castle and then back at us.

"We don't celebrate here in Robotica," it answered. We stood there for a moment, and I spoke up.

"Well, that's what it's all about! We're celebrating not being beings of celebration. We were enforced specifically by the Noctria that came to visit."

"Ah, I compute. Well perhaps I can join your side?"

"Oh no, this is a private celebration of no celebrating. I'm sorry to be rude but it must be this way," we swiftly walked by the Mechid as it watched us leave.

"Celebration of not celebrating? *Really?*" Kursus whispered towards me.

"Well, like any of you had any ideas! It got us by, didn't it? You're welcome, by the way," I said sarcastically.

We continued to walk by all of the Mechids, who stopped what they were doing to stare. It was very uncomfortable. Something told me they knew but they weren't sure somehow. Perhaps it had something to do with their programming. I looked up into the sky as towering buildings sat high above us. I hadn't noticed earlier that there were buildings that were actually floating on platforms. I was so fascinated by the sight of what looked like a new world that I bumped into Drill-Bit. They had stopped because we were at the door of the castle.

"Wow, that was quick," I said.

"Well we did walk pretty fast. Nothing matters at this point. We must get inside and infiltrate." Triumphus pulled on the door but it wouldn't budge. He reached over and slapped Drill-Bits shoulder with his cannon. Drill-Bit stepped forward in Triumphus's place and fired up both his drills, and digging them into the door of the castle. The Mechas, Triumphus, Kursus, Ectus and I stood as a wall around him to block site of our invasion process. Mechids walked by and watched in confusion as they heard the loud, drilling sounds of Drill-Bit. We waved awkwardly at them as they looked at each other in confusion and tilted their heads at us.

"Fine weather we're having," Ectus yelled awkwardly. I bumped him and gestured to keep quiet. We turned around to tell Drill-Bit to hurry.

"I'm going as fast as I can. These drills are meant for stone and scrap metal, not eight-inch steel!" He hissed as he nearly reached the other side. The handle of the door fell off and the front door began to slowly fall forward. We all watched in horror as it continued to fall. It hit the ground with a mighty thud that shook the ground.

"Yes! We made it inside!" Drill-Bit yelled in excitement. We turned around quietly. To our terror, the Mechids had moved in much closer as they watched our plan of entrance.

"Oh, hey fellas. Quite the party of not partying that's going to happen here," Triumphus boomed.

The Mechids stared at us. They were greater in numbers and even the 8-Bits and the Tech-Z's huddled above, staring at us. To make matters worse, the red glowing veins in the Mechas suddenly began to blip out and fade away. We stared at the Mechids as they stared back until a Mechid in the front broke the silence, pointing straight at us.

"The living are among us!" It buzzed.

We quickly ran into the castle. Both Drill-Bit and Triumphus lifted the door and blocked off the sea of Mechids that were trying to break through.

"Go! We will weld the door shut. You three go find Dante and the Noctria! Once we're done here, we will locate the power supply!" Triumphus yelled over the booming sound of the tidal wave of Mechids at the front door. We nodded and headed into the castle.

The castle was also metallic, but unlike the outside, it was still glowing green on the inside. This must have meant that it wasn't on high alert. We ran down the long hall that held a purple carpet with what looked like coding of some sort through out the carpet.

"All it says is *Death to the Living*," Kursus said. Ectus and I looked at Kursus in surprise.

"What? I used to read binary coding to kill the time. It was a hobby, really," Kursus bragged. Ectus and I rolled our eyes.

"They must really hate the living," Ectus said, "So, does that make me an enemy?"

"There is a possibility that you are not, considering you are only partially living. Let's not take any chances though, ok? Now remember, we only have two more ancient spells to cast, so let's use them wisely."

We made it to an opening and nearly walked into the middle of a large Mechid gathering. We jumped back and peeked around. The Mechids were fully armed. Some of them had what looked like large cannons attached to their shoulders. *Great, just what we needed; beefed up robots with beefed up weapons.* There was no clear way to get passed these Mechids.

"Hold on, I have an idea. Watch my back," Ectus whispered.

He vanished, which caused us to look around for him. We heard a loud, crashing Noise. it sounded like something large falling over, and all of the Mechids ran towards the sound, yelling "the living are among us! The living are among us!"

Ectus popped out of thin air next to us, nearly giving us a heart attack.

"Let's move," he said as he took the lead. I was a bit impressed in Ectus. He's grown so much since we met. He used to be quite the coward. Now he's coming up with ideas and taking the lead.

We headed across the opening, pressed up against the wall. There were dozens of electric eyes towards the next door followed by a couple 8-Bits and a dozen of Tech-Zs. The door was massive.

"That must be where they all are," Kursus said.

"Are you sure?" I asked.

"Yes, see how heavily guarded that door is? It's got to be," she said confidently. I walked out into the open and stood up straight and cracked my neck.

"Darkus, what are you doing?" Kursus asked frantically.

"Don't worry, I got this," I said to Kursus, then gave her a wink. She looked at me bitterly. Ok, so maybe that wasn't exactly me. I relaxed a bit and looked at her seriously.

"Don't worry, this is nothing. I've got you two behind me to watch my back, right? I trust you guys." I walked out towards the large mass of robotic defense.

"Hey, robo-scrap! Yeah, I'm talking to you!"

The Tech-Z's whirled around me as they glowed red with power. I put my hands in the air and spun on my heel, as I shooting a wave of energy throughout my hands. The Tech-Z's fell in pieces to the ground. The 8-Bits charged me. One jumped on my back and surprised me by digging its sharp saw into me. I reached back above my head. Grabbing it by the head, I threw it into a wall ahead of me and it shattered in pieces. I jumped on one of the 8-Bits and rode it as it tried to buck me off. I punched the side of its hard casing and its liquids poured out. It fell to the ground. The last two tried to charge me from both sides. I timed myself just right and ducked as they jumped, colliding with each other and covering me in glass in the process. I kicked one of them just for the hell of it and stood there with my arms cross, feeling a little cocky.

"Well, what are you two waiting for?" Kursus rolled her eyes and walked towards me. Ectus, on the other hand, had a large smile on his face.

"You sure are something else, Darkus." Ectus said, joining Kursus.

We blasted the door down and marched right in. There, in plain site was Dante and the Noctria, surrounded by Mechids. The Mechids lifted their arms and readied for fire.

"It can't be," Dante said, stepping back. The Noctria smiled.

"Well, well, if it isn't the infamous Darkus and his clan…I see your little friend recovered just fine from the GG3 I stuffed into her veins," the Noctria growled.

"You could say I'm more human than human," Kursus said as she pulled out Vengeance. I pulled out my pistol and pointed it directly at the Noctria's skull. I cocked it, nice and slow.

"You might as well give it up; we brought backup, not to mention we learned a few words of wisdom on our way here."

Dante looked at the Noctria in waiting but the Noctria smiled, keeping calm and stared at us in the most mischievous way I had ever seen. His goggles were tinted but I could almost see its eyes glowing behind the lens.

"How rude of me, I know your name but I have never given you the gift of knowing mine. I am Sadu; elder of the wise Noctria. Did I say elder? Oh, how silly of me. See, I'm not just the elder; I am the Crophix.

Yats lliw uoy dnuorg eht no,"
On the ground you will stay,"

Sadu said in Ancient Voice. Kursus and Ectus were thrown to the ground, unable to move. Sadu looked at me momentarily with a frown, and then smiled.

"Fascinating," he said. I reached out with my hand and spoke back to him in Ancient Voice.

"*Tuo edisni eht morf tsrub lliw hself ruoy*"
"Your flesh will burst from the inside out," I yelled.

But nothing happened. Sadu tilted his head back and laughed dramatically as his tongue stuck out. He looked back at me with a manic look in his eye.

"That was a very nice try monster, real cute. But there is one thing I think you personally will be fascinated to know. You see, there is only one thing throughout Remains that Ancient Voice doesn't work on, and that is a Crophix. Hmm, really? Don't you find that a little interesting, considering you are still standing?"

I stared at him blankly. *Can this be*? Was I...was I a *Crophix*? Sadu must have seen the light click in my head.

"Yes, you get it now? Ladies and gentlemen, Darkus is a Crophix, which is why he hoards such great power and which is why Ancient Voice doesn't work on him; how bizarre. You and I, monster, we are the only two Crophix throughout the land that can not only speak Ancient Voice, but don't seem so large. We are but the size of these insects," he pointed at my friends, and even Dante, whom looked a bit taken aback, the Philosopher's Stone glowing bright in his hands.

I looked down at Kursus, who looked up at me in shock. I looked over at Sadu and leered at him, "What are you getting at?" I asked. Sadu smiled.

"You and I...we could rule these lands, monster. Think about it! We could make these humanoids do whatever we please and there is nothing they could do to stop us." My fist clenched tight and I lifted my pistol once more.

"Sorry freak, not interested." Sadu's large ear to ear grin became a long frown.

"Look who's talking. So be it. I assume you're looking for this," He reached down to grab the empty flask and held it out in front of him.

"Oh, but what is this? It appears to be empty. Now where could it have gone?" I thought a moment.

"Oh, and Dante here has your stone. Good luck ripping it out of his hands. He's gotten a bit stronger ever since he obtained the thing. Weird, I know!" Sadu cackled. I ignored his sarcasm.

"Where is the elixir?" I demanded. He raised both his arms and tilted his head, "Not where, but *who*. You're looking right at it."

"No," Kursus muttered.

"That's right, I drank it all; every last drop. You see, I wanted to save the surprise for later but I just couldn't help myself. I'm confident that you won't live to tell a soul, considering you're in the middle of a death trap. I had to find the perfect place to hide it, and then I thought to myself; gee, what better place to hide it then in plain site! It was the perfect hiding place. If people saw the empty flask that held the elixir, I figured it would send them running in other directions; except you three. It turns out, you're much smarter than I had expected. *Sad face*; looks like I'm going to be around for a very long time! The only way to get what you want is to bleed me dry!" Sadu laughed in a craze. I began to pull the trigger but we were interrupted by the sound of gun fire coming from behind us. A shoot out broke loose as the Mechas joined our side, shooting down the Mechids. Dante and Sadu fled to a back room.

Kursus and Ectus regained their strength. They got up and joined my side. We looked over at the entrance and to our great surprise, there walking through the door firing at the Mechids and joining the Mechas side was Professor Milder. We looked at Milder with awe as he shot at the Mechids.

"Professor Milder!" Kursus yelled. He smiled and laughed as he shot at the Mechids, pushing them back.

"Go get Dante and that foul Noctria!" He beckoned. We continued to stare at him.

"*Go*! I will explain later, comrades. You must go now!" We began to run towards Dante and Sadu's escape route, still looking back at Professor Milder.

Dante and Sadu ran quickly up ahead, shooting at us from over their shoulders. Mechids stepped out from the suurounding walls and corridors to shoot at us, slowing us down. They began to flood the area.

"*erom on sdihcem!*"

"Mechids no more!" Ectus yelled.

Every Mechid in the immediate area evaporated into thin air. It made the run much easier and clear. We chased them around a corner, but once we got around it they were nowhere in site. We stood there for a moment, then caught site of a door closing.

"There!" I yelled and pointed. We ran towards the door, then through it. We heard the sound of a large engine starting up. It made a large zapping noise that sounded like it had some serious power behind it. We made it to the entrance. We found ourselves on top of the castle where they had entered a large, futuristic ship. It appeared to have duel turbo engines that seemed to move on their own. The ship was covered in those red veiny lights. It began to draw electrical power from the four towers that surrounded it, sending arcs all over the place. We began to run after it as it started to lift. I jumped up as high as I could and grabbed the bottom of the lift. Kursus and Ectus were almost too late, but Ectus picked up Kursus and she grabbed onto my ankle. Ectus flew above and pulled us up. Soon Robotica was out of site and we were flying over the Sea of Shame towards Lanteria. The ship gave off an electrical purge similar to Milder's pest control button. I absorbed the electrical flow but Ectus screamed in pain and was sent into the Sea of Shame.

"Ectus, no!" I yelled, reaching down towards him.

I had to move towards the inside of the ship. I couldn't think about Ectus for there was nothing we could do at the moment. My arm stayed out reached where he fell and I stared at where he had fell. Ectus had disappeared for the second time from an electrical zap. Only this time he didn't look too good as I saw him free fall into the depths of the Sea of Shame looking unconscious. I glanced at Kursus, who was full of dread; the wind blowing her hair in all sorts of directions.

"We need to dismantle the ship! Go inside and keep them from getting away! I'm going to rip this ship apart!"

"No, that's ridiculous! I'm not a Crophix like you. I won't survive something like that!" She yelled. She had a point. Her being on the ship kept me from sinking this thing into the Sea of Shame. I grabbed her hand and we climbed our way across the shell of the ship finding the latch of an entrance to the inside.

We jumped down and the first thing I felt was a kick to my jaw. I flew back and Kursus ran to help me up. Sadu stood there in a battle stance as he pulled out a large blade that had a cog spinning near the base of the blade, just above the handle.

"Clever monster; I didn't expect you to be quick enough to catch the ship," he said as he swung at me. I knocked the knife out of his hand and he reached for my neck, snapping it and throwing me to the ground. I fell hard. I reached up to my neck and snapped it back into place. I immediately kicked him in the groin. I saw Kursus grab the knife and run to the deck of the ship to find Dante. I grabbed Sadu by the neck and flipped him over me with my foot in his stomach. He hit the latch that opened the back lift, causing it to open up. He grabbed me and the first thing he tried to do was throw me out of the back. I countered his attempt and threw him towards the opening. He slid to his face and his head poked over the edge. I jumped on his back, burying my knee in his spine, and began to bash his head against the edge of the lift.

With great force, he pushed himself up and I flew back into a wall. I pulled out my pistol and shot a large ball of energy at him. He nearly missed it, ducking to the side. The energy ball tore out a chunk of the ship. He shook his finger at me.

"Ah, ah, you wouldn't want to send your precious humanoid into the abyss, now would you?" I threw my pistol at his face, breaking his nose. He held his face for a moment, then he looked up at me as blood dripped down his face. He licked his lips as the blood trickled down, showing me his sharp teeth, which had a coating of red on them then charged me. He threw me against the wall once again and began to strike me in the head with his elbow over and over. I put both my hands on his head and purged energy through my hands, filling his skull with energy. He hollered in pain as I blasted him, causing his face to distort as he fell to the ground. He lay there for a moment, and then slowly got back up. He looked at me through a broken skull and smiled. My pistol had slid back towards me. I picked it up and stuffed it in my holster.

"You're such a dirty fighter, monster. I can't wait to bleed you out."

He reached in his pocket and threw something at my face that held compressed steam. It burned my eyes and I yelled in pain as I put my hands on my searing skin. I couldn't open my eyes.

I braced myself for impact as he threw me up against the wall once more. He was quite predictable. Before he had thrown me up against the wall, yet another time, I had reached for the Screech Box in my pocket and let it rip. He yelled in pain. I heard his knees hit the steel ground. His yelling was below my waist. I took my long fingernails and drove them straight into his eye sockets and heard him stop screaming. I felt warm liquid run down my hands. I took my other hand off of my face and reached down to firmly grab his head and with all my might, I tore his head right off of his shoulders. I heard splattering on the floor as blood began to drain out of his head. As I slowly regained my sight, I reached down to get his flask.

I drained every last bit of his blood into the flask, then dragged his body to the edge of the lift. I kicked his head and his body off of the ship. I watched his body hit the water at high speed, skimming across the top of the water as his arms flailed like a dead weight and his head spun from the impact and began to float.

"Not if I bleed you out first," I said as I was looking down.

The ship started to list and I slid out and grabbed its edge, nearly joining the newly deceased Sadu. I lifted myself up with all of my might, got to my feet and headed to the deck. The ship was rolling out of control, sending me to the roof and back down, knocking the wind out of me. I had to see what was going on up there.

I made it to the ship's large pilot house. I saw Kursus being thrown around like a sack of flesh as Dante threw her around with one arm. I could see the Philosopher's Stone glowing bright green, held tightly in his other. The site of him throwing her around only made me raged. I could feel the black energy trying to force its way down my arms, but if I could sneak up behind him and take it from him; it might work. *Hang in there, Kursus.* The ship ventured forth and through its large windows in the front I could see us flying over Omitis, then Lanteria.

Dante kicked Kursus once more as she lay there clenching up in pain.

"This stone; what powers it holds! I thank you and your little bundle of joy going out of your way to obtain it for us," Dante hissed through his teeth as he kicked Kursus again. "You see, originally we were just going to come over to Robotica and follow our plan. After meeting with the Elders about the rumors of Darkus collecting the Philosopher's Stone, Sadu and I became business partners. We both agreed that it was time that Remains had a ruler. But we would need help from a powerful source. We gave the Mechids the chance to make up for their cruel, selfish behavior by taking their frustration out on the natives that suffocated us in Remains. They all stick to their stupid ancient ways of living." Dante kicked her once more.

I walked around the edge of the wall, slowly, staying out of his sight. Kursus looked up in agony; face bleeding. She saw me. Her eyes grew wide and I gesture to her to stay silent.

"I don't mind telling you the plans since you're going to die! After the Mechids killed off those stupid, naïve, unintelligent cultures, the only ones that would be left is us! But of course, we'd have our plan underway to terminate the Mechids the moment they moved onto us. They agreed to take their aggression out on the weak, see. So, we helped them build a large, robotic Meenrale to push the island over here without making a sound and a surprise attack on the land of Remains. The plan was going fine until you bumbling fools spotted us. But you were far too late, for this will all take place in only hours, and you will be far too dead to warn a soul."

Dante lifted up Kursus and threw her across the room. She hit the wall with a thud and fell to the ground. She reached out shaking.

"Stop," she said faintly.

Dante laughed, "or else what? You're going to cast some ancient voodoo on me? I'm allowing you to live. Well, at least long enough to know the truth then you will die with those last words! You and your ignorant monsters brought the ancient artifacts right into our hands, speeding up the process. With the stone and the elixir, we were able to gain the strength we needed to build a mighty Meenrale and to keep you little piles of filth at bay."

I reached down to pick up the knife Kursus had dropped, as he continued. He walked up to Kursus and looked down at her. He reached down and picked her up, holding her above him.

"Thank you so much for these extravagant gifts. I feel terrible since we didn't bring you anything. Your tribe and the others couldn't have had what was coming to them if it wasn't for you and the rest of Tinkarius's stupid little bags of flesh." Dante began to laugh, throwing Kursus once more. He walked up to her and pressed his foot on her neck, as he lifted the stone high above his head.

"With this stone and the elixir, we can have whatever we desire! And there is nothing you and your little monster can do about it, anymore!"

With the knife firmly in hand, I lunged forward, slicing it straight through the hand that held the stone. His hand fell, clean off, still clenching the stone. He began to scream in pain, holding his arm as it gushed out blood. Kursus reached down and picked up the hand, the stone still in its grasp. Kursus removed it, now holding it in hers. She stood up quickly, cracked her neck, then walked up to Dante, whom was still on his knees. He continued to scream at the sight of his missing hand. She reached down and grabbed him. She lifted him up high and began to throw him all over the room. When she got her fill, she pressed his face hard up against the glass, forcing him to look out at the lands that we had flown over.

"You see that? That is mine; *my* land, not yours. Take a good look at it, you pathetic humanoid, because it's the very last you will ever see it," she said through clenched teeth.

She continued to press his face against the glass until it began to crack, and finally shattered. She threw him out of the cockpit. He fell behind and got sucked into one of the turbo engines, shooting his blood and parts everywhere. The ship began to shake and sink to the side and we began heading straight for the surface. Kursus held the stone tightly in her hand, sat down in a seat that controlled the steering and put a safety strap across her. I did the same.

"Do you know how to fly this thing?"

"Nope," she answered. *Great*, I thought.

She grabbed the wheel tightly and tried her best to level the ship out. We gained speed and Lanterian soil became closer and closer through the glass. We held on tightly and embraced ourselves for impact.

**CHAPTER XI
THE WISH**

We hit the surface hard, our nails digging deep into the arm rests. Kursus and I got whiplash from the force of the impact. The ships nose dug into the surface, causing us to flip a few times. We skid a good half a mile across the Lanterian soil towards Muckraid on the ship's side. We held on tight as the ship slowly came to a halt. Smoke filled the inside. We unlatched our safety straps and climbed towards the exit. We exited out into fresh air. Smoke poured out from open areas of the ship; the glass towards the front and the exit, as well as the back lift that was still open. The engines were totaled and on fire. We climbed down the ship and walked out into the Lanterian land. We walked about fifty feet away from the ship, and just in time too. The ship exploded behind us, causing a huge mushroom cloud high above.

"Lurt!" I called out as loud as I could. There was nothing for a moment, so I continued to yell, "Lurt! Listen to me; this is not about us. Robotica is heading this way."

There was a moment more of silence, and then I heard something uprooting about ten feet ahead of me. Lurt came crawling out of the ground, stood up, dusting himself off and making sure there was a good distance between us.

"What did you just say?" he croaked.
"You heard me," I said, walking towards him.

He took a few steps back and realized I was coming at him and began to try digging his way back down.

"Oh, no you don't," I said, pulling him back out by his stem and lifting him high into the air.

"Please, don't hurt me," he begged. I gave him a good punch in the face. It felt so good.

"Oh, now *why* would I do that?" I answered sarcastically. He took a deep breath and sighed.

"Please let me down," he asked.

"Not until you answer the question," I demanded, "then you can go crawl back into your hole of shame."

"Ok, alright. I bargained with the elder of Omitis to take the stone from you. In exchange, I gave him a humanoid from Muckraid." he said, then swallowed and continued, "Word spread quickly about you obtaining it. I was going to just get my hands on it to gain the power I needed but he took matters into his own hands, apparently. He didn't show up at our meeting spot so I assumed he took off with it. I know what happens when you have both the elixir and the stone…but apparently he did not."

"You sack of rotten tomatoes!" Kursus hollered, reaching for Lurt. I held my arm out to keep her from ripping him to shreds.

"Well say, thanks for all that trouble partner," I said sarcastically, "Now you've really done it. We just came back from Robotica. Nice place by the way, if you take away all of the raged Mechids. Oh, and just a heads up; they built a robotic Meenrale that is shoving the island this way, as we speak. Dante and Sadu made a deal with the Mechids that if they helped them get to shore they could kill us all in revenge and take over. They had plans to sit back and sip on a glass of the Dose while this all went down, and when the Mechids went for them next, they were going to destroy the Mechids, once and for all. Give me one good reason why I shouldn't squish your stupid little head," I hissed through my gritted teeth, bringing his face closer to mine. I could feel the warmth of the flame from his skull.

I could see that Lurt felt ashamed and responsible.

"Please, let me down. I won't leave, you have my word. I may be out matched, but I am not one to leave my mess for others to clean; unlike *some* people," he finished bitterly. I slowly put him down and he straightened his robes and began to pace slowly towards the opposite way with his hands behind his back.

"What have I done?" Lurt said quietly, bowing his head. "We have gone against everything in the Book of Law to protect our tribes. You were created and gave us all a scare so we acted out of our ways. It was then we started having severe problems. We have broken the word of law to recover peace and now we will all suffer for it. Chaos will reign upon us and flush us out. It's too late to stop what we have started. The gears of our future are already in motion. If you haven't been created in the first place, this would have never happened."

"Don't go blaming others for your mistakes. It was your idea to trust a Noctria," Kursus said coldly. He turned his head towards Kursus and scowled at her.

"I was desperate. Our Crophix, Bombadicus was unstoppable until Darkus entered Remains. You don't know what it's like to be that vulnerable. We are a tribe without magic or technology. You should know how it feels, considering you broke the rules of your tribe. Sometimes it's not enough." Lurt continued.

"You actually believe that scribble? *'Beings who write the future'* do not exist. There were all kinds of trouble before Darkus had come into the picture. You're all just desperate and pathetic. We could all burn away the books now and call it good if we wanted to. We could combine our practices to create a superb world," Kursus retaliated.

"How *dare* you speak such filth in the presence of an elder? You cursed us all when you chose to veer from the path. If there were no rogues to begin with there wouldn't even be a concern for war. If you had followed your path and obeyed, our tribe may still have a Crophix." Lurt yelled.

"Yeah, we feel for you and all that but we've got bigger problems here. Robotica is coming straight at us. What do you intend to do, you sobbing vegetable?" I spat. Lurt looked over at me and glared, then took off his pendent that held the aura flame.

"The only thing we can do; call a meeting of the Elders. You may want to disappear; the others won't be happy to see you here."

"Unlike you, I don't hide in fear. This is a matter far more important than a little grudge. Now hurry it up and bring the elders."

He gave me one last glare and crushed the pendent in his hand.

"As you wish," he said.

The blue flame engulfed Lurt's hand and he threw the flame high up into the air. The aura flame stopped high in the sky and began to grow large in size, acting as a beacon. Once it grew as large as it desired, multiple little aura flames dispersed from the large one and went their separate ways, out towards different parts of the land. The large flame continued to sit high in the sky. The Lanterians began to rise from the soil, not looking too happy to see me. They started to move in on me and Lurt put his hand out.

"Now is not the time, brethren. There are much more important matters in the works. I've called for the Elders to meet here. It appears I've made a terrible mistake. Robotica is hurtling towards us at high speed, as we speak. We must gather together and discuss what we must do; together as a whole."

Lurt then turned to me.

"The only reason we are having this conversation is because my tribe depends on it."

"Yeah, well you are welcome. I could have just been the cold-hearted monster that I am and just walked away and watched them destroy you and your people," I joked.

"Why *did* you tell us, monster?" Lurt asked.

"Because I'm not as evil as you think I am. I'm trying to survive, just as much as you are," I answered. Lurt looked at me oddly. I could tell he had something else on his mind.

"We must wait here for the Elders to visit us. I would like nothing more than for you to leave my land, but in dire times like this I must ask you a question. A question I dare never to ask you in any other situation; will you stand by and aid us?"

"Well, I guess," I answered, "Just a second ago you were trying to get me to leave, but don't get too cozy. The moment one of you decided to fire at me, I'll turn you to ash, is that clear?"

After waiting quite a while, I saw elders from every corner hone in on us. Some of them could already see me and I heard complaints and yelling of anger. I stood my ground and was ready for anything, as did Kursus. I saw her father coming from Muckraid, Zint was coming from the skies in a gravi-tone from Redemption Tower, as well as a Noctria at full speed, Rip Van Lorenzo walked from Cemetrica, and even the Mirror elders hovered slowly behind him. Ladidya from the Ectos tribe came out of the ground only inches near us, as well as a new creature I haven't yet seen. He looked like a large beast human hybrid. It must be the Moon Walker I heard about. Webra, the spider hybrid, walked side by side with Rip. I could see her and Rip arguing over something. Lastly, there was a larger Glirbette that waddled towards us, behind Sulfus. It had a long, gray beard that hid under a large wooden mask. The

Glirbette's mask had a scary face carved and painted into it. It held a cane and had a large belly.

They all gathered to the circle as each one of them glared at me, Zint even tried to rush at me, but Lurt stopped him.

"What in the *hell* is that monster doing here?" Zint yelled.

"What is the meaning of this, Lurt? This monster has done nothing but spread fear and terror, not to mention the large amounts of destruction he left in his wake throughout these lands. He is enemy number one! Are we all here to destroy him?" Ladidya yelled.

"Good luck with that," I said, with my arms crossed. They began to argue and reach for me and Kursus. Sulfus, Kursus's father, stood there glaring at Kursus.

"Enough! As much as I would love for all of us to rip him limb from limb, believe it or not there are more tragic events to undergo. Darkus, creation of the one we despise the most, has just informed me about some terrible news," He stopped at the site of Rip, and the others followed his eyes. They all looked at him in awe, and then began to glare at him.

"Hello fiends, remember me?" Rip gloated, bowing down. The beast man snarled.

"How did you get out of your imprisonment, traitor?" He yelled. Rip gestured towards Kursus and I.

"I had a little help from my friends," Rip said with a smile, then looked at Webra and frowned. "I cannot believe you left your brethrens for these creatures. You should be ashamed. They abandoned you for being a hybrid," he said towards Webra.

"I decided that I wanted to be on the good guy's team. Such evil foul friends you keep for company, Rip. I did what I had to do," she answered simply. *Evil side*? The way I see it *we* were the good guys. The creatures glared at us.

"Obviously Tinkarius's creation is causing quite a problem. He must be stopped. He is only unraveling what we've tied down," Zint beckoned.

"You do realize that I am standing right here?" I hissed bitterly.

"In time, it is true that he has done nothing but stir up our way of living, but we must first deal with a new matter. As we speak, Robotica is hurtling towards us at great speeds."

The Elders gasped, and of course the first thing they did was began to blame me.

"How can we know he's telling the truth?" the unknown beast hollered.

"Is this his doing?" Zint demanded. Lurt looked over at Zint and frowned, "Unfortunately, this was something that was triggered with the help of Dante, Zint; as well as Sadu of Omitis."

The Noctria became appalled and began to yell in a language I couldn't understand.

"This is an outrage! Our elder would never do such harm no matter how important it is for us to bury the rest of you ancient fiends," Zint argued.

"Now wait just a minute," Sulfus yelled back.

"Enough!" Lurt yelled over the two, "this is my doing. I hired Sadu to steal the Philosopher's Stone from Darkus," the elders looked at Kursus and I with shock.

"That creation of Tinkarius obtained the stone? How can this be?" Sulfus said.

"Because I helped him get it," Kursus answered, glaring at her father.

"So, did I," Rip answered. Sulfus slammed his rod into the ground and pointed at Kursus and said through clenched teeth,

"I should have killed you long ago, you pathetic excuse for a Flintkus."

"Well that's just fine father, but you didn't and now I've joined sides with Darkus and Tinkarius, so you all keep that in mind after we get this situation taken care of. Darkus isn't just a monster; he is a Crophix."

The others gasped once again. I looked up at them and smiled, as Lurt continued his explanation.

"But that doesn't matter. We followed Dante and Sadu to Robotica where they made plans with the Mechids to come and strike terror on all of you while they sat back and waited for it to happen. I know this because Kursus and I killed both Dante and Sadu for doing what they did. If any of you would like to set me straight, please do."

"So, the Steinlocks and the Noctria are working together to rule the lands, huh? I will keep that in mind," Ladidya said, crossing her arms and looking at Zint and the Noctria.

"It was about time our Elder took the risk to conquer you all," Zint yelled, putting his fist in the air. "We all knew that he was going to make plans to do so, we just didn't know he was going to kill us off as well. What a traitor."

"Yes, poor you and all that," the beast hybrid spat, "regardless of our beliefs and our dislikes for one another, we can all agree that this is something that needs to be done. We must stop the island of Robotica from getting here. After that we will continue to hunt this wicked creation of Tinkarius and his friends," the beast said, looking at me, as he snarled his teeth. The Glirbette Elder finally stepped in and held his hand up; he was much shorter than the others.

"You all are such violent, vengeful creatures. The Glirbettes have to suffer because of your acts to destroy one another. Why not work together rather than tear each other apart?"

"Well, why do you think we're all here?" Ladidya spoke, "You just don't realize what is standing in front of you; Darkus here is a weapon of destruction. He is the reason for most of the troubles that have been caused lately."

"I was created originally for the better of the living. I was then created to fight by Tinkarius's side because you banned him. And to make matters worse, you put a hit on him because he was unique and different." I shouted.

"It doesn't matter what you think. In the end we will have to terminate you in order to keep our tribes safe," Ladidya finished. An answer of a creature full of ignorance, I thought to myself.

"Good luck with that," Rip said, putting his hand on my shoulder. The others glared at Rip.

"So, Rip has joined Tinkarius' side as well. Is anyone else taking the side of this foul creation?" Lurt boomed. No one else said anything. Lurt looked over at Rip and shook his head, "what has changed you so?" Lurt asked.

"You all are selfish creatures, full of false pride. You push your beliefs onto others and oh, I don't know, casted me away to an imprisonment in another dimension. So, go ahead, plan away. When Robotica is taken care of, I will continue to aid Darkus in his quest," Rip spoke proudly.

"Then you will be taken care of as well, with Darkus and Tinkarius, once we find him," Lurt countered.

"So be it," Rip answered back.

"So, what are we to do?" The Glirbette Elder spoke. Lurt's face became full of horror as his eyes caught a glimpse of something from out in the distance. He walked slowly through the circle and stared. The Island of Robotica was already close to shore.

"It's too late to discuss that, Robotica is already here."

The others gasped as they caught site of the massive island heading their way. We stared at it as its size grew larger and larger.

"Sound the alarm and bring what forces you all have left. We're going to need whatever we can get. Someone alert those Psychozoans as well," Lurt spoke.

Zint put his gravi-tone in full throttle and went soaring through the skies towards Redemption Tower, leaving us in a cloud of smoke. Ectos called for the spirits. They immediately rose from the ground, as well as the Voids. Lurt struck the ground with his staff and the rest of the Lanterians dug their way out from below the surface. Sulfus stood there, ready for battle, as well as the beast hybrid.

"I will risk the humans no more," Sulfus said, "They will not join us in battle."

"Except me," Kursus said, looking at her father. He glared back, and then slightly nodded his head.

In what only seemed like moments, we were surrounded by thousands of creatures, ready for battle! It was a bit uncomfortable being surrounded by everyone who hated you, but I knew I was safe because they knew I could do a number on the Mechids. But I had to watch my back the moment they were destroyed; I'm next in line. The main reason I was helping them was because, honestly, I didn't want the Mechids to take over Remains; regardless of my dislike for most of these creatures. This is also my land as well and I am going to defend it, at all cost!

The sound of a small stampede grew behind us. The Psychozoans came running at full speed, with weapons drawn and an overwhelming display of war paint. They hollered and laughed hysterically as they drew near. Everyone stood back in defense just to make sure they weren't coming right at us, but they joined the lot and hollered. They would get close and push the Elders but the Elders would shove them off and get angry as the Psychozoans laughed. In the skies, I could see Steinlocks by the dozens flying down in their flying devices. They moved in battle formation. There were two ships similar to the one I took down with Dante and Sadu, that landed in the distance. The abbreviations "11-F13" was read on its side. I could see Steinlocks unloading quite a few Monstruts in well-organized chains, as well as 8-Bits and Tech-Z's that swarmed quickly out of the ships. The beasts that were called Moon Walkers ran on all fours up to the battle field. Once they were in position, they stood up on two feet and howled angrily at the sky.

We soon became large in numbers with all kinds of creatures side by side ready to fight, together. It was an odd feeling; every single one of them made it a point to look at me with complete disgust. I had noticed that no one had said anything about summoning their Crophix's, but I figured I was good enough. Perhaps they weren't ready for the ultimate last resort quite yet.

As a large group, we began to run towards the Sea of Shame where Robotica was only yards away from striking the surface. Kursus and I had moved towards the front, ignoring the possibility of being stabbed to death by the hundreds of haters directly behind us. I put my hands down and they began to glow. I got ready for whatever was coming for us. The island struck the surface and made a large booming sound that rattled the lands. It grew silent as we all waited. We heard a loud screech that came from under water. Suddenly, large robotic tentacles came shooting out of the water and opened up their large red eyes. There were about eight of them and they all began to glow.

"They are going to shoot lasers!" I shouted. Everyone jumped out of the way as quickly as they could as eight large lasers were shot out from the tentacles. I looked back in horror as a good number of our fighters were turned to melting ash. At that very moment, I knew what my goal had to be. I had to get that robotic

Meenrale taken care of. I began to run towards the massive island that had touched base with our lands. The metal plant life that surrounded the island began to spill out what looked like hundreds of Mechids.

The large tentacles began to hit the ground and swat at us like we were flies as the Mechids ran at full speed shooting lasers and ripping through the living. I searched for Kursus for I had lost sight of her, but I found her eventually in the mess of things. She was taking care of herself off in the distance, blasting away at the cores of the Mechids. I looked up at the tentacles and decided that perhaps it would be a lot easier to get to the Meenrale's body if some of the tentacles were destroyed. I ran towards one of the tentacles as it towered high into the sky. I saw the one I was focused on looking down at me. It quickly threw itself down at me as I jumped, just right, and it barely missed. I jumped back and grabbed a hold of the tentacle and began to pull, trying to rip it out of the sea, but it lifted up with incredible strength. I began to ride it as it threw itself around, trying to toss me off. I took my pistol and shoved the barrel right into its large red eye and shot a large ball of energy directly into it. The eye shattered and the large robotic Meenrale screeched in agony. The tentacle was sucked back into the water. I jumped off just in time, nearly going down with it.

I hit the ground, rolled, and quickly got back on my feet. One tentacle down, I thought proudly. The Lanterians brought out their large catapults. They hurtled large Lanterian heads full of fire at the Mechids; they weren't able to get too close, they were better at long range attacks. The impact of their weapons knocked the Mechids over, but the fire didn't do the least bit of damage for their outer shells were incredibly resistant. I then watched as Sulfus's eyes glow bright red, like in the forest. His jaw dropped low as he began to scream. He shot a massive ball of fire out of his rod that pushed the Mechids far back, hurtling some of them to their doom as they were thrown into the Sea of Shame. They buzzed and crackled as they choked their last breath. That's when I realized that perhaps we should all work on trying to push them into the water.

"Push them into the sea!" I yelled. To my surprise everyone listened and changed their tactics. They began using their forces to send them into the abyss. Rip casted a large spell towards the sky, opening a portal of some sort. Large, ghostly tentacles came shooting out down towards the Mechids, like black lightning. It began to push them over the edge of the shore; falling endlessly into the abyss.

The Steinlocks flew over the Mechids in unison, shooting down a wall of laser attacks that pushed the Mechids back. This was followed by the Monstruts running full charge across the lands, taking a surprising amount of damage from the Mechids firepower and using their forces as a wall to push them into the waters. The 8-Bits and the Tech-Zs continued to attack and join fire power with the

Steinlocks. Some of the Mechids succeeded at bringing down a few of the Steinlocks, as well as the Tech-Zs. At that moment, the Mechid's more advanced 8-Bits and Tech-Zs came swarming out of the island, focusing their attack on the Steinlock's 8-Bits and Tech-Zs. A majority of our damage was in the Voids and the Monstruts, which was the sole purpose of their existence; meat shields. A majority of the Lanterians took a heavy number as well. The Ectos used a constant technique of pushing Mechids with energy bursts and throwing themselves into the Mechids. Ladidya succeeded in a possession or two; taking control of one of the larger ones and shooting his comrades until the others caught on and fired down the rebel Mechid.

The blasts from the tentacles were constant and horrendous. I continued my attempt at bringing them down. I heard a whistle, followed by a hollering that I had recognized. Our Mecha comrades, as well as Professor Milder, came running out of the metal shrubbery on Robotica. They began to fire from behind, knocking down quite a few of the Mechids in a surprise attack. Drill-Bit and Triumphus came running out, side by side, mauling down a cluster of the Mechids.

"Did you miss us?" Triumphus yelled as he shot large rounds of energy out of his arm cannon. When a Mechid got too close, he would use his large clamp hand to grab them and squeeze them until their core gave out. The Mechas were all lined with the red, veiny coloring on their outer shell caused by the Dose. Professor Milder came out guns blazing, full of the Dose. He had a large plate of armored exterior all around him that took in the Dose. I hollered at them in excitement and Drill-Bit and Triumphus came running after me, nearly getting struck by the tentacles, dodging and destroying Mechids.

"What is your plan of attack, Darkus?" Triumphus yelled over the war that sounded like advance technology versus ancient magic.

"I'm taking the tentacles down. They are the main cause of the destruction! If I can take most of them down, I can take care of the rest! I'm going to need the Philosopher's stone to power me up. My mission is to lure the Meenrale out of the water and onto our turf. That way we can all fire at it, but right now there are way too many Mechids!"

"Not to worry! I will continue to locate the power supply. If we shut it down, everything will stop functioning, including the Meenrale!" Triumphus yelled. "Drill-Bit will aid you at taking down the tentacles in order to slow it down. We will rendezvous here sooner than you think!" Triumphus yelled. He pounded sides with Drill-Bit and ran back onto the island of Robotica. Drill-Bit jumped higher than I ever could, and grabbed one of the other, bringing and brought it down to the ground with him and stuck his drill into the eye. The tentacle whipped around and dissapeared back into the sea.

Only six more, but I wasn't going to take them all down. I just needed the front tentacles to be destroyed so I could plan my next attack. I wanted to take two more down.

I told Drill-Bit the plan and he ran for the other as I tried to tackle the tentacle on the left. With ease, I saw Drill-Bit repeat his method to destroy the last tentacle. He jumped up and brought the tentacle down and continued to drill into its eye. I had to wait for the tentacle to swing at me, and then grab. Once I have it, I'll wrestle it until I can shoot its eye out. That task will be much harder for me than it is for Drill-Bit. The tentacle looked down at me and began to glow. It shot a large laser down at me and I dodged it as it burned deep into the ground, but then it took a few bullets from a near Mechid to the back. I reached out and stuck my arm through its core and ripped it out. To my surprise, the Dose filled one whole side of my body with its red, veiny Dose coloring. I couldn't believe it. Kursus had been wrong about it not being used for my purpose. It made sense. I'm more mechanical than humanoid. It reacted to my system like any other mechanical or robotic structure. I held the core in my hand and looked up at the tentacle and smiled. *Come on, swing at me*, I thought to myself.

The tentacle whipped back and swung down at me. I grabbed it and instantly felt a high level of power that I didn't have before surge through me. I pulled with one arm as hard as I could. The sound of metal tearing from its base was clearly heard, and soon enough I had ripped the tentacle clean off and threw it towards the tall towers of Robotica. The robotic Meenrale screeched as it withdrew the rest of its tentacles.

"Great going!" Kursus yelled, as she ran towards me. "I need the stone," I said quickly. Kursus reached into her robes and handed me the glowing, green stone. Her eyes caught the red glowing veiny side of my body.

"Is that the Dose?" She asked in shock, "Oh my, it appears that I had been wrong! But in my defense, it doesn't seem like its taking its full affect on you. What a remarkable discovery," she finished.

I felt no different, but I knew I had supreme power. The mix of my Crophix strength with the stone, along with the Dose was plenty to send this Meenrale out of the waters.

"I'm going to bring the Meenrale out of the water!" I yelled at Kursus.

"You're going to *what*?" She yelled back in shock.

"If I bring the Meenrale to land, it's more vulnerable for attack. We have to destroy it," I answered loudly over the sound of war and battle.

She looked at me with disapproval, but reached up and kissed me on the lips once more. She then let go and patted me on my chest.

"Take care of yourself, Darkus!" She shouted. She turned around and blasted away at the Mechids. I smiled, then turned towards Robotica. The Meenrale screeched and hollered as if it was calling me out.

"Don't get your scrap metal in a bunch," I said to myself as I began to run towards the shore.

I dived into the depths of the sea and swam. My eyes began to glow once more. The light glowing from the stone and the Dose's power helped me to see as I darted through the grimy waters. I was a creature of glowing reds, purples, and green that lit up the thick abyss. Every mechanical bone in my body felt the chill and fear of reliving my fight with the previous Meenrale. This robotic one was fierce and quite destructive.

I searched for its face or its mouth and came to a halt when I swam right in front of the eye, like before. But unlike before, this eye was large and red, and without a pupil. It began to glow bright as its mouth opened wide to expose what looked like a large whirlpool of jagged razor teeth. It began to inhale, trying to suck me in! I could hear the roar of a large engine from inside of its mouth, along with several other large mechanical sounds. I have got to bring it to the surface of the sea floor. I swam fast towards the sea floor and it followed with speed I didn't comprehend. I hit the ground and looked up as its massive body swam towards me, face first and mouth open wide. Its eye was glowing hot. I timed it just right and stuck my fist out, punching it as hard as I could with the stone held tight in my fist. With greater force than I had expected, the Meenrale went hurtling up with tremendous velocity and out of the water which caused a large flash to be expelled from our impact. I quickly swam to the top of the surface just in time to watch the robotic Meenrale hit Lanterian soil with a large thud, causing both creature and Mechids to be sent flying from the impact.

I jumped out of the water and stood there looking at what was now left of the Meenrale body. I held the Philosopher's Stone in one hand, and the Dose core in the other. Its body was the size of a massive water drop; its remaining tentacles flailed around violently as it tried to use them to pick itself up. Unfortunately for the Meenrale, it was on its back completely stuck and helpless.

"Fire at the Meenrale!" I shouted.

Immediately upon my command, every creature of the land began to fire at the Meenrale, but then stopped. To our surprise, all of the firepower ricocheted off of its polished surface. The Mechids had made it resistant to most powers. All was silent, except for the loud flailing and screeching of the Meenrale. I was running out of ideas until I heard a loud noise. It sounded like something huge was being shut off.

"Everyone, look at Robotica!" Rip yelled.

We all looked up at the large island and witnessed its glowing colors begin to flicker and turn off. I looked over at the robotic Meenrale. It suddenly began to fight for its life as it began to shut down. It squirmed and screeched, then slowly died down until it moved no more. The Mechids also began to power down and fall to their sides, blipping off and buzzing. To surprise me even more, the core I held in my hand from the Mechid died and the veiny colors in my arms, as well as the ones in the Mechas, dimmed down and faded. We watched in victory as the Mechids fell in large numbers. We all began to cheer and jump for joy. Triumphus must have found the power supply! I looked up in the sky to witness the Steinlock's gravi-tone veins begin to fade as they started to hurtle downward towards the ground. Most of them jumped out while others fell to their death. The Tech-Zs and the 8-Bits fell and powered off. Just as I had thought, Triumphus ran out of the metal plant life of Robotic with his arms high in the air.

"She's going to blow!" He screamed. He ran and jumped to his face and covered his head. I ran towards the Meenrale and got under its massive weight and began to lift. I screamed and hollered lifting the massive metal robot over my head as the others looked at me in awe. I slowly turned towards Robotica and with great power I threw the robotic Meenrale towards the towering buildings with its tentacles flailing behind it, hitting with great power and crashing through the large towers, causing a loud thud that was felt throughout the lands.

Just as I did, the island exploded, sending us all flying backwards as its destruction grew larger. A large cloud of smoke shot up through the air and the island began to sink. We all rose slowly to our feet and began to cheer and jump in victory as we watched Robotica sink to its doom. We watched and hollered, pumping our fists in the air until the island was no more. Kursus ran to me and embraced me, as well as Rip, Professor Milder, and the Mecha clan. The other creatures regrouped and began to walk towards us. For a moment, I thought perhaps they were going to thank us for our help, but I was sadly mistaken. They all stared quietly, glaring at us as hundreds of creatures circled us.

"Aren't you going to thank us?" I said out loud.

"Professor Milder, what a pleasant surprise," Lurt said, ignoring me completely.

"I thought you were killed and murdered by the hands of our kind," the Noctria panted.

"That's what I wanted you to think so I could lay in hiding long enough to rebuild my empire and help Tinkarius in his quest. You're welcome by the way," he said.

"Well that was mighty kind of you, but now that the threat has been taken care of, we have to move our matters to the next; which is destroying the next largest threat; *you*." The creatures and humanoids lifted their weapons and began to charge them.

"But we helped you all survive!" Kursus yelled in anger.

"We only used your powers to succeed in our mission; now we must rid of you. Welcome to war," Sulfus said, "*daughter*." She looked at them in horror as they charged their weapons and energy. Rip jumped in front of us and stuck his hands high in the air, screaming a spell in Ancient Voice. We were instantly engulfed in a large protective sphere of some sort.

"Not yet, we're not," he yelled, and in a blink of an eye we were gone, completely.

I watched as Lanteria transformed into Cemetrica right in front of us. The creatures vanished and we were suddenly inside of Rip's crypt. Kursus and I blinked, taking a moment to allow our minds to comprehend where we were. We looked back at Rip, who had his arms crossed behind him. He turned with his head low and walked towards the window, and sighed.

"I admit I knew they would turn on us," he spoke, "but it was for the greater good to stop those Mechids. What horror they had brought, and that metallic Meenrale." Rip turned to us and smiled slightly, "what fortune we were all in for. You heading towards Robotica for your personal needs. If you hadn't set out to do so, who knows what terror they would have brought among us. With that I, personally thank you both," He said firmly. He walked up to me and Kursus and put his hands on our shoulders.

"I'm so sorry about your friend, Ectus. Being a spirit, there is a possibility he's out there somewhere. But if he was charged with an electric force such as the one those 11-F13 ships create, there is a chance he is not." He took his hands off of us and walked towards the front door.

"Where are the others?" Kursus asked softly.

"I teleported them to where they slumber. They are all fine. We must lie in hiding for a while to let things cool down. The good news is you finally have what you've been searching for. You have both the Philosopher's Stone and the Elixir of Life! With those, you will finally be able to find our Professor Tinkarius. How exciting," Rip slightly raised his spirits. Kursus and I looked at each other and smiled. I had almost forgotten about that. I reached down to grab the flask and the stone and held them both in my hands. I felt so relieved to have them both, finally, that I totally let the betrayal of the other cultures roll down my back.

"Well, what are you waiting for?" Kursus asked. I reached for the stone in my pocket once more and held it tightly in my hands. I then reached for the flask of the elixir with my other hand. I popped open the lid and smelled the rancid smell of the Noctria's blood.

"Oh my, what is that?" Rip asked bitterly.

"It's mixed with Noctria blood. Sadu hid the elixir in his system. He felt that hiding it in plain site was genius. Obviously, he was way over his head, so I bled him out and took it back. Fortunately, Kursus, nor I, are pure so we won't be affected by the nasty side effects," I explained, holding the elixir up and glancing into the thick, reddish coloring it held inside. I sniffed the lid once more, giving it a look of disapproval and began to lift it to my lips, but Kursus stopped me.

"Wait," she pleaded, "If you don't mind, I'd like to have some." Rip looked appalled, "my dear, why would you ever want to live forever? You could live a full life, and rest in piece from old age. Large responsibilities will come with such a choice. You will grow tired and possibly even insane. Surely you've at least thought about it."

"I've been thinking about it since I met Darkus. Honestly, someone is going to have to take care of him," she said, smiling at me. My heart swelled and I felt a bit warm, not to mention a bit in shock.

"You…you're willing to risk your mortality for me?" I asked.

"I'd love nothing more than to be by your side, forever," she said, her smile getting a bit wider.

"I hate to impose, but those are all of the wrong reasons for wanting to be immortal," Rip added, sticking his long boney finger up.

"Its quite alright, there are other more selfish reasons to be immortal, that's just one of them," Kursus said. She took the flask from me and without hesitation she swallowed a bit of the elixir. She swallowed hard and her eyes shut tight; it was obvious that it wasn't pleasant. Her skin began to bubble and crack from the Noctria blood, but then slowly vanished. Her head lifted up high and light shot through her eyes and mouth, and just like that she was back to herself, looking at us in shock.

"Owe," she said in monotone.

"How do you feel?" Rip asked.

"The same honestly," she answered back, almost disappointed by the less dramatic change she had expected.

"Well, you won't feel that way much longer. Forever more, you will stay as you are." She looked down to observe her body, then looked up and smiled.

"I'm ok with that," she replied.

Kursus handed me the flask and I hesitated for a moment, drinking in the moment. At last, I am able to find my Creator. I waited for a moment, thinking about what exactly it was that I wanted. He sure would be surprised to find out that I was clever enough to find him. I wanted to know how he made me, and his side of the story. It was almost like wanting to ask a father questions that I wanted to hear just from him. I wanted to ask him how he's been so tricky and if he would allow me to fight by his side. I must have been obviously thinking about such things because Kursus commented on my smile.

"It's a lot to think about, isn't it?" Kursus said, "You probably don't even know what to ask him or what to say."

I could have sworn she was reading my mind again. I looked over and smiled, then looked back at the flask.

"Finally, I get to meet my Creator," I said with a relieving sigh.

Nothing mattered at this point. I began to take a sip and Kursus stopped me again. "Oh, what now?" I said impatiently.

"You are doing it wrong; you're supposed to make your wish, then drink it. Think about nothing else but your wish. Just watching out for you," she added.

I rolled my eyes, and then closed them tight, but then I thought of something; even at a time like this I wanted to go down and thank the Mechas and see Milder once more. I slowly put the artifacts away and sighed, looking at both Kursus and Rip.

"What is the matter, Darkus?" Rip asked curiously.

"I know this seems like a horrible time to do so, but we need to go back to our hiding spot once more. I need to see Milder and the Mechas before I do this. I know it's silly but I have to thank them properly." Rip and Kursus looked at each other, then at me and sighed.

"This anticipation is killing me," Kursus spat, "but I suppose you are right. Let's just be very diligent on getting back. Last thing we want to happen is getting the artifacts taken away, or being jumped by the elders and my father," Kursus said.

"Indeed, what a good monster you are. It is obvious that your morals are correct and in line. Alright then, make haste and tell them I said thank you as well, and let Milder know that I'd like no more disappearing acts," he finished. Surprisingly, he gave Kursus a hug and held his hand out to shake mine. I reached out and firmly grabbed his cold, boney hand.

"Tell the professor I'd like to have a glass of wine with him," Rip said with a smile.

"I will," I answered. Rip stuck his hands out and the large stone doors swung open. We walked out and gave Rip one last wave, and the stone doors shut tightly behind us. We climbed down the stairs into Cemetrica.

The walk out of Cemetrica was silent and cold, as usual. No monsters or attacks for a change. We exited the gates and I had fantasized about Ectus waiting for us at the gate like once before, but no Ectus. Kursus and I walked West towards our shelter, looking behind us every five seconds; just to be safe.

"Where do you suppose Ectus had gone to?" Kursus asked, breaking the silence.

"Not a clue. I only hope he's ok. Being a spirit, a synthetic one at that, I don't necessarily understand the science behind it. I only hope he is alright. He's a tricky little fellow; real or not." I said confidently. Kursus bowed her head down, but nodded in agreement. I could tell it made her feel a little better.

We walked to the stump that hid the secret passage down to Professor Milder's tunnel. We entered and climbed down the long shaft. The same one we used to shoot MechaTon out of. Soon, we reached the top of MechaTon. We noticed that the Dose used to powered MechaTon, and a part of the tunnel, had stopped running. We continued down the tunnel towards the living area. When we reached it, there sat Milder. He was drinking a bottle of Aged Creeple sap, but only for a moment I thought he was. It was a potion bottle of some sort and he was putting some sort of ingredient into it. He was hacking and coughing, and slammed his fist down hard. I took a look at his fist and it appeared to be white, which was not the color of his skin. We began to speak but to our surprise Drill-Bit was off to our right and out of our sight. He applauded us.

"Well, if it isn't Kursus and Darkus! Professor, take a look at this!" Milder turned in his chair and laughed, nearly breaking the bottle on the table from him slamming it down in his excitement. He ran up to us, grabbed us both and lifted us off of the ground. He gave us a massive hug. I could feel the air leaving my lunges. He put us down and insisted that we have a seat.

"Please, you two, sit!" He hollered as he hid some of his ingredients in his coat pocket and throwing away his old potion bottle. He went to his freezer chest and grabbed a couple bottles of the Aged Creeple sap. Kursus and I looked at each other skeptically, until I saw the bottles of Aged Creeple sap. I licked my lips and my mouth began to water. Aged Creeple sap was exactly what the doctor had ordered. He popped them open for us and we began to chug away. Professor Milder fell hard in his seat and lifted his bottle.

"You two are incredible, you know that? I mean, the power and wisdom you both hold together! What do I have the honor of having you two both here, once more, in such a short notice?"

"Well, we've finally got the stone and elixir as you know," I answered.

"Ah, yes! I had almost forgotten. I didn't expect such a quick visit after all of that. What horrid, back stabbing creatures they were after we helped them out. Some things never change. I guess we're all still enemy number one, only now they know I am alive. But it had to be done, so it's just fine. I kind of missed stirring things up with the locals, anyways!" He laughed, almost falling backwards in his chair.

He stared at us both as we grew a bit silent.

"What's the matter, you two? For winning such a battle and sending those Mechids to kingdom come, you sure look down in the dumps," Milder spoke much softer. Kursus and I looked at one another, and then I began to speak. "We wanted to come thank you, but we also thought you were dead," I said softly. Milder's face grew long and serious as he nodded his head slowly.

"It's true. Honestly, I only know who you two are because Drill-Bit and Triumphus told me every intricate detail about you. I feel like I've known you from the start. But the truth is, we haven't properly introduced ourselves; I am the *real* Professor Milder. You met a Capsule of mine, which was one of my survival methods. Most didn't know that I actually had not died. I was captured by the Mechids, and both Dante and Sadu had been apart of that as well. They heard about my attempt to stop the Mechids, through the other Elders and followed me. They sprung out of nowhere and stopped me dead in my tracks. I was on to something until I had realized that Sadu and Dante were working with the Mechids. So, they locked me up, until Drill-Bit and Triumphus found me and released me. When you both ran off to fight, we stayed in hiding once we heard the Mechids talking about their arrival to the lands. That's when we planned our surprise attack. I'm sorry I never got to tell you both or get a chance to properly meet you. I am so thankful that you two had helped out my Mecha tribe and kept our place in hiding."

A single teardrop ran down his cheek. He wiped it away and raised his bottle of Aged Creeple sap up and we followed.

"To our victory and to new comrades," he boomed and chugged down his Creeple sap. We followed once again. The three of us slammed the bottles down on the table and smiled.

"Well, just to let you know, *again*, I'm your biggest fan. I've followed your work for a long time, which is why I was banned from my Flintkus tribe. As you are more likely aware, it's forbidden to practice mechanics in my culture," Kursus explained once more to the real Professor Milder.

"That is quite incredible, giving up your tribe for my work. What a great honor, and to which is why I'd love for you to help me with a large underground project," Milder said. Kursus smiled wide.

"You really want my help?" She asked, shocked. "Of course, Professor Tinkarius had told me all about you." He got up and walked towards the vial of toxin. The Professor picked it up and looked at it. "And wasn't it you who captured this toxin?" Kursus nodded with a large smile on her face. "Then this will be our first experiment. We are to find the antidote for this and use it as a bargaining tool with the others. Thanks to you, we could even possibly bring back your Flintkus tribe. Imagine the look on your father's face if he heard that you had been the one to do so."

Kursus fantasized for a moment. "That would be something," she said, "but I won't do it for him."

She thought for a moment longer as her face became lost in thought. She looked up at Milder once more.

"Did you notice that when Robotica was destroyed, the Dose was no longer usable?" It was clear that Professor Milder hadn't realize it.

"How fascinating. I had not realized that. Which means the source was coming from Robotica. That just throws me in all kinds of confusion. We will have to look more into that as well. We won't have to worry about the Steinlocks for long since they run only on the Dose. Ha! What idiots; I knew one day they would regret it. This is why it's important that we always practice the ancient technology that we know."

I had nearly forgotten about my Creator. I wanted to finally meet him. I stood up as Kursus and Professor Milder watched.

"I think it's time to meet my Creator," I spoke out. Milder smiled.

"Yes, it's about time," he said, "I bet this is a moment you have been waiting for, Darkus. I'm quite excited for you." He finished his Aged sap, stood up and saluted me. "You tell that talented Creator of yours to stop running and realize he's got friends to help him out. Though his genius, pure and fine, there is nothing wrong with a little bit of help," he continued. I had noticed the arm he saluted me with was the arm that looked pale white, which was now the proper color of his skin.

"What were you drinking earlier when we had come in here?" I asked him.

"It is a recovery potion that heals the wounds. It's just a quick little potion I had learned from the Flintkus is all. It comes quite handy," he said and winked.

"Oh right, those ingredients did seem a bit familiar. Was it the Divine potion?" Kursus had asked.

"That is affirmative," Milder answered. It didn't explain his arm, but perhaps I was seeing things. I was quite tired.

I removed both of the artifacts from my cloak. Milder smiled down at them as the glow pressed up against his face.

"You've come along way and experienced much from your quest. Now you finally get to meet your Creator," Milder said softy, "What an accomplishment! I'm proud to be apart of this moment. What will you ask of your creator? What is it that you desire?" He asked.

I looked at him and sighed, "Not exactly sure, but I will know when I see him I guess," I answered. Milder nodded and held out his hand. I reached out to shake his large, warm hand. He held it in a tight grip and we shook.

"It's been an honor fighting by your side. Don't be a stranger, and hey; tell that Tinkarius to stop being such a loner. I'm sure it will startle him good to see that someone was quick enough to catch him with his pants down," Milder continued, followed by his hardy laugh. Kursus stepped forward and gave me a hug, then punched me in the arm once more.

"I will be here with Professor Milder once you've completed your task. I've got some help to lend for a good man. Don't keep me waiting, you hear?" She demanded, then gave me a kiss on my cheek. Her warm lips brought heat to my cold, clammy face. She stood back next to Milder and waited. I smiled at her.

"Thanks for everything, Kursus. Perhaps…when I get back, we can talk about standing closer together, rather than just in the battlefield." Kursus's face turned a little darker and she smiled.

"I'd like that," she answered.

"Alright you two, you're making me ill! Enough of the suspense! Make your damn wish!" Professor Milder hollered. I closed my eyes and held both of the ancient artifacts in my hands and without further wait, I said,

"I wish that I could find my Creator," then quickly took a sip of the Noctria's blood.

The taste was foul and my skin began to burn a little, then I could feel my system fighting off the toxin. I thought hard of the face of my creator and meeting him. My body felt light and I opened my eyes to see Professor Milder, Kursus, Drill-Bit, Triumphus and the hide out turning to light. In the faded brightness I saw Kursus wave me goodbye with a smile on her face. Milder saluted me once more. The light mutated to dark trees on a large mountain in the night. The wind was blowing hard with a bite to it. I looked around frantically, eager to find my creator. I saw a red light blipping off and on in a nearby opening.

"Creator!" I yelled, "Are you there?"

I ran towards the red light, and as I continued to run after it, it seemed to be moving away from me.
I continued to chase the red light as it zipped around the trees trying to shake me.

"Creator it's me; Darkus!" I yelled, "No need to run!"

But the light continued to dodge me. I ran faster and faster into the darkness on this large unknown mountain. I chased it until I saw what looked like a floating red torch that threw itself quickly into a large cave. I jumped out of the trees and followed it into the cave. The cave howled from the wind swirling around at its entrance. The rhythmic sound of dripping echoed further down. As I continued to walk with one hand on the wall, my eyes began to glow dark purple, then a sensation I hadn't felt since living rattled my brain. My head began to vibrate as I felt the antenna on the back of my head activate for the first time. I reached up to feel it. It was vibrating and making a subtle beeping sound. A red light began to fade in and out above me, indicating that my antenna was active, similar to the red light I had followed.

As I climbed deeper and deeper into the cave, my head rattled more and more as the sound of heavy machinery echoed through the cave. I grew eager and moved quicker down the tunnel, almost falling to my face from tripping over jagged rocks that aligned the ground. I kept at it for a bit longer and found an opening. Bright lights had shined through the dark tunnel and I could see all kinds of equipment and objects that I had remembered seeing in my shelter. I looked around before entering, then slowly stepped into the area and walked quietly as I observed the room. There were a few monitors that were offline on the walls and a bunch of shelves with books. There was a slab that looked like mine in the shelter that was out in the middle with arcs on either side that had an electric beam going from side to side.

I continued through the room and heard a metal object fall to the ground.

"Creator?" I asked much quieter.

I slowly walked around the corner and to my surprise there was my creator, hunched down and working on something. He was so focused and efficient. He moved so quickly that you would have thought he was a Mecha or something. After watching him for a moment I took a deep breath and entered the room, walking closely towards him. I walked until I could touch the other side of his table. I couldn't speak; I was so anxious to be this close to my creator that I couldn't find it in me to speak. I finally shook off the worry and cleared my throat.

"Professor?" I said.

My creator halted to a stop on his work and he grew still for a moment, then he stood up straight and slowly turned on his heel. At first, he had a frown, for perhaps he didn't know it was me, or how I even found him, and then a large smile spread across his face. He slowly put his tools down and stood there for a moment admiring me.

"Hello Darkus," my creator spoke, "What a pleasant surprise."

To listen (and download) The Rise of Darkus: Awakening soundtrack, visit Soundcloud.com and search The Rise of Darkus: Awakening.

To order a physical copy, visit Createspace.com and Search The Rise of Darkus: Awakening Soundtrack.

Facebook.com/tickertwizted

Twitter.com/tickertwizted

Manufactured by Amazon.ca
Bolton, ON